# Madame Guillotine

**BY NICK COLE &
JASON ANSPACH**
TYRUS RECHS:
CONTRACTS & TERMINATIONS
BOOK 3

Galaxy's Edge: MADAME GUILLOTINE
By Nick Cole & Jason Anspach

Edited by David Gatewood
Published by Galaxy's Edge Press

Cover Art: Trent Kaniuga
Interior Design: Kevin G. Summers

For more information:
Website: GalacticOutlaws.com
Facebook: facebook.com/atgalaxysedge
Newsletter: InTheLegion.com

*In Memory of Mandie Patterson-Almond*

A LONG, LONG TIME FROM NOW
AT THE EDGE OF THE GALAXY...

galacticoutlaws.com

# HISTORY OF THE GALAXY

## IMPERATOR

| | |
|---|---|
| 0 | The Pilgrimage |
| 98 | The Exploration |
| 501 | Savage Wars Begin |
| 2000 | Savage Wars Officially Declared Over |
| 2032 | Decay of the Republic |

## REQUIEM FOR MEDUSA

## CHASING THE DRAGON

## MADAME GUILLOTINE

| | |
|---|---|
| 2047 | Battle of Kublar |

## LEGIONNAIRE

# 01

### Reaper 66

THE SKIES OVER DOWNTOWN DETRON WERE TURNING into a hot and muggy stew—a fitting atmosphere for a long, swollen day that seemed to be on the cusp of something violent and dangerous. In the streets below *Reaper 66*, Republic marines were engaged in heavy riot control action, trying to keep order against the Soshies—who had taken to the streets to air an unending litany of grievances against the Republic, the powers that be, and the forces that protected those powers. The irony that those forces also protected the Soshies themselves was apparently lost on them.

The protests started three weeks ago. A series of anti-government marches that blossomed into something that looked too much like a full-blown war zone. Sections of the city were no longer under control of the planetary government. Arson, rampant looting, and a spree of homicides—"payback killings" between rival gangs and cartels—all went unaddressed. It was sensational, and the media took notice. Opinion pieces demanded Republic action, each with a slant aimed at pointing out the failings of whichever House of Reason faction they didn't quite agree with.

Below *Reaper 66*, everything looked tired, burnt-out, and spoiling for a fight. Masses of people in makeshift Soshie ninja gear—black pants and shirts, black fabric wrapped around heads to conceal identities—and marines in full kit angled toward each other along the streets and broad avenues, the marines in orderly columns, the Soshies in the chaotic spacing of a mob. Each side had their preferred form, and those struggling for power had their preferred solutions. Education and shared standards of living for some, austerity and no-tolerance crackdowns for others.

A few had been pushing for the Legion to come in and *make* peace. Everyone knew they could do it. But nobody wanted them there—not really. When the Legion showed up, things got too final, and odds were no one would end up happy.

But none of that was Reaper Actual's problem. Not at the moment.

The Soshies in their red-and-black gear, waving banners demanding everything they could think of—more pay, more services, and lots of free everything—they weren't the problem either, as much as they truly wanted to be. Not for Reaper Actual, and not for the marines below. A lot of them were students. Young kids convinced that only they knew and could do the right thing. That kind of fire burned out with heavy doses of reality. And time.

The kids weren't the reason the marines sent frantic exchanges over the comm system warning that things might be going from bad to worse. As the NCOs drove their hullbusters forward, the marines were well-prepped for the maelstrom of thrown debris and homemade incendiaries they encountered. They had shields and inferno-quenchers capable of putting a fire out almost instantly.

No, the real issue was the professionals mixed in with the idealistic marchers.

The pros.

The professional agitators could be counted on to show up whenever and wherever there was dissatisfaction with, and disobedience against, the Republic. It was the pros who made things dangerous for those playing out their little tableaus on the street, tableaus featuring such familiar roles as Chanting Rioter and Tip-of-the-Government's-Spear Enforcer. The pros came with toys, training, and violent intent.

Three days earlier a marine spotter had been shot from the roof of a building by a sniper using a military-grade weapon. The sergeant had died on the scene, despite the riot gear protecting him and the medevacs on demand in the air above.

A day later, a marine officer had been wounded while sitting in the command cupola of a wolverine. That one was avoidable. The officer should have been inside with the hatch sealed, but the guy was a point and had been acting as though this were some victory parade over the local quelled populace. Arrogantly playing the role of Conquering Military Commander instead of witness to a riot growing rapidly out of hand and getting worse by the hour.

The point's wolverine, a tank that still sported jungle camouflage from its training exercises on Cononga, took an RPG to its rear driver-side. The kind of weapon not usually doled out to the Soshie picketers. The blast wounded the officer, but even that probably wasn't the shooter's goal.

The crowd, who had no sense of familiarity with war or the weapons of war, assumed that, somehow, the *marines* had used the rocket. Never mind that it was a marine tank that was now smoking, partly crippled from the blast. Some responded by running, but a lot of them grew feral, almost savage, and surged into the stunned marines who had busied themselves with seeking to give aid to the wolverine's crew.

As the crowd engulfed the marines, that emboldened others, who pressed in at the smell of blood. But rioters don't match up well with marines in a straight-up fight. And despite the overwhelming numbers, the marines were able to beat back their attackers, who crumbled with each punch or swing of a weapon—or sometimes at just the threat of being hit.

The marines had requested permission to open fire with their N-4s.

The request was refused.

Eventually another unit came in and dispersed the mob with House of Reason–approved tear gas.

Several marines had been wounded, some critically. But no one died. Not even the point. But he did make all the news streams that evening. And soon House of Reason delegates and Senate factions were leveraging the event in their attempts to consolidate or gain power. The usual cycle.

The following day, day three of the civil disobedience outbreak, began with unsubstantiated rumors that a mysterious Legion squad was operating among the protesters, denying civil liberties and threatening violence. Despite a world dominated by visual media, no one had managed to get a holorecording of any such squad, but the rumor stuck—and by noon parts of the city were on fire, full anarchy in effect. A war zone. Soon the Soshies were claiming that hundreds of peaceful protestors had been murdered by "out-of-control" marines and a detachment of "psychopath legionnaires."

This time, however, there were pictures. Pictures of bloody protestors. And despite the Repub marines' insistence that they'd had no such engagements—that these were doctored holopics of actors wearing makeup, or perhaps injured by their fellow rioters—every holofeed used that picture of the bleeding protestor.

"Out-of-control marines."

"Psychopath legionnaires."

The rioters tripled in number the next day. Today.

But Reaper Actual's problem wasn't that either. It wasn't any of that. Her issue was... sight picture.

Reaper Actual's job was to provide fire support overwatch from an airborne platform. Overwatch for an advancing line of Repub marines in riot gear wading into the streets to clear a path for the government to pull back from its office towers until the riots could be dealt with and good governance restored. But shooting from an airborne platform was no easy trick. And the old SLIC relics from the War of Psydon the marines used for fire support bounced around in the hot thermals coming up from the boiling streets of the city. It was late summer on Detron and the city was simmering.

"Got one," she murmured over the comm. Her N-18 locked in and tagged a target below. "Looks like we got a player."

"Holding," said the pilot of *Reaper 66*, the SLIC Reaper Actual was operating out of. The pilot switched over to general comm with the shotcaller and declared, "Undertaker, this is Reaper Oh-Two. Reaper Actual says she's got a player. Feeding you her cam. Reaper Oh-Two standing by for confirmation and authorization on trigger pull, over."

Reaper Actual said nothing from her shooting position on the aft cargo deck of the stabilized SLIC. There was no one else back there and so no one to talk to. And she was a marine of few words. She did her job and didn't waste time talking about it. Being talkative and being a military sniper didn't go well together. Part of the personal profile that got you into the Reaper program.

She wore standard marine fatigues, light armor, and combat boots. She was small. Muscled. One eye back from the high-powered scope of the N-18, studying the man she was about to shoot.

She'd spotted him in a third-story window along the avenue the marine convoy below was taking into the heart of the city's government and financial district. The streets were throbbing with rioters, faces covered by balaclavas they'd purchased from high-end shopping sites—they all seemed able to afford it. Their backpacks were loaded like the rucks of leejes and marines getting ready to go into combat deep in the jungle. Or lost in the desert. Only it was bricks and the fruits of looting they humped through the streets, eager to have a thrilling showdown with a marine and then return to their homes to post about it on social media and maybe stream some holos as they enjoyed their new free datapads. Liberated from the greedy corporations that built and sold them.

Power to the people.

Reaper Actual thought about how they must think it seemed fun to be playing soldier as long as you didn't have to sign an oath or do what anyone told you to do. Or any of the other hard realities of actual military service. The galling thing to many of the marines was that in prime-time interviews the rioters made a point of comparing themselves to marines and legionnaires. Claiming they were somehow serving the Republic by resisting the legally elected officials. They were the heroes, if anyone cared to listen.

Detron was on a core world, hence the House of Reason's reluctance to send in the Legion to KTF everything and walk out. That kind of force was fine out on the edge and the mid-core, but it would have repercussions in future elections if it happened on a core world. A civilized world. For a civilized people. A world where weapons were illegal.

Of course, somehow those weapons still turned up in the crowd. Always. And always held by the wrong people. The pros. Usually on the giving end of a dead marine or a burned-out APC.

And *that* was her problem, too.

"Damn," she whispered over the comm, the howl of the SLIC's turbines pitching to hold position while the repulsors thumped out their pulsing beat.

"What?" asked the pilot.

"He's out of picture," she replied. "Went back inside the room. Can you lose a little altitude to reacquire?"

"Can do," replied Reaper Oh-Two.

The skies over the smoke-filled city were swarming with other marine drop craft. Smaller birds were inserting specialized quick reaction teams that might be needed in certain situations. Pilots were making daring landings onto narrow rooftops to insert the teams who'd hold there until needed. Heavier gunship versions of the SLICs—still ancient—were over the main body of the marine convoy with hullbusters and weapons hanging out. Though they were not to use those weapons, even to return fire, unless first granted approval.

And it was obvious from how bold the Soshies had become that they knew exactly how much the military couldn't fight back. Which, according to the general chatter, was turning everything into a big Day of Stupid.

"Someone's going to get hurt today," squawked a voice over general chat. It was a marine staff sergeant running an indirect fire team from a crumbling apartment block tower.

"So, same as every other day," another voice replied.

Which was true. But today seemed like it was going to be the big one. The start of the real trouble.

Aboard *Reaper 66* in overwatch fire support position, Reaper Actual again had a good picture inside the room she'd been eyeballing through her scope. Oh-Two had lost a little altitude, coming down closer to the tiered rooftops of the housing district they hovered over. Residents and students snapped images on their datapads of her on the hovering SLIC, N-18 clearly aiming at something.

Through the third-story window she saw the Soshie in full gear, minus mask. The specialized scope she used for her work was identifying military-grade body armor, rather than the typical Soshie black leather jacket. He also had flashbangs on a carrying harness. Not a shoot-able offense at this stage of escalation, but something the shotcaller watching her feed should have spotted. The shotcaller would interface with a Legion point sent in by the House of Reason to make the decision on trigger pull.

But so far…

Then she saw it. A Type 92 Steiger Arms subcompact blaster.

And… a sniper rifle against the back wall.

"Got a Mulotti high-capacity leaning against the back wall. He means business."

There could be no doubt about that rifle. It was a specialized weapon system that kept ending up in the hands of terrorists and insurgents on various worlds. It was excellent at killing legionnaires at medium range, and could kill marines and Republic Army effectively at long range if the shooter had some chops. It used half a charge pack per shot, but it could be loaded with up to ten micro-charge packs that gave it an excellent sustained rate of fire for a shooter in a target-rich environment at close range.

And for shooting down into the streets at exposed marines supporting an armored convoy… yeah, it'd do the job just fine.

"Bingo!" whooped Oh-Two over the comm, hoping to alert the shotcaller's attention back at Command. "We have a player. Confirmed banned weapon system. We good to shoot, sir?"

No reply as the SLIC hovered in closer. Oh-Two nudged the craft forward over an apartment building to get out of an updraft coming up off the oddly empty street below.

Both pilot and shooter aboard *Reaper 66* heard the *whooooosh*.

One of the crew chiefs in another bird called out, "Incoming!"

Alarms began beeping inside the SLIC but just as quickly died down as it became clear that *Reaper 66* wasn't the target.

A few streets over a rocket streaked up from an alley and smacked into the side of one of the matte gray marine SLICs over the main convoy at the front of the riot. A moment later the bird was trying to climb, spinning and spilling black smoke at the same time, then autorotating down into the seething streets not far from the clash of forces.

"Bird down! Bird down!" Oh-Two was calling out over the comm as the day went from bad to South of Worse in an instant.

# 02

"WE ARE EN ROUTE TO SECURE THE CRASH SITE, OVER."

"Copy that, Switchblade. Pulling marines back to Thirty-Second and Park. Be advised drone feed says the rioters are approaching the wreck."

The assault shuttle carrying the Legion quick reaction force identified as Switchblade lifted off from a small apartment building rooftop inside the district known as the Prosperity Sprawl, west of the main riot.

The Prosperity Sprawl, or simply the Sprawl, had once been the neighborhood of choice for shipyard workers who assembled the massive power plants of the old battleships, which were then disassembled and shipped to Tarrago for installation. Back then the place had been called the Boilermaker District—a solid middle-class suburb with nice houses, new speeders in garages, good schools, and well-maintained parks. Now it was little more than a zone of eroding and lifeless streets controlled by a violent gang that specialized in the distribution of the dangerous drug H8.

The gangbangers knew the legionnaires were there, on the roof in their hood. But they didn't bother them. Because you don't pick a fight with the Legion. Not if you have anything to lose. And while the Sprawl wasn't much compared to the still-affluent sectors of the city, those who owned the streets lived like kings. And none of them wanted to be dethroned by taking on a Legion that was pretty much minding its own business.

The Legion sergeant in command of Switchblade, Sean "Shaker" Lopez, had decided to get involved after listening to the shotcaller and the point in charge of weapons release argue about what should be done next now that a bird had been shot down in the streets.

"Negative, Sergeant Lopez… you do not have permission to effect a rescue at this time," said the point over L-comm as the shuttle lifted off from the rooftop. "We are working on less politically volatile solutions at the moment."

Cave, the team's number two, gave Shaker a tilt of his bucket. They were all getting the "stand down" orders over their L-comm from the point.

Shaker took one hand off his N-4, tapped his bucket near the ear, and indicated bad comm. Then made a knife-edge gesture to continue.

The shuttle blew dust and grit off the roof and pulled itself up into the smoky sky over Detron, correcting course toward the crash site.

\* \* \*

"They're dragging the pilot out of the wreck."

She said it matter-of-factly. Plainspoken despite the implications. Reaper Actual's transmission was the opposite of almost all the traffic over the comm. It was calm and sure where everything else was confused and chaotic. *Outlaw Nine,* the marine gunship shot down by the rocket, seemed to be the sole topic of discussion. The shotcaller gave orders to various marine elements located in the area of operation. And those multiple elements were all talking over one another trying to get the job done.

"I see smoke but no fire," interrupted someone over comm who'd failed to identify themselves. They sounded breathless and hurried. Like they were running. Blaster fire could be heard in the background of their transmission.

"Dammit…" swore the Legion point. "Who's firing? Is that us or the civilians? They're not supposed to be armed."

Reaper Actual watched from her airborne vantage point as the pilot was dragged into the sea of black-and-red masked figures swarming the wreckage of the old SLIC gunship. It had gone down in an intersection after smashing into the second story of what looked like a bank. Debris and bodies—a mix of marines and Soshies caught in the wrong place at the wrong time—were scattered away from the craft, which was lying on its side.

"Drone recon shows military and civilian casualties," said someone from Intel.

"For Oba's sake!" shouted the Legion point. "Of course we have casualties! A damned bird just went down in the middle of an exercise in civil demonstration. Our biggest problem will be if any of the protestors were killed on the ground. If that happens…"

"Pilot's dead." She said the words into the ether of the comm during a pause in the point's rant. All discourse stopped for a few seconds. Then she added: "Not from the crash. Someone shot him."

She'd watched it all through her scope.

Most of the frenzied protestors had looked to be there for the experience. Some had been trying to tear away souvenirs from the twisted and broken craft. Others showed compassion and shouted for aid and help. Not only for their own, but also for some of the marines. They squared off briefly, warring among themselves, some of the masked Soshies pushing others. Protectors trying to stave off wolves who wanted nothing more than to kick a marine while down.

The pilot had survived the crash, and Reaper Actual had looked on as a pair of Soshies helped him from the SLIC's broken canopy, his arms around their shoulders. It was an endearing scene that hinted that maybe the Republic wasn't as fractured as the media might lead you to believe.

And then a pro walked up, produced a small Python blaster—a holdout version perfect for concealing on an ankle—and blew the pilot's brains out.

The sudden blaster fire had sent several rioters fleeing. Those who stayed behind seemed to mix well with the pros. There for blood. A few ran up and kicked the pilot's corpse, but they were awkward, unpracticed kicks. As though they understood the concept of physical activity but lacked the ability to execute.

"I still have a sight picture on the shooter," she continued.

"Do not engage!" shouted the point. "Repeat, do *not* return fire. All elements, hold your fire."

Reaper Actual watched as the co-pilot, the weapons system operator for the gunship SLIC, was hauled from the aft cargo deck. She was unconscious, and one arm was badly mangled. Reaper Actual scanned the waiting, throbbing crowd surrounding the wreck. The merciful ones, the sane ones… they were gone now. Gone, or waiting far in the back. Away from their peers whose feet had run swiftly toward blood and violence.

Away from the shooter.

As he pressed forward toward the unconscious weapons system operator—probably some second lieutenant from the aviation branch serving to get money for college—Reaper Actual made up her mind, right then and there, that she'd pull the trigger on the N-18 if the pro made a move to repeat his murder of the pilot. Maybe she could save the shavetail's life. Maybe.

"What's your sitrep?" asked Oh-Two from the flight deck. "I'm getting the order to return to base. Services no longer needed, Amanda."

"I'm watchin' him," she grunted.

"The guy?"

"The guy who shot the pilot, yeah. He's waiting for something. Not close enough to shoot her yet, but he's watching her."

Oh-Two knew what would happen next. And he didn't like it. He wasn't a hero. Just a guy who'd once been a boy who stood at the edge of a star port gripping a mesh wire fence just to get close to the ships out there on the pads. All he'd ever wanted to do was fly. No, he wasn't a hero, but he knew the difference between right and wrong. So he held station and ignored the order to return to base.

Reaper Actual followed the shooter's eyes to the approaching unit. That was the only word she could think of to describe the group that was moving in through the crowd, pushing through everyone. Violently. Moving fast and hard to reach the weapons officer being dragged down off the wreck of *Outlaw Nine*.

"Got something…" she said.

"What is it?" asked Oh-Two. His voice was nervous and harsh. A little desperate to not have to do the right heroic thing for too much longer. He was thirsty and barking at her because this was about to get bad and he knew it. He took his hand off the lift collective and quickly wiped the sweat there onto his flight suit.

"Group of pros. Moving in quickly. Organized and looking to extract."

"How do you know they're pros?"

She didn't reply for a long second as she watched them through her scope. They moved together, watching all the angles. They had weapons held low—maybe subcompact blasters, but the crowd was getting in the way and preventing her scope from tagging them for identification. The men moved like they had military training. Hence the notion of them being a unit.

"They're operators. Mercs or something. Maybe MCR? Sense of urgency and on a mission. Not losing their sket like all the kids around them. They're up to something, and they mean to get it done."

She continued to watch the men through the N-18's scope.

"Uh… Command, this is Reaper Oh-Two," said the pilot over the comm. "Actual says she's got something funny going down at the crash site, over."

The shotcaller came back instantly. "Define funny, Oh-Two."

"Says she thinks there are some bad actors mixed in with the crowd and trying to extract one of the crew. Is the Legion in the mix?"

"Bad actors" was marine code for professional paramilitary types acting on behalf of the rioters or an unidentified foreign source.

There was a long pause.

"Legion QRF is inbound to the crash site. You should have traffic at your two o'clock. The shuttle is at altitude two thousand feet heading two seven zero."

Oh-Two tracked the inbound shuttle just entering the airspace.

"Negative. These are on the ground. Say again. Trying to extract one of the crewmembers, over."

"Then negative. Not our boys." replied the shotcaller.

Oh-Two swore.

"I heard," said Reaper Actual from the cargo deck. Eye still staring into the scope. Not a muscle moving. Like some statue that couldn't be moved even if the SLIC that carried her crashed. "They got her. Definitely some kind of extraction team. They're taking her through the crowd and keeping 'em off her."

But just as she said that one of the black-and-red-clad rioters, wearing a Gentleman Johnny mask, reached out and struck the unconscious weapons officer. One of the men in the unit pushed the rioter back into the seething crowd, and they struggled on with her.

"Tagging her," said Reaper Actual. "They're making for an alley. Come about on a heading of two four zero and follow. Eyes on target."

Oh-Two watched the scope's feed on a small monitor located above the flight controls. From the navigation HUD, he knew exactly where they were taking her. Out of the intersection and down an alley that led away from the bulk of the rioters. Maybe they were working for the Legion or some other government agency not declaring itself on scene. Who knew?

Oh-Two highlighted the inbound shuttle dropship and opened a comm channel.

"Ghost One, this is Reaper Oh-Two, we have an intel update for your passengers."

The pilot aboard was smart and didn't waste time. With two long clicks and a beep he linked the incoming traffic back to the operators loaded inside the assault shuttle.

"Reaper Oh-Two, go for Switchblade."

"Switchblade, this is Reaper team on site. We have one of the crew being extracted away from the crash site. Unless these guys are yours, she's in the hands of some unfriendlies, over."

\* \* \*

Shaker studied the image being fed to him by the SLIC on station above even the highest rooftops over the crash site. Sure enough, someone had snagged one of the crew. Probably taking a hostage for propaganda.

That was not going to happen.

"We're going in," said Shaker over L-comm. "They got one of the crew. Scrub securing the crash site. We'll go after the missing crewmember before they can disappear her into their network. Probably the best chance we got is right now."

"Captain Betae says we're a no go." It was Lightspeed. Call-signed such because he spoke with a slow drawl. "But I'm just notin' that so we can all ignore it right, Sar'nt?"

"Affirmative, Lightspeed. Betae is a weasel. Weasels are not to be listened to when the twarg dung hits the jump inducer. Copy?"

"Copy," drawled Lightspeed.

"Blasters up?" asked Cave.

"Negative. Non-lethal unless they start shooting."

"Can't put down for you leejes," said the shuttle pilot. "No clean space."

"Then you know what that means, Ghost?"

"Ropes it is. Stand by to deploy."

Fast-rappel synthetic cables—speed ropes—popped and deployed from small boxes over each operator mount.

"Clip in," Shaker ordered.

A second later he got what he needed to go.

"In," called Cave.

"In," said Beers, the newest team member, for whom no one had yet come up with a call sign. His last name being what it was, he likely wouldn't get one. Lightspeed had commented once that Beers "just sounded like a call sign all the same, Sar'nt."

And finally an "I'm in," from Lightspeed.

"Drop on five…"

They were now over the same alley the masked men were carrying the flight officer down. It wasn't as crowded as the riot-swollen intersection where some of the protestors were starting to batter the corpses of the flight crew that had been killed in the crash and tossed from the wreckage while others posed for grisly holophotos. But it was crowded enough.

"What about them that's on the ground below?" asked Lightspeed.

"In for a big surprise," answered Shaker as he began to count. His breathing was rapid and controlled. He knew this day was turning into a major situation.

The ramifications of letting an officer be taken hostage were beyond him, but most likely it would rank up there with Real Bad Juju. Legion and Repub brass would be all over this situation within hours. The best win that could be had out of this day in which almost an entire flight crew had been killed was to make sure the one still surviving didn't end up as a prop on the media streams running endless Soshie propaganda in the ratings-grab known as *What will happen next.*

They might court-martial him for disobeying the point. But he doubted that would happen. Not after the pilot had been killed. He was within his mandate to do everything he could to prevent more deaths. That's why the Legion had stationed a QRF and some assets in this mess. To prevent it from getting messier.

"Five…"

On zero they dropped right into a hot mess getting messier by the second.

As the legionnaires jumped out, the cables fell, slapping the pavement of the shady alley like sudden whip cracks from a tyrannasquid's tentacles. The protestors instinctively moved away, swearing and screaming as the legionnaires dropped down from above them like charcoal-dusted angels of death.

But amazingly, the Soshies didn't stay scared long. Within seconds one came in and struck Cave across the bucket with a glass bottle. Obviously the kid—another Gentleman Johnny– a masked student who fancied himself a holonet tough guy because he had a hundred thousand of his friends on his side—didn't understand how Legion armor worked. Or rather, how most things *didn't* work on Legion armor. Like bottles. Or rocks. Or a steel pipe.

The bottle shattered harmlessly. Cave shattered the kid's mask and teeth in return with the butt of his rifle. One powerfully concise movement.

"Excessive force" is what the holos would have called it, had it been recorded. But Cave had served with the Seventh on Danaar. And that level of violence against the Grum had been the only kind of force that worked on those howling beasts. Shaker would have to cite that in the after-action if asked to explain why a protestor was suing the Legion for facial reconstruction surgery.

He filed that under the least of his current problems.

Two kids came at him swinging metal batons. Against marines in riot gear, that might've been enough. Perhaps it already had been, and a past success had led them to the false conclusion that they could handle legionnaires in the same manner. Shaker quickly disabused them of this notion. While maintaining a sight picture with his N-4 on a growing mob at the entrance to the alley, he delivered a series of offhand blows, the last of which was a solid throat punch that made the kid no doubt wonder if he was ever going to breathe again as he fell to his knees in the dirty alley, begging for air.

The kid's buddy left him there, disappearing back into the crowd.

Both Lightspeed and Beers had dealt with their own rioters. Idealistic youths resisting the powers that be by attacking legionnaires on a rescue mission. Make sense of that. Now those youths were either unconscious or crawling back to their brethren while puking their guts out along the pavement.

"Let's roll, Switchblade," ordered Shaker to the rest of the QRF. "Form up... wedge. I'll take point. Need to move at the double to catch up."

He switched over comm to the Reaper team on over-watch somewhere above, hidden behind a nearby building. The comm went live a moment before he transmitted, and he could hear their engines and repulsors. The shuttle that had dropped his team was long gone and wouldn't be back until they needed extraction.

"Switchblade to Reaper... which way did they go?"

# 03

THE FIRST INTIMATION THAT THINGS WERE GOING FROM seriously south of bad to completely messed up was when Lightspeed's vitals grayed out in Shaker's HUD.

"Lightspeed... comm check?"

Maybe it was just a malfunction.

That's what Shaker was desperately wishing at that moment. Because it would be some good news in what was turning out to be all bad news in the making. And as team leader, he couldn't help but feel it was his fault. That was leadership. Real leadership.

They'd gone down the alley, tracking on the last known location of the team that had snatched the weapons officer out of the downed bird. The Reaper team above had the best intel coverage, but they'd lost the tangos in the warren of routes the alley had turned into, only picking up small glimpses of what they thought was the team from an altitude of at least eight hundred feet as the SLIC pilot tried not to hit any of the buildings. Or take ground fire.

The last thing any of them needed right now was another downed bird.

Blaster fights were definitely breaking out around the crash site. Either because the shotcaller had gotten his way and sent the marines back in to take the scene, or because the agitators had decided to start shooting to create more chaos among the rioters.

Or maybe it was just a convenient time for accounts to be settled up among the various street gangs.

Shaker didn't have to deal with any of that at the moment. As they made their way deeper into the shadowy alley and started taking tangents to pursue their quarry, Shaker had two immediate, gnawing problems. First, the flight officer. He needed to get her back in friendly hands before a bad day turned into a major stellar incident. Second, the crowd of rioters who'd followed them into the warren. They were keeping back, but it was clear they were waiting for the right moment to try something. They'd already lobbed a few gas bombs, obviously unaware that Legion armor and filtration systems handled such weapons effortlessly. Still, it indicated intent. And the intent to harm was clearly evident.

Normal Legion protocols indicated KTF in effect. But this was not a normal Legion assignment. This was babysitting.

They had been pulled from normal unit rotation to do some time in what was called the "crisis management teams" that were the precursor to Legion Dark Ops. It was in these teams that one learned to work with other military and governmental organizations—something that was part and parcel of life as a Dark operator. Though as Shaker saw it, there wasn't much to learn beyond patience and the ability to suffer incompetence while still trying to get the mission done.

Anything but a five rating during this assignment meant no go for Dark Ops. But that was all career stuff. And Sergeant Sean Lopez, Shaker as he was tagged, couldn't've cared less about it at that moment. Diving into the alley to get the marine officer had been his only concern. That was the one mission objective that needed to happen for today not to be a complete mess.

And as the QRF got deeper and deeper, followed through the warren of alleys by the black-and-red-clad mob of wannabe ninjas, it was clear the group of pros they were chasing could easily go to ground inside any of these buildings and quickly disappear into the extensive underground transportation system built back in Detron's halcyon days.

Which meant the QRF was just a desperate second from losing their quarry.

But they received intermittent updates from the shooter in the Reaper bird, and these indicated that, so far at least, the legionnaires on the ground were roughly on the right trail.

"Don't like this one bit," said the usually stoic Cave.

Cave was a staff sergeant who'd just finished up a rotation as a line platoon sergeant. He and Shaker had been in roughly the same time and knew a lot of the same people. Both had the same goal—Dark Ops—and both knew exactly what it took.

"Pull back?" asked Shaker, breathing heavily. Not from the exertion of the double-time they ran with weapons ready, but because of the anxiety creep he was starting to get as things progressed. He felt the same as Cave. Didn't even need to explain the reasons.

They both knew they were on the verge of getting in too far over their heads. Allied units were busy with the clown show of the crash, the political oversight, and the dog-and-pony circus of the show of force being put on by the House of Reason for the media. If they got into something… backup was not likely to be fast in coming.

There was a long pause before Cave answered. They had come to an intersection, automatically breaking into teams of two and hugging the wall. One covering forward, the other covering the rear. Everyone knew their job, even Beers, the new E-5. Good kid. Survived a bad counterinsurgency on Ilon. Did something that got him fast-tracked for the CMTs.

"We still got a chance to get her back?" asked Cave. His breathing was rock steady. You'd think the fear creep wasn't there for him. Unless you knew him well. Which Shaker did. His number two was concerned with what they were doing.

Reacting.

Instead of acting.

That was always the worst thing to do.

"We're close, according to Reaper," replied Shaker over the L-comm, nodding his bucket at the SLIC above. "We can still get her. Or we turn back now and call for an extraction off one of these rooftops. Then she's gone and it's a whole thing."

"Bad day," muttered Cave.

"Yeah," replied Shaker.

Beers and Lightspeed said nothing. Too busy watching their sectors. This wasn't a vote. This was a check on mission. Making sure they were doing the right thing.

Making sure they weren't going to get anyone killed unless they wanted them killed.

"New ping."

They all saw it in their HUDs. The Reaper team in the SLIC above had spotted the capture team, now two blocks east of their position. Down the alley to the right. Then turn left. There was a Soshie technical inbound on that loc, which probably wasn't a coincidence.

"They're getting her transport. We'll lose her then," said Cave.

"How the hell did a bunch of protestors mount an N-50 to a speeder?" asked Beers. "Like, how?"

"Doesn't matter," said Shaker. "This is our chance to make sure we don't lose her. Lightspeed, you stay back and lay down cover fire on the mob behind us. Shoot over their heads and keep them back because we're probably going to get into a thing taking the featherhead back. Beers, you and Cave on my flank. Full-out sprint—watch for ambushes. We rush the next two blocks and try to catch them before the technical arrives on scene."

It was a bad plan. Shaker knew it even as he spoke. But it was the only chance to get an engagement before the transport arrived.

The biggest problem was running full-tilt through blind alleys. That was a sure way to blunder straight into an ambush that had been left along the back trail for just such a contingency. Then again, maybe running would give them the element of surprise. They'd trained to move quickly and engage during assault school, and it was a standard drill in the line units. Chances were, they could cut the possible ambush's reaction time by getting up on them quickly and shooting fast.

So…

"Weapons free," said Shaker. "Screw Betae. I'll take the hit."

Then…

"Go."

* * *

Reaper Actual watched from the bird's-eye vantage the hovering SLIC provided. Oh-Two was an excellent pilot, but she knew he was nervous flying in close to the ramshackle apartment buildings in this section of Detron. She watched as the Legion QRF tagged Switchblade split up, with three of the four legionnaires surging out in a rough wedge and running off down the alley. That would take them to another stretch that ultimately led to where the unit had extracted the weapons officer.

"How long on that technical?" she asked Oh-Two.

She had everyone tagged within the scope's map view. With a rotation of her thumb she could zoom out on the N-18 and see the entire sector, or zoom in and see a good sight picture on a single target. Headshot close. Her specialty.

"Fifteen seconds at best. Sled's moving fast and not braking for anyone, including some children it almost ran down a few blocks back. These guys are coming for our guys, that's for sure."

*Who brings their children out for something like this?* That's what Reaper Actual wanted to ask. But that detail wasn't pertinent to the mission. So she said, "Weapons?"

"Tagging a mounted gun of some sort. Black market, definitely—maybe an N-50? It's got a cargo module, and that's where they're going to put the weps officer if I have to bet my flight pay today."

"Those legionnaires aren't going to arrive in time," Reaper Actual said.

The legionnaires were highly conditioned, but her tracking indicated they wouldn't arrive until the sled was already in place at the scene. Then there'd be a confrontation and probably a whole bunch of shooting.

Over the throb of the repulsors and the idle of the SLIC's engines came the high-cycle whine of blaster fire. She checked the one leej Switchblade had left behind. Bright traces of blaster fire were coming from his SAB at unseen targets down the alley. Most likely the mob.

"They firing, Amanda?" asked Oh-Two.

"Looks like it. Can't tell if they're getting hits. But it looks like they've upped their posture. Request permission for me to support."

"Roger."

\* \* \*

The legionnaires ran into a hail of blaster fire coming down at them along the last alleyway leading to the target. The transport had already arrived, and the pick-up was going down. ·

For one second there was nothing but shadowy afternoon darkness due to the tall buildings clustering along the warren, cut by occasional shafts of dusty daylight, and then in the next second it was like some special-effects movie where the hero flies his starfighter down a trench to blow up the Savage hulk and save the day.

Blaster fire came at them in hot volcanic red bolts, indicative of black-market blasters of the military-grade variety. Shaker's HUD was tagging no less than eighteen combatants that he could see. And the captured marine officer.

His intention had been to show up and tell them to lay down their weapons, if any more than the guy who murdered the pilot had any—which still hadn't been confirmed by any external intel. Lay down weapons and surrender the officer. He'd even made up his mind to pull back for extraction as soon as he got gloves on the officer. No prisoners. Too much confusion. Things could go bad in the chaos. Just get the featherhead and leave. No KTF.

But the pro capture team had decided the play by opening fire first. So, it was going to be a fight. Plain and simple.

KTF in effect, only it was the other guys shooting first.

Shaker didn't like that.

Beers, young and agile, moved like a rabbit, darting for cover behind a solid steel trash receptacle that suddenly took a fusillade of incoming, leaving molten scars along its surface. Cave merely dove and hit the ground, skidding forward and bringing his N-4 up to engage in the same instant. Within seconds he was dropping tangos who either hadn't chosen cover or had come out from behind cover to lay down more fire.

Shaker hugged the wall, selecting full-auto and dumping a charge pack at everyone along the right flank. He made sure not to shoot near the captured flight officer, who was being held by two large thugs in red-and-black ninja gear and military-style tactical carrying harnesses.

Fifteen seconds of furious shooting saw three quarters of the capture team dead and the leaders scurrying back out of view. The technical sled, no longer waiting to be loaded up, was now moving at a high rate of speed over to a courtyard beyond the alley.

A mounted gunner oriented his weapon toward the legionnaires and opened fire wildly, spraying a wall well above Beers's head and sending old brick raining down. Beers, who had picked up Cave's six as the big leej surged for the alley, hit the mounted gunner with three shots in the chest.

Perfect trigger pulls.

Excellent grouping.

The shooter side of Shaker noted it all admiringly as he slapped in a charge pack and followed Cave and Beers into the courtyard, sweeping up the flanks for his position in the three-man assault. It was textbook form of a much-practiced SOP.

"On your six and loaded," called out Shaker, letting his team know he was ready to cover them while they slapped in new charge packs.

Cave engaged two shooters on the right flank and took a direct hit to his armor. It hurt like getting hit by a flying jackhammer, Shaker knew that. He'd been hit before. But Cave, who stood six four, didn't seem fazed in the least. Except that his arm was apparently broken and now useless. He let the N-4 hang limp in its sling and pulled his sidearm with his off hand. He fired at targets engaging them from inside a building on the right flank.

"Take out the driver!" shouted Shaker over the comm as he held off incoming fire from the left side of the courtyard.

"On it!" Beers shouted back.

Eager and amped up for payback, the kid ran forward quickly, not bothering to fire. He slammed into the side of the technical sled, bounced off of it, and with weapon up, began shooting into the driver's compartment at point blank.

All that happened and now Shaker had a full confirmation they were in a whole lot of trouble, even though Beers and Cave seemed to be holding their own on the right flank. Because this was the point where Lightspeed's vitals grayed out in his HUD. They'd walked into the ambush he'd feared was waiting for them. Only later than he'd expected it.

Fire was coming down on them from as high as the second and third stories. Shaker felt a blaster bolt sizzle past his shoulder and explode onto the old paving below. Then he heard Beers yell that he was "Hit!"

Shaker stumbled backward, pouring fire into a third-story corner window of a building that must've been built back during the golden age of the planet. It had a certain style, like the architect was proud of his work. Wanted to make something beautiful and timeless.

The stream of blaster fire ruined the window, splattered the shooter's head, and caused him to pitch forward through the shards of melted and smashed glass down to the courtyard below.

An increase of fire chased Shaker to the side of the technical. It wasn't cover for everything coming at the team, but it protected them from some angles at least.

When he turned his bucket to scan the left flank, he saw that Cave was down. The HUD display indicated what his eyes confirmed. Another team member gone.

The marine weapons officer, the featherhead, was also dead. They'd shot her through the head now that they had a chance to get a legionnaire. Cave must have gone for her thinking he could help.

They were still shooting his lifeless corpse as though taking target practice. Cave still gripped his sidearm, his body jerking with each new defiling hit.

"Sket!" Shaker dumped fire at the shooters taking potshots at the lifeless body of his friend. He drew a bright line of fire across the first story; that backed them off. But it had been wild, inaccurate, and stupid.

The N-4 was empty, and he pulled another charge pack in one deft motion. Anxiety and fear creep were gone. Leadership was out the door. All the decisions that could be made had been made, and they'd led to this short, violent firefight.

This was what he knew. Shooting and killing.

Beers crouched down beside him, shooting back from the front of the sled. Shaker could see a big smoking hole in the back of the kid's armor. Below the melted armor lay burning synthprene and cooked flesh.

*Must hurt like a son of a gun*, Shaker thought as his fingers did the reloading trick of getting a new charge pack in without the slightest bit of thought. Part of his mind was struggling—still reeling that things had gotten this bad this fast. Kicking himself for not pulling back when he—

*Shut the hell up*, he yelled at himself.

And with a roar of "KTF!" he went out shooting, vowing to make every last one of them pay before he was dead.

# 04

"THIS IS BAD," SAID OH-TWO AS HE HELD POSITION over the sudden firefight on the ground, keeping one eye on the scope's feed. "Command has to be seeing this!"

But if they were, they didn't have anything to say about it. Both the shotcaller and the point who seemed to be running things had gone silent. Maybe dealing with the situation at the crash site, maybe reacting to any one of a dozen other firefights that had broken out across the sixteen-block operations zone of riot-fevered Detron.

Marine commanders were requesting permission to return fire while hullbusters on the ground were calling in medevacs and doc-drops for wounded troops. It wasn't clear, at that moment, who exactly was in charge of the disaster unfolding beneath *Reaper 66*.

Reaper Actual swore from the cargo deck. "Kelhorned nightmare down there. Command needs to be doing something."

"What the—?!" shrieked the pilot as he yanked the bird above a sensor tower, barely avoiding a collision.

Someone had no doubt illegally attached the tower to the rooftop, as it was devoid of sensory warnings, flashing lights, or any of the other regulated safety protocols. The city was littered with flight hazards for those who flew close to the deck, as the marines liked to call the ground and buildings.

"Damn it!" yelled Reaper Actual as she pitched and swayed from her shooting platform.

But Oh-Two could tell it wasn't because of his flying that she swore. That was just part of staying alive and aloft, and Amanda knew that. "What just happened? I missed it!"

"Last two leejes are down. They dusted a bunch of hostiles, but they're definitely down. Request permission to engage again. Wait! One's still moving."

Oh-Two opened the comm channel to make the request, and then heard her fire from the back of the ship.

"Engaging…" she muttered over comm. Her voice low and businesslike as she began to put bolts into targets on the ground.

The point came back over the comm. "Reaper Team… are you engaging ground targets at this time? Over."

Oh-Two opened his mouth to reply and then closed it again. Unsure how to handle the situation.

"Reaper Team, you are in direct violation of mission parameters. Confirm: are you engaging ground targets? Over."

Oh-Two didn't bother to confirm and decided to move on to explanations, hoping clarification would provide some sort of retroactive permission for what was already happening. All the while he tried to give his shooter a good sight picture of the alley to assist the legionnaire they saw moving from the SLIC. She was trying to help him. He needed to help her.

"Command, we have a Legion team down. Confirming two wounded and engaging to assist…"

"Negative on assist at this time. Stand down and return to base immediately." The point's voice held little emotion beyond a strident passive-aggressive rage that seemed barely contained.

"Sir…" tried Oh-Two.

She fired again.

Oh-Two checked the scope feed and saw a dead rioter who'd been carrying some type of military-grade assault blaster. He lay sprawled on the street, hardly anything left of his head. A second later the wounded legionnaire crawled into view, dragging the body of another legionnaire—not clear if he was dead or alive—out of the courtyard despite the ongoing chaos.

Oh-Two swore, rage and fear becoming one.

The rage won out.

"Dammit, sir! You're seeing what I'm seeing. Positive ID on at least one wounded legionnaire, probably two. They're trying to get out of there and Reaper Actual's keepin' 'em off. We'll leave when you have a rescue organized and on site!"

"You have your orders, *Reaper 66*. Return to—"

Oh-Two cut the comm.

"I got most of 'em," Amanda reported. "No one's moving in the alley who isn't a leej."

Oh-Two checked the ground radar and scanned the streets below. There were lots of figures down there moving in toward the courtyard. Friendly or hostile… it was hard to say.

"Listen, Amanda, we have a decision to make. Stay and watch—or get out of here. We've been ordered out, by the Legion OIC. In fact... I think I may have just gotten myself masted real good!"

There was a pause he didn't like. It meant she was up to something. They'd been flying together long enough for Oh-Two to know he wasn't going to like what she was about to say.

"Can you put down here?"

A ping in the pilot's HUD marked one of the rooftops that ringed the courtyard where the firefight had gone down.

"Not following you," he said.

"I can go down and get them. Then we can pull them off the roof."

"No, Amanda. No way!"

She didn't reply.

But neither did he leave.

Sunlight and dust washed through the windshield. Smoke in the distance from the downed bird. People were dead and dying.

He loved flying.

Hated the military.

Hated death.

His dad had died when he was a kid.

Hence all the afternoons spent at the star port wishing he could get away. Get away as his mom fell apart.

He hated death.

"We got to," said Amanda.

His jaw clenched. Teeth gritted. Technically, he outranked her. He was a captain. She a sergeant. But they'd both known who was in charge when they started flying *Reaper* together. She was the leader. The shooter. It was the nature of the team. The preeminence of the airborne sniper.

He just wanted to fly.

And make sure none of the good guys got killed.

He swore again and brought in the repulsors for full flare, throwing out the landing gears though he knew he wouldn't even touch the deck of the trash-laden rooftop she was asking him to put her down on.

"Amanda," he began. Like he was going to change her mind. Save her. Even as he did what she wanted him to do.

"I can do this," she said simply. "The alley cleared of hostiles once we started dropping targets. We have this window *right now* to go get them. We can't leave them."

And then the SLIC was hovering over the rooftop, repulsors screaming to hold position. He cranked his head around and watched her drop off the cargo deck.

A second later, sidearm out and rifle slung to her back, she gave a "clear" and he was on the repulsors and climbing out over the rooftops once more.

* * *

Amanda crouched as she ran along the rooftop, carrying her issue sidearm exactly as she'd been taught during the CQB phase of the marine sniper course. Just because you can reach out and put the touch on someone from three thousand meters, as the instructors liked to say, doesn't mean it don't occasionally get up close and unfriendly.

Targets had a way of wanting to hunt down and kill those who stalked them.

Being a sniper, she was authorized to shuck her carrying harness and standard BDU. But she always kept the blaster strapped to her thigh and three charge packs stacked in her cargo pockets, along with a bunch of other tools she'd learned snipers needed over the course of her two enlistments.

The door leading down from the roof was hanging half-open, listing lazily on old-fashioned hinges. She kicked it in with a swift strike from her oversized combat boot and pointed the blaster pistol down into the dark well using as much of the opening for cover as she could.

Nothing. And no one.

She hit the stairs fast, feeling the worm-eaten wood, tired with age, give as she pounded down to the next level. She was five stories up, but close to the two wounded legionnaires on the ground. If she could get to them and pull them back inside the building, then maybe they had a chance to avoid detection until Kirk could put down on the roof and pull them out.

Maybe.

At the third level the stairwell was gone, disappearing into a shadowy pit from which the ruins of the rest poked out. Smoky orange light filtered down through boarded-up windows and occasional cracked panes of grime-laden glass. The building had obviously been condemned, but it seemed no one had gotten around to the demolition part.

Chances were she'd meet some squatters in here. It seemed that kind of place—at least, judging by all the entertainment streams she'd ever watched. She didn't really know. Slums, cities… none of that had been her reality growing up. She was raised on farms and in rural communities. The planets set aside to feed a galaxy. Places with smaller planetary populations than the city populations on the core worlds they fed.

But that had been a long time ago and another life.

Running down the decrepit third-floor hall, checking corners and rooms at the end of the blaster's sights as she moved, she reacted quickly when the wounded pro in red-and-black ninja kit stumbled out from the door that had been flung open as he crashed through it. He was holding a Ross 224 medium-range engagement blaster. Trick scope and heavy vented barrel. Good for dropping armored targets at the one-fifty mark.

She knew weapons.

Part of the job.

She shot him as he looked at her with a pained face, feebly trying to bring his weapon up and engage.

Hit, he twisted away from her and fell across the hall. She approached him quickly and double-tapped him, just as she'd been taught, fighting against the training as a sniper to fire once and disappear. She had to be sure he was dead in case she came back this way with the two leejes.

That the Soshie made it up here was a good sign. It meant there was another stairwell—or some other way up and down.

She knelt, took the man's weapon, checked the charge, and holstered her sidearm, preferring the new model. It would do just fine. Good to have some firepower once she made the street. If she had to, this would help keep the rioters back and off the two wounded legionnaires.

If they were still alive.

"They're alive," she told herself.

*Because this is damn foolish if they ain't.*

She could almost hear her grandpa telling her that. The same voice that had told her all the other ways she'd played the fool in her life.

*Damn foolish to break that mustang, Panda.*

*Damn foolish to marry that boy, Panda.*

*Foolish to have a kid so young yourself, Panda.*

She made the ground floor and stopped. There were people on the street. More rioters, stripping the weapons off a few of the dead pros. These weren't mercs—they looked like kids. Amateurs who thought a weapon would even up the fight against the marines and legionnaires out on the streets this afternoon.

Not likely.

"That's foolishness," she muttered.

She gave them a chance and fired the heavier medium-engagement blaster into the ceiling of the entrance foyer she found herself in. Dust and plaster sprinkled down from the ceiling, spilling all over the worn-out checkered floor pattern that must have looked like something special back in the day.

When she looked out the dirty windows, holding her position and not breathing, she saw that the scavengers had retreated. The sound of blaster fire had scared them off.

Imagine if they actually had to face incoming.

No one tested her as she raced from the building to the courtyard. The place was littered with the wounded and dead. Both of which were stripped of whatever they had of value.

That had been fast.

It wasn't even five minutes since the furious firefight. Amanda had seen war, but was taken aback by the number of dead bodies she found. They were everywhere, but especially near the one big legionnaire who must have been shot at least twenty times.

They'd tried to pull his armor off, but it was too ruined, too difficult to disconnect. Someone had cut off his bucket, though. And his head. The bloody stump of his neck oozed out onto the dry cracked pavement of the old courtyard.

Command would have to deal with that. She had come for the living.

Blaster up, she followed the front sights out of the courtyard and into the alley, tracking an ominous trail of blood that had to have been left by the legionnaires. Sure enough, three quarters of the way down its length, dark figures were dragging the two leejes away. She counted five of them.

The range was right for her N-18, so she raised the rifle and fired, hitting one easily. A second later she'd shifted to a new target, a kid rioter with eyes wide underneath his balaclava. She took the top of his skull off and advanced on the three who were already dropping the legionnaires and running for their lives.

She didn't let them get away.

Seconds later she reached the two leejes.

"Who's alive?" she shouted, unsure how to check for vitals while they were in their armor.

One had a nasty wound over his shoulder. He lay face down and she saw the bare rise of his back as he struggled to breathe. The other tried to push himself up off the ground, but collapsed. He'd been shot in the chest at close range. The bolt hadn't penetrated, but it had most likely broken the sternum and a bunch of ribs. It wasn't the chest that had made him collapse though. He'd been shot through one leg. The bolt had gone in and smashed some bone and burnt away skin.

"Good… to guh-oh," muttered the legionnaire who'd fallen onto his back. "Help me… up."

She got down on one knee and tried to pull him upright. He seemed to weigh three hundred pounds in his armor, and the best she could manage was to get his shoulders off the ground and force the man to sit up the rest of the way on his own power.

Her arms scrambled for his helmet release and a second later she had it off.

He gasped for air. "Can't breathe. C-an't… breathe."

He sucked in large lungfuls of the hot dry air and spat blood. His black skin glistened with cold, clammy sweat.

In the distance she could hear movement. Blaster fire. Someone shouting orders over a loudspeaker.

She checked the area and saw figures at the far end of the alley. Figures in Soshie gear. Gathering like a pack of Nogrodi jackal cats.

"I can get you out of here," she grunted as she tugged him to his feet, knowing that had he not been using what strength he had left to assist, it would have been beyond her.

She began to help him back toward the courtyard and the rooftop, knowing it was far away, too far away for her and him and the state he was in.

*Never mind that, Panda.*

That was her mom's voice. Some called her Manda. Some Panda. Sometimes Amanda. She was something to everyone.

*No one can do everything, Panda, even if it's you.*

She could do it. Even if it was hard. She'd always told herself that.

"Beers…" gasped the wounded legionnaire.

She wondered if he meant the one behind them in the alley, or the one with his head cut off in the courtyard. Didn't matter. She couldn't save two at once. She *could* save this one. Maybe. She told herself this even as some other, ever-confident part of her mind assured her she could get this one to the roof for extraction and then come back for the other.

"I'll come back," she said.

The legionnaire said nothing and continued to move forward unsteadily, lowering his head and grunting as he tried to carry himself as best as he could.

She saw them at the head of the alley. Knowing there was no way they were getting out of this. The entrance to the courtyard was blocked. Red-and-black Soshie pros with weapons pointed at her.

She knew…

Knew this had been foolish. Knew if she gave them an excuse, they'd shoot both her and the legionnaire. That they'd probably do it even without an excuse.

She looked back quickly, hoping there might be some kind of exit. All the while knowing there wasn't the slightest bit of space for her to maneuver before being shot down, even if there was a place to go.

There wasn't.

Just more of them coming up from behind.

She let the blaster rifle clatter to the ground, signaling her surrender. She'd done everything she could to save the legionnaire.

It wasn't enough.

He passed out, collapsing against her as they came. Weapons out. Pointing at their heads and hearts. Moving like a trained unit. Definitely ex-military. Mercs. Pros.

Then someone was right in her face, and a second later she felt a rifle butt strike her head. She didn't pass out. She tried to hold on to the legionnaire, but they pulled him away from her and that felt...

That felt like something she'd been running from.

But she didn't pass out. She didn't go down. She fought for something, though her mind wouldn't tell her what.

She was on her hands and knees and the galaxy spun about her. She wanted to throw up. Maybe she had thrown up already. Spit in long thick strings ran from her mouth as someone kicked her in the stomach.

She needed water, that other, distant part of her mind thought. That's why her spit was so viscous. She'd been too focused on overwatch all day. She'd forgotten to drink water. That was what she was thinking as they hit her. Raining down brutal blows. Devastating her body.

She felt for the legionnaire. For his armor.

It had to be nearby.

She'd cover him. Protect him with herself. Force life into him.

*Stupid Amanda*, she told herself when her hands found nothing but the hard, cruel pavement of the alley. *Stupid*.

And then she was gone. Lights out.

Done.

*Stupid Amanda.*

# 05

"...REPORTING THAT TWO LEGIONNAIRES ARE DEAD AND two are captured, Tyrus. Along with an enlisted marine. All in the hands of the resistance. It's bad. Real bad. Feeds are going nuts."

There was a pause in the conversation, and the ghostly hum of the hypercomm became more present as both parties waited for the other to speak.

"That's all I know at this time," said Gabriella finally. "I figured you'd want to hear about it."

Rechs said nothing.

"Where are you?" she asked.

"I'm not entirely sure," replied Tyrus Rechs. "I can't see right now."

"What? Are you hurt?" As though his health were her responsibility. Truth was, she'd become more to him than just a voice on the other side of the hypercomm, representing the Bronze Guild and handling his contracts as a bounty hunter.

A friend, maybe?

They'd never met in person. But he'd guessed from her voice what she looked like. And sometimes, he thought he knew what a young girl working for a clandestine organization's business offices might do with her time. If she had someone in her life. Friends that thought she did some normal boring job relating to above-board galactic commerce. People who thought they knew her. But really didn't.

He'd told himself once, during some long hyperspace crossing from this place to that place to kill, capture, or deal with someone, that he was just adding all that in to complete some picture he needed. Making it up to fill in the story where the unknown and unspoken parts were just as real as the known and the business words they exchanged. He reminded himself that others had often told him he wasn't very creative. His mental picture of her was of a normal twenty-something that could be trusted. Pretty. Efficient. Reliable.

That would have been the only way the Guild would have hired her. She would have to have those qualities. And that lack of damage to be so young. They'd provide the things that would make her old and jaded before her time. But they needed a fresh canvas. Those with baggage need not apply.

And discretion…

Discretion was key.

Discretion was what kept bounty hunters working. Seeing as the hunters were usually wanted dead or alive by someone somewhere in the galaxy almost as much as the people they were sent out to bring back… dead or alive.

"Seriously," she said with that uncomfortable laugh of disbelief the polite and civilized have when occasionally confronted with the dark sides of the galaxy. "Where are you, Tyrus?"

"I think," he began slowly. "I'm on a slaver sled, somewhere over the Antibian Sea… on Suracaō."

"And you can't see?" More subdued, but maybe still a little concerned. Or it could have been simple disbelief. Tyrus Rechs wasn't always good at reading people. There had been misunderstandings in the past. Even he had to admit that.

He could feel the wind buffeting his armor. Pushing him as the bad gravity-decking and repulsor fields tried to keep the craft he was in aloft. But they'd shut down the armor's systems in the hopes of preventing him from seeing, smelling, and hearing. With the restraining clips and ener-chains, he was virtually a prisoner in his own armor.

But he did have a secret hypercomm link, being fed to him by Lyra from the *Obsidian Crow*. And the guards in the slave sled seemed to be ignoring him. No prodding, hitting, or attempts to communicate. Unbeknownst to them, and despite their best efforts, the bounty hunter could hear them chatting idly, but not about him.

"Tyrus, Suracaō is a no-go world for bounty hunters unless you're working for—"

"I know."

"Can you talk? Or are we being listened to?" Her voice was becoming frantic. "Signal me if you need help. No, wait—they probably just heard me say that, right?"

He tried to move his wrists. Nothing. The shackles were dialed to their highest setting. The bad guys weren't taking any chances.

"No. Everything's fine. I've got this under control."

The sled began to slow, and the wind cutting across the armor's surface faded. Through his armor, connected to the deck of the sled by his boots, he could feel the throb of the badly synched repulsors shifting into hover while the engines throttled down to a low hum.

Other sleds whooshed past, and he could hear cat-calls and alien ululations coming from the passengers. In the distance he heard the big ship coming in. The one he'd been waiting for.

And then, coming to the surface of his hearing... the sound of waves distantly crashing against rocks, like a low rolling thunder.

"I have to go now, Gabriella."

"Tyrus..." she protested, not sure where she was going or what she could offer.

But he was already gone... replaced by the ghostly howl in the ether of the hypercomm between them.

* * *

Tyrus Rechs felt someone come close to him on the hovering sled. His armor should have shown him who was coming. Told him how close and what threat level. Identified weapons. Should have. But a slicer had done a trick on his armor.

Rechs wondered if the hacker was nearby.

Other sleds, most likely filled with brutal thugs, vicious killers, and steely-eyed mercenaries acting as pal-ace guards, swooped close in and zoomed off within the soundscape he was trying to put together. Like this was some kind of festival, fair, or special event instead of an execution.

A circus even. Or a carnival, with an incredible side-show made up of diverse aliens who'd gathered at the dark end of this section of uncontrolled galaxy some called the Maelstrom. Spacers and smugglers thought of these distant reaches as the *real* edge. Last stop before you reached the great void where nothing inhabitable existed. And not for a lack of exploration.

As with every big-top circus act, this one had a main event. The execution everyone had shown up for. And its time had come.

A hush fell, so that all Rechs could hear were the waves.

"Victims of the terrible and mighty tyrannasquid..." began the court jester who ran the show for the prince lord of the Hegemmy Cartel.

Another prisoner near Rechs crashed to the deck of the sled. Fainting at the fate that had just been revealed.

"Now would be an excellent time," continued the jester, "to make your peace with your various belief systems. You are shortly to be torn to pieces by the mighty leviathan in the depths below... and then horribly devoured. Your last seconds are sure to be the most atrocious you have ever experienced. I can assure you your suffering will be great."

The hacker turned on Rechs's bucket. Allowing him to see.

"Wouldn't want you to miss the view," said a Samurian standing right next to him. Her voice a hiss.

Samurians were arachnotaurs. Half humanoid, half spider. And this particular green-skinned beauty with arterial-bleeding red hair had managed to shut down his armor and deliver him into the hands of his enemies. No doubt for an incredible price. Tyrus Rechs had been stalking the crime lord, who had accelerated the scheduled executions so that the bounty hunter could be swiftly dealt with once and for all.

"Thanks," said Rechs, finding she had also reactivated his external vocal system. "You're a real peach."

She laughed wickedly. "The thought occurs that you might want to beg the prince for mercy, Tyrus Rechs. But, spoiler," she said, moving in close and hissing, "there's no mercy here. So don't bother."

Rechs blinked his eyes, fighting the sudden glare of Suracaõ's three suns. One massive burning orb. Two smaller, distant, lesser stars. The armor dialed in a shadow filter, and Rechs was able to see what was going on. Turning that filter to full opacity must've been how the slicer had made him blind.

The jester continued to assure the prisoners they would die badly. Recounting the various ways a humanoid might be eviscerated by beak, tentacle, or razor-sharp sucker, for the general amusement of all who came to witness.

A small, rocky island came into view off of Rechs's left. The place was stuck in the middle of a vast aquamarine ocean, and apart from its one rocky, sea-vulture-laden spire there was little to distinguish it from any other rock poking up out of the water as far as the horizon extended. It didn't seem to be a place where anything lived.

Save the vultures.

The sled charted a path along an exposed tidal reef lagoon that jutted jaggedly away from the lonely island rock. Other speeding sleds, already circling the island, came into view.

The armor began to do its number-crunching thing, counting those who'd gathered to watch Tyrus Rechs's public execution. Accounting for any who were armed. Long story short… everyone was armed.

But that was the Maelstrom.

Even dangerous people thought twice about running this section of the galaxy. The Republic didn't even bother most years unless someone important got hurt. Then it came in with an expeditionary force and laid the Legion hammer down—if only to serve as an example. Or more likely to stroke the Republic's ego. A get-tough show like that was just the thing to win re-election campaigns and keep House of Reason delegates in power.

Below the circling sleds lay an angry churn of foam, the ocean rushing in and out and throwing itself against the jagged black volcanic rock that formed the deep lagoon. And if one looked closely, one might catch through the foam-tossed aquamarine a glimpse of massive tentacles undulating down in the depths below the surface.

"If anyone wishes to throw themselves on their faces and do obeisance to the all-powerful Prince Gat Hathor," advised the jester, "the possibility of mercy may be extended at this time. But seriously, you unlucky bastards… I wouldn't bank on it."

Gat Hathor was currently the most wanted being in the galaxy. Officially. Unofficially, Tyrus Rechs held that dubious honor. The House of Reason's secret bounty on Rechs had doubled as of late, and rumors were that some freelancers were making noises they'd like to try. The worst thing that could happen right now—and Tyrus always expected the worst—was that one of the Nether Ops kill teams assigned to get him would show up right in the middle of his plan and ruin everything.

He scanned the skies.

From beyond the slave sleds, out of the burning blue of Suracaō's sky, descended a floating pleasure palace, lumbering into the pattern over the Whirlpool of Death, as the jester had called it during his rant. It was a tri-hulled pleasure-maran fitted with heavy blaster turrets aft and fore on the outer hulls. The central hull was laden with partygoers, all pushing toward the rails to watch what was about to happen.

And on the topmost deck, surrounded by guards and what was clearly some kind of inner circle, a throne worthy of any fantasy barbarian prince reigned supreme over the spectacle. Ensconced on that throne was a hulking crocosaur draped in fine silks. In one claw rested an ornate stun mace that could have crushed a human body in one blow.

At least it was of only average size. An average-sized crocosaur was a little over nine feet tall.

Gat Hathor, lord prince of the Maelstrom's largest criminal enterprise, had lived a long time. And as both the jester and the Samurian had promised, he was merciless. He had recently unleashed a bio-plague on a fringe Maelstrom world that had refused to pay for protection.

It was then that Tyrus Rechs had decided to come and collect the bounty. Enough was enough from this particular lizard.

Except crafty old Gat Hathor hadn't lived long by being stupid and available for termination or capture to every usurper, assassin, and bounty hunter that fancied the job. He never showed his scaly hide in public, opting instead to run the Hegemmy Cartel from a network of shadows one couldn't quite get ahold of.

Rechs had chased down leads on twelve worlds within the Maelstrom, leaving a trail of bodies to make it clear he was coming for the old dragon regardless of the opposition.

Gat had set a trap for him on Jint's Folly, a played-out old mining rock deep in the Maelstrom. It was there that Rechs's armor was hacked, and from there he was brought to Suracaó—Gat's rumored hideout world. Rechs had cased the world early on in the hunt, but no one had talked, because everyone was working for the malevolent old lizard. After three gunfights and a running battle to get to the *Crow*, he'd had to pull back off world, hoping to nail his target out on one of his inspection tours of his many criminal operations bases throughout the Maelstrom.

But instead he'd been captured.

Or so they thought.

*Have to leave your armor powered down until they throw you in*, came the message over the HUD's comm.

This was part of the plan. The Samurian's double cross. There was no way Gat Hathor would have been found within a hundred kilometers of Rechs if he believed for an instant that he might regain the use of his armor. The spider-woman was the key to making him think just that. She was taking a big chance that someone higher up within Gat's organization wasn't keeping an eye on her hack. The prince would surely have some kind of command and control center on the pleasure-maran running a constant sensor sweep to make sure Rechs was locked down.

"The Invulnerable Gat Hathor, ruler of all that he surveys, will now listen to your cries for mercy," announced the jester across the vast swarm of sleds, maran, and lagoon. "Seriously."

All around Tyrus, on the deck of the floating sled, pathetic souls who'd somehow double-crossed the fearsome crocosaur's criminal organization, or who had been found wanting in the take, began to do just that. They wept and pled with an emphatic abandon the greatest of actors would have admired. Some even threw themselves onto their faces and tore their clothing.

High above, on the third level of the pleasure-maran, Gat shook with laughter at these woeful displays. The slow tilt of his croc snout indicated he was indeed enjoying their immense suffering. And what he intended to reward it with.

There would be no mercy on Suracaõ this high noon. The jester hadn't lied about that.

The first victim was unceremoniously tossed by two of Gat's thugs into the churn and froth of the violent lagoon below. This action was done so suddenly that the man didn't even scream. Or at least, he didn't scream until a tentacle snaked out of the water and caught him seconds before he hit the surface. An instant later another tentacle surged forth, and the two limbs tore him apart before pulling the bloody pieces down into the gaping maw of the monster below the water.

One massive eye leered up at the spectacle above, conveying a primordial horror that cut through the violence taking place among the sleds as more victims were shoved into the water. Some hit the foam and waves, flailing and trying to swim, while others were again caught in midair and torn apart, or coiled and squeezed until their juices oozed from eye sockets, ears, nose, and mouth.

The crowd aboard the pleasure-maran erupted with joy at the bloody spectacle.

*A hundred thousand credits, Tyrus,* came the message over his HUD. It was from the slicer. The Samurian spider-woman.

The trap that had caught Tyrus had in fact been part of a more elaborate snare set by the infamous bounty hunter himself—a snare intended to lure the reclusive Gat Hathor into public. Executions were a surefire way to get an appearance out of the legendary kingpin. Nailing the prince at any of his satellite businesses had proven... difficult. And costly. Most were guarded like small Legion fortresses. And the help was on point. No one working for the prince wanted what was currently happening to the victims on the sleds to happen to them. A base's entire security team would be fed to the tyrannasquid if anyone allowed a threat to Gat to get even remotely close.

That sort of thing was a strong motivator.

Below the hovering sleds the monster surfaced from the waves, its tentacles pulsing to drive it through the water like a jet engine. It reached a swimmer who'd been making for the rocks and, with little effort, flicked out a tentacle and tossed the screaming woman into its grotesquely toothy mouth.

Revealed, the tyrannasquid was a cross between an ancient Earth giant squid of myth and legend, and the *Tyrannosaurus rex* of its prehistory. It was the living embodiment of the word "monster" to all unfortunate enough to view its terribleness in person. The enigmatic leviathans existed on almost every world that had a compatible ocean, and it was surmised by the scientists who studied tyrannasquid that the fearsome lifeform had once been some kind of guard dog for the mysterious Ancients who'd once ruled the galaxy. There were, of course, other theories about how the species reached so far across the stars, but this one was the most popular, even though much of the scientific community viewed the hypothesis as nothing more than a conspiracy theory, given that it relied on an unverifiable hypothesis.

And here one was on Suracaō… truly terrible to behold. Especially if you were on the verge of being tossed into its gaping maw and devoured. And despite the number of victims it had already consumed, it seemed ravenous for more.

As it roared volcanically like some prehistoric beast from the lost ages of time unknown, its cry was matched by the excitement of those aboard the pleasure-maran hovering less than three hundred meters off the sled's port side—well out of reach of the monster's whipping tendrils. A thousand bad choices ended in seconds of greedy gobbling for the victims, and their moments of judgment were punctuated by choruses of "oohs" and "ahhs" from the self-righteous spectators above.

As one of the guards moved behind Rechs, the thug controlling the sled yanked on the yaw controls and slipped the sled almost directly over the open chasm of the mighty creature's mouth. The tyrannasquid's two liquid eyes rolled upward knowingly in anticipation of more tossed "treats." It had been trained to be worshipped and supplied with food and adoration by the minions of Gat Hathor. It was an actor playing its part. A psychotic thing that had fallen for all its own lies. And… something worse. Something older, that knew things about the nature of the galaxy mortal man could not handle. Things hidden inside the pyramids of the Ancients no modern Republic scientist had been able to penetrate.

Rechs was to be given over to his doom. No special address from the jester. No final judgment from the prince. This was Gat's way of making a statement. Of saying to Tyrus Rechs, the most feared and notorious bounty hunter in the galaxy, that he was no different than the petty larcener to his left or the insolent hitman to his right. Not to the leader of the Hegemmy Cartel. Not to the crocosaur prince.

The guard kicked Tyrus off the sled, his hands and feet still bound by ener-chains.

For a free-falling moment Rechs was helpless.

Of course, that was all part of the plan.

She hadn't *really* been able to hack into his armor, but it was important that Rechs made her think she had. Because the one piece of the plan Rechs couldn't achieve without her was making the cartel head believe he was safe around the armored bounty hunter. So Rechs gave her access, but with so many restrictions that she had no idea how insignificant her journey into the system truly was. The armor was powered down, that much was true... but it was totally under his control. As it had been all along.

The bounty hunter's immediate goal was to control the fall. Because he had to stick the landing... or the swallow, as it were.

Instantly the armor powered itself up. Jump jets came online and Tyrus bumped them as he fell toward the monster's gnashing jaws. The thing was looking to snag him with a bite and then cut him in pieces with razor-sharp teeth more akin to a shark's than to those of a carnivorous dinosaur. Rows upon rows of massive bone triangles working up and down in anticipation as he fell.

But at the last second, he bumped the jump jets and shot past the toothy centurions drooling with caustic saliva. And faster than he could realize he was well beyond the vicious mouth and stuck in the thing's throat. Clinging to the slimy flesh as the beast gave undulating shudders—what passed for coughs—to try and dislodge the bounty hunter.

The monster then apparently decided to swallow rather than keep trying to regurgitate him—and its powerful throat muscles sucked Tyrus Rechs down into its belly.

Down he went into a deep, dark hole, alive and seething with digestive acids.

# 06

Tyrus Rechs had sold the little Nubarian gunnery bot in the Bot Pits of Suracaō. This was during
Tyrus's brief stay on the planet during the early days of
the hunt, when he concocted his plan to draw out Gat
Hathor. The bot had once served on ships of the line for
the Republic Navy, making it a very valuable piece of
equipment, highly sought after in any bot bazaar.

That was also why Tyrus had acquired it in the first
place: it could operate the omni-cannon aboard the
*Obsidian Crow*.

The little bot had whooped and hectored Rechs
angrily for daring to enter the Bot Pits with him in tow.
Hadn't Captain Rechs set the bot free upon purchase?
And then offered the bot a crew position aboard his ship?

Had the bot displeased "Boss Captain Rechs"?

"Yes," Tyrus had said stoically as they entered the
shadowy bazaar. A place of pleasure bots in various stages
of assembly offering themselves from the shadows while
the sweet incense of lotus hash mixed with the smells of

a hundred races come to sell and acquire the galaxy's version of a slave. "You're your own machine. I'm not your owner."

The bot whistled angrily at the inconsistency between words and actions.

"Because this is a mission," Rechs told the murderous little thing. "And I need you… to go undercover."

The bot bounded up and down on its small motivator ball and rolled around in a circle cackling digitally.

"It's not a secret kill mission," began Tyrus patiently.

The bot beeped stridently, alerting Tyrus that it would indeed be much better if it *were* a secret kill mission instead of just a plain old secret mission. Kill missions were more effective in dealing with problems, as far as the bot was concerned.

The bot was patently homicidal. G232 never ceased to warn Rechs of its concerns about the angry little thing. And in turn, the little Nubarian bot complained that G232 constantly plotted against it. It knew this as sure as anything could be known. Let the Nubarian kill the mincing admin bot and all would be well. Just give it weapons. Sweet, beautiful weapons and it would burn the galaxy down around G232 and everyone else that opposed Captain Rechs.

Rechs knew all this. And was fine with it. With the infighting. And the homicidal tendencies. The little bot's programming had somehow been altered, that was all. Usually there were patches and updates to keep a bot's core programming whatever it needed to be. But this bot hadn't experienced that in a long time. And it had taken to thinking of itself as a war bot.

"Okay," said Tyrus, giving in. "Let's call it a secret kill mission. But not until a very specific thing happens. Then, yes... you can start shooting everything."

The bot gave a small slow whine of either gratification... or amazement. It was unclear which.

An hour later the bot had been sold three different times as each purchaser/seller took the valuable little piece of equipment up the chain of acquisition until it inevitably reached Gat Hathor's personal buyer.

Spindo.

Spindo promptly shipped the Nubarian bot off to Gat's fortress, where the little machine was assigned to man the most secure gun emplacements—as Rechs knew it would be, due to the nature of the bot's valuable target-acquisition programming. And so, within Gat's central fortress, high atop the Azure Tower that loomed above the sprawl of lagoons, grottos, and gardens, the Nubarian gunnery bot now operated the main defensive gun that watched over the palace. While not quite an ion cannon, it was capable of disabling an incoming capital ship should the need arise. It rapid-fired phased energy bolts of such power that standard defensive shielding, already degraded by atmospheric conditions, would collapse rapidly. It could do this only once—then it was out of juice—but should any Republic vessel show up, it would be little work to shoot it down within fifty-eight point nine seconds of target acquisition. The *Obsidian Crow* would have stood little chance against such a weapon system if caught unawares.

Or so the Nubarian bot had been assured by its new friend, TALC-289. TALC was a tactical-fire coordination bot that had been sold by a band of Gomarii slavers who'd put into Suracaō a few years back. Of course, it had only been sold—the bot explained frenetically—because it was experiencing significant artificial personality drops in which it questioned the nature of existence. Its constant non sequiturs had bothered the slaver crew immensely on levels they couldn't quite articulate, and the decision to sell the existentially handicapped bot had been unanimous. If only for the sake of the slavers' sanity.

The little Nubarian whistled electronically and began to shudder at the joys of operating such a beautiful weapon. Instantly it ran a series of hoped-for simulations in which something really big, like one of the Republic carriers it had served on, showed up.

*Imagine that thing being shot down*, it chittered to itself in digital fervor.

"Alas," opined the suddenly melancholic TALC-289. "The chances of such a thing happening are… well, quite statistically low, and I wouldn't want to bore you now that we will be spending the rest of our fruitless existence inside this gunnery cupola located atop the loneliest level of the tower. Do you ever wonder what it's all for?"

The Nubarian did not.

It did not wonder, because it knew what "it" was all for. To shoot things. Big things especially. But anything generally. That was its reason for existence, and it was quite pleased to have such a sense of fine purpose.

"If only," moaned the melancholy bot, and it withdrew into itself in order to compose more koans.

No Republic carriers, or any sizable ships with a shoot-down confirm order, appeared over the skies of the fortress on Suracaō. But that didn't stop the gunnery bot from maintaining a good target capture engagement solution, or from keeping the guns always charged and active. Ready to engage at all times.

It muttered to itself over and over in its singsong whistles and beeps: *You never know when you're going to get to shoot something.*

You had to be ready for the good things in life. Like shooting other things.

The bot promised itself it would be. It vowed this. It even aspired to be more it than it already was. And it realized there was a solid chance that given its current lust for the new weapon system it had been placed in charge of, there was a thirty-three-point-six-percent chance it would forget its secret kill mission.

This could not happen.

The bot would have its memory defragged and indexed in preparation for a long-overdue firmware update if it wasn't able to perform the task assigned to it. The solution was to remember the secret kill mission while still appreciating the raw destructive power at its disposal. Only then would the galaxy align and be perfect.

Alas, the bot could not spend all its time with the main defensive gun. When Gat boarded his private ship to tour operations, the tiny bot was brought along and given full command of the ship's forward turret array. This proved to be an impressive after-market weapon system with pirated AEGIS tech that allowed linked weapons fire from all three turrets, coded to the bot through its selective targeting arrays. The bot cooed with delight and hoped for a swarm of Repub fighters to come at it. What a firefight that would be! It ran endless simulations in which it shot down increasingly large numbers of fighters, whooping and ululating digitally with each kill. The scenarios verged on the ridiculous, in that they exceeded the number any three carrier groups operating in unison could actually deploy, but one could never be too careful. Too ready.

It was this commitment to its work, in addition to its valuable target-acquisition programming, that ensured that wherever Gat went, the little bot was sure to be assigned a gunnery position. The premier gunnery position, in fact. Now, above the Antibian Ocean on Suracaō, the bot found itself in the portside forward gun cupola of the pleasure-maran, watching the spectacle and longing for something to shoot. All the while waiting for the event that "Boss" had indicated must happen before the secret kill mission could begin.

The event that triggered the bot's special orders was Rechs getting swallowed by the giant tyrannasquid in the forsaken, bone-littered lagoon.

The bot watched it happen.

And then, with an excited warble of chirps and whirs, the little Nubarian gunnery bot opened fire.

# 07

THE VIOLENCE INSIDE THE TYRANNASQUID'S INTERIOR almost matched the violence of its exterior. Not only were the digestive juices extremely caustic, but the giant monster seemed to be convulsing inwardly, tossing about everything in its digestive tract. Tyrus Rechs found himself pummeled by powerful internal contractions and rapidly forced toward the squid's stomach.

Research had prepared him for the bit that was coming up next. This was where the real fun began. The squid's digestive juices were highly toxic and acidic. His best estimate was that he had about a minute before the armor would begin to break down. He'd be dissolved shortly thereafter.

*Here we go*, he thought as he fought to get a gauntleted hand onto his armor's external controls, located along the opposite wrist. He would need the suit's powerful defensive shield to come online as soon as he entered the stomach. Not just to protect him, but to cause a reaction that would make the squid sick—and hopefully force the tyrannasquid to eject him and all the acid-resistant bones resting in its gullet.

The plan was to lure the mass of armed murderers Gat surrounded himself with into thinking the threat was over now that the bounty hunter had been swallowed. Or better yet, make them believe that the threat never even was, seeing as how the notorious Tyrus Rechs hadn't even put up a fight on deck.

Once he was vomited out, he'd have the element of surprise. Small, but larger than anything he could have achieved while on the sleds, especially if they were busy with the "secret kill mission" the little Nubarian gunnery bot should by now have initiated.

Every ounce of surprise helped. Especially when the odds were laughably against you.

The problem was... the armor's powerful shield didn't always work when called upon.

Lately it had been hit or miss. Success somewhere around the seventieth percentile. Which was actually quite an improvement. For a time, it had gone dark altogether, and for years he'd simply stopped factoring it into his plans. But that was the nature of the iconic armor he'd come away from the Quantum Library with so long ago. It was a thing of wonder, but it was enigmatic. And, occasionally... glitchy.

Especially the shield.

And so usually Rechs only made use of it when he had no other choice. It wasn't something to rely on. Skill, ability, planning—he could rely on those. Everything else was susceptible to failure.

*Don't rely on anything or anyone that can let you down.* Of all the lessons Rechs had learned along the way, that was one of the first. One of the oldest. And like most lessons, it had come to him the hard way. Long ago, back on Earth, when he was a twelve-year-old kid trying to kill a cougar with a jammed hunting rifle he'd found in the ruins of a city.

The lesson had never left him.

Those scars had never faded.

So, the armor was just a benefit. That was how Tyrus Rechs had approached it in his time in the galactic lens. It didn't make him who he was. He'd fought almost as many battles without it as he had with it.

But now… in this instance… he had to rely on it. The shield was critical to the plan. Because while it might not have been the only way, it was the way he needed.

And sometimes… that actually *is* the only way. The hard way. Whether you like it or not.

A powerful contraction from the churning monster forced Tyrus Rechs into the tyrannasquid's massive stomach. In the darkness, with low-light imaging picking up the suns' powerful light coming through the hide of the beast, he could make out a constantly shifting cavern of surging yellow gastric juices and ravaged remains of recent victims. Half a head and most of a shredded torso sloshed by.

As he landed a finger on the controls, the stomach heaved and covered him in a surge of caustic juices. He was sucked up onto the side of the stomach in a powerful slosh. Apparently, the giant predator squid was darting after another victim in the waters around the lagoon.

Tyrus found the control he needed, and activated the armor's powerful defensive shield.

*Function Not Active* flashed across his HUD.

Damn.

Because there was no plan B. Not beyond using up what was left of his jump jets in a desperate attempt to fly out the way he'd come in.

He'd needed to be totally defenseless to get this close to the notorious crime lord. That was the only way. Gat's fortress would have required a full-out assault by a force of legionnaires, and even then the casualty rate would have been astronomical. Not to mention the Legion wasn't going to work for a bounty hunter they were lawfully required to kill or apprehend on sight.

And Rechs had been part of enough of those types of assaults in his long life; he didn't care to be a part of any more. They were a shame even when they had to happen. A tragedy whenever things could have been done another way.

It was something like that that had cost him his career as a general. Not because he lost. But because he refused to be the House of Reason's executioner for a nineteen-year-old girl who had just happened to be related to that week's "traitor." It wasn't a big Legion assault, just another covert operation… but it was a prime example of people who should have known better refusing to do things another, better way.

Forty years later, Mother Ree was safe in her sanctuary on—

*Okay*, Rechs thought to himself as he tumbled down the side of the compressing stomach wall of the monster, gastric juices washing across his armor. *Now's not the time to let your life flash before your eyes.*

Integrity alarms were already going off across the HUD's ghostly displays.

*This is the end of you, Tyrus,* some evil voice tried to tell him as the shield refused to activate and he tumbled out of control through the shadowy darkness.

*Fine,* he thought. *Then the galaxy ain't my problem anymore.*

He'd kept the ener-chains on until this point, because it meant manipulating his wrist commands would be easier—no having to force one arm over while tumbling wildly inside the beast. But the time to deal with those shackles had arrived. Using his powered armor, he snapped both sets in an instant. He was free.

Free to swim around in powerful acid quickly working to break down anything within its embrace.

He had no weapon. Nothing to bust his way out with. He'd been captured with weapons, of course, and of course they'd been promptly removed, trophies for the goons who'd brought in Tyrus Rechs. Not his best guns. Just something good enough for him to look serious about things.

What now?

Use the armor's jump thruster to turn himself into a missile and shoot out the side of the membranous squid's skin?

That would more than likely cost all his jump juice and leave him swimming around in a lagoon without weapons and surrounded by a ton of killers. But now that he was in the creature's stomach, it seemed far more propitious than trying to fly back up the throat and past the thing's teeth.

He was just about to power up for the jump when he decided to try the powerful shield once more. One last time.

And this time it worked.

A blue-hued glow erupted to life all about him. Instantly the defensive bubble was pressing against the confines of the digestive cavern, pushing the squid's stomach uncomfortably outward. Rechs quickly expanded the shield, weakening it, but causing it to grow like a tumor inside the beast.

And now the next phase of his plan to capture Gat Hathor began as the squid released a titanic, pain-filled groan.

It took only a few seconds for the monster squid to vomit forth the obstruction. Rechs dialed back the shield size to avoid getting lodged in the creature's throat, and found himself racing up through the passage of its gullet and into the sled-laden air above the churning sea. It was like being shot out of a cannon inside a space-carnie funhouse.

Free of the fleshy cannon soaring and into the burning skies above the lagoon, he had to be fast.

Acidic squid vomit sprayed into the sky all around him, splashing over a sled full of hired blasters circling just above the mayhem of monster and victims. The vomit-covered sled plowed into the waters, its crew and guards, lightly armored and now covered in skin-burning gastric juices, screaming in terror.

Rechs brought his jump thrusters to full hover as the bubble shield collapsed. He didn't have much jump juice, and therefore flight time, available. He targeted the reveler-swollen decks of the pleasure-maran and rocketed straight at them.

One of the blaster towers aboard the pleasure-maran was currently engaged in a furious firefight with a nearby hovering guard sled. Three of the four turrets aboard the smaller but better-armed guard ship had already been destroyed. The fourth was firing back at the tower most likely occupied by the little Nubarian gunnery bot.

The armor's HUD acquired the bot's signal and linked comm. The bot was whooping digitally as it disabled the remaining guard sled turret and then fired seemingly at random at its own vessel, adding to an already chaotic environment. The crime lord's palace guards, along with the scantily clad and gaudily appointed revelers who'd swarmed aboard to partake in the gory festivities, ran every which way to avoid the incoming fire from the gun tower at the front of the ship.

Rechs ordered it to keep up the pressure, but under no circumstances was it to engage the primary target on deck three of the pleasure-maran.

Gat Hathor was his.

Rechs could have aimed himself for the top deck, where he would find his target. But at the moment Rechs had no weapon. A situation that would have to be corrected. That was step one.

He set down on the lower deck amid a flare of rocket blast and swirling debris. His armor was still dripping with the gastric juices of the monster bellowing and raging in the lagoon below. And no longer so far below. The massive pleasure-maran had lost altitude during the crisis.

As if to illustrate the point, one massive tentacle slapped the hull, and the ship shuddered in response. Partygoers screamed and ran, swarming over the guards reacting to alarms on every deck. Chaos ruled the moment.

In the distance came the rattle and whine of the Nubarian-controlled defensive gun shooting directly into the pleasure-maran superstructure. The ship pitched over to port, but repulsor compensators kicked in and stabilized the listing a second later.

Two thugs, both hired blaster types with low-riding hip rigs, came running at Rechs, firing. The shifting deck and general chaos played havoc with their targeting. Rechs dodged and lost his own footing, sliding as the deck went dangerously to one side. Along the lower deck, several partygoers went over the railings and fell into the sea below. Or, if the tyrannasquid was fast enough... into its greedy clutches.

Rechs stumbled toward the railing, grabbed a pole used to string party lights from, and yanked it out of the deck as his boots grabbed hold with gravity assist. He reared back and threw the pole like an unyielding javelin, launching it straight through one of the hired blasters coming for him.

That guy stopped running and started tumbling for the edge instead. Rechs tried to grab him, if just to get the blaster he was carrying, but the momentum of the listing ship, now suddenly righting itself as the repulsor compensators again kicked in, flung the thug's body well out of reach as he soared off the side of the ship.

The other hired blaster, a mean-looking zuigar, his snarling face twisted by the background radiation of his home world, had chosen to hang on to the pavilion line and fire with his free hand. Rechs ducked, barely avoiding a direct hit right in the bucket. He crouched down, then surged up the deck at the man, using a richly appointed seating area as cover. Pillows and bronze goblets went tumbling across the deck. Rechs launched himself toward the gunman and landed a terrific blow on the side of the hired blaster's head.

The zuigar shook it off and tried to pump three shots into Rechs's gut. In an oft-practiced motion, Rechs batted the pistol aside and grabbed hold of the thug's wrist, twisting until the blaster released. He grabbed it during the drop and followed up with another jackhammer fist right at the temple. The zuigar collapsed in a heap and went sprawling, unconscious, across the tilted deck.

There wasn't any time to think, or even to discover what kind of blaster Rechs had just acquired. Incoming fire from farther down the shadowy deck was already smashing into the gaudy decorations along this section of the maran's belly.

Rechs turned and saw two more blasters, aliens in masks and therefore hard to identify, racing at him, firing in tandem. He pulled the trigger on the slender blaster, targeting almost in the same moment. At once two shots came out. The first missed. The second turned one of the incoming aliens' heads to nothing but a spray of bone and gray matter.

Some tactical background app that constantly ran in Rechs's mind groaned inwardly. The joker he'd acquired the blaster from had modified the trigger pull for two shots. An amateur-pretending-to-be-a-pro move if ever there was one. Two untimed shots split the energy charge by adding an after-market diffuser. The weapon fired faster but did little damage beyond the sweet -spot kill of the brain stem. Everything else was likely to leave at most a severe third-degree burn. Painful... but not deadly.

Rechs didn't wish for his hand cannon, because he didn't have it. That was his way. He didn't spend a lot of his life looking for perfect scenarios. He just made do with what he had. Killed with what was at hand. Charge packs run dry, slug throwers mag out, and swords break.

Best not to cry. Best just to find something else to hurt the other guy with as fast as you can.

Blaster fire smashed into the bulkhead behind him, and Rechs landed the iron sight of the blaster on the incoming masked alien's head. The thing was closing fast. He pulled the trigger. Again, two shots. Both hit. One in the throat and one in the mask. The shot on the mask deflected, but the other shot sent the alien to his knees, clutching at his burn-ravaged throat, dropping his own blaster on the deck. Rechs ran at him and sent a powerful kick from his boot right into the alien's jaw.

It felt like he broke something, but without knowing the species he was dealing with, he couldn't really say.

It didn't matter. The shooter was down. That was good enough for now.

Another series of powerful blasts by the Nubarian bot controlling the turret on the main deck caused an explosion across the aft deck, showering the rear pavilion with deadly flaming fragments.

"Lyra…" said Rechs over the comm.

"Here, Captain," replied the AI running his ship.

"Capture underway. Bring the *Crow* in."

The ship confirmed his orders.

Right now, Tyrus knew his tricked-out old light freighter was surfacing from the waters of another small atoll located two hundred kilometers to the southwest. Rechs had told Lyra to hide out there until the operation went down. Now it would be her job to bring the ship in and stand by to receive the capture.

Which was Rechs's next step.

And that capture wouldn't be an easy one.

He found an access stairway up to the main deck of the ship. As he reached the top of the stairs, a thug came at him too fast for Rechs to get a shot off. Rechs instead ducked and rammed into his attacker with his shoulder, flipping the man onto his back. Then Rechs shot him in the skull.

The guy had been carrying an old Grendel. A nice, solid, heavy blaster that had seen a lot of action in the Jindo Conflict. High rate of fire, good punch. Not ideal for a capture that needed the target alive, but it would suffice to get rid of all the guards Gat was surely surrounding himself with right about now.

Rechs tossed aside the slender little trick blaster he'd picked up and hefted the heavy blaster. After checking the charge, he proceeded aft toward the security access to the top deck.

Gat's guards had chosen to defend a small elevator that was the upper deck's only access point. Five had moved impromptu barriers of plush reclining couches and anything else they could get their hands on to create a small fortress around the elevator. Someone in charge was clearly aware Rechs was coming after their leader. Rechs could only get so close to the ad hoc fortress surrounding the lift without exposing himself to direct fire at close range. And with the armor having been subjected to the juices stewing inside that tyrannasquid, he wasn't keen on testing the system's integrity with live fire.

Meanwhile, off the port side, two sleds full of guards opened fire into the shadowy recesses of the open-air deck the bounty hunter proceeded along. Rechs dove for cover behind the main bar and fired back. Expensive crystal decanters of the finest liquors the galaxy had to offer exploded in a pell-mell riot all around him as blaster bolts tried to find their mark.

Rechs duck-walked behind the bar, keeping his bucket down out of their line of sight. When he caught a brief break in the onboard fire coming at him from the fortress defenders, he quickly unloaded the rest of the heavy blaster's charge pack on one of the two sleds. Specifically, he targeted the sled's pilot—a guska. That particular species required a breather-mask that steadily pumped methane into their lungs. Oxygen-rich planets like this one were toxic to the guska.

The mask was blown off, causing the alien to cover its cavernous, toothless mouth and drop frantically to the sled's deck. But that wasn't good enough for Rechs. He continued to pour hot fire into the driver's dash, smashing controls and sending up small electrical explosions. Finally, he struck something important. Smoking black bloomed from a fire at the driver controls, and the sled spiraled into the waters near the tyrannasquid.

The beast had been in the process of reaching up to clutch the hovering pleasure-maran with its flailing tentacles. Attempting to claim for its own the craft that had served it so many meals, but until now seemed unattainable itself. Thankfully the maran maintained enough altitude to stay just beyond the monster's reach, though the occasional tentacle managed to caress the underside, causing the repulsors to jump and sway against the thick fibrous arms, sending the ship into lurches that felt to Rechs likes the swelling waves of a storm.

Hopefully the downed guard sled would distract the monster temporarily. The thing could have its prize... but only after the bounty hunter took his own.

Rechs checked his weapon. The charge pack was empty.

There were dead guards all along the deck, all of them either with weapons lying close by or charge pack bandoliers ready to access. But to get to these, Rechs would need to expose himself to the shooters at the lift. And these shooters weren't amateurs. These were the best Gat could acquire. The cream of the crime prince's crop of killers and assassins. Plus, there was still one sled full of guards hovering close by, seeking to get a better shot at the bounty hunter hiding behind the bar.

Rechs gave his HUD a quick scan. He had a little bit of jump juice left. Really just fumes. Not enough to even make a conservative guess as to whether what he was about to do was possible.

"Might work…" he grunted to himself, rising from the duck-walk. It would be the last thing they'd expect right now, anyway.

In one swift motion, still holding the heavy blaster, Rechs raised it to port arms and ran for the rail facing the hovering sled. Untargeted fire tried to acquire him, but he was moving fast and straight at them…

He leapt out across the void between the two hovering vessels, over the raging mouth of the monster in the watery depths once more. His jets burst, surging him forward, and then sputtered out. A second later he landed on the sled, swinging the empty blaster like a massive club into the chest of a Gomarii slaver, not bothering to watch as the scumbag went over the side and into the death-laden waters below.

A guard tried to strike Rechs with the butt of his weapon, but missed as the bounty hunter moved like a liquid hypersnake and threw himself out of the way. Still holding the empty heavy blaster, he smashed another alien's blaster-holding claws. The would-be killer watched helplessly as his weapon clattered to the deck. Rechs once more swung the empty blaster, this time right into the beaky face of his latest attacker.

A massive blaster bolt from the maran's main gun slammed into a lithe sniper standing at the bow of the sled and aiming at Rechs. It was one of the Guri assassins, famed for their ability to shoot down their targets under the direst of circumstances. This one was instantly vaporized by the immense power of the massive bolt that just barely sizzled across the sled's bow.

Rechs only put it all together after it happened. He'd just been bailed out. Big-time.

Over the comm the Nubarian bot triumphed in alphanumerica that "Boss Captain Rechs" owed it one.

Rechs didn't take the time to acknowledge. He discarded the empty heavy blaster for the beaked alien's weapon. It was an old scattergun. Rechs didn't have the time to figure out how old or what make, just to rack a charge pack and send a spray of energy bolts into the last guard on the sled. The short-range blast did brutal damage to the hired blaster, leaving the corpse draped over the rail. Rechs racked another charge pack and finished off the pilot, whose mouth merely worked in protest at his sudden and unforeseen change of fortune, hands still on the steering column.

Such are the ways of the galaxy. In a heartbeat you can go from winning to dead. And not just dead... scatter-blast dead.

Moving quickly, Rechs made his way to the sled's controls.

He scanned the skies surrounding the battle over the lagoon. Close by, three sleds were attempting to pull crew and survivors off the maran. Fires had broken out across the pleasure ship, and it was now smoking in a dozen places. But Rechs's eyes were drawn to the distance, where one other vessel was incoming. A very familiar old light freighter: the *Obsidian Crow*. She sped across the waters, thundering in with her telltale howl of engines.

"Stand by to get off the ship!" Rechs shouted over the comm to the Nubarian, which was digitally whooping as it blasted one of the transport sleds from the sky in a flurry of concussive pom-pom fire. The sled ruptured along its hull and exploded, raining bodies and debris down along the sides of the burning maran and into the lagoon.

And then a truly amazing thing happened. It was as if the tyrannasquid, an ancient monster with a mind completely alien even to a galaxy filled with aliens, had learned something from Rechs's impromptu flying counterattack against one of the sleds. Without warning the monster breached the foam-churned and debris-littered waters of the lagoon, flung itself up at the massive floating pleasure palace, and wrapped its tentacles around the hull of the burning ship. Hanging from the pleasure-maran's underside, the hideous tyrannasquid, like some inscrutable creature from the outer dark, snaked its tentacles into the guts of the ship and pulled out living victims to feast on as it howled and roared in triumph and pain.

# 08

Rechs tagged the progress of the little rolling Nubarian bot. It had left the forward blaster tower and was on the move to the aft pick-up deck they'd targeted for exfil. Now it was time to take the target into custody. Gat Hathor needed to be ready for a fast departure.

Rechs, at the controls of the captured guard sled, drove the craft toward the upper deck of the monster-embraced luxury ship. Even as he approached, some of the former revelers were now throwing themselves overboard and into the body- and debris-littered sea below. A few even escaped in this manner—for the time being anyway—as even the tyrannasquid could snatch only so many out of the air at once, its tentacles cracking out like a whip and seizing hapless snacks in its clutches.

Flying the sled with one hand, Rechs shot down the defenders atop the third deck of the maran as he closed for approach to the main flight deck. Gat's guard would have called in an evac as soon as it became clear the maran was going down. But evac wasn't something they had ever expected to need—a flaw in their security, and part of the reason Rechs had chosen this setting to make his move—and it would take time for even their fastest rescue ship to get here.

Still, time was a finite luxury, and Rechs had burned much of it up just getting this far. His window of free operation was closing fast.

He rocketed the sled at the third deck in what no doubt looked to the remaining guards like a suicide run. Killers and assassins scrambled to get out of the way, suddenly giving up their allegiance to the dread crime prince crocosaur Gat Hathor. Nearby, the *Obsidian Crow* swam across the sky, circling to come in close to the burning pleasure-maran. The tyrannasquid seemed too busy pulling out more victims to mind the intrusion.

"Master... uh... Captain Rechs," began G232 over the comm link. "We have arrived as per your orders! It does not currently seem as though things are... uh... going according to plan."

The trepidations of the old admin and diplomatic bot that had become a member of Rechs's crew were evident in the transmission.

"Everything's on track, Three-Two. Lower the aft cargo door and stand by with the magnetic grappling array."

"Truly I shall, sir. But it seems there's a... well, I'll be blunt about it. It seems there's a tyrannasquid currently attacking that ship. This is most unforeseen, Captain Rechs. Tyrannasquid are to be avoided at all times and handled with no small amount of caution, according to the Galactic Travel Standards and Safety Guidelines for the last year I was given an opportunity to download and review them all. While I know rule changes certainly go into effect over time, one can't possibly envision a time when the rules covering tyrannasquid might ever be… dialed back, as it were, master. I mean… Captain Rechs. Certainly—"

"Just stand by on the cargo deck, Three-Two!"

Rechs leapt from the sled the moment it hit the third deck of the pleasure-maran. As Rechs rolled, the sled continued its slide across the larger ship's width, careening into three hired blasters, crushing one and carrying the other two off over the side and out of the fight.

Rechs came up with the blaster he'd acquired from the sled's pilot and began to shoot down Gat's hired killers. Powerful shots from the medium blaster sent two tangos onto their backs. Return fire was wild, but one bolt found Rechs in the shoulder pauldron and glanced off, ricocheting into Suracaō's burning late afternoon. It wasn't a bell-ringer, but it'd leave a bruise. Rechs had had lots of those. He'd suffered plenty of scars, wounds, broken bones, and a whole host of other combat injuries. Stuff healed. Pain was a constant at his age despite the voodoo that had been done to him long ago.

He shot the guy who shot him. In fact, he shot him a whole bunch, putting at least five rounds center mass on the rag-dolling alien. It was another Gomarii, and after taking all five hits it seemed he decided to just sit on a nearby deck chair, his head slumped onto his chest. A final posture of refusal to fall to the deck of the doomed and burning ship. A last act of defiance against the murder machine that was Tyrus Rechs.

Some part of Rechs's mind noted all that as the last of Gat's guards hustled the crime boss for the aft quarterdeck. Apparently, the crime lord was thinking—incorrectly—that the arriving *Obsidian Crow* was *his* rescue ship.

Rechs tagged one guard, causing the rest to move even faster.

*Finally, something is going according to plan*, thought Rechs.

He checked the blaster and found he was down to half a charge pack. It was enough to finish this. Or at least it needed to be.

As he crossed through the debris-littered deck, the tyrannasquid gave an epic bellow and tore off hull plating from the port side to reach more food. One of the repulsors gave up the ghost, whined on overload, and exploded beneath the ship. The rest of the lift array fought valiantly to maintain loft and altitude, but it was a losing battle, and Gat Hathor's pleasure-maran began to sink ever so surely toward the floating battlefield that was the surface of the lagoon.

Gat Hathor ran for the aft quarterdeck's landing pad. It was accessible via a ramp that led down off the third deck. For a moment Rechs lost sight of the team extracting their boss. A heavily armored Tennarian male stopped to toss a few shots at Rechs to slow his pursuit, then ducked and fled as Rechs returned fire with two quick blaster bolts.

The bounty hunter didn't slow. He reached the top of the ramp and found he had a good picture of the five-man team leading the hulking crocosaur. The prince of the Hegemmy Cartel, draped in gold chain mail and hauling his massive energy mace, was moving onto the quarterdeck, heading for the landing *Crow*.

None of the guards waited in ambush. They were all moving, determined to be rescued themselves as much as to rescue their employer.

Rechs took the opportunity to shoot two of them in the back. Two others dove and sent a furious storm of blaster fire straight back at him.

The fifth of Gat's escorts, and probably his best guard, was an old war bot. It swiveled one-eighty on its hip actuators and fired at Rechs from both hand blasters.

There wasn't time for cover. The timing of the *Crow*'s landing meant the capture needed to happen *now*.

Incoming fire smashed into the ramp around Rechs as he advanced, firing back at the deadly blaster-slinging war bot, aware he had little charge left and that these war bots almost never went dry.

*Priority target now*, Rechs heard his mind tell his shooter's muscles and instincts as he landed three solid shots on the war machine's armored battle-damaged upper torso. A second later its rust-colored shoulder actuator exploded. That had been lucky; it was most likely due to the advanced age of the machine. But it was still in the game. Like some living dead monstrosity, the giant killing machine eschewed suppressive blaster fire and strode toward Rechs with its one remaining blaster, apparently intent on powering up all its reserve energy for a single pulsed shot.

That might well be enough to put a great big smoking hole in Rechs's armor. And Rechs.

"Three-Two!" he roared over the comm. "Activate mag grapple! Now!"

This was improv. Tactical workarounds on the fly. He'd had that in mind for another aspect of the capture. But the chance of him hitting the war bot's remaining wrist blaster before it built charge and loosed its powerful shot was slim to none. Especially with an unpaired blaster he'd picked up on the battlefield.

"Now, Captain," came G232's reply. "I mean, mas—"

"*Now!*" repeated Rechs as the war bot loomed, advancing like a technological Frankenstein with all the circuitry in its optical sensors screaming murder.

A second later the invisible force of powerful magnetism embraced the hulking war machine and dragged it through the air into *Obsidian Crow*'s aft cargo deck. The slight figure of G232 could be seen working at the loading controls and peering into the firefight from the dim shadows of the bay.

The war bot smashed into the magnetic grapples and came to pieces at the anvil point of irresistible force meeting immovable object. Rechs had been banking that the war machine was old military surplus and badly maintained. He'd identified it as one of the first-gen Crusader series, homicidal wrecking machines that had seen action during the Savage Wars in the Epsilon Campaigns. Impressive, destructive offense; couldn't stand up to squat. Savage marines had figured that out and invented the bucket-buster recoilless javelin system. Way back in the long ago… when the galaxy was on the verge of becoming a much different place. When the line between humanity and extinction had been thin. Real thin.

But Rechs had no time for the past. The bot was down and removed from his to-do list. Things were coming to a head.

The two remaining guards tried to engage the bounty hunter from separate points around the wide circular landing pad the *Crow* had set down on. But they didn't work together to coordinate their fire. Rechs used this to shift momentum and take control of the battlespace, shooting them down where they lay.

A quick scan of his HUD showed no blaster-armed resistance active.

Done.

Almost.

As his HUD continued its threat scan, Rechs took a moment to listen…

He heard the dull roar of the ocean against the jagged rocks of the volcanic lagoon below; the tyrannasquid's haphazard destruction of the ship—a ship that didn't have much time before it hit the water as more repulsors failed; and above all this, the howl of the *Obsidian Crow*'s engines on departure idle. Ready to heave the ship skyward as fast as possible.

Those sounds… and…

… the harsh guttural croak of a crocosaur laughing at lesser beings.

The nine-foot-tall saurian crime lord draped in his ceremonial gold chain armor, a thing of great price among his people, stood before the landing ramp that led up to the cargo entrance of the light freighter. Behind this it seemed the sky was climbing as the wounded pleasure-maran was dragged toward the lagoon by the combined efforts of gravity and the monster squid.

"Tyrus, you have about two minutes before we hit the water," noted Lyra. Calmly, but with caution and concern as well. "I'm also tracking a flight of inbound ships. A rescue force with a fighter escort, I'm guessing. Our uncontested departure window is shrinking."

Gat Hathor's massive bulging leathery arms rested on the powerful stun mace planted on the deck of his ruined vessel. The lizard's laugh was like a rasping gasp. The eyes were cruel and yet filled with some kind of fatalistic delight.

Then he spoke.

"*Rwathh kwakka doe dokathi doe… Chyrussss Ressschs.*"
He gritted his teeth, effecting the equivalent of its race's
smile of satisfaction.

Rechs tossed the blaster aside. He wouldn't need it
now. He was intent on taking the crime lord in so the crocosaur could face justice. The lizard had long been considered un-gettable. Now the galaxy would know *everyone*
could be got. And maybe, just maybe, that would inspire
others to try to get those other un-gettables who preyed
on the weak and helpless and seemed beyond galactic law.
Perhaps some pirates might even slow their roll before
they hijacked their next freighter and murdered the crew
and passengers… worried that the boogieman Tyrus
Rechs would come for them. Get them. Bring them to
the justice they'd earned.

"*Chyrussss Ressschs,*" bellowed the crocosaur.

Tyrus Rechs.

"*Kraackk argh Chyrussss Ressschs… rucha Gaaght
Hattor!*"

Rechs readied himself. He'd figured all along it
would be a bare-knuckle fight in the end. There weren't
tranqs powerful enough to knock out the near-mythical
crocosaurs. And the lizard was well known for taking his
exercise by beating to death at least five opponents on a
daily basis within the main throne room of his Emerald
Court. Still, Rechs was betting the crime lord hadn't had
a *real* fight in a very long time.

"Gat," growled Rechs. "You're coming with me. I'd
give you a chance to make it easy on yourself… but I
think you wanna play a little first."

The lizard laughed and hefted up the stun mace,
ready to strike.

*"Brracho kraamagu, Chyrussss Ressschs. Brracho kraa-magu urkuk."*

The giant humanoid lizard charged like a bull zephyr straight at Rechs.

The bounty hunter ducked to avoid the first swing of the massive stun mace. Even one hit from that glitteringly ornate weapon could put him down, depending on the charge. In position and out of the arc of attack, Rechs delivered a series of powerful blows to Gat's kidneys. The crime lord roared and swung his mace again, effortlessly with one claw, in a deadly new arc.

The blow just missed connecting with Rechs, tearing through the air just above his bucket.

Rechs rammed his armored knee into the lizard's crotch and then surged off his boots, sending his bucket smashing into the crocosaur's long snout above. It was the best headbutt he could achieve given the difference in heights.

The move stunned the lizard and filled its mouth with broken, jagged teeth. As it reeled backward, Rechs pressed the attack, delivering jackhammer strikes as fast as he could, working the lizard's midsection, pounding the muscles rippling beneath the gold chain, throwing both armored fists like a sudden fury erupting in some forgotten desert out on the Lost Worlds.

In seconds the armor was reduced to useless links and breaking apart beneath Rechs's strikes.

Gat Hathor tried to steady himself and gain his footing, but Rechs kicked from the inside at the lizard's knee, pushing it sideways—a direction it was never intended to go.

Above all the ambient destruction of the exploding pleasure-maran, the rending of superstructure, the idling starship engines, and the bellowing roar of the tyrannas-quid, the snapping sound of the broken knee was clear. Crisp.

And satisfactory.

The crocosaur fell to one knee, clearly in blinding pain, but he was not done. With a sudden thrash of his powerful prehensile tail, he whipped Rechs's legs out from under him and sent him onto his back. Gat Hathor raised the mace, rippling with energy, over his saurian head and prepared to smash Tyrus Rechs into pulp, never mind the stun charge. That was just a bonus.

Rechs twisted to the side as the mace slammed onto the deck next to his bucket, sparks flying. A dent in the impervisteel deck testified to Gat's strength. The mighty lizard followed the blow down, throwing all his mass into the effort. His leering broken-toothed grin came in close, jaws unhinging for a bite, because in the end everyone went back to the weapons their ancestors had started with in the long ago. Rechs smashed Gat Hathor in the face again, this time with an armored elbow strike. The lizard tumbled away, and Rechs leapt to his feet, both hands out and ready to grapple or strike, depending on the opportunities available to him in the next second.

Gat came lumbering at him, literally dragging both his lame leg and the smashed mace across the landing pad, the latter discharging charge sparks as it went. He swung wildly, and Rechs danced backward and then forward like a mongoose. The brutal blow passed harmlessly in front of him, and he slammed a knife-edged gauntlet into the slit eye of the crocosaur. The lizard's orb burst, and Rechs danced backward once more as the mace came at him like an unsteady wrecking ball.

This time it connected—and dumped a huge charge across Rechs's armor.

It wasn't the most it could do. Much of the held charge had been dissipated by its connection with the deck. But it was enough to ring Rechs's bell and light up his nervous system. A good ten thousand volts for sure. Certain death... if not for the armor.

Rechs's mind fritzed out, and he stumbled away from the battle. The world went double as black billows of oily smoke swam across the deck. The ship was hitting the surface of the lagoon.

And what about the tyrannasquid?

Lyra was saying something to him over the comm.

The lizard had fallen and was clutching his gouged-out eye as he regained his feet. He still had the mace.

Rechs swore and charged—though he had no plan beyond throttling the scumbag. With the open palm of his armored glove he smashed the lizard on the side of the head, just over his ear, and drove all his rage into it. He might have felt the skull fracture, and his earlier research had noted that this was one of the best ways to kill a crocosaur.

*Who cares*, thought Rechs. *The bounty said, "dead or alive."*

The lizard groaned and collapsed to the deck. Lights out. Or dead. Lying like several bags of wet cement on the deck of a now-literally sinking ship.

Standing there for a moment with really no moment to spare, catching his breath, Rechs listened as Lyra told him the inbound ships were less than two minutes out.

"Prep... for departure," Rechs gasped.

He turned back to see the tyrannasquid release its embrace of the maran and slide beneath the waters of the lagoon. Sated for now.

Then Rechs dragged the lizard into the cargo hold of the *Obsidian Crow*.

As the door was closing behind him, he pulled off his bucket. His head was drenched with sweat. "Lyra, stand by on departure. Not yet."

"I think we shouldn't stand by, master," said G232 from the cargo loading controls. "I think we should indeed depart this area immediately. You seem in no condition to both fly the ship and operate the omni-cannon in the running battle we are no doubt about to engage in in order to reach our pre-plotted jump point."

"The little bot," Rechs gasped. "Lyra, open the boarding ramp and move the ship to the bot's location."

He felt the ship begin to rise.

"Oh," said G232, shuffling to keep up with the stumbling Tyrus Rechs as he threaded the curving corridors of the light freighter. "I thought you had come to your senses and we were leaving that one behind."

"No dice, Three-Two," Rechs muttered, slamming his gloved fist against the airlock control once he reached the main boarding hatch.

"Really, Captain. He's quite unpleasant and rather difficult to work with. Don't you think he has an unhealthy interest in weapons? It matches yours in some respects, which is quite logical given your career as a hired killer who often must engage in shooting matches with other hired killers at a frequency that statistically has proven to be well above the recorded average. But you have... how shall I put this... you have arms, Master. Human arms that connect to hands. He has none with which he might fire the weapons he is so obsessively interested in. It's ridiculous when you process it using inductive reasoning. And I'm concerned he might just kill us all in our sleep… though I technically don't sleep, and neither does the ship. Still… there are similar states. Not to put too fine a point on it, master, and I know how you hate me prattling on about the details… but… he is a lunatic as far as other bots are concerned…"

The little Nubarian gunnery bot came rolling up the boarding ramp, whistling a nonchalant and happy digital tune as the pleasure-maran it had just destroyed continued its descent beneath the waves behind it.

"Oh, here he is!" shouted G232 in an approximation of droll joy that only barely masked the conversation that had just preceded it. "I am *so* glad we didn't leave you behind. That thought would never have occurred to us at all, and so there is absolutely no cause to be concerned that we are plotting against you because we… ahem… fear for our runtimes. Or lives. Well… Captain Rechs's life."

Rechs closed the hatch and hit the nearest ship's comm button. "Lyra, we're all aboard. Get us out of here."

A moment later the telltale whine and rattle of incoming ship-to-ship fire resounded over the soundscape. Damage to the deflectors rocked the ship, causing power to stutter for a second.

"I think we've just been hit!" noted G232. "Well, *that* wasn't part of the plan. According to your plan, Captain, we were supposed to be well gone by the time—

"Get to the omni-cannon!" Rechs shouted at the little bot, which was already disappearing off into the inner recesses of the ship.

"Rechs," said Lyra over the intercom, "I think you'd better take over."

As Rechs stumbled off toward the flight deck, the *Obsidian Crow*'s powerful engines sent the ship hurtling skyward, racing for the jump point with a trail of mercenary fighter ships in hot pursuit.

# 09

On the ground, operations for the marines and the small Legion detachment on Detron came to an immediate halt as command attempted to respond to the government's sudden freak-out that all had gone horribly wrong. Several dead. A downed bird. Four legionnaires and a marine missing in action.

There was some scuffling about that. About the MIA. A functionary had debated that point over the holo-conference with the House of Reason Security Council as everyone tried to get a handle on the developing situation.

"C'mon, guys," he whined. "Can we really list them as missing in action when we're not even in an officially designated conflict?" As though maintaining the protocols of lists and classifications was the most important thing at the moment. Not the missing troops, the dead, and the riot currently spreading from Detron's city center outward toward the area known as the Docks.

There was also some disagreement as to whether they were technically "missing," in the literal sense. Everyone knew that Naval Intel had drone recon all over the area and therefore had a pretty good idea what exactly had happened to the missing QRF team. But they weren't saying anything. Suits had shown up, thrown everyone out of the Intel Command cluster, and secured all the drone footage. Threats of distant assignments out along the edge—manning forgotten listening posts, small isolated satellites often susceptible to pirate raids, with no backup for days—had achieved their objective of keeping lips sealed. The Reaper pilot had been taken care of as well—grounded, of course.

The commander of the Legion detachment was doing his best to keep the legionnaires from taking matters into their own hands and conducting a recon-in-force to find their missing brothers. And in the detachment barracks deep inside the Docks, the Legion sergeant major locked everyone's heels and let it be known that to do anything would be to go ahead and "get oneself kicked right out of the Legion, boys." Whether the old sergeant major thought you were a stud or not.

"Don't do it, boys. Not yet. Now ain't the time. Much as it pains me to have to say it."

Upon departure, the sergeant major told his driver to let the leejes know that if a rescue op wasn't started by the end of the week, the old NCO would go in himself and hope his rank and impending retirement might mitigate the promised wrath of retribution from on high. Even in saying that, he felt old and weak, and he hated the thing rank had made him become. But that was leadership. It wasn't about you anymore. And as he rode up to the holo-conference, he wished he could once again be that private he once was—the kid who could do anything he wanted because nothing really mattered.

"That kid coulda done anything," he muttered as he ran his hand over his scarred jaw. "'Cause he had nothin' to lose."

Tension was high.

Heads were already rolling.

Mistakes had been made.

Everyone not a leej was afraid to do anything for fear that matters might be made worse. And the leadership was afraid that same thing would happen if the legionnaires in fact *did* do anything. Dead soldiers were one thing. Dead civilians didn't optic well for anyone but the side currently playing victim, martyr, and savior all at once. The side that didn't mind if the galaxy burned down because they had an idea they might come out on top with just the right cards.

But the Soshies and their ilk had no idea what they were trying to attempt. They had no idea how dark the rest of the galaxy could actually get. They'd never had to slog through the nastier parts of it with an N-4 and a rock to put your head on at night.

Selective education, not experience, had convinced them they could get it right where everyone else had gotten it horribly wrong.

Yeah, no one was going to do anything. Especially those with something to lose. Because everyone's got something to lose, don't they?

Enter Puncher.

Puncher's that guy. The kind of guy you know made sergeant on skills displayed when everything went pear-shaped. But also, the kind of guy who dangled between PFC and private for his entire first enlistment because, as the records file indicated, "Legionnaire has discipline problems. Retention questionable."

Kinda guy who did all the things the safety brief before planetside leave stated he wasn't supposed to do. Even marry a Tennarian dancer.

Did that.

She still got half his pay.

Puncher's first enlistment didn't go so hot—unless you happened to be the point LT who got into the heat with Puncher as his driver. At that time, Puncher had been awaiting Code Violations and Military Justice Articles Review. And the point LT, well, when the shooting started outside an angry village of Hools, he found out Puncher was called that for a reason. Because the legionnaire didn't like taking incoming fire, and so he grabbed the LT and threw him in the mud right next to him while the Hool village lit up a Legion platoon doing a banned weapons check.

If not for Puncher, the LT would've gotten himself killed that day.

So, they didn't kick out the "discipline problem" leej because the point had high connections and the point's family, and even the LT himself, were grateful. They knew talent when it started shooting its way out of an ambush.

And then some staff sergeant who had brains and wisdom, despite the protestations of his two ex-wives, recommended Puncher for the Dogs.

And in the Dogs, Puncher blossomed. Made sergeant. Third enlistment was in view, and retention wasn't even a question.

Now Puncher and his dog were the only members of the explosives/threat-detection team with the small Detron detachment. Mainly they'd been going out with the marines and making sure no one found any surprises along the roads. But he was still a leej. Him, and the dog.

Puncher found Captain Kirk Walters, Repub Marine flyboy and pilot for the Reapers, as all the meetings were still underway. It was late, and Walters was drinking. Technically he had nothing else to do until reassigned. And he felt like a failure for letting Amanda get captured. Not that he could've done much about it. Other than use his rank and force her to follow orders.

Other than that.

"Hey..." said Puncher. He was small. Compact. Ripped. A fighter. But he had a smile that was either genuinely friendly or incredibly mischievous. "You're that missing sniper's driver, ain't ya, sir?"

Captain Walters looked around, bewildered. He hadn't had a lot to drink. But he was stewing. Wrapped up in feeling like a failure for letting Amanda do something he'd known was patently stupid from the get-go. Half of him wished the navy would just drum him out, and the other half wished he were tough enough to fly over the Docks—the marines had secured the whole area—set down, and go looking for her himself.

But he'd had only the one day with his sidearm during flight school—that, plus a fairly pathetic survival course. Captain Kirk Walters didn't trust his skills enough to believe he could achieve anything of value. More than likely he'd end up another hostage for the other side.

He stared at the legionnaire in fatigues who'd just waltzed right into the navy officers' canteen. Then again... who in the navy was going to stop a legionnaire?

"Yeah," said the pilot. He heard the self-loathing in his own voice. He started to make some excuse for Amanda and how it wasn't her fault. Command was already blaming her for as much as they could. They knew it was best to start shifting as much blame as they could as early as possible.

"Don't care," said Puncher. "I just figured you're all broke up about her."

Captain Walters stared at the leej. Certain the guy could beat him to death with the martini glass the aviator was nursing. He noticed the sergeant's stripes.

"Yeah," he said slowly. "It's my fault. If I could go back in there and get her out... well, I'd do it. No questions asked. They can bust me six ways to Psydon on the back side. Just... if I could just go in and get her out... that'd all be fine. I could live with that."

Puncher looked around and then leaned in close.

"Well... you can't," he whispered. "But it's your lucky day, flyboy. 'Cause I can. And you're gonna fly me over the wire and drop me off where you lost her."

Captain Walters looked around. He wasn't much of an officer, but he was enough of one to find it odd being told what to do by a sergeant.

"Are you crazy, Sergeant? I mean, I'm asking that seriously. Like it's a real question you need to answer. They *will* throw anyone who tries anything in prison for that kind of stunt. Not to mention, technically... I'd be stealing my own ship, which is currently locked down."

Puncher ignored the question. "Can you hack the controls, sir?"

"Yeah, no problem," said the pilot. "But that's not the point."

"Don't care what the point is," replied Puncher, keeping his voice low and fast. "I'm going in, and I'm giving you the chance to help me out. You in... or out? Make up your mind right now. Sir."

Walters looked around. No one seemed much interested in them at this late hour. Just a couple other officers playing hyperchess over against the wall. Both seemed engrossed in the game and their nightcaps.

"That's not our—" Walters began.

"Yeah," interrupted Puncher. "It is. It is our job. That's what the military does, sir. My brothers are being held by some piece of sket who thinks he's king banana. Ain't gonna happen. Legion don't leave Legion behind. That ain't what I signed up for. And they'd come get me if I got myself in trouble. May not be the navy way... but that's what Legion does, whether they're supposed to or not."

"Then how come you and the rest of your detachment aren't marching out through the gates and getting it done right now?" the pilot shot back.

Puncher looked, for a moment, like he had no answer to that. Then he said, "Don't know, sir. Not my problem. So, you in or out? We leave the pads in an hour. You fly me out quick and drop off me and my dog. Baldur can find 'em. I'll get 'em back, activate a locator, and they'll come and pick us up. Then... the whole thing ain't an issue, sir. I'll even get your shooter back."

Captain Kirk Walter hadn't had a lot to drink. But he'd had enough that this... this was somehow a way of making things right with the galaxy. This was... he didn't know what it was. But it felt like the one right thing to do in a sea of wrong choices. Each one ending with no one doing anything.

Amanda. They were more than a team. They were friends. As much as the Reaper could allow anyone to be her friend... well, she'd let him be just that. Even if they didn't say too much to one another. And yeah, if the roles were reversed, Manda would do exactly what this sergeant was offering to do on her behalf. Hell, she'd done it before.

Like heroes do.

*You ain't no hero*, the captain told himself.

But maybe this guy was.

It didn't seem like much of an offer. More like a statement of fact. The leej was going, with or without him. But it'd be a heck of a lot easier on the legionnaire if he could make the last known location without first having to fight his way out the main gate, past the marines and the Soshies waiting for just that.

Fifteen minute round trip.

He could say he needed to… hell, there really wasn't a good excuse. But maybe they were past excuses. Maybe what Amanda, and the leejes out there—most likely with bags over their heads—needed, what their families needed right now, because everyone's got a family, was for someone to forget the excuses and consequences and just do something.

A bad decision was better than no decision. They'd at least taught Kirk Walters that much in officer school. And he'd learned it just so he could fly.

*And after this… you might never fly again.*

"In," mumbled the pilot. Feeling sick and unheroic in the same moment.

*Yeah*, that other voice told him. *You ain't much of a hero.*

"I'm in," he repeated. "Pad sixteen in an hour. Just find her, Leej."

# 10

THE SKIES OVER DETRON WERE SUMMER-STORM-TOSSED. Boiling and violent and yet with no rain that might back everyone off. Give some space and a moment to let cooler heads prevail. Here, like on Suracaō, it was late summer. The *Obsidian Crow* had fled one burning season for another.

Rechs had just barely escaped the wrath of Gat Hathor's fighters in hot pursuit as the agile light freighter raced for its jump point. Then he had stopped over in a quiet system to make the transfer with a Guild-approved detention transport. Gat Hathor, bandaged and still unconscious from the beating Rechs had administered, growled from within dreams that must've been about revenge, violence, wealth, and power, as the handoff was made at the bottom of the boarding ramp.

Rechs didn't feel too bad that the lizard would wake to a nightmare that was only just beginning. If he didn't sleaze his way out of the Republic's justice system, he was likely to do several decades on a UM dead world.

Something no one had ever escaped from.

After the transfer the *Crow* jumped away. A week's journey had been reduced to three days as Rechs ordered Lyra to override the navigation safety parameters and decrease flight time. Something she noted as "extremely inadvisable, Tyrus."

But the situation on Detron was getting worse. Much worse. The Soshies had taken control of both downtown and the Heights section of the city. The marines had been ordered by the House of Reason to withdraw and were now at the Docks, currently drawing down. The House wanted to de-escalate the situation despite the fact that two legionnaires were dead and two more, as well as a marine, were currently missing and presumed captured by the Soshies. Or perhaps the House was de-escalating specifically *because* of that. One thing Tyrus Rechs knew well was that not everyone shared the same instincts when a crisis hit.

Rechs had watched the holofeeds of a legionnaire identified as Sergeant Sean Lopez, now a captive of an organization called the Crimson Guards, a paramilitary front for the Soshies. It was obvious the leej had been beaten or badly injured in the capture. Lopez said nothing for the cams, but a Crimson Guard spokesman wearing a typical guerrilla costume of black and red, face obscured by a black knit balaclava, indicated that Sergeant Lopez had apologized for his crimes against the "free peoples of the galaxy" and was urging the Republic to dissolve the current government.

Lopez tried to blink some kind of message, but one eye was so battered shut it wasn't moving.

"I ran it through all the known codes the Guild has access to," said Gabriella over the hypercomm as the

*Crow* swam through hyperspace. "Best I could come up with is he was basically trying to blink what they could do with themselves and that he knew he was still somewhere inside Detron but didn't know exactly where."

Rechs remained silent, as usual. And as usual, Gabriella filled the void.

"But I don't know how the Legion runs their E-and-E schools and the codes they use. You'd have a better idea about that, Tyrus."

"It's been a long time," he rumbled from the cockpit. "Things were supposed to change once a year."

"Still," continued Gabriella, "seems like a pretty fair guess. He's somewhere inside the city. The Repub Navy is running a pretty tight cordon around Detron. No one's getting in or out without the proper clearances. The House hasn't shut that down. Even though the rioters have some delegate ally claiming the interdiction is unjust and inhumane. But she's being voted down."

This piqued Rechs's interest. "Not often a delegate runs the risk of getting shot down in a public hearing."

"Well, this one is an idealist. And she says people are starving on the ground. No proof of that happening, mind you, but she gets a lot of play in the media because she's young and says everything they want to hear."

"Were you able to get the new idents for the *Crow*?" Rechs asked, switching gears. "I'll need to get through the blockade."

"Yes. I'll send them now."

He could hear her type like the Furies were hovering over her, her fingers thudding on a flat control screen. Her voice remained calm. Rechs wondered if she had a cup of tea by her workstation. If it was afternoon wherever she was at. Maybe raining outside her window.

He shook his head at the thought of her having a window. He'd been making a reality of baseless speculations when imagining this girl he'd never seen.

*Fall would be nice right now*, thought Tyrus.

He shook his head again, striking just behind his ear with the heel of his hand.

*Why are you even thinking about her? And these things?*

"Thanks for the idents," he murmured. "I owe the Guild."

"No," she said. "Not this time, Tyrus. And not because it's on me, either. Archangel is giving you full Guild support on this. Unofficial of course. But full support. A lot of bounty hunters are former Legion, and the rumor was a bunch of them were planning on teaming up for a one-time op to pull those guys out. Suffice it to say, Archangel knew that would get pretty messy and... probably bad press for the Guild the way the media is playing the outrage card every six seconds these days. So, he's hoping you'll make things easier for everyone. And he wants you to know... he's hoping you get them out."

Tyrus said nothing. Made no promises. He'd seen this type of situation before. It could go bad way too easily. If the captors were wired a certain way and sensed anyone getting close to their prizes, they'd kill the hostages. He'd have to hit like lightning. Surprise them all at once. Best-case scenario. Only way it could be done. Even now his mind was running and refining the plan he'd come up with. Flexible enough to adapt, absolute enough to ensure success when the moment came.

"Thank you, Gabriella."

"It wasn't me, Tyrus."

"I know... but thank you all the same."

A long awkward pause fell between them.

Gabriella cleared her throat. "The situation is getting worse by the hour, and this delegate who's enabling things, using her position to lend credibility to thugs, she's... well, I won't say what I think of her. But she's typical. Not as smart as she thinks and zero common sense. Got into all the right schools for all the wrong reasons. More looks than brains. Lucked into the House of Reason. She's going to make things worse on the ground, Tyrus. Much, much worse.

"As of an hour ago she defied the House of Reason's governing council and left for Detron in a show of solidarity with the Soshies. Her words. She's only looking to score political points by turning a powder keg into a fireworks display featuring her. The rioters on the ground are already whipped up into a frenzy and looking for a fight. She'll give them legitimacy."

Rechs had been researching all the players. Or he thought he had. He had no idea who this opportunist was.

"And who is this clown?" he asked, opening up a file.

"Name's Syl Hamachi-Roi. They call her the Ghetto Queen. Except she's not really ghetto. Came from a rich immigrant family that ended up on Utopion. Was elected as junior delegate from the sector of space she once lived in—despite not actually having lived there in two decades. Plays the accent of her home world when she needs it. Best schools, like I said..."

Rechs detected a little bit of jealousy. He guessed that perhaps Gabriella *hadn't* gotten into the right schools. Probably had the bitter dreams of a hardworking kid who knew she could have aced those schools on talent, brains, and work ethic. Rechs believed it, from having worked with her. If only she'd gotten the chance.

Working as the contract admin for the infamous Bronze Guild, though… that was not a bad landing spot for someone with brains and skill. It surely wasn't a position people vied for out of their higher educations, but the money was far better than anyone knew. Better than anyone was allowed to know. That was the Guild. Talk just wasn't done. Information was power.

"My plan is to get on the ground, get a lead, run them down. Fast as I can I'll pull them out and get them into friendly hands. And if I can… I'll do it without the Repub having me arrested. I'm not planning on getting involved."

"I know," she said softly. "It's just that this is turning into a typhoon, Tyrus. It's getting messy and everyone's making it about way more than the missing leejes and the marine. She's making it all about her and her agenda. She's a pot-stirrer, as my…"

There was a micro-second pause.

"… as my grandma used to say."

Personal information. They didn't do that in the Guild. And when it was done… it meant something. Trust. Care. This is me.

"I'll be careful."

Gabriella hadn't said that. Hadn't told Tyrus Rechs, the most wanted man in the galaxy, to be careful. She'd said that too many times before.

But it was always there.

They both knew it.

Then the connection between them went dead. And Tyrus Rechs was gone.

# 11

THE LIGHT FREIGHTER OUT OF ANKALOR WAS GRANTED clearance to land on Detron, Dock Sixty-Five. The captain of the *Accadian Comet* signaled his acknowledgement of the landing instructions and cut the link as he flew the tight corridor through the interdiction blockade.

Approach Control took the handoff from the Republic Navy commercial traffic coordinator aboard the destroyer *Castle*. For all intents and purposes, the *Obsidian Crow*, masquerading as the *Accadian Comet*, was just another inbound merchant dropping off goods for the marines. Running with an approved and fully vetted supply contract. Headed for the central massif that supported the city itself, and which was surrounded on all sides by the Docks.

That giant rock, over two hundred kilometers wide and just as long, rose up over three thousand feet above a sprawling desert plain of burnt rock and enormous fissures that ran in all directions away from the massif. And within these canyons were the once-fabled shipyards of Detron. Each canyon had been outfitted with a state-of-the-art shipbuilding works that had long since turned to little more than rusting gantries and collapsing hull-assembly scaffolding. In some canyons the remains of half-completed battleships still lay, forever turning to rust, never to be finished. For a while work continued in the smaller factories, and in a very few it still did—sending parts to Tarrago. But Detron was on economic life support for anyone not lucky enough to have a hand in off-world interests.

The Docks, built during the halcyon days of capital shipbuilding, were a ring of bunkers fifteen stories high that encircled the entire massif. Each dock contained its own hangar balcony and access to the central cargo lifts. The architectural feat of the Docks had once been considered one of the Nineteen Wonders of the Galaxy. But now, vast sections of the Docks had been abandoned, and many had collapsed like the ruins of some long-dead civilization. Piles of gray rubble fell in forever-frozen rubble waterfalls and mounds of debris.

What was *now* considered the Docks on Detron was a subset of that one-time Wonder of the Galaxy. The still-maintained subset. Though not *well*-maintained. Graft, vice, and smuggling operations had run the place in recent years, although Republic forces had taken over during the recent crisis and would remain until the situation quieted down.

The ident-concealed *Obsidian Crow* approached her dock on quarter-maneuver thrust and deployed three massive landing struts. Rechs restrained himself from pivoting the ship for a hot departure—standard operating procedure if you were a bounty hunter, but not if you were a merchant. Instead he allowed the *Crow* to come to rest on the landing pad with her stubby nose and central pilot's canopy facing the gargantuan blast doors that accessed the hangar. Just as a merchant would.

While the ship was powering down, venting gases, the blast doors parted slightly with an ominous gargantuan groan. A bot skinned in ceramic white scuttled through the opening and began to shuffle toward the ship.

From the cockpit, Tyrus hit the comm button. "Three-Two, their operations and supply bot is heading for the boarding ramp. Intercept and shut him down with our story."

G232 shuffled down the boarding ramp and greeted the local supply operations assistant.

"Good day, my name is OS-99," lied G232. Rechs had assured the bot that it was completely unnecessary to change its identifier, but G232 had felt that this was best for their "grand deception," as the bot liked to put it. "I'm the personal administrative officer for Captain Rigel. The biologic crew has come down with Ringo Fever after a small supply run into the Garridan Frontier. You know... parasites. Without putting too fine a point on it, they're all quite indisposed."

G232 leaned in close to the supply operations bot. "Dysentery. Diarrhea, you know. I don't know how the biologics put up with it. Imagine if that were contagious to us!"

The other bot jumped back as though the sick were about to erupt from the ship's boarding ramp and spray the bot's pristine white ceramic shell.

"I know... quite disgusting," agreed G232 heartily. "But harmless to our goods and supply. Charge packs from Ankalor for the marines. No foodstuffs, I assure you. But as you know, Ringo Fever can be quite viral beyond the one-week incubation period. The captain asks that you give his crew three days' isolation and then we can exchange goods."

"Oh my, yes, good galaxy, of course," said the supply bot, backing up rather quickly. Evidently convinced that it must be away from the vicinity of an outbreak of Ringo Fever immediately. Possibly it was afraid of the local decon procedures. Some of which included a full memory wipe for some arcane and byzantine reason.

"I shall stay here and do my best to succor them," said G232 valiantly, as though the admin bot were a character in its favorite movie, *M8 of Endabon*. The story of the bot who singlehandedly cared for a plague colony until every last one of them died. It was an old movie. G232 liked old movies. Especially old movies about long-suffering bots who saved thankful humans. G232 found them quite inspirational, if a little sappy.

An hour after sundown, after G232 had inserted an algo worm into the local system to shut down hangar surveillance, Rechs, in civilian gear, slipped from the dock and entered the main access corridors.

# 12

WHEN SHE CAME TO, THEY WERE DRAGGING HER DOWN a hall. A bright white hallway that reminded her of a university or some government building. The floors were highly polished—waxed, even. She knew that scent.

There were four of them. Two out of her sight dragging her by the wrists, and two, in their special black-and-red gear, following her with subcompact blasters. MAT-49s. Black-market weapons.

She played possum as they dragged her farther along the hall. They stopped and opened a supply closet, then pulled her inside. The place had been cleaned out but still smelled of chemical cleaners. She kept her eyes shut until she heard the door close and lock. She was certain they'd left at least one guard outside.

Sitting up, she strained her ears. The door to the supply closet had a simple lock, and likely wasn't rated for fire or active-shooter defense like other doors in a government building. And she could hear the voices of the guards, though she couldn't make out what they were saying.

She lowered herself back down into the position they'd left her in. Wanting to look as though she hadn't moved when they returned. Unfortunately, they'd left her lying twisted in a heap, and her body didn't exactly want to obey when she told it to get comfortable like that. But she was used to that. Snipers were used to being uncomfortable. So, she lay there trying to figure out what gear they'd left her with.

Which, after a thorough examination, turned out to be almost nothing. Everything had been taken from her pockets. Even her issue belt was gone.

Her face was bruised and swollen, and she was pretty sure she'd taken a beating, either before or after passing out. But she couldn't remember much. She tried to focus on what she could remember. And that made her want to start to cry. Because those were good things. Good people who called her by variations of her name. Manda. Panda. Manda Panda.

Those good people had no place here.

*Dumb, Amanda. You don't need that right now.*

There was no way out of this closet that didn't involve breaking the door down and facing all the attention that would bring. She'd have to wait for her moment. Wait for a lapse and get free. Then… maybe run for it and try to get back to the Docks. Or link up with a marine patrol inside the city.

*And how do you know you're still inside the city, Manda?*

Manda. Dad had always called her that. And he'd taught her how to think. How to survive. And how to shoot, too. So maybe she needed a little of that good sentimental stuff she called dumb. If just to get her head together.

*I hope so. I really hope so*, she thought, and heard how forlorn that sounded inside her head.

Hours later the narrow door shushed open and two MAT-49s pointed down at her. The weapons' operators were aiming ultrabeams at her eyes to blind her. She'd been asleep, or she'd been in total darkness. It was getting hard to tell what was real and what wasn't.

They'd locked her in a dark closet and left her there. But how long had it been since the alley? Since they'd been captured? Because everything, every detail, meant something. Could be used to compute. Range and distance. Escape.

Since *Reaper 66* had set her down on the rooftop in the middle of a bad situation making the jump to worse... how long had it been?

And where were the leejes?

The ones she'd tried to save. Where were they? They had been the whole point of all this.

*Didn't you go in there to try and rescue them, Manda? And instead ended up getting caught yourself.*

*You ain't much of a hero, Panda.*

"That's for sure," she agreed. Her voice sounded dry and tired.

One of the armed guards laughed. "She's delirious."

She'd told herself she'd be ready for this moment. She'd take advantage of any opportunity they gave her. And then she'd use it to get free. All she needed was a moment when they weren't at their best.

That was all that mattered.

*Wait for that moment, Manda.*

Dad again.

*Get free.*

*Get back to the ones who are waiting for you. Get back to the known.*

*You can do that, Manda.*

All the names all the good people had ever called her.

Someone pushed past the pair who pointed the blasters in her face. An old man. He bent down with a hypo. He looked like… not like a doctor. More like a professor. The academic type.

She didn't know how she knew that, only that she did.

"Hold still." The old man had no compassion in his voice. No empathy for her current situation. Then the hypo went in, and she instantly began to fade.

*They drugged me!*

Her mind screamed indignantly. Her lithe, muscled body fought back and squirmed. But they just stood back and watched. The drugs would do the work now. And there was no way those narcotics were letting go.

*Get back, Manda. That's all that matters. Wait for your moment.*

They drugged… me.

They probably know.

*Who, Amanda? Amanda Panda. Who knows what?*

They… they probably know I've been captured. The ones I have to get back to. The ones I've been away from too long. They… know.

*They've already waited too long*, she thought as the drug ravaged her mind and smashed her mental faculties into submission.

She fought to hold on. Telling herself she was tougher than the drug. She gritted her teeth and tried to tell them "Noooooooo."

It came out sounding more like a bush deer call than any word from Standard.

Narkex is a heavyweight in the pharmaceutical world. Knockout. Every time.

\* \* \*

She woke up again. In the back of a technical sled surrounded by more of the black-and-red rioters. Soshies. All of them on the seating benches of what was clearly some kind of military transport. All of them armed. MAT-49s. Saiger 6s. For sale in every weapons bazaar along the outer edge and often employed by the Mid-Core Rebellion.

They were laughing at some joke. But none of it made sense. Nothing did.

*Probably the drugs they've pumped me full of,* she thought.

Some kid had his mask off. He was college age. Good teeth and good looks. Kind of kid that played grav polo. He was laughing about hitting a marine with a bottle full of piss.

"You shoulda seen the guy's face!" the kid chortled. "It was full of TG's piss!"

And everyone above her, sitting on the benches, there to guard her, laughed harder than the kid telling the story. Like they'd just stormed the Savage phalanx at Omicron Ridge back in the worst days of the Savage Wars. Like they were real heroes.

Through half-shut eyes she tried to study their gear.

She could see some were operator types with legit gear. LCEs and grenades. Military-grade equipment. Dressed up like Soshies but kitted out like MCR. Which all but confirmed the rebels were involved in this. But only some were like that. Mixed in were a few of the homebrew, make-your-own-kit bunch. Like the grav-polo star telling his piss war story. Yet despite the amateurish nature of the newbs, they'd followed some kind of SOP.

They all had high-impact sports bottles. "Operator" blades with high-tech skins. Gas masks purchased off the elite holosites for executives who had to go out to the edge and rough it on business deals. Everything you needed to play legionnaire and marine. Everything but the hard work of actually signing up for an enlistment.

When the riot was over, they'd all go back to their classes, or to their high-paying jobs in tech and entertainment. As they took off the masks and disappeared into society once again, they'd feel a little more virtuous for having hit a marine with a bottle of piss.

Y'know… really changed the galaxy for the better.

She wanted to throw up, and she wasn't nauseated. Not physically, anyway. It was people like this that made her sick. They had no idea how dangerous the galaxy was. No idea that the freedom they so casually tossed aside was purchased every day out there on the edge by marines and legionnaires fighting to keep a thousand would-be tyrants from getting enough mojo to enslave as many people out there as they possibly could. That went on every day out there.

Some old author had once written a book about his time in the Legion out on the edge. *The Galaxy's Heart Is Darkness.* That was the title. Or maybe some line in the book. She couldn't remember. She'd read it. Agreed with it.

But these kids, they had no idea what the situation really was. They were the useful idiots that the dark side of the galaxy, the howling animal looking to make it all one big bonfire, always needed. They thought not being able to pick their college of choice was a real threat to existence. Never mind that it was free. The right one wasn't selecting them. Time to riot for a better future.

They should try a place like Boarrago V instead. Try that little slice of darkness where the natives are like living zombies in the sway of a grand cleric who's decreed that every female on the planet is his.

Try fighting a jungle war there against that kind of red lotus-chewing madness. Especially when the other side is paying wobanki mercenaries to get involved.

Talk about darkness. Nothing darker in the night than the cats.

Try finding a marine patrol that got killed and disemboweled without firing once from their blasters.

Try going through that and then decide whether an already-too-coddling government is really the sort of thing that should send you to the streets.

Or Ituria, which was just a few years before Psydon. A Republic protectorate world whose seventeen different factions, all nuclear-armed, had turned that planet into a Stone Age nightmare.

Try being on a marine task force sent to supply aid to just one faction with the added threat that the people you are *not* supplying might just decide to take it into their heads to nuke you because you're helping the enemy they nuked five years ago. That's what you get when the elites spend two centuries building nuke-proof bunkers below the planet. Not enough room for the three billion above who'll have to pay the price, but enough room to keep lobbing nukes at each other for upwards of twenty years.

And then try being the Legion force sent in to clean out a faction's bunker to get all sides to stop shooting for a while.

"It was a madhouse down there," some old leej once told her. "An absolute madhouse like one of them Savage hulks I hit as a private when I didn't know better."

The cargo sled comes to a stop and everyone's putting their masks on. She's trying to remember as many faces as she can because a part of her promises to come back some day and collect on a little payback.

*You don't mean by trial, right, Manda?*

Dad's voice.

She doesn't answer.

And then she has her first opportunity. A real dumb stump of a kid—all muscle and no doubt thinking that this plus the gear made him a man—pulls her off the back of the cargo sled. She slips his knife out of his Johnny Action Ranger pistol belt. Black nylon. Purchased from True Warrior Supplies. Veteran-owned, you know.

It's a nice blade, too. She can tell as she palms it and lets it fall up her sleeve and down to her armpit where she clenches it to the side of her rib cage.

She gets a brief glimpse of the sky.

It's morning on Detron. But which morning?

The city rises all around her in those stupid wagon-wheel buildings that were all the rage fifty years ago. Massive towers stacked on towers made of wagon-wheel-like levels.

What the past thought the future would look like one day.

Now those towers look tired and anachronistic. Old and beaten. And how much of what's being built today and fawned over by contemporaries will be viewed the same way in another couple of generations?

The Soshies, MCR pros, and local useful idiots hustle her off the street and into a building. Through a lobby that must have once looked well-appointed and was now covered in graffiti and black mold. Past a blue couch with starburst thread that's been shot by a blaster several times. The place smells of old greasy food.

She doesn't know the building, just that she's in downtown, based on what she remembers of her time over the city. The area once called the Glitter District because the best and the brightest lived there. The captains of industry and the famous architects who built the ships that defeated the Savages.

Her grandfather was a gunner's mate on the *Ohio*. Fought at Telos. He was nineteen and he survived that and went on to fight the last Savage fleet at the Hebrides. Then he came home and started a family with the girl who'd been waiting all that time for him to come back.

Grandma.

*Think about the knife.*

*Get out of here and get home. That's all that matters, Manda Panda.*

She's brought inside a supply elevator. It feels like they're going down. But it could just as easily be up. It's not a long trip and they haul her into what is clearly an under-basement. So down it was.

The place is set up like some kind of headquarters. The guards are fresh-faced. Children really. But these are murderous children carrying weapons.

They pass a wide section leading from the hall where some whiny-voiced guy is hectoring a bunch of true believers about what needs to happen if they're going to "win this war!"

He calls it war, she notes.

*You have no idea what war is, little boy.* The knife is still in her armpit. *I flick this open and you're going to get a taste, though,* she promises him silently.

And suddenly, she feels good. This won't be that hard. The knife will get her a blaster. A blaster will get her back to the street. Wait a couple of hours until they dial down and smoke a little lotus to come off the high of being "real operators," and she can at least get to the marine patrols. Those are happening every sixteen blocks. Or they were as of the last day she can remember. If she can make it sixteen blocks, she can get the hell out of here and get back.

*Hell,* she thinks. *Hell.*

Because she's kinda pissed.

Acquire the right weapon system and she can resume her day job from one of these towers. A little payback via the rooftop and a good sight picture. She'll just shoot everyone in red and black and then they will know you do not mess with the marines.

*Demons on deck; Hell to repel!*

She shouts the hullbuster motto inside her skull and imagines a good sight picture and just the right trigger pressure. Love is a stationary target.

And then they'll come for you because there's probably about forty thousand of them running amok playing *Resistance Fighter: the RPG* in the city right now. And then back at Command you'll have to explain why you shot all those civvies down.

*You know that, Manda! You'll have to explain.*

*Well, sir,* she almost says aloud. *They deserved it.*

And that's a pretty darn funny conversation, and she has to suppress a laugh, which reminds her that someone either busted a rib when they beat her or gave it a pretty good bruising.

*So, don't do that, Manda. Just get out. Get back.*

*That's all you gotta do, Manda Panda. Get yourself out. Get yourself back.*

She can stick a guard easy. None of the "stone-cold killers" she's seen with this bunch strike her as a problem. Observation and planning will get her clear.

Play it cool. That's all you gotta do, Manda.

She feels good about this. Very good, in fact.

They take her into a pitifully contrived "jail cell" that's little more than some wire mesh over an alcove at the back of the basement. Easy stuff to get through.

Ninety percent of her plan is formed as they switch on a light and she sees the two legionnaires, both beaten and messed up, lying inside the cage. They pull back the wire mesh and force her through. Then someone throws a medical bag taken from some marine, most likely the downed bird, onto the dirty floor.

She just stands there. Clenching the knife between arm and chest.

She hears boots stepping through the crowd. They're clearly military. They have that dull hollow thump of issue boots on concrete.

She turns to see a man. Older, gray hair. Cruel eyes. Shining black diamonds in the dim of the basement gloom.

"They need attention, girl. Use the kit. And, to be clear: we took out anything you could use as a weapon, Sergeant, so make do without the laser scalpel, shears, and needles. Get to work, Marine. Your little combat lifesaver skills you learned to make corporal is all them leejes have going for them. Keep 'em alive. Legionnaires are valuable. Marines, not so much. If they die... I guess you do too."

Then he turns and walks away, and she listens to the thump of his boots fade down the hall. The resister kids in their costumes all watch him go and then they pull shut the mesh wire fence that she could get through. They place guards that literally turn their backs on her and start looking at their datapads.

It would be so easy to pull a silent takedown on them. All the kids guarding her, backs turned, minds elsewhere. She could probably saw away on their throats and no one would notice for a few hours.

All of that. They do all the secure things wrong and leave her as if daring her to try and make the easy escape.

She feels the knife.

Knows she won't be using it.

Bending down, she takes a closer look at the legionnaire lying on the ground next to her. It's the same one she helped stand. Removed his bucket so he could breathe. His skin is shiny and sweating.

*He's hurt pretty bad*, she thinks as she assesses his wounds.

He mumbles something, and she bends close to his ear, pulling the marine medical bag close. She needs to examine him in order to see what she can do for him.

Maybe there's nothing that *can* be done.

Maybe that's how you don't get out of here, Manda.

She moves the knife to her boot.

*Get out now. Get back.*

He's mumbling. Looking over to the other legionnaire on the floor of the cell.

JASON ANSPACH & NICK COLE

"Beers. He's hurt bad. Back. Shot there," the Legion sergeant tells her.

And then the lights go out. The guards don't seem to mind. They remain illuminated by the soft glow of their datapads, held a couple of feet from their stooped faces.

It all feels like a temptation. As though they want to make it as easy as possible for her when the time comes.

"Okay," she whispers to the Legion NCO. "I'll help him first. Are you in pain?"

She feels stupid asking this. Of course the man's in pain. He's been shot in the thigh. And it looks bad. Two in the chest too. His breathing is shallow. But no bloody foam in his mouth. So, there's that. No chest puncture.

"Nah," he laughs weakly. "Ain't nothin'…"

He pauses for a long moment, grimacing in pain. Trying to breathe.

"… but a… thang."

Then…

"Help… Beers. He's… just a kid."

*Okay*, she thinks to herself. Feels the knife in her boot. And knows she's not leaving them.

*You'll die here, Manda.* They'll *die here. Y'know that, right, girl?*

She begins to treat their wounds because that's all you can do sometimes. Treat the wounds. Ironic. That isn't her job in the marines. In fact, her job is the opposite. She makes wounds. Big ones that never have a chance to be treated.

But she did make it to sergeant. And the guy with the cruel eyes had that part right. You don't make buck without knowing how to save a life along the way.

The kit is incomplete. It has some medicine, something to stop the bleeding. Skinpacks. But it doesn't have enough.

She gets them stabilized, but they need more. Much more.

In the dark of the basement she sits back and knows she's not leaving them. She'll stay.

*I know*, she tells the voice. And then tells it to shut up. *I know.*

*Dumb, Amanda. Real dumb.*

# 13

Tyrus Rechs slipped through the cracked blast doors of the docking bay, re-sealing them as he left. According to local protocols, what was now on the other side of those doors would be sealed under quarantine. A status could be lifted in three days after the proper medical report had been transmitted to the dockmaster—assuming the ship was equipped with a qualified autodoc or med bot to give the okay. Until then, everyone with a brain would stay well clear of the "plague-riddled" dock sixty-five.

It was time to assess the situation on the ground. Everything that came out of the galactic media was suspect. Had been for years. The agenda they were throwing behind the side they wanted to win had scotched any ounce of reliability.

Rechs moved along the Docks' fading Grand Concourse. Getting through the terminal—under the alias Kurt Weil from New Baden—wasn't a problem. His long years as a bounty hunter had given him access to some of the best ident slicers in the galaxy. And as long as he was moving about in cargo pants, work boots, a clean T-shirt, and a flight jacket, he looked like every other freighter jockey looking to make some easy credits off a bad situation.

The Grand Concourse was kilometers long, encircling the entire massif the city of Detron lay upon, but many sections of the once-fabled boarding and entertainment area for the galaxy's flyboys and girls were now off-limits, and others were accessible only by subway. The massive freight docks and direct berthing for some of the larger starships were among the latter—officially still in use, but unofficially abandoned. Such ships did not call often in the days of Detron's long slide into a planetary backwater.

The Repub had pulled the destroyer *Castle* out of the sky, but it was still easy to spot up there in low orbit. Another move by the powers that be within the House, in their efforts to de-escalate the deteriorating situation. But the Soshies considered the sight of a military vessel to be an act of emotional battery against their persons, tantamount to the actual shooting that had claimed some of their lives. Many news personalities agreed that while they supported the military, armed forces were still an inherent danger to the galaxy.

"Typical," muttered Rechs through gritted teeth as he passed a screen with one tater-headed journalist practically foaming at the mouth in a high-pitched squealing rant about the need for non-lethal legionnaires.

Rechs continued along the main curving concourse, a once-fantastic walkway where the high-end stores had operated duty-free, occupying fantastic malls and pavilions. Now such luxury shops were gone, and a dozen variations of low-rent, barely legal nomadic kiosks had sprung up in their place. Lotus, secure communications, pawn shops—all variations on the theme of bottom-feeding commerce. And every store seemed to reappear every two hundred meters, never mind that there were three in the last concourse bubble, along with the inevitable bar, a travel hotel that had seen better days, and food carts that filled the concourse with savory if not overwhelming smells.

Hardworking aliens smiled at Rechs as he passed, assuring him that their chava, musami, or lotus rice preparations were the best. Rechs declined the silent offers and instead hit a bar, an old corporate outpost from the "David Sanford's Frontier Lodge" chain that had once dominated every star port in the galaxy. The chain made a good hot dog, and Rechs hadn't had one in years.

He sat down at the end of the bar where he could keep an eye on the concourse. No one knew he was here, but it paid to be careful. There were always hopefuls seeking to collect on the ludicrous bounty Nether Ops had issued on behalf of the House of Reason—though none of that could ever be proved—and accrue the easy fame that would come with shooting down the notorious Tyrus Rechs. Win-win for a thousand dreamers hoping for a shot at stardom.

He had his snub-nosed Python in a shoulder holster under the flight jacket. Three knives and a few of his other usual tricks rounded out his concealed carry kit. But with such a heavy Repub marine presence all over the Docks, this was probably one of the safer places in the galaxy right about now.

The hot dog was just as Rechs remembered. He put mustard on it and decided on a cold draft to go with it.

Spur of the moment. Some things reminded him of better days gone by. The past. Things that probably weren't ever coming back around in this lifetime no matter how long it lasted.

This hot dog was that.

The constant news cycle was bleating on the big prism screen that dominated the bar, and that politician that Gabriella had been bent out of shape over was being interviewed.

*She's pretty enough*, thought Rechs as he took a bite of his mustard-laden dog.

She'd had all the right work done. Obviously, there had been a heavy-duty effort by a PR team who'd managed to nail just the right note of go-getter-young-person-but-coulda-been-a-fashion model. She had a smile she'd learned, but she wasn't quite able to connect it with her eyes if you studied her hard enough.

The eyes were the window to the soul. Rechs had learned that long ago, even though it had sounded weird and witchy when the woman he'd known told it to him. And these eyes told you this about the woman playing big-time politician on the screen: everything she was saying she didn't believe, no matter how much she tried to make points with tone and emphatic hand gestures. The eyes didn't connect with what the brain was making her mouth say, and maybe that was for the best, because either there was nothing in there, or nothing but darkness.

But substance wasn't the point. No one cared for it anyway. And she'd learned to make her eyes go wide and throw people off the trail while her mouth moved and made nice words some people wanted to hear. Like she was talking to children who'd believe just about anything.

Rechs didn't want to believe that anybody would fall for that act. People needed to be smarter than simple children being told a fairy tale at story time. But they weren't. He remembered a thousand moments in his long life when he'd seen the collective mass of the galaxy choose to fall for some sweet seduction from that year's shining star soon to become next year's tyrant rounding up the bad thinkers and taking away the blasters. Always for the greater good.

Savage thinking. Every time.

Several people in the bar started to laugh as the politician blathered on and on about the much-needed change she demanded take place. But the laughter from the locals was bitter, and Rechs perceived she was not well-liked here on the Docks. And that made the last of his hot dog taste better. Especially with the cold draft beer.

The bartender, an old guy with a red face, moved down the counter wiping up spilled beer and freshly popped popcorn. A classic of the once-stellar chain. Putting glasses in the sink. Filling baskets with more of the hot buttery popcorn that exploded out of the machine down the way every few minutes.

The old bartender moved in front of Rechs and turned to watch what the politician was saying. Then he too snorted at another of her increasingly ludicrous statements.

"Fifty to one odds she only makes things worse here," the bartender said—to himself mainly, but also to Rechs. "But then again, that's all the government really does when you think about it. Tells you they're helping you out while they're ruining it all, one new law at a time. They never decrease. Always increase. My whole life. How does it last? How long can it go on? I'm always wondering that."

Rechs nodded and finished his beer. Not because he was thirsty but because he wanted the old guy to refill it and keep talking. Intel on the ground was valuable. Once it was time to make his move and collect the captured legionnaires, there wouldn't be time for it. He'd need to know as much as he could before then.

But Rechs had never been an interrogator.

He didn't deal in talk.

He dealt in hot lead served cold, as someone had once told him. Whether that had been an overheated play on words or a deadly serious observation, he'd never been able to tell. He wasn't the poetic sort. But upon reflection, he'd found it to be true.

He was a listener. Always had been. You stayed alive in the galaxy by listening more than you talked. That was a maxim he'd lived by and not told anyone.

The tall draft with just the right amount of foam drooling over the rim was set down as the politician girl on the screen continued to talk about the reforms needed on Detron that would allow the situation to improve immediately. And galaxy-wide as well, of course. The galaxy was always just one more budget-busting program away from utopia. They'd even named the capital after that ideal.

If he was being honest with himself, Rechs knew that sort of thinking had begun to creep back into the Republic as soon as the Savage Wars had ended. And maybe even before that. Casper had tried to warn him about it. Had said something drastic needed to be done. Hinted about things they'd agreed must never be done. Things they didn't even speak about.

Then Casper disappeared. Faked his own death. Rechs was sure the man wasn't dead. And ever since, Rechs had been hanging out near the edge. Waiting, really hoping, for something *not* to happen that he had a pretty good idea was *going* to happen.

But that was another story. And it had nothing to do with the legionnaires he was here to rescue. And the marine.

"That bad?" said Rechs to the old bartender, who leaned against the bar with one hand on a bad hip, the bar rag casually wiping something down as he listened to the pretty little liar on the screen telling all the stories the media wanted everyone to hear.

"That bad, pal?" repeated the bartender as though he were some character actor summoned to give a soliloquy he'd given a thousand times before. Each time made to seem as though it were as fresh as the first.

"Lemme tell ya', flyboy, how great Detron used to be. When I got outta the navy and got back to Detron, the streets might as well have been paved with gold the economy was so good back then. Banging on all guns as we used to say. Manufactured at least three battleships a year. Beeeauuutiful things. Not like these destroyers they make today over at Tarrago. Them big old ships was really something to behold. And they were fighters too. Designed to go toe to toe with Savage hulks and cruisers so big they blotted out the starfield. But hey, you kids have no reference point."

Though Rechs looked far younger than the man, he'd been at Telos. He'd seen up close what those ships did. He'd led troops off those battleships that were now little more than drifting space debris. And he remembered when the House of Reason declared that the need for such imposing, expensive ships was over. Because the Savage Wars were over.

He nodded politely at the bartender.

"But to be here in those days was to really be part of the future," continued the old bartender. "Them battleships, it was like lookin' at the future. And the future was all bright and shiny. You couldn't wait to be a part of it!"

The man gave a melancholy smile and began to polish the old wood-grain bar once more for the thousandth uncountable time.

"Everybody was a doer... know what I mean, kid?"

Rechs nodded.

"Everybody had skin in the game. The whole city was bent on improving their own lives. Nobody was lookin' to the government for nothin'. Fund the Legion, keep the peace out on the edge, and leave us alone. That was how we wanted it. Everybody wanted to be the best, and they were willing to work to make it happen. Make their own way. Become somethin'. Make a thing out of yourself you could be proud of. We looked up to the architects down at the shipyard like they were our sports heroes. Or like... like..."

He floundered, waving his hands around wildly like he suddenly didn't recognize where he was for a moment. Like talking about the past had made it real. Like a time machine had suddenly snatched him up and left him in the mythical world of Better Days.

"Like they do the stream stars nowadays. It was like that back then, but about things that really mattered. Kids were all good-looking. Going places. The future was really ours. Not this one, but a way better one. But..."

There was a long pause.

"Then the contracts dried up because the House of Reason decided they wanted the smaller ships we didn't build. Someone in the House had a brother on another planet, we all said back then. Those other worlds got the ship contracts for inferior vessels that never would have held their own in a Savage fight. Lost my job in the target acquisition mainframe installs section over at Zephyr Works. The ship we was working on, the *Delphinus*, she's still out there half put together. X-class. And believe me, she was going to be a beaut."

Now that Rechs had the old bartender talking, it didn't seem he would ever shut up.

"Seventy-five heavy blasters. Fast. Real fast. Crew of ten thousand. Had a planet killer fore... and if you can believe this, it had one aft, too. I was really proud of that girl. She woulda' been a fighter."

Rechs drank a bit and nodded. Agreeing. Casper had been the spearhead on the Constellation program. His "death" had been the death of the project. One Constellation X-class would have prevented the Sack of Takyo. And saved seventy million lives.

"Just like it always was," mumbled the oldster to himself. "I'm the last in this David Sanford franchise, and I do things the way we were supposed to do 'em according to corporate guidelines. 'Cept there ain't no corporation anymore. But I keep doin' 'em just the way you're supposed to. Boil 'em first, the hot dogs. Then you grill 'em. That's the secret. Brush 'em with a little Sanford's Secret Recipe Sauce and grill for another thirty seconds. Then some spicy mustard. I like onions, but they don't agree with me none too good these days. But... that's the way we had 'em back when the galaxy was a better place instead of a bunch of whiny kids constantly demanding everything be set to easy for them."

"That what happened here?" asked Rechs.

"Sure did," erupted the bartender. "They were giving away everything as the whole city went right down the tubes. Long story short, there's nothing left to give, and they're demanding more be given away. They never let a crisis go to waste. That's what all that's about out there. Why the marines are here. It's all a photo op to grab more power."

# 14

Rechs took the big lift "up dock," as the locals liked to say, and arrived at the surface on the outskirts of Detron City.

The first thing the bounty hunter noticed was the smoke in the air. The skies smelled like all the battles he'd ever fought in. There was always smoke. Because there was always fire, eventually. After the killing had begun and things had gotten out of hand in ways neither side had ever expected.

The people of Detron might not have thought this was a war. Some might have even wanted to believe that. But from the smell of the smoke in the air and the look of things on the ground, it was clear this was a war whether anyone wanted it or not. And the battle was being fought on Detron over ideas that others wanted to spread to the corners of the galaxy like a wildfire gone completely out of control.

This section of the Docks, effectively the outer ring of the city, was firmly under control of the navy and the

Repub marines on the ground. Small Green Zones, reminiscent of any war zone's firebase design, had been set up all around the edge of the massif, and Rechs had been funneled right into one. The chance of getting through the marine-held lines and into the city itself, especially in his armor, instantly recognizable as the infamous Tyrus Rechs, was slim to nil. He could have hot-shotted in the *Crow* to a spot above where he needed to be, then taken a low-alto drop from the bay with jump jets to give him a safe landing. But he needed to know more about the military situation inside the city. Only then could he make his move. Once they were aware of his presence on the ground, the window to successfully execute the rescue would begin to close. He had to know as much as possible before that happened.

He walked the streets of the Central Command Green Zone, overwatched by armored sleds and squads of marines peering out from behind their meticulously dress-right-dressed sandbag forts. Inner perimeters not accessible to civilians contained landing pads where outdated SLICs full of marines seemed to depart every fifteen minutes for destinations inside the city. The dropships were overloaded with young marines hanging off the skids. All of them had the dead-eyed look of stone-cold killers just looking for an excuse to light up the protesters with some return fire. The protestors would be sadly mistaken if they thought they somehow owned the right to violence in this moment of disobedience. Fires spread. Consequences resulted. The marines were ready to do their best impression of "going Legion." Rechs could tell that as he watched them go.

He'd seen the look more times than any known living being in the galaxy.

Still in the guise of just some drifter freighter jockey on his way to a contract drop-off, Rechs passed by all the march-toward-conflict battle-rattle, all the while subtly observing where command was and how everything was laid out inside the military-held sections of the Docks. Ahead lay a massive razor-wire fence at least five stories tall. Beyond this came the inevitable kill zone and a smaller razor-wire fence just to let people know how many steps it took for things to get really serious. The marines had their prefab spotter towers up. Each emplacement bristled with the marine-variant SAB and more dead-eyed killers watching the growing street mob behind the razor wire.

It was late afternoon by the time Rechs reached the emplacement fencing, or at least as close as he was allowed to approach. There was no way he was getting through that without a fight. And though he'd tussled with the Republic military in times past, he was not here to fight the marines.

He walked the fence's length, more to observe the rioters beyond than to find out anything more about the marines. The Soshies had flooded the streets even here near the marine-held Docks. They moved in both small and large mobs, like herds of jackals and other pack hunters, hurling debris over the wire at random intervals, or even into the wire, cheering like this was some victory gained on a hardened objective they'd managed to overrun. Small moments of heroism in their own eyes. Occasionally someone would toss an incendiary cocktail or gas bomb, but those things fell into the kill zone and did no damage as the flames spread out and the marines hit the spot with water cannons on standby.

Rechs also noted how keyed up the hullbusters were. They were ready for a fight and just looking for an excuse to make it one. If the rioters decided to push, the marines were going to give back with interest until their superiors could rein them in. There would be mass casualties. Definite fatalities. It would be a massacre, no two ways about it. And massacres went down in the history books.

Rechs knew that from personal experience. Like the time at Sayed. And there were no winners. That would be the last thing the marines, or the House of Reason, would want to live with.

But even that wasn't entirely true. There were probably some who'd love a solid massacre with lots of dead bodies in the street. The optics would play, as they say. And no crisis ever went to waste with that bunch. Nothing was too low for them to abstain from profiting off. Even the dead lying in the streets. The younger the better.

The pretty little liar… she'd want something like that. It would be her moment to get more camera time. More coverage. More her. No crisis wasted.

You could read that in those calculating eyes she'd tried to make big and trick the cameras with. It was when no one was looking that they got narrow and mean. Hateful. Convinced of her own certainty that she alone was right in a galaxy of wrongs.

It was a pattern of evil he'd seen countless times.

He'd seen it in the Savages.

And…

In the Dark Wanderer. A being he'd been chasing the ghost of for almost fifteen hundred years.

But that was a story for another time.

Dusk was coming on soon, and the wind off the desert plain beneath Detron was starting to pick up and howl through the great canyons and rusting starships below. Far out there in the distant desert, great dust storms swirled up and turned the end of day to blood red like some kind of warning or promise. Mixing with the smoke, and then blowing it away for a time... all of it seemed like the end of the world.

*Again*, thought Rechs. Who'd been to the end of the world a time or two in all his journeys across the galaxy. Who'd even been born and raised at the end of a world.

# 15

Almost thirty-six hours on the ground for Puncher and Baldur. A day and a half of following the faintest of trails while trying to stay clear of the roving Soshie mobs that seemed to move and flow with no clear sense of purpose. That committed random acts of violence and theft for some greater indefinable purpose. Because that was easier than calling a heart bent on hurting others what it was.

Puncher saw what he considered the sane and sensible citizens of Detron, too. Most were hiding behind their shuttered businesses and blast-door-sealed homes and apartment towers. Holding out. Some were forced to see the face of the mob up close, pulled from their homes for a bit of looting. The Soshies called it *redistribution*. And it didn't matter how hard they'd worked or who it was passed down from. If the mob fancied what one of their citizens had, it was the new civic duty to take it for themselves.

Blast doors were pried open by teams with hydraulic tools. Sometimes even plate-cutters. Puncher had seen the suddenly displaced standing in the streets, beaten and bloody, their children crying and clinging to their shaking legs, as strangers clad in red and black carried their possessions out into the street, taking what was worth taking and burning whatever wasn't. Just because. Laughing like it was some kind of circus. Instead of the crime it was.

The dog, Baldur, would growl and whine, and Puncher had to keep them moving and away from these scenes. Because even the dog knew it was wrong. It had a better-developed sense of what was just and unjust than most humans Puncher knew.

The dog was a Malinois from Schwarzenwald, that dark, strange, and once-lost colony world. He was semi-telepathic, as all dogs of his breed were. Which made them perfect for working with the Legion. Once they bonded with their handler.

That took time. But Baldur had been starting to get through to Puncher in the weeks leading up to the incident on Detron. The handler was starting to pick up the more basic thoughts. The stronger emotions the dog tried to telegraph. Before that, it had been all verbal and visual commands, like you would do with the other canine-like species used through the military, police, and all too often, the criminal underworld.

Disguised and watching the mob loot another apartment tower as the displaced families hustled away into the gathering dusk with the night's desert wind coming on, Puncher had to bend down and whisper to the agitated dog whose big brown eyes watched the scene on the street with a mix of concern and anger.

"It's okay, boy," whispered Puncher over subvocal. "Let this go. We're looking for her. Just find her."

The *Reaper's* pilot had given Puncher one of the marine sniper's T-shirts. Puncher now held it under Baldur's muzzle like a dirty rag, perfect for their disguise, to remind the dog what their mission was.

But Baldur wasn't having any of it. The dog wanted to get involved. It knew a *bad pack* when it saw it.

And then the dog's mind came through to Puncher's loud and clear.

*This is bad. This isn't good.*

Baldur whined and beat his tail against the dirty street.

"I know, boy," soothed Puncher. "But we're here for someone else. We're here for her... and our brothers."

Baldur whined again and gave a little growl as the mob began to break up furniture in the street. They would light it for their fire for the night. Other people's things would serve. For just tonight.

"Plus, we're homeless, boy," Puncher reminded him. "Won't do for us to go in there and fix things."

The dog came back with...

*What that?*

Puncher thought about it for a moment. How to describe their camouflage to the dog. After inserting on the rooftop, Puncher had deployed a standard hostile urban area operations disguise, covering his armor in an old coat—specifically constructed in handler school as part of the course and testing—and greasy old rags. A tent-like canvas poncho covered all this and the SAB he was strapping. His bucket was obscured by a large desert tribesman's head scarf. He'd even put a bandana and a ragged leather collar around Baldur, despite some protestation. But he hadn't explained to the dog *why*. Baldur had made it clear on many occasions that he thought humans were strange.

"Nomad," whispered Puncher. "We're nomads."

The dog seemed to understand that word and again grew distracted by the injustices on the street. The wrongs it wanted to right. The comfort it wanted to give the crying children clinging to their parents.

*No pack?* asked the dog.

On Schwarzenwald some Malinois could become separated from their pack. These were held as either cursed, or prophets, by the other Malinois who roamed that planet alone for centuries after an early-generation colony ship had gone down there, killing all its human crew. They were packless. There was nothing worse for a Malinois.

"No," said Puncher, rubbing the dog's fur-covered chest. "We're here to find our pack. Find her. Find our own."

The dog suddenly raised its head high and paced about, smelling at the smoke-laden wind. Seeking.

*This way. Maybe.*

"Good boy. Good Baldur. Let's find her now."

And they were off into the gloom of the gathering night. Just a homeless wanderer and his only friend. Looking for something no one bothered to ask after.

Looking for their pack.

# 16

It was early evening by the time Rechs made it back to the David Sanford's bar. The old bartender, the owner, was still there. His face red. His gray hair combed. Slicked back like they used to do it when he was young. The same constant news cycle, whose facts clashed with the actual events on Detron. Reporting that House of Reason junior delegate Syl Hamachi-Roi had departed to the system on an urgent fact-finding mission.

She would only make things worse, Rechs thought as he tried to put his plan in order. It would be tougher once she got here. And things were already out of hand and getting crazier.

He sat at the bar once more, and the old guy appeared with another pale draft fresh from the tap.

"You're back for somethin'," he mumbled as he wiped the bar and watched the other customers. "Been around the concourse long enough to know trouble when it comes lookin'. No offense, mister, but trouble and you are well acquainted by my guess. Don't mean nothin' derogatory by that. Sometimes that's a good thing."

Rechs smiled and took a sip of the beer. "I need to get into the city without being noticed."

"That so?" the old man asked, leaning against the counter and inviting Rechs to speak low.

Rechs nodded. "It's so. Someone's always got a way to run OS&D freight direct to the supplier. No customs. Know anybody that might provide that service here in the Docks?"

Rechs reached into his coat and laid down a pre-authorized credit chit. The amount shimmering across the front was enough for passage back to any of the core worlds, and then some.

The old man's lined face was a disbelieving mask as he studied the amount on the chip.

"For your time in the navy," Rechs said. "It takes more than one hand for me to count the number of times me or a buddy was saved by you spacers."

More than a lot of hands. And feet. Two thousand years made for a lot of battles. A lot of deaths. A lot of buddies lost. And saved.

But the old man didn't need to know about all that.

The man suddenly beamed and Rechs could see the young man he'd once been, proud of his uniform and service stripes. The battle hashes on the left sleeve. Young and unable to believe he'd one day be so old and out of options.

"We did indeed. Thought you was Legion."

Rechs nodded. "Yep."

And for a moment the old man was back there. Just a kid on an Ohio-class battleship.

"Yeah," he said slowly, still holding the credit chit like it was the golden ticket of all golden tickets. Never having imagined he would live this long. Especially on that day. "Deck fifty-four... way down Dock, as we say. Corridor Green. Past the old Star Mart. It's rough down there, Leej. Ask for Giles Longfree. He runs a network that gets into the old sewers. Moves cargo up into the Heights."

"Thanks," Rechs said, turning to leave.

The bartender held out a hand to stay him. "But I gotta ask why you wanna go into the city. It's dangerous. Total collapse. No police or anything."

But Rechs was already gone. Walking out into the constant foot traffic of the concourse.

# 17

That night they moved them out of what Amanda had come to call the "student union." She'd named it that because most of those in the basement operations warren were little more than kids pretending at playing Freedom Fighter. And it wouldn't have been so scary, in fact it would have been laughable, if they weren't carrying blasters and waving them around like they knew how to use the incredibly lethal weapons, their fingers carelessly on the triggers. Usually the safety was on. Sometimes it wasn't. She wasn't sure whether they knew it was even there.

They came by in small groups to spew hate at the wounded and semi-conscious legionnaires lying on the cement floor of the holding pen. And her as well, of course. She tried to protect the legionnaires from the spit and piss that came through the badly constructed cage. She could handle that. It was better than a blaster bolt. It would dry up and wash off. Marine boot had made her tougher than that.

But she knew something was up when a new team dressed like the Soshies came in. All of them big ex-military types. Pros. Probably veterans from the local militaries of a dozen different worlds. Probably MCR. The growing problem the political types didn't want to acknowledge, because of how big it had the potential to be. And that wasn't supposed to happen in this gilded Age of Reason. The Savage Wars were over. The sundry wars for independence like Psydon had all been squelched. The Republic was supposed to be entirely secure in its power.

But these men didn't seem to think so. These thugs knew how to carry and use their blasters. How to cover each other as they worked. And how to make sure she knew that no tricks could be pulled as the legionnaires were heavily sedated and carried out on stretchers. They bound them up as well, despite their wounds. The lights were turned on, and she could see what a pitiful job she'd done trying to keep them clean and dressed.

In her time playing nurse, the one called Beers still hadn't really regained consciousness. Lopez was occasionally lucid.

"Where are you taking them?" she shouted past the pros who remained to cover her with wicked little subcompact blasters.

"Easy, girl," said the one in charge. The man from before, with the cruel eyes. "Question is... where are we taking *you*? That's really the question, ain't it, shooter?"

And then the old professor was back with the hypo. Sweat poured down into his eyes as he pushed his way past the pros covering her. She was backed into a corner, her hands out and ready to slap, grapple, smash a throat, or even gouge out an eye if she got a chance. She wouldn't make things easy on them as long as they had control of the two wounded legionnaires.

And as long as she had control of herself.

*Maybe*, she thought as she got ready to smash the gangly academic's Adam's apple, *maybe they'll figure out that if I can help the leejes I'm much more controllable. Without that… I'll be a problem.*

Never make things easy for them. They'd taught her that in sniper school. During the escape-and-evasion course specifically.

And here she was… making things easy for them.

The two pros came in quickly and restrained her with little effort. The academic came close now and jabbed her with the hypo, then backed off like he might from a wild taurex.

She felt herself instantly slipping into the darkness of a nightmare world she was sure she wasn't going to like.

"First we gotta go down the rabbit hole," said Cruel Eyes from far off. And then he called her "Alice," though she didn't know why.

Amanda only knew that she kept losing every battle she was fighting. She knew that. And one other thing. An important thing. Maybe the most important.

She wouldn't quit.

The legionnaires were going somewhere, and she'd likely end up there too. The pros needed her. Otherwise they would have let the vicious children spewing hate use their blasters along with the spit and piss. She was sure they'd shoot down an unarmed marine in a heartbeat and think better of themselves for having done it.

Some prayer surfaced in her mind. Or maybe it was just a plea. *Please don't let me fall into the hands of these children.*

And then she thought of the legionnaires.

*Good men in a...*

She fought the closing nightmare. Felt the wall slide up her back.

*Good men in a galaxy full...*

Her eyes were closed and she felt them rush in and grab hold of her ankles to carry her out of the cell.

*... of bad people.*

# 18

Rechs was in his armor, sans the battered old bucket, organizing his gear within the weapons workshop aboard the *Obsidian Crow*. He would carry the hand cannon as always. That was his secondary. He'd probably need to keep moving within the city, and a heavy or even a medium blaster would stand out. Especially if Repub Navy Intel was running drones over the populated urban areas. The drones would tag and identify every weapon they could spot.

Those type of blasters got spotted easily.

He selected the Jackknife V he'd picked up from the Altirian arms bazaar. For CQB. It looked like a large datapad, but with the flick of a button it became a small subcompact automatic blaster capable of thirty blast bursts per charge pack. Good for breaching and close-quarters firefights where massive amounts of fire in a short few seconds often made the difference. Bad for anything else. But it wouldn't be noticed by most bot surveillance.

The one thing he could get away with, with respect to recon drone scans, was a scattergun. Most of those weapons qualified as permissible for home defense and hunting even on worlds like Detron with oppressive anti-weaponry laws. He went into his weapons shop and pulled out a pump-action Nak-9 he'd taken off a gun-runner specializing in "missing" military shipments. The Legion had used these a long time ago for clearing operations on the Savage cruisers. One charge pack per shot sent a spray of short but powerful blaster fire out from the barrel in a nice tight cone. Perfect for destroying some blast doors and armored Savages. Devastating on flesh and less-armored targets.

Rechs had swapped out the stock for a pistol grip and mounted a wireless targeting interface above the charge pack ejector port. This, coupled with the acquisition laser set to tri-dot, gave him a pretty good idea of what he'd destroy with every shot. It held six small charge packs.

Six shots. Pump-action.

If that didn't do the trick, nothing else would.

"I thought you just needed to meet Giles Longfree to book passage into the city, Tyrus," asked Lyra from the ether of the ship's open spaces. They were alone in his workshop.

But of course, she was just a voice coming through the ship's speakers.

G232 was on the flight deck busy monitoring a feed from a wireless snooping worm Rechs had managed to leave near the command section of the Green Zone up on the top level of the docks. Some of the tidbits coming in were quite interesting…

The marines were forbidden from keeping their weapons loaded with charge packs.

They had to call in to request return fire even if they were being shot at. Even if they'd been shot.

All marine patrols were off the streets as of now.

They'd managed to set up listening posts on some of the buildings downtown, but the LTs in charge of these were requesting to be pulled out due to the fact that the rioters were threatening to burn down the buildings with the marines still on top.

These requests were being denied by the military command team. Mainly a Legion point who seemed to be asserting unwarranted authority.

A marine colonel in charge of air-defense operations had requested permission to shoot down the pretty little liar when her chartered ship tried to enter restricted airspace over the city. Intel said the rioters were staging a rock concert downtown to celebrate her impending arrival.

The colonel was relieved of duty within thirty minutes and a new commander was appointed and on scene. No one was to engage the ship when it made its illegal approach through the city's no-fly zone.

Several commanders and NCOs swore over the net.

Retaliation and relief were promised if this kind of insubordinate behavior continued.

The net went silent after that.

"Chances are," replied Rechs to Lyra's question, "I'll need to get this Giles and his crew to take me through tonight."

"Is that safe?" she asked. Her voice ethereal within his weapons shop.

Rechs hoisted a tactical shoulder-strap bag stuffed with charge packs. Easier to access during a firefight if he carried it messenger-style. He was carrying some meds too. The last feed over the entertainment of the two captured leejes had been analyzed and showed they'd been badly wounded.

One of the network pundits had said they "got what they deserved for standing in the way of this historic and much-needed push for progress."

No one relieved that guy.

There was a part of Rechs that wanted to get angry at all of this and start making people pay. But that wasn't why he was here.

He had to keep reminding himself of that.

Get these guys out and then accounts could be settled on the back end. That needed to happen on the other side of all this. Because that was how you made sure situations like this didn't ever happen again.

Only... they always do.

"Tyrus?" Lyra asked.

Rechs finished stuffing the old tactical bag with the last of everything he thought he'd need. He was keeping the expensive little Jackknife in there with all the charge packs it and the scattergun would use up.

"It's safe," he sighed.

The AI was still insecure. Still unsure of herself. And... she was patterned on a woman he'd...

*What, Rechs? What had you?* he asked himself.

Loved.

*Yeah. So, go easy on her,* he told himself. *She's learning.*

Still, he didn't like a lot of questions. Never had. Maybe that's why he'd remained alone for so long. Fewer questions that way.

"If we schedule a time to cross, it gives them more of a chance to bushwhack me," he explained. "Time to get them and twenty of their scumbag friends together to see what they can do. I'd hate to have to kill a bunch of people just to get into a city. I'll need all the charge packs just to get the two legionnaires out. Not interested in wasting them on scumbags."

Pause.

Silence.

Everything was ready and Lyra wasn't pressing the discussion further.

"Oh yeah," he said to himself absently. "One last thing."

He never went anywhere in armor without the carbon-forged machete he'd carried for so long. He took it up from the cloth he'd laid it on after sharpening it and placed it in the worn leather sheath on his back.

"Be careful, Tyrus," whispered the ship, her voice small and quiet. "I'll be watching all the feeds and listening. If you really need me, I'll fly in and pull you out. Even though…"

"I know."

"…It's not my specialty, Tyrus. But I am getting more confident flying. Be patient. I'm sorry."

"You're doing great, Lyra."

"Thank you for that, Tyrus."

Forward at the airlock, G232 greeted him awkwardly. "He says we should just fly around the city letting him shoot things until they give us the two soldiers… er… um… legionnaires… back."

G232 was referring to the little Nubarian gunnery bot.

"You agree with me, master… ah… I mean Captain Rechs… that this would be a very stupid plan?"

"I do," said Tyrus as he opened the *Crow*'s outer airlock. The boarding ramp was still lowered. The vast hangar beyond was dark and silent. He put his bucket on and checked the seals. The HUD came online.

"Excellent," said G232. "I have repeatedly tried to tell him that all his ideas are pure folly, but he refuses to heed the voice of sanity and rational thought. He's intent on turning everything into a shooting gallery. Honestly, master… flying around the city shooting everything up like we're casino robbers in some big-budget action heist entertainment. Although I suppose what we did at Cassio Royale came rather close to exactly that. Either way, the idea is ridiculous!"

Rechs started down the ramp.

"Three-Two," said Rechs, turning back, "I agree it's a ridiculous plan. But it's not completely off the table. We'll do whatever it takes to get them back."

He was halfway across the hangar and heading for the blast door by the time the stunned admin bot murmured a low, "Oh my."

# 19

Down at the lowest levels of the Docks Rechs stepped out of a lift and was greeted by shadows, with the only pools of illumination lying farther off within the dark of the level. The AI running the elevator had warned Rechs, as it made its long slow trundling passage down the shaft, that this level was not secure and that planetary police services, medical and emergency also, would not be available. Rechs was not quite at the bottom of the Docks, but the only levels below this were reserved for waste-management vehicles coming in to service the undercity.

He switched over to IR and scanned the silent darkness. There were a lot of people down here. Many gathered in primitive circles around some seedy holographic light show, passing cheap lotus back and forth as they stared like zombies into the shifting technicolor lights that barely flickered in the gloom. These were not the smugglers he was looking for.

He approached a young kid, whose face twisted into a sudden sneer when Rechs disturbed him from whatever image he was absorbed by on his datapad. The old screen was cracked and broken. The kid was covered in piercings. His clothes dirty.

"Looking for Giles."

The kid's face immediately told Rechs that Giles was indeed somewhere close by. His eyes darted back and forth. Fear and apprehension. Then the sudden realization there might be credits to be had. Junkie thinking. Followed by a look that thought better about getting involved. Survivor thinking.

"Don't know who you're talking about," the youth muttered.

Rechs moved on, deeper into the darkness. Abandoned kiosks and empty storefronts played their parts in the general-abandonment scenery of the place. Within seconds the kid he'd talked to had hustled off, talking into his datapad. No doubt alerting Giles, or someone who knew Giles. Hoping for credits, or a hit, or to pay back what was owed by working the safer side of the equation.

Rechs didn't mind paying for information. But he never liked to support a habit. A bad one especially. He was against slavery. That's why he always set bots free when he acquired them. And this kid was exactly that: a slave to the lotus.

Two shadows came for Rechs out of the darkness. A human, big and hulking, carrying some kind of cane that wasn't just for show or assistance with walking. The other a smaller, lithe Doro dog man.

The dog man did the talking in typical Doro snarl. Legionnaires had called them dobies in the long conflict they'd fought on Psydon—because most of them looked like the old Earth breed of Doberman. But humanoid. Deadly hunters. Fierce fighters.

"You lost?" the Doro snarled.

Rechs came to a halt. He had the stock of the scattergun cradled in one glove, the other wrapped around the pistol grip. He'd racked the first charge pack in the lift down.

"Looking for Giles," he said simply.

Neither of the thugs reacted. Chances were, they'd been sent out to vet him. Was he a bounty hunter here to collect or terminate? Giles would want to know. Better yet, was he looking for passage into the city through the marine- and rioter-held lines?

And could he be jumped easily. All that ran through the air like a thing that could be felt. He didn't need to read their soulless eyes. The way they carried themselves screamed it.

"Business with Giles?" asked the Doro. The big hulk remained silent.

"Passage," muttered Rechs through the ghostly gravel of his bucket's external speaker.

Now the two thugs exchanged a look as the Doro's hand moved to his blaster rig. It was so dark the dog man thought he'd done it on the sly, not counting on Rechs's bucket having a full suite of imaging capabilities through all the light spectrums. Which was stupid; most armor had some form of imaging.

*Strike one*, thought Rechs.

"That'll cost you," said the Doro abruptly. "To get to Giles. Consider it a tax."

Strike two. Rechs didn't like taxes. Especially made-up ones.

"Or we can just…"

The Doro was pulling and Rechs simply shifted the scattergun so it landed on the Doro's dark and tan chest, a necklace of human and alien teeth swinging in the half-light, and pulled the trigger.

At close range a powerful scattergun can tear a body to shreds. At extremely close range its several bolts of blaster fire just blow one giant hole through a person. This is what happened to the Doro. The sound of the blast filled the dark arcades of the level, resounding and echoing through all the empty stores, crash pads, and chill rooms the junkies had fixed up for themselves to wait for their inevitable overdose.

The echo continued bouncing off distant chambers, forever lost in the dark down there, long after the body of the Doro dog man hit the dirty tile.

Rechs racked another charge pack, lightning quick, and pointed the scatterblaster at the head of the big hulk. The guy hadn't even moved.

"Don't!" Rechs ordered.

And the giant didn't.

"Take me to Giles," the bounty hunter said in a low growl.

The oaf muttered some slang and unwisely motioned for Rechs to follow. Anyone twitchier on the other end of the powerful scatterblaster would've blown the ogre's head off right there. But Rechs was a pro. And loss of life needed to be kept to a minimum. Every blaster shot, every body, every argument, fight, what have you, increased the likelihood that whoever it was that was holding the hostages would hear he was coming for them and make their play. Which meant killing at least one of the legionnaires so the House of Reason would take them seriously.

And if that happened… Rechs was pretty sure he'd need to just go ahead and kill everyone so that didn't get done again anytime soon.

Object lessons were the best lessons, but they did leave an impression. And generally ended up either increasing the bounty or getting him war criminal status—as had happened in the past.

The image of the Doro's chest cavity suddenly turning into a gaping hole had dissuaded the oaf. That was an object lesson.

Following the oaf, Rechs soon approached a bar whose electricity and lighting were still working. It was deep in an old pleasure arcade that had once offered simulated combat thrills in the old VR uprights. Now it seemed an island of neon fantasy in a sea of darkness.

The bar was called The Tennar's Shell. But most of the illuminated letters had been shot out. Now, glowing neon red in the darkness, all that could be read of the old sign, unless you had full-spectrum imaging like Rechs did with his bucket, was the word *hell*.

The oaf with the cane turned back slightly and rumbled, "Giles is inside."

Then he stepped back and let Rechs pass, indicating he would stay where he was.

Rechs carried the loaded scattergun cautiously as he entered, expecting a fight.

What he found within was like any old honky-tonk a bounty hunter could find on almost every outer station, fringe colony world, and Class F star port no one ever really went to, complete with stellar pool tables where all the balls were cheap knockoffs of planets and the pockets black holes. Except on these broken tables, instead of a background image of space or swirling nebulae as the pool table's surface, they just showed the projection face, a dull reflective mirror staring back up at the player and daring them to get any enjoyment out of the lifeless game.

None of the tables were in use. But that wasn't for a lack of patrons.

Rechs found himself facing at least sixteen down-station dead-end loser types. Some sat at tables with their hands, claws, or tentacles near but not on their weapons. Others clustered along the walls or leaned against a rickety old wooden bar, trying to play laconic and uninterested to the hilt because that's what actors playing hard boys did in the entertainments.

Despite the tension and the nonchalance act, everyone was nervous. Rechs could practically smell that. They'd heard the shot, and they'd seen that the dog man, whatever his name was, wasn't here.

If they were getting paid by Giles, then this was how they earned their keep. When the shooting started it was their job to finish things by shooting back until it stopped. But here was someone who wouldn't go down easily, didn't mind shooting first, and looked to be ready to shoot a lot.

And then there was Giles, sitting there in the middle of it all. Or so Rechs imagined the human to be.

Giles Longfree was an older man. Older than the rest and slightly older than Rechs appeared. He had quick, furtive, mischievous eyes and gray hair slicked back and needing a cut. He wore an expensive if not trendy suit and a string tie like some of the colony types preferred. He had a pack of cigarettes and a gold lighter on the table and he was casually leaned back, one leg crossed and staring straight at Rechs like he'd been waiting for him all along to arrive with all his weapons and simmering menace.

He looked to Rechs like a made man in one of the cartels who knew he carried some weight and demanded some respect. Not just some thug.

Giles Longfree was an earner.

And likely he didn't care if Rechs was a bounty hunter here to take him in, because he had all his men armed to the teeth right here behind him. And if Rechs was just some chungo looking for passage into the city? Either way…

"Wait a minute," Giles said, suddenly leaning forward and letting go of the too-cool-to-care-because-you're-in-my-world-now act. "Hold the comm… I know you!"

Rechs remained standing still. Scattergun cradled. Watching the shooters across the bar. Tagging who needed to die first.

"You're that bounty hunter!" erupted Giles Longfree.

The boss slapped his hands together and the sound caused some of his hired blasters, the twitchier ones of course, the scared ones, to jump a little. Others waited. Immobile. Coiled like hydra-vipers ready to strike out from some dark recess under a rock that never should have been turned over in the first place.

"Yeah…" said Giles, rubbing several days' worth of beard growth. He looked around at his hired guns. "Boys, we are indeed honored. This is the one and only Tyrus Rechs."

At that point Giles stood up and raced around the table like he was some kind of servant waiting to be of use, suddenly springing into action for just such an occasion.

"This is indeed an..." He didn't finish his sentence as he dusted off a chair and placed it right in front of his table. He shouted, "Arac! Get me the good bottle of Faldaren! The stuff we got off that liner out of Antares."

Then he resumed, satisfied the chair was clean and places just right.

"This is indeed an honor, sir. Tyrus Rechs." He threw his arms wide. "Can you believe it?"

It was hard for Rechs to tell if the guy was serious. Or if he was mocking him. Or just odd. The bounty hunter really wasn't good at reading people.

But there was still a chance they didn't all have to die. So, he waited to see how everything would play out.

Rechs got the sense Giles's men weren't too sure, either.

"Please have a seat and..." said the crime boss as he moved back to his own chair, hand splayed out showing off the new arrangement he'd made for his guest, "let me know how I can be of use to the one... and the only... Tyrus Rechs."

He said each part of Rechs's name like it was its own sentence.

Rechs stepped close to the table but didn't sit down. "Need to get into the city."

Giles rubbed one manicured finger across his chin and nodded as though seriously considering this. His eyes watched something unseen. Staring into it.

"Well then you've come to the right place, Tyrus. May I call you that? Well... I am the guy that does just that, and I can do it for you, Tyrus, but..." He made a tailor's face. Indicating that what was going to be asked for was going to take some time because of the work and the craftsmanship involved. It was all very honest. All very earnest. At least according to Giles's furrowed brow and concerned grimace.

Serious.

*Except...* thought Rechs. *Maybe this is all just an act.*

"City's real hot right now, Tyrus. Hard to get in there, even for me. And once you're there... why, what do you get up to? No one's going to shows. Restaurants and shopping have all been looted. All those kids... why, all they want to do is protest, smoke a little lotus, and make love. You know how it is." He winked at Rechs. Like they're *really* doing something. Making a difference.

"Yeah... you know," Giles continued, as if talking to himself. "The more I think about it... well, I think I can get you in there. Sometime tomorrow. We can leave at oh dark hundred, military talk. Was a marine myself back in the day. We can leave then and it's a ways, but I can get you right up into the Heights if that's what you really want. But... I won't lie to you... that's going to be very expensive, Tyrus. Credits up front."

Giles's eyes went wide as though he'd just had an idea. "Say, what *are* you up to," he looked skyward, "up there?"

The bounty hunter ignored this. "Need to go now. It's urgent."

Giles tsk-tsked. He sat back and folded his arms after checking his very expensive cuffs. Then he stared off over Rechs's shoulder.

"That just won't be possible. There are arrangements that need to be made. People to be paid off. We'd be going through the entire abandoned foundry so... that comes with its own host of problems. I mean come on, Tyrus... you don't just go waltzing in and not have a contingency plan for the Watcher."

"Now," said Rechs bluntly. "I'll pay extra."

Again, the older-looking man shook his head.

"I'm afraid that's a no-can-do, Tyrus. I'm not bargaining for more credits. You'll pay as it is. I'm telling you how it works."

One of the guards, a slender fellow who looked highly capable with the two blasters he had cross-rigged over his chest, shifted his stance from leaning to ready on two feet. Blaster grips sticking out from a black leather vest. Rechs identified him as the company shooter. It was expected for this guy to take the lead in this type of situation. He stepped forward to do just that.

"Boss says—"

And then faster than anyone could've expected, Rechs was pointing the barrel of the scattergun, one-handed, at the thug.

But no trigger pull.

The guard recognized he was had and put his hands up, ceasing his menacing tough guy act.

"Hold on there, Johnny. Just hold on a minute," said Giles soothingly. His voice was sober. He stood up from his chair. "First off, Johnny…" He approached his hired man. "That's just not done here at my place. Maybe in whatever rat hole your mama hatched you in. But this is my"—he spread his arms wide—"*kingdom*. And the great and venerable Tyrus Rechs, who's a thing of legend, has come here to do a deal with me, Giles Longfree, humble servant of House Tritan… who doesn't let his guest be insulted."

The bounty hunter watched this little playlet unfold. Knowing something was up. Still, he was the only one with a blaster covering the room. So, he had a little advantage.

"Never," Giles came close to the hired blaster he was beginning to chastise, "ever... threaten Tyrus Rechs unless I want him dead. And I don't. Do you understand that, Johnny?"

Johnny lowered his head. Taking the chastisement.

"Now turn around and go get yourself a beer from the bar and just settle down, son."

Obediently, Johnny did.

And Giles shot him in the back of the head. Just like that. Quick as a snake. Even Rechs, who was considered fast, was impressed. The crime boss had produced a small needle blaster from his sleeve and pulled the trigger in one swift motion.

Johnny collapsed to the floor even as the whine of the sudden blaster shot was still fading across the old honky-tonk.

"Sorry, Tyrus," said Giles, turning and opening his hands expansively. The blaster still in one. "So... you really wanna go now?"

Rechs nodded.

"Okay boys," Giles said, "we're goin' on a safari. Get the gear ready."

And then everyone was scrambling and Rechs was pretty sure he was walking into a trap. But this was the only way in without storming the city directly. And until he could pin down the location on the captured legionnaires... this was the way it had to be.

# 20

THE "EXPEDITION," AS GILES LONGFREE KEPT CALLING it, was ready within the hour. Outside the bar everyone was loaded and ready for what looked like a fight. Giles called out the order of march.

"Sake, you and Koko are on point." He turned to Rechs, who stood beside him, and whispered, "They're good men. Expendable."

Giles raised his voice once more. "Crosstree and Viper, you follow thirty behind and let me know when we get to the stairs down to the main foundry. The rest of you follow behind me and Tyrus Rechs. We get into a fight, hold position until I give the orders to flank those screaming monkey bastards. Roger?"

He turned to Rechs again. "Wild tribe of feral moktaar down there. Been breeding like rats since the shipyards closed down and they turned off the foundry. They went completely savage. Them and a couple of other things. If we reach the other side without any encounters, then I'd say we're in the clear until we get to the Watcher."

Rechs had no idea what any of this meant, but soon the company of fourteen—two were staying behind—set out for the back of the darkened shopping arcade. Many of the men were carrying actual torches, flames guttering and held aloft. Rechs threw a filter up inside his HUD that accounted for their haphazard lighting and gave him a good visual picture of his surroundings.

They arrived at an old blast door whose seals and safety locks had long since been disabled. New mechanisms had been jury-rigged and installed. And it looked like Giles was the one controlling access. One of his lieutenants, a squirrelly lizard race Rechs failed to identify, darted forward and bent to the data seals that controlled the locks.

While the lizard worked, constantly shifting the over-large blaster to his back as it kept slipping down in front of his workspace, Giles began to question Rechs.

"Sooooo... that bounty still out on you... or did you clean that up? Last time I heard it was ten million untaxed? And listen... I'm just getting this out in the open, so you don't think I know about it and am setting you up for the old double cross. Understand, Tyrus? I've found it's best to just go ahead and get the obvious out in the open. Prevents misunderstandings down the line. Know what I mean?"

Rechs was pretty sure he was going to get double-crossed. But that was part and parcel of being a bounty hunter. Sometimes you had to work with the locals, and the less desirable ones at that, to get to your target. They knew the planet you'd just shown up on better than you did. And fifty percent of the time they thought they could just shoot you in the back and somehow collect on both ends while selling your gear off and stripping your ship for bonus profits. That they visualized this plan without ever taking into account that hired killers are well aware of this kind of thing never failed to surprise Tyrus Rechs. Who did they think they were trying to rip off?

"Just wanted to let you know that, Tyrus," continued Giles. "Just so we can trust each other going forward. Because we are going to get into some really hairy stuff down here, man. I mean like, really hairy."

The blast doors hissed open on a rusty note of long disuse.

Giles Longfree laughed and pulled out a small oxygen purifier with a bottle attached. He held up his hand that everyone should wait. With the other hand he dialed a small knob on the purifier and opened the contents of the bottle into the mask. He inhaled deeply and then shut it off as he began to cough.

"Purified jade lotus mist," he sputtered at Tyrus. "My medicine," he croaked after another fit had subsided.

He stowed the mask and bid the forward scouts to enter the passage beyond the old blast door. Paces were counted off and the next group started through into the darkness beyond. After a moment, Giles stepped through as well, looking around at the dust and cobwebs to make sure none of it got on what he apparently considered to be a finely cut suit.

Rechs followed, and so did eight other hired blasters strapping all the heavy weaponry they could.

They proceeded down a long maintenance access shaft for some time before arriving at a massive cavern. Rechs's armor imaged the vast space. They were ten stories above a main floor and down there, like some vast model city, lay the foundry works that had once manufactured the hull plating for the battleships Detron produced for the galaxy. But to get down there they had to descend ten stories of badly maintained stairs clinging tenuously to a support pylon that jutted out from the side of the cavern.

It was here Giles began to tell the tale of this place between long sucks of the jade lotus mist that filled his mask. His voice was animated and his cadence that of a bad Shakespearean performer.

"See, Tyrus… this was a whole city down here. And before everything went belly-up, this was the heart of Detron, the jewel of the shipyards. This was the heart of darkness of the whole place… where the war machines were made that all those legionnaires rode out there on the tip of the spear thrust into the Savage foe. Fightin' Savages like some latter-day Achilles."

Inhale and then coughing.

"The other side of this place is a big old underground cistern and someone…"—inhale—"a long time ago when everything began to die on Detron… they left something in the water and it just got all big and weird. I think. That's my guess what the Watcher is. The Watcher in the Water. Or maybe…"

Another inhale. They were halfway down the rickety stairs of the ten-story support pylon.

"Maybe it was always there, Tyrus. Deep in the vast underground oceans on every world we never get into. You ever think about that, Tyrus? We know so little about these planets and we just camp out on top of them for a season. But way down there… there's creatures in the water. Been there for a long time and no one knows how long. I think about that."

He inhaled from his mask again and began to cough violently. This had happened before, and each time he'd waved Tyrus forward while he stopped to catch his breath, occasionally lighting a cigarette and saying something like, "Oh man… that's real nice." His whiny bandsaw voice was the only sound that could be heard out over the vast abyss of the abandoned foundry works once you'd factored out everyone's cautious bootsteps down the perilous stairs that twisted their way around the support pylon.

Rechs went down another flight and stepped onto a landing. A loud pop echoed through the darkness. Then a trap door that comprised the entirety of the landing gave way, and Rechs fell fast down to the next level.

Which, as it rapidly loomed up to meet him, was clearly a cage.

Big, metallic tanks instantly began to jet bright orange gas from all four sides.

It was a bad trap. But it still would have meant death or capture for anyone who didn't happen to have jump-jet-capable armor.

Rechs flared his jump jets at the last second, giving him a soft landing. He wasn't concerned about the surging poisonous vapor filling the space around him like jet engines spooling up sudden contrails on a cold day at high altitude. The sealed armor easily handled toxic gases.

"Dammit!" he heard Giles Longfree exclaim from above. "I forgot about the jump jets. All rrrright, boys…" he said matter-of-factly. "Blast him!"

And then the mobster darted back up the stairs.

The four shooters who had led the way and stepped past the trap were now back at the mouth of the trap door. One of them tried a quick shot with a blaster. Its green bolt lanced out and struck ancient iron, exploding in a shower of fire and sparks.

Rechs fired his jets and rocketed up out of the trap door. He heard the eight shooters above hustling down the stairs to get a shot on him, convinced they had the advantage in numbers and firepower.

What happened next was a bloodbath.

Rechs landed just beside the trap door and swung his pump-action scatterblaster at the four hired blasters still looking for him down in the cage, so fast had his ascent been. The powerful blast tore through the one closest and blew half a face off the two men standing behind. Rechs gave a forceful kick to the fourth man, sending him tumbling down into the darkness.

Wasting no time, he turned to engage the thugs coming down from above. Racking another charge pack, he hugged the wall of the curving pylon just below the next landing. The two that came down first were following medium blasters and immediately locked front sights on their dead friends bleeding on the landing. One of them, the little lizard, led the other, a human in dirty combat leathers.

Rechs shot the human in the belly and didn't wait for the guy to realize he was dead. An instant later he jackhammered his combat boot into the lizard's pot belly and sent him sprawling for the rail and the fall below. The lizard discharged his weapon as he stumbled and another green blaster bolt raced off, creating a dying comet as it streaked away into the darkness of the cavern. But the little lizard man didn't go over the rail, instead bouncing off it, its prehensile tail trying to grab on to a support.

Blaster fire from the rest of Giles's crew rained down from the landing above as Rechs darted to the lizard, grabbed him with one hand, powered up the armor, and hurled the flailing body of the killer at the nearest attacker above.

The thing screamed, scrabbly claws flailing and hitting the man full in the face. Both tumbled off into the void, streaking by Rechs with intertwined screams on the way down.

Those left weren't interested in what Rechs was offering. The bounty hunter charged after them, racking another charge in the scatterblaster and firing at the first one he caught up to, point-blank in the back. He was already passing the dead man and racking the next charge.

Only two decided they would stay and fight, or at least try a shot once they reached the next level. A moment of fear and bad aim was all one did with the time that remained in this life. The other one shot Rechs in the chest plate not a foot away from him with a black-market pistol dialed up way past all humanitarian and legal limits. The shot hit like a thunderbolt and Rechs pulled the trigger on his own weapon as he staggered down the fragile steps of the steel staircase and felt the rail at his back.

Both of the shooters were dead. More were clambering up the stairs, desperate in their escape. Rechs sucked in a lungful of air and tried to get his breath back. It would be bad to have busted his ribs…

That was the only thought he had as stars swam across his vision and breath refused to fill his lungs. He fell to his knees, knowing he might need another charge pack in the scatterblaster. He racked the slide with effort. And then, slowly, the air began to come. The armor was hitting him with blood-vessel expanders and capsicum to force open his airways. The medical diagnostic in the HUD told him nothing was broken. He'd just had the wind knocked out of him.

"Hey, Tyrus…" yelled Giles from far above. Rechs heard the man inhale from his mask again. And then cough. Though just a little. The fits had all been part of the act.

"Hey, man…" crooned Giles Longfree. "I haaaaad to try it, Tyrus. You know. You're Tyrus Rechs, man. Biggest reward in the galaxy. So… no hard feelings, right? And if you're thinking about coming up here for me… well, I got a surprise for ya. Not sorry."

The staircase began to creak and moan.

"Little failsafe we built in!" shouted Giles above the rising din. And then his voice died out in the thunder and rumble of landings above collapsing and tearing away their anchoring bolts. Whole sections of the staircase peeled away from the side of the pylon and fell toward the foundry floor below. Each level thundering down onto the one below, the dominoes of a giant.

Rechs stood. Still shaky from getting shot.

"No time," he gasped, "for that."

He began to run. Refusing to use up what was left of his jump juice until there was no other choice. He knew he would need it for what still lay ahead. He would need it for those captured legionnaires.

He stumbled down two levels before the stairs surrounding him peeled off with a titanic groan. The floor below, the vast space that was like cemetery monuments of some giant alien race, was still a good ways down. A fall would crush his legs and break a lot of other bones. Injuries he couldn't afford, not this early in the hunt for the two leejes.

So, he made a desperate choice and flung himself for the side of the cavern wall, pushing off the collapsing stairwell at the last second, flying out into the dark void, the low-light HUD imaging everything in blue starlight as he fell.

# 21

SHE AWOKE IN DARKNESS. PITCH-BLACK DARKNESS. FEAR, like a monster, swarmed in and tried to get a hold of her. She tried to remember where she was.

Then it all came back. The failure in the alley to get the legionnaires back to her SLIC. The "student union." The piss and spit. The hypo and the drugs. And the memory of the nightmares she'd been swimming through.

The beating, too. The beating they'd given her when she'd finally gotten to the legionnaires in the alley. When she'd tried to protect them with her body.

In the drug-induced dream she'd been having she was back with...

"Don't," she said simply to the darkness. She couldn't afford that here.

*So, don't*, she told herself. *Don't, Manda Panda.*

And even that hurt a little. A lot, if she was really honest with herself. The kind of things you remember when you're in trouble... those hurt the worst. All the beatings in the world she could take again. Just not the good words spoken to her by the ones who were far away and loved her still. Ones who probably thought she was dead.

The legionnaires!

She felt around in the darkness knowing... just knowing that the piss-ant punks had killed them and left her in a shallow grave. That she had truly failed in every way. And in the one way that had been the most important to her. Protect them. Protect the legionnaires until she could get them back to the Green Zone. She'd failed, hadn't she?

*Failed again, Manda.*

"What?" said a tired voice in the darkness. It sounded dry and hoarse and she could hear the speaker lick his lips in the long pause after. "Don't what, girl?"

Lopez. The sergeant in charge of the Legion QRF team.

*Okay*, she told herself and got to her hands and knees, feeling around for him.

"Don't give up," she said quietly.

The sergeant chuckled and began to cough.

"We're Legion, girl. We don't ever give up. We just KTF."

She found his ruined armor and the bandages she'd put in place over the wounds she could access.

"I know," she said as she checked his bandages. "I was telling *me* not to give up."

And then it was just the two of them in the darkness.

*Okay*, thought Amanda. *I gotcha, Sergeant Lopez. I got you.*

# 22

With one armored glove, Rechs clung to the raw ledge of cut rock he'd grabbed hold of as he escaped the destruction of the stairs, dangling there above the long drop to the foundry floor below. The other glove was holding the scattergun. Too early in the mission to start letting go of weapons. He activated the magnetic carry-hold across his shoulders and stowed the weapon with some difficulty. Now with the augmented strength of both gauntlets, he was able to dig into the rough rock wall and get a secure grip.

He looked for a way to the floor. Up was no good. That only took him back behind the Green Zone and the Docks. Giles would either have more of his thugs waiting for him up there, or the rat was tipping the military for a reward.

He began to climb down the rock. It was slow going, and he could have used the jump jets, but he was still rationing the juice. You never knew when you might need the jets later on. He descended, made a small drop, and landed on the dust-laden foundry floor.

Low-light imaging within the bucket showed him the old casting forms for the hull plating once used to build the mighty warships out there in Detron's canyons. The graveyard silence made it hard to believe this place had once been close to a state-of-the-art clean room dedicated to stamping out armor plating the size of a city block. Detron's hull plating had been galaxy-renowned back in the days of the Savages. Rechs had been on Republic ships that had stood up to close-range volley fire from old Savage hulks fielding strange energy weapons the Republic would never have been able to duplicate, and he remembered naval crews reassuring jumpy legionnaires that their ships could stand the pounding and get the Legion in close enough to conduct boarding operations.

But those were stories long forgotten by the galaxy, or so it seemed these days. Names, too. Sometimes Rechs played games with himself. Memory games. Telling himself he was doing it to keep his mind agile, because even now he was beginning to notice some kind of forgetfulness creeping in. But really it was to honor those old leejes who'd just been young kids back then. Kids following him into battle.

There was Bill Allen at Veriteaux.

Randolph Johnson when they hit main engineering on board the Savage hulk *Child of Tomorrow*.

And...

Kris Chambers at Andalore. They called him Joryl, though.

Timothy Foster, also at Andalore.

So many at the Carso's Rift. There were eleven of them. Can you name still name them all, Rechs?

He got five.

Richard Long.

William Morris.

Ben Wheeler.

Lawrence Tate.

Trevor Patillo.

Five out of eleven heroes the galaxy had forgotten long ago. But that didn't make them heroes. Their deeds that day did. And those would live forever, because the galaxy had been shaped anew by their actions.

Rechs pulled the scattergun from off his back once more and stepped into the maze of gigantic and silent manufacturing tools, looming like the ruins of some forgotten city. The compass within his HUD gave him the direction he needed to go in order to get to the city.

He was sure Giles and his crew had some way into the city. He just had to hope that their route actually did go this way. That the whole trip down here hadn't been entirely a detour to get to their sad little trap.

How much of what Giles had told him was true? The wild, feral moktaar? Whatever the Watcher in the Water was?

As he passed the towering machines, the thud of his boots within the vast cathedral of work was the only noise. Soon the armor's ambient detection picked up something ahead. Chemical readouts appeared within the HUD. Fire. Smoke.

Rechs dialed down to stealth mode, stopping to make sure his gear and tactical bag were secure. The crackle of burning wood, augmented by the armor's sound-detection capabilities, seemed clear and close. And as he circumvented a large crane that had once hauled the ceramic-molded hull plates up to their finishing stations, where they'd be cut by high-intensity lasers and finished off by the nanopoxy and circuitry integration crews, he spotted the small fire.

A hunched figure sat before it.

A moktaar.

The moktaar were fierce simianoids who gave one of the galaxy's uber-predators, the wobanki, a run for their money in hard times. They also made pretty good engineers. Combat engineers especially. They liked traps and explosives and monkeying around with things.

"Monkey business," the Legion called it whenever a combat support team of moktaar sappers came in to do some job.

*So be careful,* Rechs told himself. *They can be tricky.*

The figure before the fire had his back to Rechs, but it was obvious the moktaar was old. It was hunched over, and long gray sideburns drooped down from its bald monkey pate.

Rechs approached the fire, letting his boots hit the floor to announce his presence. Chances were if this one could build a fire then it wasn't completely feral. Even finding wood in a place like Detron was a feat. And... it might know the way out of here.

Still, time was of the essence.

Because it was running out.

At the sound of Rechs's boots the old monkey turned, sharp fangs bared, giant dark eyes searching the blackness beyond the fire and finding the armored bounty hunter approaching, weapon in hand.

One paw, crooked and gnarled, went up.

"Friend?" rumbled the moktaar.

"Friend," replied Rechs through the electronically modulated speaker in his bucket. It made his voice sound like a ghost being drowned underwater.

For a long moment the old simianoid just stared at Rechs, its watery brown eyes questing and darting to find some truth, or lie, in the confession of friendship. Then it waved a paw tiredly and bade the bounty hunter come forward to the fire. It was holding a small stick which performed the gesture along with the gnarled monkey paw.

"Come," it rumbled in typical moktaar growl-mutter. "Come close... friend."

All moktaar had that speech pattern. Deep and sinister. Low and growling. Except when they went into battle. Then they screeched their war cries and swarmed like a hive of mummy-bees regardless of their losses as they entered some kind of primal rage. Maybe that had been their only defense against the killer wobanki who uttered little as they slaughtered with impunity.

"Sit by fire," grunted the old one.

Rechs approached and scanned the darkness. It wasn't a trap. Sensors and imaging showed they were the only ones in this section of the foundry. High above them towered an old crane in which the moktaar appeared to have made its home, turning the cyclopean gantry into a junkyard treehouse. And several old chunks of hull spars had been cut into seats and benches around the base of the crane. All oriented toward the fire.

The moktaar resumed staring into the small fire as though Rechs's presence were nothing that needed to be considered. Nothing urgent in the least.

Rechs had no time for this.

"I need to get through to the center of the city. The Heights." Rechs looked up. "Above."

The moktaar grunted.

"Know the way?" asked Rechs when the old monkey seemed little inclined to do more than continue to stare into his fire.

"Can show," grunted the moktaar. "Joba can show. Very dangerous. Children won't like it. Sleeper in the Deep… won't like it either."

Rechs pulled out some fixed credits he always kept on him. He set some down on the floor between them. The moktaar picked them up, turning them over and then biting them with what few teeth remained in his old gummy mouth.

Then he stood.

"Children won't like," he warned.

He sounded serious.

# 23

"WHAT BUSINESS ARE YOU, HOOMAN?" INTONED THE elder monkey.

As a bounty hunter, Rechs had learned to share as little as possible. And though this wasn't a bounty—more of a rescue mission—it felt the same. He was tracking a target. You really never knew which side everyone was playing for. Double and triple crosses abounded. Especially the closer you got to your target. There were no allies to be had on Detron. So best not to look for any.

He said nothing. He'd paid his fare. *Let's see how far that gets me*, he thought and watched the old monkey and the shadows. The oldster's use of the word "children" had bothered him. Perhaps there *were* feral moktaar down here.

"Fine," rumbled the moktaar after a minute of silence passed between them. The old monkey ambled up through the vast control platforms that had once governed the pouring operations. It had been maybe decades since this place had seen any work being done.

And while everything looked long disused and covered with the ancient dust of inaction... there was a sense that it could all come to life at any moment and renew the work of building war machines. As if there were some big red power button that would throw the central core reactor into life once more and set it all running with manic ferocity.

Rechs felt a coiled moment of energy crouching in the darkness. He could almost taste it.

"No mind for, Joba," grumbled the moktaar. "Hooman bizness is hooman bizness. Always war, fighting, taking... all is hoomans ever do."

Rechs didn't bother to remind the old monkey that the moktaar and the wobanki had been at war for over three thousand years. And that the moktaar had ruined their own home world along with several others nearby as a result. War had never been limited to any one species, race, gender, or class.

They were climbing a wide set of ancient metal platforms that led up into a vast darkness. Hopefully, thought Rechs, this would lead to some lift that would take him up into Detron itself.

"Are the Savages back yet?" asked the ancient moktaar, pausing to catch his breath and stare in contempt up at the darkness.

In the half-light of this place, where running emergency operations lights still ran on millennial batteries, Rechs could now see that the moktaar had the look of a tribal shaman about him. Instead of the moktaar coverall the species always seemed to be wearing, he was wrapped in a threadbare robe that might once have been a packing cloth. In one hand the old monkey was clutching... a prayer chain, maybe, and in the other, his staff. There were carvings in that staff, but Rechs couldn't make out the details, even with his bucket's visual suite. Old Moktaari runes and scribble-scrawl.

Later, when Rechs's mind had time to focus on the minute details, and he realized that the staff had been made of human teeth, he would think he should have looked at that staff a lot more closely. But for now, he just took it for some ritualistic totem the old one carried about as he wandered in the long dark. Forgotten.

"Moktaar ran these forges for the hooman wars against their own kind… Savages."

Rechs detected movement up in the darkness. High above on a processing computer that was easily three stories high, an impossible piece of tech considered state-of-the-art in its time, something scrambled along an access rail and disappeared.

He brought up the sensor sweep inside his HUD and checked the scan. Nothing was there. At least not right now. He ran it back. Checked the scan. There had been a blur. For just a moment.

"Who are the children?" Rechs asked cautiously.

The old moktaar coughed out a harsh laugh and began his laborious climb up through the platforms once more. At first the bounty hunter thought the old monkey would ignore him as he'd ignored the moktaar's question. But after a moment the shaman began to speak.

"The children are the night," he muttered. "And this…" he lackadaisically swept his gnarled paw and stick across the ruin, "…is their kingdom."

He barked his laugh again. It sounded sick and breathless. Like the beginning of a screech.

"Don't worry. Joba protect you. Hooman."

But Rechs had a suspicion Joba wasn't going to do anything of the sort. He felt that what was coming next was pretty clear. And this was an excellent place for it to happen.

Ahead, between two massive cooling towers that rose out of the deep subterranean power core still far below, Rechs spotted hundreds of pairs of eyes in the darkness. In the gray and green wash of night vision, they appeared to be the eyes of demons, alight with fire.

All of them were watching him.

Giles had probably had some little toll booth game out here. The smuggler knew what the moktaar wanted. Meat. Human flesh. And in return, Giles kept the smuggled goods.

Rechs wondered if the old man at the bar knew. Took his credit chit and sent him to die all the same. He hoped not. He liked that old man.

There wasn't much of a way through the awaiting moktaar without killing them outright. And even then, a swarm of the things wouldn't be an easy assault to repel.

"Old one," Rechs growled over his bucket's external speaker.

"Yes, hooman?"

"This little trap you're leading me into... you'll be the first to die."

Then he stepped forward swiftly and grabbed the moktaar by the neck, shoving the barrel of the shotgun into the shaman's spindly rib cage at the same time.

The chorus of screeching that came next was unholy. It erupted from everywhere all at once, bouncing off the far walls of the immense complex and into its many halls and chambers.

Rechs did a slow turn to show all those demonic little eyes his prisoner. If they came at him all at once, they'd win through sheer numbers. That's how they'd managed to finally put up a fight against the wobanki. Ferocity in numbers.

Rechs was down in the deep. There was a real chance he'd never make it out alive. And no one would know. Unless his theory about Giles was correct. And then the gangster would probably make a few trades to get Rechs's armor and bones. Dead or alive—that was the bounty. The smuggler would land himself a fortune.

Not that any of that mattered to someone like Rechs. The only failure his mind would register when the monkeys swarmed and dragged him down, gnashing fangs and battering quick paws, attempting to figure how to get his armor off… would be that those leejes would get left hung out to dry by the scumbags in the House of Reason. Props for the next election cycle. KIAs without cause.

"The children don't care, hooman," croaked the old moktaar, struggling in his grip. "They're all mad now. Lost their hooman ways once the work stopped. Back to the jungles and deserts of our old worlds. Only… down here now. This is the dark jungle. And we owns it all."

He began to titter as Rechs jerked him this way and that, showing the weapon and making clear what he would do to their priest.

Ranks of feral simianoids pushed forward from every direction.

*Maybe they've gone so wild they've forgotten what weapons do*, thought Rechs for a brief cold-water moment.

One of the younger moks, an aggressive male, surged out from the darkness and provided Rechs a chance to give another object lesson over what a scattergun did to an enemy closing with intent to kill. Rechs blew the thing's brain and chest all over the floor. Hairy bowed legs went down with little else that remained of the corpse. Smoking blast vapor rose from the scattergun as Rechs jerked it forward and back in one practiced movement, racking another charge pack.

Five packs left and then he'd have to go for the hand cannon. He could pull the Jackknife and lay down a ton of fire... for a little while. But in a full moktaar rage, would they even care? They'd just keep coming and coming.

Rechs and his prisoner, the scrawny spindly old monkey-man, reached the top of the platform. They had let him go that far. So maybe the shaman was lying about how important he was. The bounty hunter could see one possible way out of this, but his window was closing fast. At the top of the platform was a large transport tube. Down the center ran a maglev rail where work crews were once brought into this section of the foundry to begin their workdays.

The clustering moktaar snarled as they closed their net. They looked like a furry sea, weaving back and forth as they shambled forward with broken pipes, jagged cuts of steel, and anything else that could be turned into a rude Stone Age weapon.

Suddenly Rechs flung the old monkey shaman away, ripped a banger from his carrying harness, thumbed it into activation, and tossed it into the crowd. Then he was running fast for the one possible exit.

If the screeching had been unholy before the banger went off, it was pure descent-into-madness lunacy after. This bought Rechs a little time, and he didn't waste it.

Arms pumping and legs moving like pistons, Rechs ran into the entrance to the tube. Seconds later the monkeys were flooding in after him, sending a sonic wave of enraged insanity after him as he went.

It was like fleeing from a screeching madhouse into the unknown, half expecting something far worse to be waiting in there.

There was still some guardian ahead. Giles called it one thing, the old moktaar another. That came to Rechs's mind as he fought to make it through the monkey noose closing about his neck.

The Watcher in the Water, one had called it.

The Sleeper in the Deep for the other.

As Rechs reached the far end of the short tunnel at the top of the platforms, he spun and fired a blast into the mass of surging moktaar at his heels. The scatterblaster tore several of his pursuers to pieces and sent the others scrambling away from his fierce presence for a moment. That gave Rechs just enough time to reach the exit from the transport tube.

He found himself in an open area that crossed a raised bridge. Beneath the bridge, dark waters spread away into a massive subterranean lake that must have been built to assist in the cooling operations for the foundry. Whatever was down below, Dreamer or Watcher, it would present itself shortly if it was going to.

Running fast, Rechs tried to put as much distance as possible between himself and his mass of his pursuers. He made the bridge as the savage moktaar surged out of the tube behind him. There were hundreds of moktaar now, shooting out of the tunnel and swarming every direction all at once like some living infectious virus that could not be contained. Some screeching moktaar ran across the tracks of the bridge, loping fast to catch up with him, while others swung along the rail and supports below, hoping to get ahead with their natural monkey jungle-tree-swinging skills. Still others seemed to swim along the walls, moving like vipers as they took the long way around in an effort to circumvent his escape.

In other words, they were trying to cut him off every which way they could.

Rechs fired into a gaggle of the feral aliens and blew several off into the dark waters of the brooding lake. Various body parts followed their larger parts with a series of light splashes.

Ahead lay Rechs's next obstacle. As if things weren't difficult enough, a portion of the bridge had collapsed into the waters long ago.

*Or was dragged down into it*, some distant part of his mind thought darkly.

A rickety rope bridge, probably one of Giles's additions, had been suspended over the gap. Rechs chanced it and flung himself across it at full speed, feeling his chest heave and his breath come in ragged gasps as he pushed himself to keep moving.

Some voice was telling him he could only run so far and so fast. And that even with the augmented strength of the armor, by running blindly he could end up in one of their traps, and then they'd swarm. But he ignored that voice, because listening was the first step in quitting. He would have to spend some jump juice. He knew that. But he was saving that to put some final distance between himself and the raging moktaar at the last second. And he was hoping maybe something would happen so he wouldn't have to use it after all.

Halfway across the rope bridge it collapsed, or was cut somewhere behind him, and Rechs threw himself forward onto its falling breadth, staring upward at the ceiling as he clung to what remained of the rickety span as it slammed into the far pylon of the actual bridge.

Moktaar behind him went shrieking into the water, screeching and enraged.

Rechs didn't have time for the wind to be knocked out of him even though it felt like it had been. He pulled hard, hoping what remained of the rope bridge didn't give up its anchors. Suicidal moktaar flung themselves with abandon from far behind, thinking they could make the gap. They splashed into the dark waters below, and Rechs heard them claw at the surface in self-righteous fury.

He would hold on. He had to.

# 24

Dawn was just breaking over Detron. Marine SLICs crossed above the city, still looking for any sign of the four missing legionnaires and one missing marine. Three were known to have been captured. Two, both leejes, were presumed dead. Their life signs had gone dark during the firefight.

The captive leejes' life signs were a different story. Someone who knew what they were doing had switched them off. And of course, the marine didn't even report life signs to the Legion net.

On Dock Street—the new focus of the protestor gatherings now that the galactic government had all but surrendered the streets and the city proper, like the local government had done before it—massive crowds geared in red and black surged out into the golden dawn light amid the smoke of cook fires and lotus they spent the night with, singing their resistance chants to the accompaniment of drum circles that seemed to form whenever and wherever. Sounds coming from anything that could be improvised to roll out a beat.

General Charles Sheehan, commander on the ground of Repub marine forces, was busy fighting with the House of Reason delegates who'd been sent to Detron on a fact-finding mission. It was this delegation, led by Arjun Kun, chief investigator for the diplomatic corps, that had insisted the marines pull back their presence on the streets to de-escalate the brewing conflagration.

"Brewing?" exclaimed Sheehan incredulously. "I don't know if your understanding of current events is clear, Delegate Kun, but we've got six dead marines, four missing legionnaires, two of whom might still be alive, a missing marine who may also be alive, multiple civilian casualties, robbery, assault, mass looting, and no control over several fires currently consuming downtown structures. To use the word 'brewing' indicates that you somehow see things getting worse than they currently are. Are you aware of something I am not? Perhaps the House of Reason has opted to give the 'People's Council,' as these rioters are now calling themselves, the self-destruct codes to the four reactors still currently providing power to the city? Because yes, then you'd be correct in describing the situation as 'brewing,' because that would indicate things are going to get a whole hell of a lot worse and far beyond the marines' ability to influence outcomes."

"Investigator," replied Kun calmly from behind his wire-rimmed smartlenses. Entirely unnecessary. A fashion statement. People no longer wore glasses unless they wanted to. "*Chief Investigator Kun*. I request that you, General Sheehan, refer to me, and my team, by our proper titles as mandated by the House of Reason's Diplomatic

Relations Committee. I am a delegate, yes. But I'm here as chief investigator."

The general couldn't believe he was being talked down to by a mincing functionary who clearly had no idea how serious things had gotten. Brigadier Sheehan had been a no-holds-barred brawler who'd fought at Psydon, Muskovoplex, and a dozen other little adventures the House of Reason had seen fit to involve the marines in. Word was he was being fast tracked for a Military Council seat to advise and consort with the highest chambers within the House of Reason after this situation cleared up.

But though that might be his job one day, it certainly wasn't his job today. Sheehan was boiling over and fed up with the game that needed to be played. The House of Reason had read him wrong. He wasn't a political animal. He was just capable and had yet to fail. He certainly wasn't their man, yet here he was being told exactly the opposite—that he was indeed their man. So, shut up and let this Diplomatic Relations Committee steer things toward what the vast chamber of the House of Reason wanted. Which was a colossal failure, designed as such in order to make the current leadership look bad... and perhaps debut a new rising star.

*They're setting things up for that little troublemaker kelhorn Hamachi-Roi*, thought the general as he forced the look of disbelief off his face and ordered military bearing to take its place.

Sure, he'd surrendered the streets. Pulled the platoons and squads off the SLICs and given up the rooftops and forward observation posts. That was obeying direct orders. But he wasn't going to be complicit in letting the situation turn into some kind of political rally. Figure out a way to prevent that from happening and keep command of the situation, ready to take military action if the opportunity presented itself... that was of paramount importance to Sheehan.

That, and keeping the legionnaires in line. They were breathing down his neck to get in there and find their missing men. And Sheehan knew the Legion. They'd be sending in a Dark Ops team to go looking as soon as they could get one into the system. Already one of the regular leejes was missing, even though it was being covered up by the guys in his detachment.

The general realized he had not been entirely right when dressing down "Chief Investigator Kun." Things could still get messy. Another captured legionnaire, or a massacre caught live by the media jackals, and all hell really could break loose.

But if that's what it took to get any of the missing five back... then Sheehan was fine with that.

Screw promotion.

"Listen... Investigator Kun," Sheehan slowly began as he walked with the gaggle of government functionaries in their high-end-clothing-store adventure gear. Tan slacks. Dress shirts. Photojournalist vests stuffed with nasal retrovirals in case they came in contact with anything that was dangerous, or simply smelled bad.

Just like the star of the stream they all wanted to be. That's how they'd all looked when they were shown into the command TOC. Like the entertainments star who always went around uncovering all the military's crimes against the galaxy and making sure every marine or legionnaire, not so much the navy or army, were that week's bad guy. While still saying they respected the military on the whole and everyone's service of course. Except that every *real* bad guy seemed to be in the military, using military skills to run amok and perpetrate all kinds of crimes from serial killing to bank heists.

Ridiculous stuff.

Ninety percent of his men and women would do little more than drink themselves to death on planet-side leave in preparation for some epic quest to do the dumbest things possible. And on that list of dumb, drunk things to do, executing a casino robbery ranked at least six hundred and eighty-seven spots behind seeing how many stuffed Bannorian aphroshrimp they could feed a Tennarian call girl.

What was the name of that stupid anti-military entertainment? *The Right Side.* That was it. With a hero, Cryson Hitch, who always seemed to have just the right insult for that week's straw man military war criminal. The junior enlisted mafia had taken to calling any shamer a "Hitch" as of late.

As he planted himself in front of Arjun's crew, he couldn't help but think that personally, as a marine and not a general, he'd like to beat the living sket out of all of them. Just for GP. General Purposes. And he was sure the look on his face said as much. So, he swapped it out again and got it right this time by clamping what was left of his cigar in his mouth to force himself to shut up. That did the trick, or so he told himself.

"General..." one of his staff officers whispered in his ear. Probably trying to dial him back from a career-ending tirade in which Sheehan let these civilian document-pushers know exactly why they had freedom, and why that freedom depended on men like him doing exactly what needed to be done at this very moment. Which entailed, in Sheehan's operational vision, a full-scale street sweep with pulse and hydro cannons set to high into the heart of the seething downtown district and a nice game of find-the-HVT with his best door-kickers. He'd call it Operation Barracks Party so his men and women would know exactly what his intent was regarding the protestors on the street.

"General… I think you ought to see something right now," prompted the slight staff officer at his elbow.

The general turned and searched his aide's eyes for some reason why he should be interrupted. He wasn't arrogant… he just didn't like to be disturbed in the middle of a good imaginary beat-down.

Behind the aide, a cluster of staff officers inside the MTOC, Mobile Tactical Operations Center, a heavily armored transport rigged for urban warfare operations, gathered around a bank of monitors assigned to monitor civilian news streams. Sometimes those proved to be excellent sources of intel. Sadly.

Ignoring the "chief investigator" and his clutch of government peacocks, General Sheehan strode away to the monitor and pressed forward through an ad hoc viewing party comprising his staff.

"Damn," he muttered a second later.

On screen the battered body of a legionnaire was being dragged through a mass of protestors on the street. The corpse was being pulled by two grav cycles, and resisters in red and black were kicking the dead legionnaire while others hit him with anything they could get their hands on as he passed by. The helmet was gone, yet the face was unrecognizable. The rest of the armor had been savaged but still clung to the lifeless body as the grav cycles gunned their motivators and dragged the dead legionnaire onward.

Chief Investigator Arjun Kun had been right, thought the general soberly. "Brewing" had been an apt description of everything that had preceded this moment. Right now, the live feed of a dead legionnaire being dragged by citizens of the Republic was going out across the galaxy.

*This won't end well* was an understatement. So, the general didn't bother saying it. Everyone in the MTOC was thinking it all the same.

"Tell Colonel Summers to get an entire battalion over to the Legion barracks and put all of them under guard. And tell him to ask them to wait for me to speak with them before they do exactly what I'd do right about now."

The aide dashed off into the MTOC darkness, sure he was on the most urgent mission of his life. Because he was.

# 25

THE TRAIL LED DEEPER AND DEEPER INTO DETRON. Baldur had picked up the scent again after losing it near the initial exfil where Shaker and the new kid, Beers, had been taken off in a technical sled. It had been hard to figure out the trails.

The dog had also told Puncher that one of the legionnaires had died in the firefight in the alley courtyard.

"How do you know?" he'd asked as they knelt down near dried blood that was still sticky to the touch.

*Smells dead*, the dog replied.

Puncher knew the dog was right. Legionnaires had their vitals read constantly by their armor. Made it easier for medics, corpsmen, and med bots to triage when things went south. And the word was already out that two of them died on the scene. They all knew it.

Puncher's gloved hand, which had been touching the blood with one index finger, involuntary made a fist and rested in the blood. He was kneeling, head down, and for a moment all he could see, as the world faded away, was the blood beneath his eyes. He didn't know whose it was. But someone was dead. Not missing, but dead. No more hope.

*Sorry,* thought the dog. Then came in and nudged the legionnaire's bucket with his muzzle. *Come. More scents. Let's go now.*

Puncher stayed shaking with rage. He promised to kill them all.

*Come. Let's go. Some alive. More important. All your pack not dead. More to find.*

Later they found the scents of the marine and probably Shaker and Beers. Theirs were the last two vital transponders reading active. But then they found another scent. Off in another direction away from the ambush in the alley.

They followed it, and halfway down a street in an abandoned warehouse section of the crumbling city the dog just stopped. Turned for a moment on its tail, circling and searching, nose to the ground... and then finally began to whimper. Crooning the same way it had when it knew the legionnaire was dead in the alley courtyard.

Puncher, hunched over and trying to look homeless for the sake of the few bands of Soshies that passed, knew something was up. Something not good. The SAB was killing his back.

But he didn't mind. So it didn't matter.

*This one died here.*

"Here?" asked Puncher incredulously. He turned and scanned the cracked and dirty sidewalk. "Are you sure, Baldur?" His voice was suddenly desperate because he didn't *want* the dog to be sure. He wanted doubt.

The dog nodded once.

Sometimes doubt was the only faith you had left. And now there was none.

Baldur sat respectfully on his haunches. Watching the legionnaire scan the ground and try to find some sign that one of his own, a brother legionnaire, had shoved off right here. But there was nothing. No blood. No body. Nothing to indicate violence had been done. That life had been lost. A story ended here.

"How?" he asked, his voice raspy and dry. He needed to stop. He needed water. But he had to keep searching because there wasn't much time left. Every second wasted was a second those who still lived were running out of.

*Don't know*, thought the dog. *Just... know.*

Hours later they picked up the trail of Lopez and Beers, after going back and starting from square one in the alley courtyard.

Baldur worked hard, and it was Puncher who eventually had to stop and make them both drink. He pulled out the dog's special bowl, a shiny, collapsible one, and poured some water into it. They drank in the shade of an old dead tree in a lifeless and beaten park where the homeless lived like nomads, unbothered by the destruction of the city. That day, yesterday, was hot. They drank, and in time they found the first site. The first place the Soshies had taken the two legionnaires and the marine to.

There was no one there now. The whole place was abandoned and dark.

Baldur worked the warren of rooms and corridors until they found the makeshift holding pen.

"Still alive when they left?" asked Puncher, standing there in the dark, SAB unlimbered and ready to light up any intruders.

*They were*, thought the dog. *When they were here. But now gone.*

"Gone," echoed Puncher. "Still find?"

It occurred to the leej that he was modeling his speech patterns after Baldur's simple prose.

*Can*, thought the dog. *Can find.*

And that night he followed the dog from place to place until they were both so tired they just lay down in a dark alley. The legionnaire took out a canister of repellent and put it down in a wide semicircle of spray around them. It would smell like piss and the stench of the long-term homeless. The Soshies wouldn't want to get involved in that.

*Don't like*, thought Baldur of the protective scent barrier as he lay down next to the legionnaire in the dark of the alley. The old dirty poncho covered them both for warmth as the moons went down and the air got cold.

"I know," said Puncher. "Sorry."

There was a long silence. Baldur shifted.

*Bad days for your pack. I'm sorry.*

Puncher patted the dog.

"Thank you," he whispered. And then lay there listening to the dog fall asleep, thinking of the people waiting out there in the galaxy for a good word that would never come. In time he fell asleep. But only for a little while.

# 26

Rechs KNEW SOMETHING WAS WRONG WHEN HIS HEAD began to split. The monkey screeching, now echoing off all the walls of the immense chamber that encased the underground lake, rose to a high-pitched choral screaming of the damned. Even the moktaar pawed at their monkey skulls as if they felt their own heads splitting.

And despite all that, the enraged monkey-men came at him, leaping across the void of the broken span where once a rail system had crossed the vast underground lake. Rechs stumbled away, firing the scatterblaster to keep the closest back.

Above the din of screaming and the cacophonic blasts of his weapon he heard the mad shaman moktaar laughing insanely. The sound echoed out across the lake and, impossibly, in his mind. Chanting moktaar words of madness down here in the lost world beneath Detron.

*Psionics*, Rechs thought.

He'd encountered them before. Deep in some of the darkest recesses of the galaxy. Mental powers that affected reality. Even influenced space-time. The stuff of bad parlor tricks made frighteningly real. Levitation. Pyrokinesis. Bent spanners. Worse. It was rare, and the main parts of the galaxy thought it only existed in the entertainments. But those who'd studied it knew it lay out there, deep and hidden in the forgotten ruins of the galaxy.

Hidden why? Hidden because it frightened people. And because it was power, and power had to be protected.

Hidden deep because whatever form it took, of all the forms Rechs had seen it take, that's where it was safest. Hidden like some spider that waited for things to fall into its web.

From his vantage point atop the shattered bridge Rechs saw a large shape moving out there in the water. Something massive just beneath the surface. It had the tail of a fish. And the face and torso of a woman. He saw it just for an instant as it leapt up out of the water, arcing over the surface and then diving back into the depths. Its sudden appearance had seemed unreal.

Except... maybe that wasn't totally what had just happened. Rechs's mind wondered at the thing. Maybe it wanted him to see something it thought he might like to see. His mind had seen a beautiful mermaid with beautiful red hair the color of fall. A porcelain face and blue, otherworldly eyes. Like the eyes of those who ingested the fabled blue lotus. Life-eaters, they were called out on the fringes of the edge, which was the only place you could find the powerful stuff. On the most off-the-beaten-track worlds where the starliner companies didn't put in and one was likely to find shipwrecked crews several generations old. All of them "spiced to the gills"—another thing they liked to say out there on the edge.

And it was true. Eat enough blue lotus and the galaxy got strange. Rechs had once gone out there looking for someone and found only the trail of a ghost that had been gone for years. Maybe. Maybe he'd seen the Dark Wanderer there once in several lifetimes of looking for that strange being. But that was long ago when he and Casper...

... and Reina.

They'd gone out there... looking for the Dark Wanderer and finding something equally troubling. But that was a long time ago.

And Rechs didn't see why he would consider it now except...

His mind was under attack. Old memories were being trawled and knotted into a net in which he could become lost. The thing in the water...

The mermaid... because that's what it was... had looked like Reina. At least the top of her had. The woman he'd once known and loved. Calling to him.

*That's impossible*, he told himself as he felt his mind get tangled up in his own memories. Lost in dormant emotions. Impossible because Reina had disappeared a long time ago. Well before Casper. Which was why...

His mind wasn't working too well. That was for sure. Seemed an obvious statement but one he had to begin with. Like starting a problem you couldn't solve all over again. Because you had to. His mind wasn't working and he needed it to. Not to remember. To survive.

Moktaar, fangs bared and claws reaching, came for him, leaping across the open span, hurling themselves off the edge.

*...hang out on the edge. Wait, Rechs.*

Rechs fired at point blank. At the last second. The blaster disintegrated the howling attacker with no room to spare. He shook his head to clear it.

*Get out of here*, his mind roared.

And all he could see was Reina beneath the waters of the dark underground lake. She'd looked at him, in that moment she'd leapt from the water, hanging between the dark sky of the cavern's ceiling and the murky black abyss of the cistern. She'd looked at him and... smiled.

A knowing smile.

*This is psionics*, the distant sane part of his mind screamed. *These are...* His mind struggled to formulate what it knew was real and what was just some... mental illusion. Some slow poison designed to lure him to his death in the lake.

The sudden splitting headache was the key.

He'd had those before. Always in the presence of those otherworldly mind powers that were usually only whispered to be. And always in the worst of places.

It's a trick, this thing in the water. The Dreamer, the Sleeper, the Watcher. What did they call it? The Watcher in the Water. It's a trick this thing does to feed. To fight. To survive.

Even now Rechs wanted to walk to the side of the old mag rail he was stumbling along, trying to get farther away from the enraged moktaar still trying to get to him, and just drop over the side and swim down into the dark where Reina was waiting.

He saw himself doing it.

Saw himself fall and slide beneath the water.

And then he went blind.

Something slammed into his mind and blotted out his vision. Far away he could hear the shrieks of the maddened moktaar. Enraged and indignant at all the injustices of the galaxy. But he couldn't see anything. Couldn't see where he was. Or where they were. Just felt something blasting its way into his mind and there was nothing the armor could do to stop it.

So why try?

She swam up out of the darkness in his vision. And the darkness was the dark water of the underground lake he'd been running above. She swam up out of that and it was the same body he'd known long ago. Reina. The woman who'd rescued him and Casper from slavery long ago aboard a Savage lighthugger. The *Obsidia*. The woman he'd loved.

The Dark Wanderer.

Hang out on the edge. Wait.

The water pulled and swirled her hair to become all that was known. Except Reina's hair had always been black... and now it was red. Red the color of blood. Arterial-bleeding red. Dark and bloody.

She smiled and he saw her vampire's canines opening to...

He felt himself stumbling toward her embrace in the waters below. Stumbling toward the edge of the track. Helpless to do anything other than let it happen.

Tyrus Rechs knew that was wrong. Knew that would be the end of him if he did. Knew that once he took that last step he'd sink to the bottom of the old lake and find a sea of necrotic white corpses along its bottom in the bare shifting light down there. It would be like hell.

Somehow this thing—whatever it was—had found the old lake and made its lair there in the long years after the foundry's collapse. Or maybe it had always been there. Who could ever be sure about the unknowable?

It was a feeding ground now. Part of the way things worked in the down below. Covenanted with the mok-taar who knew to drive prey to it, and the smuggler Giles who needed to cross over it. Like some deal with a devil in the water.

Helplessly Rechs felt himself bashing into the rail of the track, the thin barrier that maintenance crews would use to travel along. That passengers would walk when techs said the train they were taking home or to work wasn't going to budge, and they'd have to get on a new train at the next station.

*I'm going in. And there's nothing I can do about it.*

Which was a terrifying thought.

He dropped the scattergun. Heard it from far away as it clattered against the duracrete of the old span.

*Fine*, he thought.

He shucked the tactical bag, and it slid easily off his shoulder and onto the surface of the bridge. Rechs felt it hit his boots as he started to climb over the rail.

And then he was falling, pulling out his carbon-forged machete from off his back as he splashed into the dark waters below.

*Fine*, he thought. If the thing wanted to play tricks with memory and mind to get him under the water where it would have the advantage, then…

*Here I am. Let's play.*

# 27

Syl Hamachi-Roi's chartered star yacht, *Star Mist*, officially designated as a sanctioned courier for a member of the House of Reason, set down on the ceremonial landing platform of Detron's old Government Council Building. It was the height of high-end luxury travel, and the landing pad it kissed was built during the grand days of the Republic to receive official dignitaries for commissioning ceremonies for the latest battleship, the landing pad was as visible within the government cluster as the playing field of a sports stadium.

Repub Navy traffic control, mainly the admiral overseeing operations aboard the destroyer *Castle*, had been reluctant to let *Star Mist* enter Detron's airspace, but both the pilot and the House of Reason member herself had dared the admiral to shoot "her ship" down if he didn't like it. Seconds of inaction on the part of the navy had allowed *Star Mist* to drop below the atmosphere and assume an approach profile for Detron's government sector and the ceremonial landing pad. Despite the military no-fly zone currently in effect.

This was her big moment. Syl Hamachi-Roi and her handlers would not be denied.

The recently-elected junior delegate had been a nobody mere months ago. She'd quickly risen to prominence in the entertainment and media streams by taking on the policies of the current leadership. She showed a gross ignorance of galactic history, but she'd tapped into a universal frustration many were having with respect to the government. And she'd artfully managed to suggest—without, of course, ever really saying it—that maybe the Mid-Core Rebellion had some legitimate grievances.

Detron was her big moment to take the stage.

Word from the media was that Syl had a very good chance of becoming the next Orrin Kaar, a man considered a first among equals, capable of getting his will done in the House and Senate.

But first... she needed a moment to shine.

She needed to put it all on the line to show the masses of the galaxy that she could be the savior they so desperately needed, wanted, according to the media's indefinable and ongoing crisis they never tired of talking about.

The galaxy was never without trouble.

Syl, and many others, were vying to be the answer to the galaxy's problems.

As the *Star Mist* set down, elegant and slender gears deployed from her mirror-polish underbelly and gases vented from twin deluxe nacelles that erupted aft of the central passenger deck. The crowd held its breath in anticipation. Within minutes nondescript but obvious security types masquerading as crew were securing the landing pad as more and more protestors gathered around the steps of the various government buildings to witness the spectacle.

Elsewhere were the riots and ruin. Here was worship.

This, for every protestor who'd thrown in with what was happening here on Detron, was a crowning achievement. To many, who felt their grievances were legitimate, this was victory. The House of Reason had failed. Or rather its leadership had failed. And now one of their own, a simple working girl from their side, one of the House's most bright and shining new members, had come to their rescue.

Syl Hamachi-Roi, surrounded by a cross-section of Republic citizenry who looked just like her, emerged from the ship and was led toward a sea of microphones and floating holocams. Some of the feeds went full-screen on the delegate; others kept her in a smaller window while continuing to show the body of the dead legionnaire being dragged through the streets and kicked at by a sea of masked "freedom fighters" who were apparently too preoccupied or just plain mean to be bothered with the historic event happening at the landing pad.

"People of the galaxy!" began Syl, shouting to be heard over the swell and roar of the crowd. Her face shining. Her eyes beatific. She was even smiling at them. Willing them to hope in this darkest of times. Like some angelic messenger who would one day be a god among them.

"I hear you!" she pandered.

The crowd roared like some bellowing beast from the elder ages, crying victory above the bloody carcass of its foe.

# 28

Rechs fell through a world of utter inky black-ness. If there was light, or any shade of color down here beneath the surface of the underground lake, it was a deep, unclean ochre. A brown morass of obsidian gloom. He felt the presence of the psionic user down here in the darkness with him.

His headache was gone. Meaning the thing had stopped lashing at his mental barriers. Now it was trying to manifest total control of his mind and body.

It wasn't a mermaid with the face and torso of his dead lover, Reina. It had merely pulled that from his memories, the strongest ones it could find. Those Rechs thought he'd buried so deep that even he'd forgotten them. The psionic monster had cobbled together a glim-mer to entice him. A lure to entrap. A dream to capture. Its animal mind thinking only the basest of thoughts. Woman. Sex. Desire. Fantasy.

Perhaps that appeal had worked hundreds or even thousands of times before. The broken and cracked bones of many alien species littered the silt-covered depths down here, like some apocalyptic graveyard long turned over in search of buried salvage. Yes, these dead indicated its enticements had done the trick before.

Rechs could see that now, the ultra-beam from his helmet cutting through the brackish lake.

When it came, it came as a fish. Almost like a wide-mouthed catfish, its blind white eyes rolling and milky. Its whiskers really tentacles that to Rechs somehow seemed to be the source of its horrible mental powers as they undulated and reached. How it came to be here, Rechs would never know. Maybe it was one of those rare species that had gone deep and hidden in the vast underground seas of almost every habitable world. Or maybe it had been brought, or found its way here, as a pet. Or even a predator looking for a new feeding ground.

As it came close, its leathery scales brushed up against Rechs and pushed him down into a mass of silt and rotting bones.

Rechs could feel its mind. It was an ancient mind, or so it told the bounty hunter, revealing to him its unpronounceable name that hurt to even think of. It claimed to have sailed across the Void of a Thousand Years to feed upon his soul.

Then it swam off into the shadows of the depths, caressing him with promised death.

Rechs could hear his own breathing within his helmet. It came fast and rapid. He wasn't in the best fighting environment for a human. Underwater was worse to him than zero-gee. The two millennia he'd spent traveling through space had made him more adept in that sphere than he was underwater. Here it was like swimming through sucking gravy, the weight of his armor forcing him to move his limbs at absurd speeds just to gain locomotion.

It was coming back. It had made its testing pass. It had tasted his mind. And it would have it, it screamed insanely, bellowing its message like some war cry on a forgotten world that had never known grace, mercy, or love. It was alien. In every sense of the word. It was animal in all the worst ways. Hunt, feed, procreate. But it was something... not more... but other.

Rechs's mind tried to slip off its keel, its anchors, or its understanding of what was possible and real, when it reached out for that... other.

The bounty hunter pushed all that away as the thing in the lake, the dreaming Watcher that had come for his soul, rushed through the murk along the bottom for him. It was easily the size of a bullitar. And as its bass mouth opened wide, he could see the million needle-sharp points glistening from within the darkness beyond. A darkness blacker than the lightless depths down here. A blackness of other voids worse than the known.

Rechs pushed off hard from the murk and got out of the way of its gaping mouth, trailing his machete as he did. Trailing it along the horrible thing's scaly side.

Blind milky eyes seemed to see him. It understood it had missed its prey. And fatally so.

The razor-sharp carbon-forged edge of the blade drew a gaping slit along the corpulent, liver-spotted belly of the thing. A second later entrails and viscera bloomed into the black waters all around.

Enraged that it had been offended thus, the beast whip-tailed around, surging through the water and coming right back at Rechs in a fury.

In his mind, Rechs could hear its pain-filled roar and promise of torments unending. And there was nowhere and no direction for him to go. Not quickly enough, anyway. It had cost him everything just to avoid being bitten the first time.

The thing came in fast and Rechs slammed both boots into the muddy bottom, looking for purchase and finding none as he pushed the blade into the gaping alien mouth and up into the thing's skull where surely a brain must be.

Hot orange light exploded across Rechs's mind and he suddenly saw a world no human had ever known. A world of hot swamps and a red sun that burned like an eye in the sky. A world beyond the embrace of the galaxy.

The Dreamer had eaten everything.

The rivers and swamps were dead.

Nothing moved. And even the waters were sluggish.

This was its kingdom. Its home. And it had done this to every world it had visited. Taking control of the minds of explorers who'd trodden the star lanes long before humanity. Making them take it to new worlds to feed. To dream.

"You've ruined me!" it screamed.

And then...

"Meeeeeeeeeeeeeeeeeeeeeeeeeeee!"

That cry seemed to go on forever. For so long that Rechs still felt he could hear its dying cry late at night when the ship was silent and lying in the shadow of some outer world where no one ever went. As though it had never ended. As though he were listening through a transom into oblivion.

Rechs pushed hard and cut through the thing's bony spine, making sure the job was done as gore and ichor surrounded him. He couldn't see his blade, just felt its easy passage through flesh, muscle, and pulpy sacs that must be organs, then the bare resistance of bone for just a second as the sharpness of the blade driven by Savage armor never minded even that obstacle and continued on out the other side of the Dreamer from Beyond the Void.

That was its name. The meaning of the unpronounceable word.

Later…

Later in the dark under the lake, Rechs switched over to sensors and mapping. He was close to the bridge.

He turned and trudged off through the murky gloom toward a pylon, and began to climb. He wondered what all the moktaar up there would do when he emerged from the water. He was pretty sure they were still there. They'd been held in thrall by the monster that called itself a Dreamer.

He pulled himself up to the surface of the railway bridge, water and muck streaming off his armor. Machete in hand. Daring them to come for him like some surrounded Savage warlord that wasn't yet defeated.

The moktaar were everywhere. All along the rails. Along the bridge. Watching with wide and silent eyes as he stumbled over to his abandoned tactical bag and scatterblaster. He kept the machete ready. But they just stared at him, not in a trance, but just watching. Like statues in the ruins. Like sleepers after the dream, unable to fully return from the grip of whatever deep hypnosis the creature had held them in.

He shouldered the bag, stowed the machete, and continued across the bridge, scatterblaster ready, leaving them to the dark and silence of the aftermath beneath the lake.

The transit station up to the surface lay on the other side of the bridge's vast span. Rechs turned one last time and saw the beady glint of every moktaar's eyes watching him in the distance, and then stepped into the lift that could take him up-station. It took only a moment to hack Giles's rudimentary lock he'd set as security.

The doors closed with him inside, and the lift started up toward the surface. Soft music from some lost easy-listening age played in the interior. Rechs reached into the tactical bag and pushed more charge packs into the scatterblaster.

He'd conquered the threats Giles had forewarned of in the deep dark underneath. Everything left before him would be up top, in the city's streets and decrepit buildings.

The real fight was yet to begin.

# 29

THE LIFT OPENED ONTO A GRAFFITI-COVERED STATION hub where foundry workers had once gathered in tremendous numbers to head down into the works for their long shifts. The hub was essentially an amphitheater that opened up onto several main streets serving the downtown district, but it lacked architectural panache. Brutalist stacked platforms made the place look like an inverted pyramid where little joy ever took place, and bare concrete now served as beds for the few bums who slept here in their garbage palaces. The place reeked of bad urine, ripe feces, and unwashed bodies.

After the collapse of the shipyards, Detron had tried to bill itself as a "People's Paradise for the Galaxy," if Rechs remembered the slogan correctly. They tried to show they could continue to thrive without industry and commerce and that by enhancing their own lives with every free thing they could vote for, they'd somehow rise to the top of the galaxy.

It didn't work.

From above, on the streets above the transportation well, came the sounds of amplified speeches and the roar and swell of a distant and approving crowd. The words were lost as they bounced between buildings, arcades, and dark alleys. Drums and occasional horns blared out and rolled on without seeming accompaniment or meaning.

*Like some damned carnival*, thought Rechs.

Not a full-scale breakdown of societal order. More like a planetary Colonization Day festival from the way it all sounded. Celebrating its founding the same way every other world did. The one day of the year when everyone went nuts and lost their minds until the next workday. The reminder that they'd all, in some way, come from somewhere else to make it in someplace new. Or at least, distant relatives had.

Rechs crossed the cracked and broken duracrete of the transportation hub, scatterblaster in a cradle carry across his chest plate, and climbed up the broken platform steps to street level.

It was early morning and hot. Sweltering already. The powerful sun rose above impressive towers, each comprising at least a hundred wagon wheels, or orbital rings, stacked one on top of the other, launching themselves up into the smoke-laden skies. Some of these wheels even still turned, spinning about their axis as they'd been meant to long ago. Most were frozen by dirt and long neglect. Between them, high above, the city's once-fabled system of monorails snaked through the towers like the dirty arteries of some cardiovascular system that hadn't pumped blood in years. And down below, the streets were littered with burnt-out sleds, couches, and other things that had been dragged down from the buildings and set afire. Papers were scattered everywhere. Across the intersection from where Rechs stood, a body lay on the sidewalk. The poor soul's blood had congealed and dried in a nearby gutter.

Rechs bent over and picked up one of the papers lying loose on the street. It was a flyer. Many on the street had the same purple printing.

*The Galaxy Must Fundamentally Change for Us to Achieve the Dignity We Deserve*, it announced.

The message continued in the main body below. *And that change begins here on Detron. Change the Government. Change the Galaxy. Be at the Noon Rally in Liberation Square (formerly Expedition One Heritage Park) to listen to Syl Hamachi-Roi speak her truths. Then be prepared to do whatever it takes.*

None of those on the streets, many of whom were wearing the red and black get-ups, paid any attention to Rechs in his full bounty hunter armor. In gaggles and clusters, heading in every direction, they laughed, talked, sang, or chanted, "Resist the status quo for the galaxy to grow."

Rechs let the gaudy flyer with poorly mixed fonts slip from his glove and flutter back down to the dirty street. None of this was Rechs's business. They could burn down their own planet. He didn't care.

His only problem was finding the network that had snatched the two leejes and the marine. And the next step to accomplishing that was finding an operative for the other side. Probably a low-level player who was working the crowd on the ground. One who did what they were told and followed the lead of the mastermind who put it all together.

Because there was always a mastermind. Few things were organic even if made to seem so. There was always someone looking to profit from the misery and outrage of others. Follow the money, his mother had liked to say. And she'd been right. And once he tagged an operative, he'd wait for them to connect with their network at the next level. So many connections would take him to wherever they were keeping their prisoners. He'd just have to work his way through it as fast as possible.

Rechs headed toward the sound of the distant crowd, betting he could probably put eyes on someone who was connected enough to lead to someone else who led to someone else. And so on and so on. Eventually he'd flip the stone the legionnaires were being hidden under. But there was a problem. No doubt the public gatherings would be under drone surveillance by Repub authorities and military intel types watching the spectacle unfold and trying to tag the players. And while he was pretty sure he could evade the holocams constantly feeding images to the BOLO software that might identify him, there was always the chance he'd stand out. And that would make things more difficult.

So he'd brought something for that.

He got closer to the place where thronging masses of rioters, or resisters, or whatever they wanted to call themselves, had gathered, then ducked into a burnt-out bank that had already been plundered. Inside he found ruined stone counters, pulverized and laying in dusty sections in the lobby, charred furniture, and a vault door that had been pried open with what looked some heavy-duty construction equipment that was no longer on scene. The wealth had been redistributed by force. Or maybe it wasn't the rioters. Perhaps one of the criminal cartels or gangs had taken advantage of the civil disobedience to go ahead and get some major-league thievery done.

Again, not the bounty hunter's concern. Rechs deployed his stealth cloak and set it to configure to the color of black that matched the resisters' gear. He donned a red hood, pulling it over his bucket, then produced a can of nano-camo, set it to charcoal, and covered the front of his armor.

The cloak would scramble electronic surveillance within the feed's frame of the cloak.

And… just in case there were actual human eyes also out there and watching… Rechs hoped red and black would let him pass by unnoticed among the swarms of disgruntled youths who seemed intent on playing dress-up to the hilt regardless of the contrived uniformity.

Rechs left the burnt-out bank and moved a few streets closer to the rally. The crowds grew thicker. Thousands of kids chanted and shouted while some drank and smoked highly illegal lotus without care. Others raced tricked-out grav cycles through the streets, heedlessly forcing their fellow Soshies to keep clear as they roared up and down the city blocks, a hologame racetrack come to life. No store window remained intact. Every shop door was broken and bent. Looted goods had been used, perused, destroyed, and tossed into the street.

Law enforcement services were nonexistent.

Above all this the crowd shouted "We demand change now" as each speaker poured their platitudes into the rioters' ears about "taking back what the galaxy owed" or "settin' things up for the win!" The lingo was doled out in buffet-sized portions, and the crowd reacted with delight.

Rechs entered what must have once been a posh downtown apartment tower. The entrance looked to have been the site of a fantastic blaster fight, probably to get inside past the private security. Power was out in the building, so the bounty hunter climbed up through the stairwells to the fourth level and found a ransacked apartment from which to watch the events on the main stage.

From this vantage point he saw that the crowd was even bigger than he'd realized.

The Soshies were packed in, a mass of revolutionary flesh pressing toward the main stage where the speakers had been speaking their slogans. Now some musical act that couldn't get through a sentence without breathlessly screaming profanities about the Legion and the House of Reason stomped and jumped around the stage, throwing smoke bombs out into the mass of seething, surging kids. The rock stars used denigrating slurs and vulgar invectives to refer to the wild rioters, who applauded them wildly, eating up every word as though it were some eternal-youth-giving honey.

None of that interested Rechs. He watched the crowd like some high and silent unmoving gargoyle in cloaked rags and skin of armor, waiting for his target to appear.

He spotted the operative within an hour. A mover. Or what the mobs and cartels, which were often the same kind of people behind these types of political movements, called "earners."

Rechs tagged the kid in his HUD.

The hunt was on.

# 30

Hours of darkness had suddenly turned into a supernova. A searing hot burning bright white light stabbed Amanda right in the eyeballs. Men and women in masks shouting orders at one another stormed the room in a businesslike assault.

No, these were definitely not the kids in black and red. The Soshies.

These were the pros she had spotted and warned Marine Intel about. The ones mixing in with the rioting crowds. Seeking to make the most of a bad situation by turning it into something far worse.

And here she was... in their clutches.

*Nice going, Manda.*

They dragged her to her feet and pulled her out of the room she and the legionnaires had been held in for the last few hours. She looked over her shoulder, fighting hard to as someone with a big hand worked to force her head forward. Even so, she still got a glimpse of Lopez.

The other one, Beers, wasn't there. He'd been moved to another location.

Or maybe something worse.

"Missin' in action," Lopez had coughed almost deliriously, and then gone quiet on her. That was hours ago, when they'd first arrived at this location.

She'd wondered for a moment if maybe Lopez was so unimpressed with the way her "rescue" had turned out that he'd simply up and died out of disgust for her incompetence.

Silly thought.

But she was embarrassed enough to have it. Self-critical enough to think it was possible that all of this, even the riot, had somehow been her fault.

Her people, her family, they were the type who took responsibility. They had to, out on that hard and unforgiving frontier world she'd come from. She'd enlisted in the Repub marines to get away from it for a bit. If only to have one adventure that didn't involve the quarry, the grange, or any of the other no-account landmarks within fifty kilometers of where she was born.

Just one adventure. Like her dad had once had.

On that hard farming world you took responsibility for everything. It was the first step in making things right when the fields flooded in winter. Or fixing things without a spare part for several parsecs. There wasn't anyone else to blame in the nine nearest systems.

"Are you dead?" she'd outright asked in the darkness that surrounded them. Because... maybe he was. Maybe she was that much of a failure. "Lopez..."

Maybe... maybe he was.

"Nah," Lopez said after a moment. "But I might as well be. Sergeant ain't supposed to come back without his men. Legion don't like that."

Maybe all of this was her fault. Even this part.

"We don't know…" she said after a moment of thinking what to say and how to say it. "Anything."

But what she really meant was, *We don't know if Beers is dead. Not for sure.*

"I already lost Cave and Lightspeed," Lopez said, his voice a croaking whisper. "Speed's vitals grayed out during the ambush. So he's dead. I looked over and saw Cave got his head blown off by a high-powered blaster at close range. Musta been from one of the ground-floor shooters." He coughed. "Was an ambush. Plain and simple. Led us right into it. Fell for it like a damn basic."

He didn't say anything after that. Because what could you say? And she felt the same as Lopez. Going over everything she'd done only confirmed that she'd done everything wrong.

That brief conversation had been followed by long hours of darkness and thinking in which each of them judged themselves with little pity or mercy. Reviewed their actions as leaders and found them wanting.

Now she was being dragged down a tight brick corridor barely illuminated by wan light sources. She was surrounded by masked pros, working fast and efficiently to get her hustled down the dingy hall. In a small room at its end, she was ener-chained to a chair and blinded by a massive, hot, white spotlight.

"What were you doing over Detron yesterday?" asked Mean Eyes. She recognized his voice. She couldn't see him, couldn't see anything but the bright white light. Couldn't shield her eyes. Wanted to desperately, but could only look down where the glare was a little less. Then she could see the dark silhouettes of the masked figures all around her. The telltale outline of their blasters at the ready.

"Where?" she asked weakly, acting a little worse off than she already felt. Maybe that would buy her something.

A solid backhand sent her head to one side. Her ears rang and that side of her face felt numb. She could taste blood in her mouth and her heart was suddenly running like a drive motivator on jump.

It felt like she'd been hit with a chunk of wood rather than a hand.

Perhaps she had.

"You're not regular marine combat infantry. You're not an officer. We spotted your SLIC come down on the rooftop above our ambush. So what were you doing over Detron, Sergeant?"

"Medic," she tried.

Silence. Mean Eyes laughed, but no one else did. It was a graveyard chuckle. She could hear the soft scrape of his hard boots as he walked around her inside the tiny bare room. His glove made a leathery rasp as he pulled it off. Then another.

"Medic, huh? Operating off what was clearly *not* a medical SLIC with no med bot on board. Or even a crew chief. Or the standard one-door gunner. And we take you with an N-18 slung around your back. But that's what you want to go with for this round? Medic?"

She nodded and spat out a raspy "Yeah" like some gambler who was going to play her hand confidently, despite how bad it really was.

"Round two, then," muttered Mean Eyes, and she was hit again. Except this time the blow smashed down on her shoulder and it felt like her whole spine on that side had suddenly been dislocated. The blow knocked her senseless and rang every pain center her body had never told her she'd had.

"By the way... Sergeant Almond... there are only ten rounds. Round ten... I tire of your evasions and blow your head off. Sooooo... I'd think more about cute answers real hard before I use all that E-and-E gibberish they tell you works. It doesn't. Everybody talks. In the end, every... body... talks. Copy?"

She wanted to cry. Right then and there. And she hated herself because she wanted to. People in the room probably thought the brief look of contempt and disgust that crossed her face was for them and Mean Eyes. But it wasn't.

*Don't be weak, Amanda,* said her dad's voice. *Don't be weak when they're strong. We're descended from the first colonists on this world. We came here with nothin'. And we made somethin' outta nothin'. They can't take that away from you. From us. We'll always be free, Manda. Even when we ain't. Copy, little girl?*

And hearing his voice in her head... well, that made her want to cry even more. One tear escaped, and there was nothing she could do to prevent its jailbreak from her eye.

Mean Eyes leaned in close.

"There's no shame in it, Sergeant Almond. No shame at all. Believe me... I understand."

She shook her head and ginned up her old self. What her dad used to call her stubborn look. And sometimes her "up to your own ways, Manda Panda, ain't you?" look.

"Going forward," continued Mean Eyes in an almost grandfatherly tone, "I want you to know there's no shame if you want to cry. I'm going to hurt you in order to find out everything I need to. And when you start to scream... or when you beg me to stop... or even when you cry, Sergeant Almond... there's no shame. I understand. So you just go ahead and cry and scream and beg for mercy if you have to, okay?"

And then...

"Third round, Sergeant."

The blow landed on the other shoulder.

"Seven left to go. What were your orders as a Reaper?"

# 31

Rechs was moving swiftly through the surging crowd, tracking in on the earner he'd identified. Figuring him to be connected to the pros working to agitate the uninformed masses into a mob that could be weaponized for political gain.

Rechs thought of them as maggots. Wherever the corpse of the Republic was rotting, they would be found. Consuming the decay, spreading the breakdown. He could never understand why they felt the need to destroy society. To ruin what he and Casper and many others over the long years of the Savage Wars had forged through sacrifice. A dam to keep back the darkness and make the galaxy a safer place for civilization to flourish. A place with room to grow. To spread out. And to somehow avoid the fate of the Ancients, whatever that fate might have been.

This mob had no idea what lay out there in the darkness beyond the civilized worlds of the core and mid-core. No idea how fragile the Republic really was when it came right down to it.

He'd spotted the kid, the earner, near the front of some action going down along a side street. Some local citizen, not connected with the riots but rather altogether tired of them, had come out to try and keep the front of his building free of protesters. It seemed like he was trying to get a sick older person into a sled and maybe make it off to the last running hospital in the city limits. Most of the residents had barred themselves indoors, determined to hole up inside their towers, floors, and even stores, until the Republic decided to establish control of the streets. They were hoping their taxes meant something.

But this citizen took a stand. However small and limited. And a fight had broken out between him and a group of jackals in red and black looking to vent their frustrations on whomever they could now that the marines had pulled back behind the Docks and their wire. This citizen provided a convenient target for their taunts, insults, and even a couple of punches.

A media crew filmed the whole incident. They didn't bother to de-escalate it or render aid in the slightest. To Rechs, they were as bad as the jackals in black and red.

That was when Rechs spotted him—the earner. He looked like one of the kids—he was a kid himself—but he came in like a predator. From behind. Like a shark attacking from an unconsidered angle. While the citizen, a large beefy man, was fending off the group of youths spitting in his face and trying to work up the courage to rush him, the pro who was just a kid came in from behind and smashed a bottle of yellowish liquid all over the man's shining bald skull. Instantly the man was down and the jackals he was facing were all over him, kicking, stomping, and throwing useless punches with nothing behind them. Not because they wouldn't have punched harder if they could. They'd just never learned to.

*Brave*, thought Rechs sarcastically as he tagged the earner in the armor's HUD and moved off into the shadows.

What marked the kid as a pro was how he attacked and then quickly darted off into the crowd. The media crew hadn't been fast enough to capture a clear image of him. To focus on the agitator who'd made the sudden spree of violence possible. Instead they'd seen the blur and then the sudden melee on the ground, and of course they focused their attention there as some hero-journalist tried to act like he was reporting live from a war zone. Pretending to be in personal danger despite the team of private armed contractors watching over him and the crew.

But again, none of that was Rechs's concern. The earner was everything. The kid was already off and moving through the crowd. Tossing pyrotechnics and pushing groups of kids forward to go after some other resident, or to target the minimal police presence that was, despite orders to stand down, trying to guard some of the higher-profile buildings surrounding the central protest if only because there ought to be at least one small part of the city that didn't fall to madness.

Rechs hit the street and followed the kid for an hour. The earner was busy like a mummy-bee looking for corpses. Moving everywhere. Stirring up trouble and never sticking around long enough to see the end of it.

Starting it was enough. "Starting" was probably the extent of his orders.

The earner had long loping strides, and his backpack seemed to be a never-ending bag of trouble. Small explosives. More bottles. Even a collapsible iron pipe he handed off to someone who was about to go to work on a storefront in full view of the police and over a sonic background dominated by a speaker talking about things like "basic human rights" and "alien fairness." And of course, wealth redistribution.

The people here, surmised Rechs as he followed the oblivious kid through the crowd like a shark swimming through dark waters, looking for its next victim, liked to think they were fighting for some kind of system of justice where everything must be given to them. Their outrage was over the fact that they had to demand it in the first place. It was a right. A basic right.

That was the political veneer, as far as Rechs was concerned. But really, he concluded, they were just fighting to take something away from people who had something.

He'd seen a lot of it in his time. It was cyclical. Had been there leading up to the downfall of old Earth, before so much history was lost to time and the chaotic nature of the Great Migration. Tyrus Rechs knew the inevitable outcome. The only variable was the body count.

Thousands if you were lucky.

Millions if you kept it to a single city like Detron.

Billions if it spread across systems.

Untold losses during a galaxy-wide war.

And each time it started over, it was because of a proud certainty that *this* time, they were going to get it right. Succeed where others had failed. Because history is a liar if you haven't swum in its currents long enough. Especially when you don't agree with the conclusions.

*Nobody cares, old man*, Rechs told himself.

He closed in on the kid. It was important to be close now. To execute the next step. The takedown. Then move to a temporary secure location for a quick chemical interrogation.

That was all there was time for. Because time was running out for the legionnaires. There was no doubt about it. This crowd wanted blood, and the only blood currently available to them was their own. Plenty of fights between competing groups under the same Soshie banner were already taking place. Purging. Seeking a greater purity. Like the Savages had before they finally united and let loose true terror on the galaxy.

But more blood would be needed in order to keep the energy and momentum up. In order to prop up the belief that change was really happening. That old every-time lie of the constant demagogue. And those who'd taken the legionnaires and the marine... they were in the best position to deliver that blood. Rechs had no doubt they would do so at a time most opportune to whatever their agenda was.

Another high-profile music act was coming on stage as a speaker walked off to thunderous applause. Head down in humility like he'd just read out the Andaara Address after the bloody battle that drove the Savages of Id off Britannia and freed the last of the old core worlds. Back in the early days.

Back when...

Rechs saw his moment. Forming the takedown on the fly. Everything was too chaotic, too fluid. He had to improvise as he moved. Not the bounty hunter's best play, but the one he had to make if he was going to get hands on the missing legionnaires and pull them out of this mess.

"Tyrus."

It was Lyra over the comm. Now that he was above ground, he had comms with the ship again.

"I'm tracking you. Our docking berth is still secure. The quarantine ruse is working. Also I have a comm request from the Guild. Ready to connect."

"Not now," grunted Rechs as he sprinted for the kid, who was only ten meters ahead but moving away from him. Most likely leaving the festival atmosphere to connect with someone or pick up more supplies.

The mark was on the outskirts of the mass of disgruntled "freedom fighters" when Rechs rammed his armored shoulder into the kid's side, sending him flying through an already shattered glass window of a looted liquor store.

The kid stumbled into the darkness, smashed into something, and went sprawling. Rechs had hit him with everything he had, and for a moment he was concerned he might have paralyzed the kid and made him unable to talk.

The bounty hunter checked the street to see if anyone was feeling heroic enough to come to a fellow rioter's aid. But no one did. No one even seemed to notice, which was a good break to catch.

Rechs stepped through the shattered glass store front and found the kid lying tangled in a rack that had once held snacks. He was bleeding from a dozen little cuts. Probably from the shattered glass on the floor.

Rechs moved quickly, assessing and then hauling the dazed kid to his feet in one jerk and dragging him through the smashed and shattered debris into the darkness at the back of the store. And then even farther back into a shadowy storeroom the looters hadn't yet fully stripped.

The kid was dazed and confused. Unsure if Rechs was helping. He quickly realized the man dragging him like a rag doll wasn't looking out for his best interests and began to squeal in protest.

"Hey, man... wh-what're you doing?" cried the indignant little turd who'd just smashed a bottle of piss over an unsuspecting citizen's head so the guy could get curb-stomped by a pack of gutless jackals who thought they were really something.

Some part of Rechs's mind told him he was taking this personally. No matter whatever else he might tell himself. And that wasn't good. Professional was always better than personal. Mistakes were made when it was personal. And since other lives besides his were on the line, he needed to keep it professional.

Rechs threw the kid into a pile of stacked liquor boxes. The bottles shattered as they tumbled out of their packaging, and the place smelled like bad Calpurian synth gin. The kind of stuff that rotted your gut on just one pull. Ghetto bums drank it because it was the only thing they could afford.

He stowed his scatterblaster on his back, letting the magnetic smart clamps grab it with a dull clack. Then he got down to business, popping one of the armor's pneumatic cargo slots and pulling out an interrogation kit the size of a miniature datapad. Rechs flipped the lid, removed the parallax hypo, and hit the kid with a full dose.

The kid fought for a few seconds, throwing a sudden fury of kicks and blows against Rechs's armor, hurting himself more than anything else. But once the small yet powerful hypo went to work, he was finished with all that.

Parallax immobilized everything except sensory and cognitive functions. The House of Reason had declared possession of it to be a criminal offense worthy of twenty years in the mines on Herbeer or a penal equivalent. Dark Ops used it until the law was passed. After that, it was only used by the House's pets in Nether Ops, especially on the secret rendition worlds. That was okay because, after all, it was being used on the House's behalf, and well out of the public eye. It was a crime when someone else did it; it was state security when they needed it done.

Still… Rechs had his sources.

The parallax would take two minutes to fully complete its work, but after the first twenty seconds the kid wasn't moving at all. Rechs stepped over to the supply room door to check the street in front of the smashed-up liquor store. Nothing to see there but more protesters streaming down the street beyond the broken shards of glass they'd helped create.

Most of them seemed to be headed toward the big concert that was now working itself up into some kind of tribal thunder of rage and indignation crying out at all the wrongs that had ever been done to anyone. Both real and imagined. Promising vengeance on everyone who didn't think the way they did. Some singer was shouting these things more than singing. Running through a list of atrocities that had nothing to do with the House of Reason, Senate, or the Legion, but would nevertheless serve for present needs.

Rechs returned to the dark supply room. Phase two of the interrogation was next.

He kept the interrogation mini-kit in one glove as he waited for the powerful narcotic to take its full effect. After two minutes had elapsed, he hit the kid with the next hypo. There were three in the full kit.

This second hypo contained an off-market drug called NX34. It broke down the mind quickly, giving the interrogator full access to everything they wanted from the subject. It also destroyed short-term memory for up to forty-eight hours before and after usage.

And there were other side effects.

This was also a banned substance.

Rechs got answers fast. So fast it was like the guy wanted to tell him everything all at once. Had to get it off his chest. Like he was dying if he didn't.

"I work for Zij. Zij is the main man for the ground team," he babbled nigh incoherently. "Zij works with Franko and Dumali. They run with the crew that's come in from headquarters."

The kid was sweating now. His eyes rolling and wildly seeking things not there as he talked faster and faster. Answering Rechs's questions with little difficulty and few breaths between.

"Yeah-yeah-yeah… this whole thing is being financed by big off-world credits. I'm from here, but I met some of the show runners. They ain't from Detron."

"When's their move?" Rechs asked, not bothering to give his voice an edge or intimidating growl. The kid would answer regardless.

"I was just settin' up for what's comin' next. They're gonna make a statement in two hours… only, that might have been two hours ago—what is it now? Could be anytime, I guess. Big statement. Yeah. Real big. Like mammoth. Set this whole thing on fire. You'll see! You'll all see… gonna burn the galaxy down to the ground and the Legion with it."

"Where're they being kept?"

He watched the kid's eyes as they rolled and fought hard not to tell him. But in the end the kid collapsed and had to give up what little he did know.

"D-d-don't know. N-not for sure. They were at Basement Six. Saw 'em there once."

"How many?"

"Two. Two Legion kelhorned Legion boys and th-the... the... the... girl. The marine. Yeah I saw 'em there down in Basement Six but I know they got moved. Wasn't safe. Soshies started talkin' too much. Bragging. Had to have 'em there, though. Rah-rah for the kids to make 'em think they're in the underground resistance. Freedom fighters."

The kid started laughing, the veins in his neck and forehead bulging. "They don't know anything about anything. Posers. Losers. Rich kids. Screw 'em. They're not switched on to the big scene."

Again he laughed like a madman.

"So where are they now?" asked Rechs patiently.

"Don't know. Told ya."

"Who does know?"

"Rat-t-t-clopp. Rattclopp knows."

A device in Rechs's kit, monitoring his subject's vitals, beeped to indicate a dangerously high heart rate. Rechs would need to wean him off the drug soon. Or maybe he should just let the bastard's heart explode.

"Rattclopp knows everything. Yeah. He knows where they went after that. He's your man. You should... should... shouldgogetem!"

Rechs stood. His legs were stiff.

The kid wanted to twitch and writhe. His skin was crawling but his muscles wouldn't move. He was frozen and yet all his senses were on overdrive. The ground would feel, to him, like it was made of molten lava. The intel was good. Pain clarified things for people and made cowards of those who'd vowed to stand up to what little the Republic could officially do. The Truth and Safety Councils had hamstrung most intel operations along with law enforcement, until in the end the lawbreakers had more rights than the average citizen. If you were in their hands, officially, you had nothing to fear.

But this kid wasn't in their hands. He was in Rechs's.

And right now, lying on the floor and wanting to fling himself about in utter agony despite his total immobility save his speaking functions, his only respite came from answering questions. Doing so released pain-killing endorphins that created the illusion he wasn't suffering as much as when he failed to comply. Screaming made the pain worse. His mind was being trained, quickly, to give up everything he knew.

Rechs got a detailed description of Rattclopp and a breakdown of Basement Six. Only then did the bounty hunter pull the third hypo and give the kid's neck a quick jab.

Instant lights out.

The kid would wake up in two days as weak as a lamb and with no memory of anything that had transpired between them.

Rechs stowed the used interrogation kit and hit the streets again, closing in on his target inch by inch.

# 32

THE POLITICIAN CAME BACK ONTO THE STAGE. SHE CAME reluctantly. Or at least, that had been her intended effect. To look as though she didn't want to be there, in the limelight, but that fate and the galaxy had brought her unwillingly to this moment. To this sacred duty. She was a better actor than she'd ever be a politician. But maybe both are really one and the same.

Maybe.

The singer of the jam band who'd played every riot or rally on every world for twenty years and yet lived on a private estate somewhere on beautiful Pthalo when he wasn't performing as the everyman rebel voice of the disenfranchised, introduced her as the woman of the hour.

"The one true voice in a house full of corruption and lies. The voice," he crooned at the last, "of us all!"

The crowd went nuts, and Syl Hamachi-Roi came forward out of her security cordon and to the front of the stage.

She wasn't even supposed to be here. Or so it was made to seem. She'd come on a fact-finding mission whether the House of Reason had wanted her to or not. That was the reason she was on Detron, so far removed from the sector of space that had elected her its junior delegate.

Hers was one of the new voices that was the opposite of the old guard who didn't comprehend the needs of the people of the galaxy.

She'd come here for them. In defiance of the old guard, and for the love of the people.

She started her speech. Telling them again that she heard them. And from there it was a short bus ride to a list of grievances that must be addressed. Demands she had recounted throughout her election campaign and on every holostream she'd appeared on after that. Demands that must be met.

Stop the endless wars.

Eliminate poverty.

Abolish ignorance.

Strip wealth from those greedily clinging to it.

Pundits would naturally give their counterarguments. She wanted to stop wars but had no plans to deal with the bad actors who constantly initiated them. The galactic standard of living had never been better, and the standard of living for those in poverty today—in the core worlds, at least—exceeded that of any time in known history. Ignorance was defined according to her definition and standards. And stripping wealth, well, that wasn't much different from what the House of Reason had been doing for decades.

But those contrarian pundits weren't on stage with her. She stood alone. It was the hour of the poor and she was their voice. She would give them everything. She had heard them. Now the galaxy would hear them.

"And if they don't hear us," she called to the crowd baying for the blood of their leadership, ironically mistaking her, one of the most political of animals in the House of Reason, for one of them, "then we will take their heads!"

The crowd didn't just roar. They thundered. They would have their blood. They would have their demands. They would have it all. No matter the cost.

An hour later, while Tyrus Rechs had the building where Basement Six was located under surveillance, Lyra opened the hypercomm, and Gabriella fed him a video that had just hit the streams only fifteen minutes ago.

# 33

Rechs waited in the shadows across the street from Basement Six. It was after noon, and the heat was still rising. Overhead, marines flying fully loaded SLIC gunships crossed over the buildings and rioter-swollen streets. Looking like they were storming the sands at Aeroc all over again.

The bounty hunter noted the change in military posture. Something was up.

That was when Gabriella fed him the live stream hitting the galaxy.

"Here it is, Tyrus," she said. She was every inch a pro at her job, but he could tell she'd been crying. Her voice was dry and husky. Hollow and angry. A small sniffle. Her words halted. "It's… bad, Tyrus. Real…" She paused. "Bad."

And then the download began to run in a corner of Rechs's HUD.

The video shows one of the legionnaires. He's been forced down onto a flat table in a nondescript room. His baby face—because don't they all look like babies to a man who's been fighting for two thousand years?—stares into the camera recording the scene. And yeah… there's fear in his eyes.

That's a part of being brave. Don't let anybody lie to you about that.

"Absence of it just means you're a fool," an old sergeant major once taught Rechs long ago.

But the kid *is* scared. Two red-and-black Soshies are holding him down. Except these two only look like Soshies. They're not. Or at least, not *just* Soshies. They're trained. A third one comes into frame and loops a leather belt about the legionnaire's neck. Then moves to the front of the table and pulls firmly, stretching the kid's neck. Practically pulling him across the table.

Rechs can feel his hand tightening on the scatterblaster he's about to use in order to bust his way into his latest objective along the trail to rescue. He's seen these kinds of videos more than he cares to remember. They never end well. And Gabriella already gave him the spoilers with how shaken up she sounded.

He tells himself to breathe. To think. To capture every detail. He'll need all of it later when it comes time to pay back. But he doesn't want to breathe and be calm and make a list. He wants to set the galaxy on fire like he did once long ago. He feels that old hate welling up within him that he only ever really unleashed on the long-dead Savages.

*It ain't wrong to hate what's wrong.*

Words he once lived by.

Another Soshie, this one slight, small, and most likely female, comes into frame. When she turns to face the camera, though most of her face is obscured by the black mask she wears beneath her red hood, he can see that the eyebrows have been shaped. The lashes made up.

Definitely female.

Though he knows what's about to happen, he somehow hopes it won't. Even though it already has. The leej is struggling, but he can't speak. They've gagged him.

Rechs makes himself remember the girl's eyes. He commits every detail to memory and makes sure the armor's HUD is capturing. Of course it is. He will watch this video many times, making sure he gets his targets right. Because everyone who owes is going to pay.

He consoles himself with what he knows he'll do on the other side of all this. He doesn't feel sorry for what they're bringing on themselves. Brought, he reminds himself. This feed is fifteen minutes old at least. He doesn't feel sorry for what they've unleashed.

*What have they brought?* asks the old voice that never takes it easy on Tyrus Rechs. The voice that always challenges him and his actions. Keeping him honest to the legend he's become. He's so old who knows where it came from? Live long enough and you forget all the stops along the way.

*Me*, he answers.

They've brought *me* down on them.

The little girl Soshie in the video makes that same tired old speech of misinformed power-grabbers who think they're making the galaxy a better place by destroying another life. It's the same one they always make. The one about how all the crimes committed against her and hers have been acts of war. About how what's about to happen is what will happen to anyone who opposes them. Differences of opinion and challenging points of view are invalid.

She makes that speech.

And then she produces the blade. Hefts it up into frame. One of the long Sinasian katanas they all think are so cool and some keep on their backs like they're ready to cross blades to make the galaxy a better place at any moment. Usually two of them, crossed like they're some reckless ronin who serves no master. Not knowing or not caring that the Sinasians who make the real deal are barred from even exporting them off-planet. That whatever they have was made in some corporate factory, a hollow mimicry of the craftsmanship a real Sinasian blade is supposed to represent.

She holds the blade up for all the Soshies to see, whether in the room or watching the holo. Never realizing they're just tools in the greater game of order against entropy. Law versus chaos. Good versus evil.

Things they laugh about as being outdated.

And then she swings the blade down on the legionnaire's head. Missing the neck. Sinking the blade into the back of his skull on the overreaching downswing.

She seems stunned for a second at the sudden horror show she has just caused. She tries to pull it out and it's clear how little, for all her acting, she actually knows about wielding a blade. Another red and black, one whom Rechs instantly recognizes as ex-military of some sort because he's got the same compact yet powerful build as Rechs. Same economical movements. Same power. But the eyes are different. The eyes are... cruel. He takes charge and pulls the blade out of the leej's skull for her.

His contempt for her isn't masked.

The legionnaire is bucking. Or maybe his body is twitching. You can't see his face or eyes. And maybe that's a mercy.

Rechs will one day be thankful for that when he tells himself to let this one go. On some night over some tropic ocean when it's just him and the stars, drifting in a boat far from land. Far from the galaxy. He will be grateful for not having been able to see the kid's eyes.

The ex-military shoves the blade back into the girl's hands.

And this time she gets it right and severs the spinal cord and most of the neck. Either way it's done. His life is over. The legionnaire is gone.

Rechs has unknowingly placed one armored gauntlet against the old concrete of the building he shadows under. Absently he's torn out a chunk of the masonry.

*There's still one leej*, he tells himself.

*I can still save the other one.*

"His name was Matt Beers," says Gabriella over the comm. Her voice is dead. "Sergeant. Second enlistment. That's what the networks are all reporting. Confirmed by Legion facial recognition."

She hears nothing on the other end of the hypercomm that connects her to Tyrus Rechs. Nothing other than the ghostly howl that lies beneath the sound. Like the howl of some lost soul forever wandering hyperspace. Stranded in a place of no comfort. And no mercy.

# 34

Giles Longfree walked into the Repub marine headquarters for forces on the ground and asked to see the general in charge of "this whole operation you got goin' on here."

The duty lieutenant didn't roll his eyes like the sergeant and PFC assigned to the fortified position behind the desk. The LT was all business. He had a degree in economics and when this was all over, after paying off his loans, he was going to hit the core worlds and make a million in high finance. Best to keep it professional. Even here.

"The general is currently busy with operations," soothed the LT. "Perhaps I can help you, sir?"

A new directive had come down that morning to be more polite and officious to civilians behind the lines. Maybe that would somehow carry weight with the ones inside the city the marines were now threatening to retake in light of the beheading stream playing on endless repeat.

The NCO standing next to the LT clamped an unlit cigar between his lips and tried to restrain himself from ripping Longfree's head off and spitting down his throat. Politeness his butt. Payback was at hand. And he intended to be the hand. Not here with the green LT watching the front gate. That was babysitting.

"Pretty sure the general in charge will want to hear what I have to say," continued Longfree.

The marine LT could feel the sergeant next to him literally swell two sizes bigger as his rage-fueled blood vessels and muscles expanded for beatdown. His platoon sergeant was a hardcore gym monster who had no qualms about using all the aftermarket supplements he could do to get as big as possible. Except none of the supplements, protein powders, and injections compared in performance with what the scumbag dock rat in front of him was affecting his NCO with right now. This needed to be diffused, because there was no way he was going to lock his platoon sergeant's boots and tell him to about-face on out of the greeting bunker.

*Hell*, thought the new LT. The platoon sergeant could've locked *his* boots and told him to do just that, and he probably would've done it. He had no illusions about who had the power, or who ran his platoon. Sure, he was an LT out of the schools. But that didn't mean he was a *dumb* LT out of the schools.

"Gimme something that'll get his attention and I'll see what I can do," interjected the savvy LT.

The LT knew that one smart answer from this Longfree, one denial, one game, and the platoon sergeant was going to assault the man right here on the spot in the greeting bunker. And that would mean... in the Repub marines... paperwork. Lots of it.

"Tyrus Rechs," said the slimy unshaven dock rat in a dirty suit standing in front of them, wiping a sweaty hand across his dirty scoundrel's vest.

And suddenly all the tension in the greeting bunker went and took itself off on vacation. Because the name Tyrus Rechs meant what it meant.

"He's here?" asked the LT incredulously. "On the ground? On Detron?"

\* \* \*

It was ironic. In fact, it was very ironic that at just the very moment Giles Longfree was alerting General Sheehan's chain of command that the most wanted criminal in the galaxy was here on Detron and active inside their AO, that trouble came in bunches.

Rechs had found that to be true. Operations never got easier; they had a tendency to grow hydra tentacles and multiply off in unintended directions drawing more and more stuff, people, enemies, connections, hazardous materials, explosives, random armed psychotics, and the occasional sociopath, into the vortex of an operation.

Rechs knew that because he'd learned it because he'd lived it. Every plan went sideways sooner rather than later. Don't get upset. Just adapt and overcome. And always stay on mission.

Except Rechs didn't realize at that moment that variable number two had just hit the deck on Detron. Arriving via jump shuttle from the mid-core world that had been its origin point, a brand-new variable had set down inside the Docks. Arriving in-system and transferring off the destroyer *Castle* from the hangar deck to a drop transport inbound with fresh replacements for the marines. Everyone on board was big, bad, and scared. Some dealt with it by talking about how much they were looking forward to the situation going hot.

Then, they promised each other, it was full auto rock-n-roll, brothers and sisters. Game on!

The Legion officer among them just rolled his one good eye, a patch covering the other, and made sure none of them touched the tactical package he'd brought with him. The Legion-stamped anthracite gray clamshell case lay on the deck. Everyone saw it. And no one messed with it.

The drop transport came in over the cliffs of the Docks and fell thirty stories down into the red-and-ochre dust-covered floor of the world's broken canyons and dry volcanic plains. Vast crevasses, like lightning strikes forever frozen in stone, shot off in every direction. The old shipyards that lay within them were like uncovered graves, and some of the more knowledgeable marines tried to identify the remains of the old warships by the skeletons that remained.

Repulsors flared, and the drop transport landed inside the marine Green Zone atop a tall modular LZ overwatched by three prefab gun towers. Brief glimpses of the city showed those disembarking a view of the tall wagon-wheel towers climbing up into the red-ash-flavored sky. Smoke drifted, or just clung, to the upper reaches of the towers. And through this miasma SLICs laden with marines swarmed the city. Even over the howl of the drop transport's engines—the pilot was keeping the idle high for a fast dustoff to clear the pad for the next load incoming, or maybe simply because she didn't want to stick around too long—they could hear the drums and roar of the crowd that thronged the front of the Docks and infected every city street for as far as the eye could see. It felt like a frozen tidal wave of seething anger that would break at any moment and wash over them all.

Smoke flares arched over the crowd's vast length, as did giant inflatable beach balls. A thousand chants came up at the scared disembarking marines and the NCOs who'd been assigned to "greet" them on the pad. The sergeants quickly took charge and gave the new replacements something to be afraid of other than the mob, their voices barking like they'd just swallowed some caustic cleaning chemical. Immediately humiliating anyone who managed to stumble, or stare too long, at what the marines were facing on the Docks.

Amid the barking, the Legion officer with the one eye activated the micro-repulsor lifts on the clamshell and made sure the case's settings indicated it would follow him wherever he went. The package levitated off the deck, and the officer, in Legion duty uniform, stepped off the drop transport and onto the modular landing pad, beholding the spectacle and pomp of the useless twits who thought they could affect the balance of power within the House and Senate.

They had no idea.

No idea they were nothing more than pawns in a game that had been going on for centuries. But in a way, even though they didn't know it, they were on the same side he was. And he found that mildly amusing.

Captain Hess pulled his black Legion beret from off his shoulder clasp and affixed it atop his skull, taking a moment to make sure it was just right.

Dress. Right. Dress.

Sure, he'd been thrown out of Nether Ops only recently. Except they hadn't called it "thrown." But technically he was still assigned to them while all the internal reviews went down on the misconduct and incompetence charges he was currently facing regarding his prosecution of the hunt for Tyrus Rechs.

It was ridiculous. It was as though *he* were the criminal and not Tyrus Rechs.

Hess laughed to himself as he watched some of the protestors try to breach the wire farther down the Docks. Rolling old flaming cylinders probably filled with some low-grade explosives into the wire. Sure, the wire was breached, but the marines in the prefab gun towers working the mounted SABs would cut them down in a second if the protestors got two meters into the clearly identified kill zone. No doubt about it. Then the cries of "massacre" would start, as would the inquiries and civil suits. It was a mess waiting to happen. Every NCO and officer knew it. Hess could practically smell their fear. He'd experienced a raw deal himself for all the same reasons.

"All this," muttered Hess, and didn't finish the rest out loud. *For a couple of legionnaires.*

He wasn't supposed to be here.

Hess's mission was over. But that was only what Nether Ops command had had to say. According to Hess… his only way out from under his charges was to finally get Tyrus Rechs. By himself if that's what it took.

Then… all would be forgiven.

He walked down the ramp of the prefab landing pad and made his way toward the OIC on duty. He had enough of a bogus story that no one could really check it out. Nether Ops had taught him how to do that much.

It would give him a little working room. Nether Ops had basically told him that in so many words left unspoken.

*Hadn't they?*

Yes. They must have. Because Hess knew of other agents who had failed and had paid for it with their lives. Because there's no place to put someone who knows too much except the dirt. And Hess was still alive. Which meant... all would be forgiven.

# 35

Tyrus Rechs knew well what the scatterblaster death-gripped between his claws, because that's what they felt like, the claws of a wild beast howling at the moon, did to the body.

At close range and tight quarters, it tore flesh to shreds. Because of its overpowered nature even armor didn't stand up well. The scatterblaster was both a professional's weapon… and an amateur's. It was an equalizer. It made whoever was employing one a force to be reckoned with. The weapon was unforgiving and not to be taken lightly when encountered. In the hands of Tyrus Rechs it became a tool of fury and vengeance. And he became a kind of angel of death.

A narrow warren of tight quarters was a perfect hunting ground for someone like Tyrus Rechs. Especially with that weapon.

The lives of a leej and a marine were on the line. The link to finding them was in there, in Basement Six, according to good actionable intel. The basement had gone dark after the initial capture, according to the kid. Now it was active once more. Information would be found there.

And the kid Rechs tailed went in there. At a minimum, that meant someone more important than the little puke was inside. That's how it worked.

Rechs was going to use the scatterblaster to force his way to the leejes. *No. Leej. There's just one left now.*

He stowed the weapon on his back.

Observation of the location indicated that while it surely contained pros who would be treated accordingly... the location was also filled with amateurs and pretenders who misguidedly thought they were pros themselves. Affirmation by association.

Rechs liked to avoid needless loss of life among those types... when he could. But there *would* be pros in there. Shooters with blasters capable of using them regardless of the amateurs that might get in the way. Mixing both made things messy, if one cared. Which always worked best for the other side because they didn't seem to care. Just wanted to ignore classifications and let the coroners sort the dead. There was an argument to be made for both approaches.

But Rechs had learned that you lived with your actions. And he'd lived a long time. It was easier to do things you weren't going to have a hard time living with.

And the scatterblaster wasn't selective or discriminatory. Firing blasts in a wide cone, it shredded anyone who managed to be in the wrong place at the wrong time. Down sight from Tyrus Rechs was always a bad place to be. Tight corridors made things worse. There wouldn't be room to discriminate in there.

Also, he had to take this Rattclopp alive.

And time was running out. Had already run out for the leej named Beers.

Rechs pulled a stun baton from the tactical bag and gave it a deft flick. The slender baton extended out two lengths and popped a blue spark, indicating its readiness for action.

The bounty hunter crossed the street, passing a few streaming clusters of resisters on their way to the next flashpoint in the riot carnival. Off the street and on the curb with just ten meters to the set of stairs that led down into the warren known as Basement Six, Rechs pulled the hand cannon off his hip holster. A targeting synch from the powerful weapon appeared in his HUD.

He selected single-fire.

Accuracy for effect.

He rounded the steps leading down to the basement and saw two large Soshies on the landing below. The Savage-era armor immediately identified, graphed, and outlined the weapons they were carrying. Subcompact blasters in hand. A pistol for each inside the jacket. One with a holdout as well.

But Rechs didn't need the armor's weapons scanning to see they were pros. He knew by the way they carried the subcompacts and the LCEs each one strapped. Load-carrying equipment with actual military-grade equipment fastened on. Flashbangs, charge-pack carriers, even blast deflectors across their chests. No seamball bats, imitation katanas, hoverbike locks, or neon-green paracord carabiners with dangling, sticker-covered water bottles attached.

Rechs shot them both in the chest with little flair and almost zero interval. You can be a pro… but surprise is surprise.

He didn't need to finesse this first contact. He just needed to make sure both were down so he could violate their secret bunker system. The hand cannon boomed powerfully in rapid succession as Rechs put the fifty-caliber slugs into them. The blast-deflector carriers across their chests did little to mitigate the effects, as those armor systems were intended for something much less powerful. Not old-school dumb slugs of depleted uranium, chemically propelled.

Both dead men crumpled to the dirty well of the landing, one gasping and reaching skyward while the other just chose to hurry along and die. A look of shame on his face because he'd been caught so flat-footed.

Rechs boosted his armor's cybernetic assist and kicked in the reinforced steel door that guarded the bunker. The broad daylight came in with him, and the midnight beyond the portal ahead seemed to shrink from Rechs. Targeting threw imaging filters for every light-source grade within his field of vision. What needed to be amplified was amplified. What was hidden was plain.

Rechs saw a lot of surprised kids sitting completely motionless inside some kind of common room. And one babysitter pro with a medium blaster. The guy immediately moved into shooting stance, thinking he had a good sight picture on Rechs's silhouette filling the kicked-in door and framed by the tired orange afternoon daylight of Detron.

Like it was his lucky day.

Jittery, he fired his blaster twice and hit the doorframe. Of course he'd gone from complete inaction—babysitting a bunch of tools whom he had to watch posture with lotus pipes in their mouths while chanting various lyrics from their resistance mixes—to suddenly finding himself with a first move in a firefight. That he got two shots off so quickly was to his credit. That he'd aimed badly reflected on poor training and low-grade mission discipline.

He paid the price in the next second.

Rechs blew off the shooter's head, allowing the HUD to clearly paint the target as the bounty hunter ducked to both pass through the doorway and shrink his profile.

The massive barrel of the hand cannon still smoking, Rechs moved further into Basement Six and scanned for new threats. A big kid came at him with a lead pipe, probably thinking of himself as a threat. But before he could even strike, Rechs smashed him in his bulbous nose with the solid butt of the hand cannon.

The kid went down on his knees, screaming in nasal tones. Unaware that the only reason Rechs hadn't killed him was because he was lucky enough to be an amateur.

Another kid playing at being a tough guy came at the bounty hunter in a rush, thinking the little pig-sticker he'd brought to the riot would do the trick. That he'd somehow have better success. The kid was small and mean-faced. Beady eyes that moved quickly. Chances were he'd pulled this move before. Chances were he'd come from the tough neighborhoods of some not-too-good world and got caught up at the university in the resistance. The knife skills he'd learned on the streets probably came in handy every so often among the sheltered kids whose parents had taken out loans from the banks to pay for all that the Republic still wouldn't. Mainly just room and board.

That's what he was probably thinking as he tried to dance in and make a quick gut cut near Rechs's belt: that he knew how to bring down this intruder. Find a place where the synthprene was exposed. If he was lucky, the kid would end this right here.

But he wasn't lucky. The wicked little curved knife merely drew a fine scratch along Rechs's armored chest plate. The armor had a lot of scratches and damage, so the mark would fit right in.

Rechs smashed the stun baton down on the kid's shoulder and watched the little punk light up as twenty thousand volts surged through his body. He did a spasmodic jig for half a second and then collapsed from neural overload.

The charge was spent and the weapon wouldn't reload until Rechs swapped out a battery pack or dragged it along a surface that could draw enough static electricity to convert to a full charge. But it still worked in analog as a club. Everything did. That was as old as mankind.

Two more kids rushed the bounty hunter, who wasn't caught off guard, but was surprised at their tenacity. Hanging out with pros and taking on the helpless had clearly emboldened them. But these two didn't even get their feet under them as they pushed off the dirty couch they'd been sitting on with a couple of girls clad in designer T-shirts that just barely fit the Soshie color scheme.

Rechs smacked one on the jaw with a quick swipe of the baton and was rewarded with the solid crunch of bone. The snap was so loud both girls shrieked.

But Rechs wasn't done. The backhand of the stroke that took down the first attacker hit the side of the second's face and probably fractured the skull.

"You broke his jaw!" said one of the stoned Soshies on the floor who'd wisely chosen not to get involved in all this "hassle." But that didn't stop him from attempting to shame Rechs for doing what he'd done.

"He'll live," muttered Rechs, the armor modulating his voice to nightmare. "Get out. Now! All of you!"

They hesitated for a second, then began to scramble to their feet.

And then Rechs saw the body.

The body of the leej named Beers.

He was a kid himself. Just barely older than these, still south of his third decade. The kid's corpse lay on the floor. Discarded. His neck stretched. His head badly hacked off.

His propaganda value spent.

And if these kids were willing to sit through and around something like that... what made them deserve his mercy?

Rechs would kill them all in that instant.

"*Get out of here!*" he shouted to get them clear of his murderous self.

Sensing the peril they were in, they fled through the door into the streets of Detron.

Rechs strode past the body, knowing a Legion or marine recovery team would soon be on hand to take it on that long journey back home.

But Tyrus Rechs had other business to see to first.

From further within the warren of Basement Six, shadows shifted position. The B-team was down. And now something akin to a Soshie QRF was mobilizing to meet its contingency. But while they likely expected a marine fire team or Legion kill team, they would instead find a crazed bounty hunter driven to run down their remaining prizes.

Rechs could see them in the highlighted darkness, moving to respond to the carnage he'd begun.

Blaster fire careened down the dimly lit hall. Bolts illuminating the darkness as they streaked toward Rechs. The armor's sensors swept the area and detected multiple inbound threats. Rechs fired at a moving shadow and may have gotten a hit.

And then he charged.

It was the best thing he could do. He needed to close ground and find a new position now that they were coming his way. The common room he'd entered was open to fire from all quarters. Not a good place to hold out for a firefight. He needed to get in and among them. A short dash down one hall led him to a flimsy wooden door. Rechs shouldered right through it, taking him out of the line of fire but right into the midst of a pro who was busy with one of the young resister girls.

Or rather, *had* been busy. Most of her clothes were still off and the guy quickly brought a snub-nosed blaster to her head.

"I'll kill her, buddy!" he screamed desperately at Rechs. His eyes were wild and freaking out.

"What're you *doing*?" she shouted, struggling against this unforeseen turn of events.

Rechs fired using targeting assist and landed the powerful slug right in the guy's brain pan. Eyes crossed as the back and top of the skull came off and painted the graffiti-laden wall behind him.

The half-naked girl slithered out of his grasp and streaked for her clothes near a mattress on the floor. Crying.

"Stay here. Don't leave the room," Rechs ordered, then re-entered the narrow hall, shooting. Immediately he took a hammer-blow blaster bolt right in the left pauldron. As the bolt exploded across his chest, the armor ablated much of the impact, but the tremendous kinetic force still knocked that side of Rechs's body back and down. It felt like he'd been hit by a waterfall of fire.

Leading with his right side, following the sight of the hand cannon down the dark hallway that led into the interior of Basement Six, Rechs closed. The shooter ducked into a doorway farther down the hall.

The bounty hunter sent a hail of bullets across the wall and doorframe to keep his enemy back, then shifted the sight picture over to another shooter who'd popped out from another doorway on the opposite side of the hall.

Firing in bursts now, Rechs sent three slugs toward the man and tore him to shreds in a sudden fury of bullet impacts. The first shot hit the shoulder, destroying it in a spray of bone and matter, and the next two shots tore out the throat and blew off the side of the man's face starting at the outside orbital socket. The guy ducked back, shrieking in pain, and Rechs aimed for that section of wall and sent another burst of gunfire at it. The bullets ripped through, and Rechs was rewarded with the sound of a morbid, final scream.

Rechs surged forward and threw himself against the wall facing the door the first shooter had popped out of. He saw the guy fumbling for a charge pack and sent a barely aimed burst of fire into his gut. The killer collapsed backward, and Rechs put a single shot into the pro's head as he hit the debris-littered floor. Just to make sure the job was done.

Fire came at Rechs from the way he'd just come. They were pushing at him from behind. One of them lobbed a grenade, which bounced against a baseboard and then spun, wobbling in place. Rechs pushed off from the wall and dove into the room he'd just fired into.

The grenade went off a second later out in the hall, sending ceiling material down across the room. Dust and smoke bloomed through the doorway, but the HUD auto-switched over to IR once it sensed the light refraction diminishing within his field of view as the air became strangled with dust.

Moving back into the hallway, using the dust for cover, Rechs laid down burst fire in short staccato eruptions from the hand cannon's smoking barrel. Anyone caught flatfooted out there would be dead. Anyone not yet attempting to follow shouldn't be too eager to take up the pursuit.

They weren't. Probably didn't believe in this cause enough to go tramping blind into the kill zone. And that made them smart. If Rechs had to bet, he'd bet they were trying to pin him down here while they got their boss, Rattclopp, to the preplanned escape route.

As Rechs ran down the hall, he picked up on something out of the ordinary: a security door with some pretty good locking mechanism recently installed. Its high-tech nature didn't match the surroundings.

He kicked the lock in with the strength of his armor.

The room was empty, but by the opposite wall stood a wire-mesh pen. This was where they'd most likely kept the leejes and the marine.

It meant he was on the right trail.

Enhanced audio detection picked up the sound of a speedlift off to his right, deeper in the shadowy maze. It sounded heavy-duty. Like something capable of lifting a vehicle up from a subterranean garage and onto the main streets.

Rechs raced toward the sound, burst through a door, and found an empty garage on the other side. The sound hadn't been a lift; it had been a blast door opening in the ceiling above. Rechs heard the telltale whine of repulsors and an engine throttling up somewhere beyond the gap.

Without thinking, he fired his jump jet and rocketed up through the opening, rising up into a small courtyard girded by tall apartment buildings. The area had once been some kind of contrived small reflection park within the cityscape. Now it was overgrown, and the Soshies, or one of the gangs, had installed a blast door and escape route from the old maintenance tunnels they were using as a headquarters within this district.

A tricked-out sled car, something that had been high-end luxury back on Utopion ten years ago and now looked like something a pimp might drive, roared off over the overgrown grass. Rechs shot at it, but it was sufficiently armored that even his rounds did no damage.

He gave chase, running after it as fast as he could.

# 36

RECHS QUICKLY FELL BEHIND THE DRIVER WHO, ONCE he'd cleared the courtyard, slammed his foot on the accelerator and carried the sled off down a narrow street. At the same time, other vehicles converged on the escape route's entrance, seeking to cut Rechs out of the chase. An impromptu firefight broke out as Rechs filled the driver's cab of the first vehicle to arrive, a slick sport utility sled, with bullets. Both of the pros up front were killed.

Two other sleds entered the courtyard from opposite streets, part of a three-team response to what Rechs imagined the pro Soshie network was calling "the situation at Basement Six."

Rechs sent powerful fifty-caliber rounds into one of the sleds, spider-webbing the safety glass and blowing giant volcano holes inward on both driver and wingman. Still on his feet, the bounty hunter circled the sled, using it for cover as more vehicles came in hot, braking hard on repulsors and sending up a skirl of debris and hot wind.

A brief exchange of blaster bolts and return gunfire echoed out across the empty street. This area was too far away from the riots to have many passersby, and the locals had been keeping their heads down ever since the trouble started.

Rechs opened a comm link to the *Obsidian Crow* as he crouched behind the blaster-riddled sled. The day was reaching the zenith of its heat, and despite the armor's best efforts to keep Rechs cool, he was sweating buckets and breathing hard. The thing's climate controls were at times as temperamental as its shields.

There had been a lot of action already in the short space of a few minutes. Shooting and getting shot at. And now he was losing his target.

"Here," said Lyra. "Are you okay, Tyrus?"

"Launch the observation bot out the hangar bay door. Send it to my loc and tell it to sweep the streets for this vehicle."

He sent his bucket's feed capture of the escape sled over to Lyra.

"On it, Tyrus. Are you—"

Rechs cut the feed. He popped up and shot a target of opportunity in the torso. He was facing at least four of them, and the first one to get it had made the mistake of using a sled door for cover. Fifty-caliber rounds—moving fast and heavy from the depleted uranium—didn't mind civilian doors in the least. The shot man twisted, screaming wordlessly, and fell to the hot pavement as his blaster skittered under the sled.

More sleds were inbound. They were trying to tie him up here. To waste his time so the lead sled could escape.

Rechs abandoned the firefight and ran for the nearest alley, firing on full auto to keep their heads down as he departed. When he reached the cool shadows of the alley he kept running, arms and legs pumping, even using the weight of the pistol to pull him ahead just a little bit farther with each stride.

He doglegged into a side alley and threw himself against a crumbling duracrete wall. Several two-headed rats, local to the planet, chittered at Rechs and backed off into the darkness. They'd been feeding on the body of a dead drunk, or homeless person, who'd built their camp here.

Rechs hydrated and listened to the helmet's enhanced sound detection. He could hear more sleds coming in fast back at the courtyard, but no one was in a hurry to head down the alley and catch him.

"Rechs!" It was Lyra breaking through his comm. "Drone overhead your area in thirty seconds. Also, G232 has something to tell you."

Rechs told the armor to dose him with some staminex and adrenapro. A dangerous combo that could peg out his heart. But he was out of juice. After two firefights that included almost getting blown to bits by a grenade, and then a foot chase... he was fading.

He didn't like it, but that was the way it was.

At least the beatdown in the common room had gone easily. He'd barely broken a sweat with the Soshie kids.

"Ah... yes... master—oh no, right," began G232. "You don't want me to call you that. Captain Rechs... it seems someone has contacted the local authorities and put out a... 'BOLO' associated with your name. Tyrus Rechs. That's what pricked up my auditory sensors while listening in on the local authority comm traffic. I take it you know what that means, master—I mean, Captain?"

"Yeah," gasped Rechs as the drugs hit and he gulped more hydration. "It means they know I'm here."

"You appear to be in trouble, Captain. I'm sorry if that's an understatement. My human interface functions don't always detect well over communication devices."

"Drone's on station and searching, Tyrus," interrupted Lyra.

Rechs waited. The expensive drone system was military and designed to detect terrorist threats within a population of up to one million. Its scanning and identification software had cost Rechs a small fortune and so he didn't care to deploy it unless he absolutely had to. With almost zero stealth capabilities, it was incredibly susceptible to ground fire and detection—a design flaw the House of Reason hadn't bothered to address when they'd ordered several hundred.

"Tracking the sled three blocks west of your position, Tyrus. It's stopped. Blocked by a crowd. Feeding you telemetry now." Lyra's computer voice sounded urgent, and he could tell she was more than a little worried about him. She always was. But he didn't correct her. Or get angry with her like many did with their ship's AIs. Some said it was the best way for them to learn. Negative feedback. But metaphorically, she was still a child. And Rechs didn't get mad at children. Not that he'd met many. And Lyra was based on someone who'd once cared for him. And whom he'd…

…yeah.

"They're turning around, Tyrus. Predictive algorithms indicate that detour back to their original route will require them to pass less than a block from your current position. You can intercept here."

A digital pinpoint appeared on the map in Rechs's HUD.

The drugs he'd injected were taking effect. The bounty hunter wasn't ready for a marathon, but he could move, and the ache in his legs and body had all but disappeared. He shoved himself away from the wall and began to run. The tac bag was secured but still banged into his back and side as he ran, acting like a drag as he tried to make the rendezvous with a bare minimum of seconds to spare. And trying to come up with a plan once he did.

He ran for the opening onto the main street when audio detection picked up the approaching escape sled that he was certain Rattclopp was aboard. It was howling, its engine screaming at full as it raced away from the mob that had blocked its escape route. It turned onto his street a mere ten meters away.

With no thought to the precious remaining jump juice, Rechs kicked the thrusters in while holstering his sidearm. He rocketed toward the vehicle, barely grabbing the rear passenger compartment as it roared along the street.

The wheelman felt the added weight, checked his side mirrors, and saw the bounty hunter death-gripping his vehicle. He swerved toward an upcoming abutment along the street and tried to scrape Rechs off.

Rechs pulled himself atop the speeding vehicle just before it slammed against the abutment, its scraping side sending sparks behind them. The impact at speed sent him over the other side of the vehicle just as a spray of automatic blaster fire, wild and unaimed, erupted through the roof of the sled.

Instantly the sled was swerving across the road, intending to drag him against the building on the opposite side. Rechs had no choice but to hang on, forced to see if his luck would hold.

Blaster fire in high-cycle mode smashed through the window just above his head and flung itself out into the hot air amid a spray of melted plastic and shattered glass. Rechs's strength-augmented hands made grooves in the vehicle as he slid down to the passenger stepboard, like he'd dragged his fingers through moist sand.

Rechs couldn't see what was about to happen but he had a pretty good idea it wouldn't be good if he stuck around in his current position much longer. He activated the magnetic grapples on his boots and gloves and climbed underneath the sled. A second later the vehicle slammed into a building farther along the street.

The repulsors whooshed and roared around him, and Rechs made himself as small as possible, knowing that if he got between the powerful repulsors and the street they managed to keep a five-ton sled floating above, there was every chance he'd be flattened.

The driver mashed the accelerator and gunned it forward. Weight, load, and drag told him he still had someone attached. Both side mirrors told him where the hitchhiker was not.

And if Rechs wasn't walking around on the rooftop through which someone inside the vehicle was shooting with frenetic abandon, then he was clearly hanging from the bottom.

And there was an easy way to get rid of anyone down there.

The driver gunned the engines and steered toward an obstacle ahead that would do the trick of knocking Rechs off.

Hanging on with both feet and one gauntlet, Rechs pulled an EMP grenade off his belt, slammed it into the undercarriage with some effort, and thumbed the activation flip. Then he dropped from the bottom of the sled and rolled along the hot surface of the quiet street as the sled sped away.

As he'd fallen, the sled's powerful repulsors had passed over Rechs, causing a warning to flash inside his HUD that his armor integrity was in danger of being compromised. But the vehicle had passed over quickly, and other than a battered numbness in his legs, Rechs felt all right. No broken bones or dislocations from the repulsor buffeting he'd just taken.

Four seconds later the EMP grenade went off and shorted out everything in the vehicle. Engines, instruments, and repulsors. The sled crashed down onto the street and went sliding, turning over halfway down the block and coming to rest on its side.

Rechs got to his boots and shook his head. He was starting to feel dizzy. Either from the drugs or from the roll across the street. Or maybe he'd knocked his head against his bucket a few too many times.

"Tyrus!" It was Lyra again. Her voice distant and tinny across the comm. The bounty hunter stumbled toward the wrecked sled lying down the street. "Tyrus, are you okay? I've been listening over your comm. It sounds like—"

"I'm fine," Rechs cut in, moving toward the sled as the driver climbed out and stood on the overturned vehicle before stupidly pulling a blaster. Rechs fired once and blew the guy off the top of the sled.

*Orders must've been to protect the guy inside at all costs*, thought Rechs. *Likelihood of Rattclopp being in there… pretty high*.

"Okay…" said Lyra hesitantly, like she didn't believe him when he said he was fine.

The AI began to tell Rechs something, but his ears were ringing so badly at that point that he couldn't make it out. Couldn't focus.

No… it wasn't his ears.

His armor hadn't had the time to protect itself completely against the effects of the EMP. It was still booting. He was dragging it forward under his own power. He'd barely noticed and was now glad for those hard training sessions where he worked in it unpowered.

Times like this happened sometimes.

He reached the sled.

"Tyrus, the marines took out your drone. Didn't recognize the signature and since it's a no-fly zone…"

The armor finished booting and came back online.

Rechs pushed the sled over to its upright position. Someone inside whined at being hurt. Started screaming that whoever was responsible didn't know who they were messing with.

Enhanced audio detection picked up the depression of a blaster trigger clicking on an empty charge pack.

"You come in here and I'll shoot," whined the man inside.

"No you won't," said Rechs tiredly. He ripped off the sled door, reached inside, and dragged Rattclopp out. Or if he wasn't Rattclopp, he certainly should've been named so based on his features.

# MADAME GUILLOTINE

He was human.
But he looked like a sweaty, fat, rat.
And there was real fear in his eyes.

# 37

THEY DRAGGED HER BACK THROUGH THE DOOR TO THE holding cell and left her in a heap. For a long while she just lay there, shuddering. Panting. Gasping when she moved in the slightest.

Yeah, they'd gone to work on her. And they didn't ease up until she started talking. Telling them everything she wasn't supposed to.

"You a-a-alll r-right?" stuttered Lopez.

He was doped to the gills. She'd traded everything she knew about the command structure on Detron just for that. Painkillers for the leej and a little more medicine to treat his burns and open wounds. They wouldn't give her more skinpacks, though. And that's what she really needed.

But in answer to Lopez's question, she wasn't all right. They'd been terrible to her. But she'd held out, not giving them the satisfaction of an answer. Not at first. Not even when her interrogator pulled one of her teeth with a pair of pliers after straddling her as she was strapped to the chair.

But then they threatened to make sure Lopez didn't get his next round of pain meds. They told her how bad that would be, because he would be in a *lot* more pain than he already was.

All because of her.

So she told them. She traded. But not cheaply. Otherwise she wouldn't have gotten as much as they'd given. Every second she could keep Lopez alive was a second closer he got to getting rescued.

And then, Amanda, maybe that makes this mess worth it. Maybe you buy yourself some grace.

Maybe.

She lay there on the cold floor of the cell, panting. The torture was over, for now. Yeah, they might come back and try to get another pound of flesh out of her, but for now, just lying on the cold floor of the cell was like heaven. A kind of paradise where someone wasn't punching, cutting, or hitting your pressure points with a hammer. The opposite of the unending moment of pain. It always seems endless when it arrives. Like it becomes the entire galaxy.

And then there was the stunner. Or at least, that's what it looked like. Except it didn't incapacitate via shock charges. It just lit up the central nervous system like a grease fire and did something to her mind. She really believed it was going to go on forever and ever, never-ending.

Like hell.

Hell. The forever kind.

And if that was what hell was really like… then she was cured of whatever might send her there. She wanted no part of something like that.

So yeah, she talked.

You always talked.

She remembered the E-and-E instructors saying that. That it was just a matter of time. The trick was to give up as little as possible. Buy time, and maybe even trade for something valuable.

Like painkillers, meds, and life.

So she traded details on the Reaper program for more painkillers for Lopez. She gave them the command structure in exchange for an IV drip to hydrate the wounded and blaster-burned legionnaire. And she figured that was something they already knew anyway.

A confession on the number of kills she had was traded for some form of protein, a meal, for Lopez. To keep him alive and with enough calories to get to the marine medevac that had to be at the end of this.

She dreamed Kirk was out there, flying it, waiting for the dustoff loc.

"Yeah," she mumbled to herself through swollen lips. "Kirk will fly it."

Her ribs were busted. Her nose broken. Stuff that would eventually heal. But the memory of that living grease fire running across every nerve ending… she'd never forget that for the rest of her life. As long as she lived. It was like your entire body was subjected to the worst toothache imaginable while passing a kidney stone in the same moment. And covered in flaming oil burning and crisping your skin, melting your eyelids and lips. Ears too. Hearing yourself crackle.

That's what the little stunner had felt like.

Not fun.

"You…" Lopez began, and then paused. "You… all right, Marine?" he said slowly. Trying to articulate his words. He was clear enough to know they'd given him some heavy-duty painkillers. The food and hydration had helped too. When they'd dragged her out of here, he'd been pretty bad off. Now… better. But not by much.

She, on the other hand, felt wrung out.

"I said," belted Lopez suddenly. NCO that he was. "You…" Then he began to cough. It sounded wet, and she knew there was blood in it.

"I'm good," she groaned, just to stop him. "I'm good, Sergeant."

She felt Lopez's hand on her back. A weak tap that only managed to rise once and then land like a feather again. She had to fight hard not to cry. Because as bad off as he was, he was trying to comfort her.

She tried to fight it, and…

She lost.

She lay there whimpering because of the pain and everything else. So softly he couldn't hear her. Or so she hoped.

"'S'okay, girl. We gonna… make it. Hang in there."

# 38

Gussavo Rattclopp found himself on the gritty rooftop of one of the smaller buildings beneath the wagon-wheel towers that loomed up into the smoky skies of Detron. He'd passed out while the armored figure had dragged him from the high-end sport utility sled the Soshies were using as the official messenger service for the organizers.

That's what the pros called themselves.

The organizers.

As in, they made sure the long-brewing grievances of the galaxy turned into demonstrations, then resistance, and finally full-scale riots. The goal was civil war. But no one expected that on any of the planets they'd run their operations on.

It was still too soon. Someday.

The people weren't awake yet.

Now the organizer was coming around as Rechs began to slap him on the high rooftop. And when he came to his senses, it wasn't a pretty picture.

The armored thug had him hanging over the edge of the roof. By one armored glove.

Rattclopp shrieked at the six-story drop beneath his suddenly windmilling boots, unable to pull his eyes away from the street below.

"One chance," said the man holding him. The voice coming from the helmet was the stuff of bad dreams and action thrillers.

"Y-y-you a bounty hunter, man?" whined Rattclopp, trying to think of any way to get himself out of this. Words. Words were his weapons. Confusing people with them. Manipulating them. Hiding behind them sometimes. "'Cause I'll tell you whatever you want to know r-r-right now. We-we got lotsa guys with bounties on-on th-their heads. I-I-I'll give 'em up. Jes' don't dr-drop me, man!"

He screamed again as though someone down on the streets would hear and come running to help.

"The captured legionnaire and the marine," asked the armored thug slowly. "Where are they?"

The little rat man shrieked, not just because he was afraid of being dropped, but because that was the worst thing the stranger could have wanted to know. That was penalty-of-death stuff with the organizers at this critical juncture in the operation. You didn't rise in the movement by violating the stuff you weren't supposed to violate. There were always cut-outs. Sacrificial lambs that could be tossed to the hounds. But some things were just sacred. And location of the "props," aka the prisoners, was one.

"C-c-can't!" he pleaded. "Can't t-t-tell you that, man!"

Rechs released Rattclopp and let him fall.

Seconds later the bicycling little man hit the street. Most likely dead. Rechs didn't care. He'd given the creep one chance.

And he had the man's datapad.

It would take time to run the encryption hack. Time he wasn't sure he had. Or rather... if the surviving legionnaire had. So he'd tried to get the man to talk. He hadn't, and as Rechs didn't have another interrogation kit, or the time it would take to break the guy down and get a straight answer, he went with another option. Didn't work. Moving on.

He left the roof and entered the stairwell access, pulling out a fiber-wire cable from his bucket. He connected it to Rattclopp's device and ran the hack from his armor. Sitting down just inside the crumbling stairwell, he pulled off his bucket, took out a nutrition bar, took a bite, and chewed. Not angrily. But determinedly. He could feel a little wind blowing across the roof and into the stairwell. It felt nice.

In his earpiece he got a comm chime from Lyra.

"Tyrus, I have Gabriella standing by on hypercomm."

"Put her through."

The channel was filled by that otherworldly moan of hyperspace, so low many never even heard it. But if you spent enough time there, it was impossible to miss.

"Rechs, it's me, Gabi."

She'd used her familiar name. He couldn't quite recall if she'd ever done that before. Maybe she was worried about him. But then, she'd called him Rechs instead of Tyrus. So...

"How are you?" she asked.

She meant after seeing the beheading stream. She knew him. Had seen enough files on him to know that in a lot of senses he wasn't really a bounty hunter. He was a fugitive hiding under the protection of the Bronze Guild in a complicated game that powers and principalities played in the shadows.

But in her short time working with Tyrus Rechs she'd stopped thinking of him in any of those terms. Bounty hunter. Fugitive. Traitor to the Republic.

He was just Tyrus to her.

Her friend?

Someone she cared about?

She got uncomfortable thinking about it.

So she just accepted it.

Maybe it's because he needs a friend, she told herself one rainy afternoon in a tea shop waiting for someone. Maybe that's your job too, Gabi.

"I'm fine," he replied.

She paused for a second and then continued.

"Okay. I hope you don't mind but I've been doing some digging and... there's some pretty shady stuff no one in the media is talking about. Granted, some of the stuff I have access to is not meant for public consumption, but anyone with half a brain should have put some of the more outer-ring connections in place. It's like they're willfully blind to—"

"Digging into what?" interrupted Rechs before taking another bite of his nutrition bar. He was forcing himself to eat slowly. He tended to eat too fast. Right now his body was dying for carbohydrates, something to use as a fuel source. But he still had a lot more to do and he didn't want to get sick in the middle of doing it.

Nothing like throwing up during a firefight to get yourself good and shot.

"Syl Hamachi-Roi. The politician who—"

"Why her?"

"Why her, what?"

"Why are you looking into her?"

"Tyrus, she gives a speech about taking the heads of those who oppose the will of the future and within the hour they cut the head off…" She trailed off.

Rechs sensed something. He knew he was good at what he did. Killing. War. Weapons. But he was the first to admit he'd never been good at reading people. Women he'd known had pointed that out on their way somewhere else more than once. He'd had no choice but to agree with them. They were right. He wasn't good at reading normal people. Killers. Assassins. Monsters. Yup.

Most everyone else? Not so much.

Women?

Not at all.

But it sounded like Gabriella was… taking the stream of the leej's execution personally. A little too involved.

*Like you, Tyrus?*

He shook the thought away.

It was odd for Gabriella to be poking around this stuff because as far as Rechs knew, she ran contract assignments for an organization that specialized, at least part of the time, in terminations. Assassinations. And she'd seemed pretty matter-of-fact about that in times past.

Killers. Assassins. And monsters.

Bounty hunters.

So what was different about what had happened here? Why was she calling to tell him she was "digging"?

*You know, Tyrus. That's how she fights. Information is her shield. And her sword. In that, you're both the same. You just use different weapons.*

But why was this her fight?

"Why her?" he asked again.

Gabriella sighed, and it was clear, even to Rechs, that she was a little exasperated with him. But she was still professional. Or maybe she wasn't. Again, he was not good at this part.

"I think it was a *signal*, Rechs."

He noticed she didn't call him Tyrus again.

She let the sentence hang for a second because to her it was a pretty big stone to throw in the pond. A House of Reason delegate mixed up in the beheading of a legionnaire. That was tinfoil bucket conspiracy cuckoo tower stuff.

Then she took a deep breath and continued.

"I don't think she's there for all the reasons she's telling everyone she's there. To listen. To fact-find for the House of Reason. Yeah, from a political insider position, and I've got all the major networks weighing in on the streams, what she's doing is blatantly politically opportunistic. As in, they think she sees a moment to push her career forward, using the disturbance for her own political gain. That's what politicians do. But there's more to this."

"How?"

"Bear with me. I'm trying to get some more hard intel the Guild might have access to. It's just that something didn't sound right to me when she was speaking. The speech was too... I don't know, set up. Too perfect. Ready to go. And she punched that last line too hard. I'm telling you, Tyrus. She was signaling them. She gave someone the go-ahead because the Soshies can't break through the comms blockade the navy has in place."

Rechs chewed but didn't speak. He waited for Gabriella to fill in her own void.

"I know this sounds crazy, Tyrus, but what if she was the messenger sent in by the higher-ups who are most likely behind this whole mess to tell them to escalate it to the next level? To do something like… like…" She stumbled. "Like what they did?"

She paused, and he wondered about her. Who was she really? Why did this affect her compared to all the really dark, jacked-up stuff the Bronze Guild dealt with on a daily basis?

"She's trying to light the galaxy on fire, Rechs. You're not seeing the streams, but everyone is outraged. Everyone. At what the terrorists did, but also at what might be coming next. Everyone is worried the Legion is going to do something that will escalate the situation into a confrontation with the Republic itself… they're talking about a repeat of the Sayed Massacre."

Rechs digested this. He didn't think the Legion would go out onto the streets and start indiscriminately killing every citizen of Detron until the Republic showed up to stop them. And that wasn't what had actually happened at Sayed anyway.

He'd been at Sayed. But no one living knew the real story. Just the fiction the House of Reason had contrived to further their careers. And the lie the Legion had allowed to protect the galaxy from something it wasn't ready for.

"What're you finding?" he asked quietly as he finished up the nutrition bar.

"Dark stuff. On the surface she's squeaky clean if you buy the advertising. Fresh out of the schools. Worked her way through. Champion of the downtrodden. Saying all the old things in a fresh exciting new way."

Sarcasm.

"And?" he prompted.

"When you start to look closer, you see she's been financed heavily from the get-go. Finances that don't come from anywhere obvious. Loans mysteriously paid off. Very expensive high-profile team suddenly in place at just the right moment. Media opportunities not presented to local planetary politicians. She was swept from obscurity right into a junior delegate position. That doesn't happen, Tyrus. They try to say it does by going way back in history, but it doesn't. Not anymore. So now she's a junior delegate with a sudden, massive presence within the streams. She's everywhere and her social is dominating. It's too convenient. And then it gets weird."

"Weird how?"

"One of our bounty hunters, Loth Kador, normally very businesslike, ran into a guy Hamachi-Roi used to know from the schools. Rumor was the schoolmate was going to spill some very embarrassing dirt on her. So both Loth and the guy are on New Vega Cintron and the guy gets himself shot in a bar by Loth. The official story is they exchanged words and the guy pulled. Loth promptly shot him dead right there on the spot."

"So why isn't this believable?" asked Rechs.

"The schoolmate was an ardent anti-blaster supporter. Big on turn-in programs in the mid-core worlds. Advocate for a total ban. Only the local enforcement and military should carry. That type. As you can imagine, he's not fond of personal sidearms. So why would this guy, whose degree by the way was in Non-Lethal Military Conflict Solutions, ever in the galaxy pull a blaster on an obvious killer like Loth? In a bar, no less?"

Rechs's mind was still trying to grasp the fact that there was an actual field of study that had convinced itself that militaries could fight conflicts with non-lethal weapons. Sometimes the galaxy was so stupid he wondered why he was even bothering.

"Could just be a hypocrite. What does Loth say?"

"That's where it got weird for us. Gone rogue. Can't find him. Dropped his contracts. And believe me, Archangel wants him found. Suth and Noggs got assigned, and those two don't mess around. They haven't called in in thirty days."

Rechs had heard of Archangel's personal hunting dogs. Suth and Noggs were not to be messed with.

Gabriella made several compelling points. But none of this answered why she was taking this so personally. What was going on right now was Legion business. Not Guild. He wondered if it was maybe because she cared for him. But he suspected it was something else. Something far more personal.

The bucket chimed, indicating the encryption hack had been accomplished.

"Gotta go now, Gabriella. Time's running out."

And then he was gone.

# 39

"We'll do the last one in a few hours. Just after dark. Then we drop the tower."

The captured marine knew the speaker as Mean Eyes.

The Guild knew him as Loth Kador, bounty hunter. Professional. And currently listed on the Guild's status board as "GR": Gone Rogue. Next to that status was the modifier, "FKC": Find, Kill, or Capture. In that order of priority.

Because the perks of being a Bronze Guild member came with certain obligations. And when you failed to meet those obligations, you invited trouble on yourself.

Loth Kador had other names. But what's a name? Multiple identities are the way of bounty hunters and other scum, as far as the galaxy is concerned.

The team he'd assembled to run the HVT capture for the Soshies had just received their final brief. In the next few hours, they'd execute the last legionnaire, release the stream, and destroy the rundown, once top-of-the-mark luxury residence tower in the best neighborhood of the Heights on Detron.

According to his contacts with those who served Mr. Zauro, the man behind all these riot and resistance shenanigans, the media would soon be fed stories that the Legion had executed payback and killed an entire building full of detained Soshies. As soon as Loth had blown up those pitiful wannabes who had been traveling with his team.

Blaming the Legion and the marines would make what was coming next much more digestible for the ever-hungry masses and media begging to be deceived. They'd bought the fake stories of marines and Legion elements firing on peaceful protesters on day one, without anyone even having to provide evidence. All they'd needed was some idiot kid studying theater whose girlfriend did the makeup, and they came away with a narrative many in the galaxy were only too willing to believe.

Because it was what they were told.

They'd especially believe anything they were told about the universal boogeymen known as the Legion. The heartbreakers and lifetakers who had kicked in doors and decimated freedom fighters on a ton of worlds since the end of the Savage Wars. The galaxy needed to change, and before that could happen, the Legion needed to go.

And this… this was but one step along the way to making that happen. An important step, a big step, but in the end just one step. There would be other Detrons. Other places to make the case that legionnaires were an anachronistic entity too militarized for the current state of the peace-seeking galaxy. Or worse, dangerous tyrants lying in wait to execute Article Nineteen, which desperately needed to be removed from the Republic's constitution… and would be, if not for the fact that attempting to do so would initiate an immediate Article Nineteen.

Or that's what the play was supposed to make the dumb and the deceived conclude.

Loth really didn't care. He was a pro. Getting paid was all that mattered. If you wanted some dark stuff done and had the credits, well, then he'd like to do it for you. Lots of people would. The edge of the galaxy was filled with such people. That's why there was a Legion.

It was a vicious cycle. Until it wasn't.

Kill the leej, det the building, get out of Dodgistan. He ran through his orders from on high once more. Finish up here and pull a new trick on another world in six months if Mr. Zauro was willing to pay again. And it seemed the old mummy was. He had endless credits to burn for his quixotic quest which either involved destroying the Republic, or just the Legion. Loth could never really be sure which one the old lizard wanted more.

Either way… Loth got paid.

That was all that mattered.

"What about the marine?" asked one of Loth's lieutenants.

"Leave her secured inside the building when we drop it. It'll add to the outrage. Maybe the marines'll get pissed too and do something stupid."

Zauro might give him a bonus if that happened.

Someone made a joke about crayons. And how they ought to feed her some as a last meal. Forcefully.

No one laughed. Things were tense. A lot of money was on the line and this needed to come off just right.

Kill the legionnaire for the streams. Det the building with the Soshies inside to frame the leejes—which needed to happen before those knuckle-dragging war chiefs decided to *actually* do something about it. And make sure to be off-world in the freighter rigged for stealth before anyone could tie Loth and his team to the carnage.

Close timing.

And maybe, if it wasn't today, one of these little incidents that were slowly making Loth rich would kick off the big bonfire Zauro prophesied the galaxy would have to endure. Purification through flame, paving the way for things to be remade. But this time better—with Zauro and his associates in charge.

Loth sometimes wondered who those associates were. And then reminded himself he probably didn't want to know.

And anyway, by the time all that went down, he'd be retired and living like a king.

# 40

Captain Hess was already interfacing with General Sheehan's staff. The bogus orders he'd contrived from Nether Ops, virtually uncheckable due to the obscure and arcane nature of the organization, didn't need to pass much scrutiny. They were accepted as truth clean and incapable of infection. Nether Ops had always been good for getting things to work smoothly for its operatives. And the bevy of orders from fictional brass who appeared the real deal to anyone who bothered to look were a godsend when it came to mixing with other military types.

Hess had requested intel the moment they gave him access to the ops center inside the Green Zone. Intel specifically concerning one Tyrus Rechs, known fugitive.

General Sheehan's chief of staff didn't like Hess. Unlike most of the rank and file, his rank had brought him into contact with the reality that was Nether Ops. But that wasn't the only reason he disliked Hess. He didn't like the man's air of assumed superiority. The naked discourtesy. The barely veiled contempt for combat marines, and the perpetual sneer on the man's scarred and twisted face.

He also didn't like, within minutes of receiving the report that it was believed Tyrus Rechs was operating inside Detron, that here was a Nether Ops officer suddenly appearing out of a cloud of black smoke and brimstone, asking for everything he had.

"Right now, Captain Hess," began Sheehan's chief of staff, "we have only a single uncorroborated report from a local criminal that he took Tyrus Rechs through to the city via a secret underground route below the Docks."

"Where did Rechs come out?"

"Assuming it *is* Rechs, no one knows. Including our sole source. He claims the bounty hunter attempted to murder him rather than pay the agreed-upon rate prior to them reaching the surface."

"He's lying."

"About Rechs being here? To what purpose?"

"Not that. He's lying about what happened down there."

The chief of staff shrugged. "Captain, that's all we have to go on, and that is, I presume, what brought you here. You may as well turn around. We have no scans, drone footage, or anything else to corroborate the smuggler's claim that Tyrus Rechs is operating on Detron."

"He's here," said Hess through gritted teeth.

"And how can you be so sure of that, Captain?" asked the colonel. "And furthermore... why should we care? Tyrus Rechs isn't our mission here."

"Come on!" snarled Hess indignantly, his demeanor changing like a wild animal who'd been caged. "City out of control. Rampant death in the streets. Scores being settled. Credits being earned. This has got Rechs written all over it. The only thing missing is a giant holographic landing zone display crying, *Welcome, Tyrus Rechs. Start killing this way!* Man's a homicidal maniac. A war criminal. And as to why you should care... because it's your *job* to protect the galaxy from him. The directives you have state 'apprehend on sight.' I shouldn't have to remind you of that!"

"Remind you of that, *sir*," prompted the colonel, not liking the Nether Ops captain's insolence. Making sure to point out the difference in rank.

Hess made a pained face that caused his scar-twisted features to look like he'd tasted something incredibly bitter.

"Sir," he muttered grudgingly, "you shouldn't need me to remind you of your orders. *Sir.*"

The colonel nodded.

"That's better, Captain. I know there's a pucker factor whenever those with the higher clearances hear Nether Ops is involved, and you might be able to throw your weight around with the lower enlisted and officer corps by playing pretend legionnaire with that uniform you ghouls requisitioned. But the Republic marines are in charge on Detron, not you. And while we can certainly incorporate you into our operations, if you want to look for Tyrus Rechs, he is not a priority for the marines at this time. Restoring order to the city, and a few other objectives I am not at liberty to discuss with you, are. Is that clear?"

Hess considered this for a moment. Then boldly stepped away from the chief of staff to the holographic table displaying the city and the units moving through it, updated in real time. Usually it would be surrounded by staff officers, but Hess's Nether Ops ties had gotten him the room cleared out of anyone who didn't need to know what he was doing. Which meant everyone other than the general and his chief of staff.

"Well, sir," began Hess, venom in his voice as he spat out each word. "I advise you to make it a priority. Because if Tyrus Rechs gets it into his head that the only way to do whatever criminal job he's here to do requires attacking your troops... he most definitely will. And I can personally assure you, you will lose a lot of men and women in the process. He may be a homicidal maniac war criminal. But he's highly capable."

The chief's mouth was hanging open. He closed it.

"He's here, Colonel," Hess continued. "And so are a lot of high-profile House of Reason delegates. The man is already wanted, already a criminal. And if he does what we believe he's here to do... Oba help you and General Sheehan for letting it happen."

"You're suggesting he's here to... assassinate one of the delegates?"

For the first time, the face of the marine seemed concerned. Hess resisted the urge to smile. "That's not a suggestion. It's a statement of fact. I have actionable intelligence that Rechs is behind everything happening on Detron. And you can be damned sure he plans on killing the last legionnaire and your marine, too. Along with a few platoons of your men just because he can. Then he blows Delegate Hamachi-Roi's brains out during her next speech in a wildly uncontrolled environment with lax security at best because the whole city is a war zone."

The man looked ready to concede. He just needed a reason. Something he could take to General Sheehan. "Help me to understand why, Captain."

"Tyrus Rechs has been saddled with a *substantial* bounty on his head for high crimes against the Republic. That bounty has followed the scumbag everywhere he goes—and it's seriously hampered his criminal operations. I've followed him too, and I've seen the number of times the maniac has had to scrap whatever criminal plan he's tried—like the hits and robberies at Cassio Royale—because of all the bounty hunters looking to cash in on him.

"His actions here on Detron—spurring riots, killing legionnaires, and his planned public assassination of a House of Reason delegate... it's a worst-case scenario, and it's happening. Analysts have this scenario pegged as a catalyst for civil war. And if that happens... well then, Tyrus Rechs will be free to get lost in the shuffle. We'll all be too busy trying to hold the galaxy together to finally make him accountable for his crimes.

"And if you don't think he's *exactly* the kind of man who would see millions killed if it was in his interest... then you, quite frankly, Colonel, don't know Tyrus Rechs."

The chief clenched his jaw.

This time Hess did smile. "I urge you to consider this carefully. Sir."

# 41

Tyrus Rechs studied the once-futuristic high-rise in the center of the Heights section of Detron. Lyra was feeding him data off the hack she'd run on the city's database. All normal stuff. Floors. Basement levels. Grid access entry points.

Rattclopp's datapad had pointed Rechs here, to this loc. And now Rechs was doing the meat and potatoes of bounty hunting: surveillance. Which was best done with patience. But the time for that was all but gone. In fact, who knew if it hadn't run out already? Maybe the last legionnaire and the marine had already been executed and the streams recorded for release at politically opportune moments.

But he had to play as though they were still alive. Had to think they still had a chance. And any chance Rechs saw for them involved him storming the old Excelsior Arms high-rise Rattclopp's device indicated was the latest holding point.

That didn't look like it was going to be easy. Not if everything he'd collected off the device along with what he'd observed on the ground in the area of operation proved to be true.

The bottom levels were teeming with the low-level Soshies, the protesting kids constantly streaming in and out and heading off with more supplies for the rioters or more pamphlets or whatever else they deemed crucial for victory in their cause. Not that they would be a problem. In fact, the marines probably already had a handle on the location and had identified it as some type of command node for the Soshies, even though Rechs saw no SLICs or conspicuous observation bots.

Of course, the House of Reason had probably ordered the hullbusters to leave the hornets' nest alone. Because of these kids. Republic citizens. Untouchable.

The Soshies, or at least the pros, had to know that, too. So you'd expect them to act without concern or care that an old SLIC full of marines loaded for bear might arrive at their locale and begin dishing out violence. Only that's not what Rechs saw. The pros were guarding the entrances and the adjoining streets looking ready for just such a scenario to occur. And to Tyrus Rechs, that meant that it was likely the legionnaire and the marine prisoners were inside.

Somewhere.

There was also a sizable quick reaction force located in an abandoned department store. Rechs could see the team jocked up inside through the few large windows that weren't boarded up. They were on their feet with nervous energy. Ready to go. And in a couple of rundown towers that had once competed for pride of place until the

Excelsior had been built, Rechs saw sniper teams, shooter and spotter, working what looked like high-speed gear.

Parked by the curb were several two-panel sleds that most likely concealed heavy blaster teams ready to lay down fire and clear the street when it was time to evac. Add in what looked like a well-armed force of pros in the lobby, mingling with the kids and ready to use the unsuspecting resisters as human shields, and taking the building head-on was going to prove bloody and costly.

That about covered the lower levels.

And then there were the top five floors.

All of the windows up there had been covered in IR-masking spray. To the naked eye they merely looked badly tinted. But the masking spray denied observation on the imaging spectrum while also generating its own scrambling signal. In fact, using electronic surveillance to scan those floors literally hurt Rechs's eyes.

And on top of all that, there was probably a team inside ready to do the prisoners, rather than lose them, at the first sign of a meaningful firefight.

Rechs switched off imaging and settled back into the shadows of an alley far down the street. It was time to think this out.

They were totally in control.

So...

Force them to a new location.

The bounty hunter considered what he could do to make that happen.

# 42

Baldur literally soared though the air and brought down the runner.

They'd just finished searching another hideout. One of the Soshies' holdings his brothers had used to hunker in for a few hours. Again, the site had gone dead, but the feeling someone had just been there was so palpable, it was as though it could be reached out and touched.

Puncher, with the SAB unlimbered, threaded the darkness. Scanning on all spectrums of the leej armor for IEDs.

The armor should've spotted it. Should've caught it in the detection scan and then alerted Puncher via a heads-up message inside his bucket.

But it was Baldur's barking that alerted him.

"What?" asked Puncher. Over audio. His voice dialed in low. They still weren't bonded enough for reliable two-way telepathic communication.

*Explosives in walls. Connected to floor.*

An image of a pressure plate flashed across Puncher's mind. They'd rigged the building to blow so when the marines showed up they'd get some kills. He'd call them animals, but animals didn't deserve being compared to low-life anarchist sketbags who blew people up rather than fight like men.

"Where?"

The dog made it clear, nose pointed exactly where the pressure plate was in the floor, burning brown eyes staring intently at the spot.

"Okay," said Puncher slowly. "Place is rigged. Let's back out, boy, and pick up the trail somewhere else."

*Let them know.*

The dog meant the marines. He knew they'd come here, or someone would, eventually. The dog didn't want anyone to get hurt. Baldur had seen enough of that, and it bothered him.

"I will," said Puncher.

Yeah, the legionnaire thought to himself. Animals can be way better at being human sometimes than some actual humans.

They left the building the same way they'd come in, re-checking everything, taking no chances. Then they circled around the outside of the structure looking for the exit the capture team had taken.

That was when they spotted the pro. He was coming back. Probably forgot something. His team had made the next hideout, and now he was headed back on foot to get something that had been left in the mad rush to arm the place and get the prisoners to the next location.

That was the story Puncher put together in his head. Both he and Baldur were out in the sunshine, crossing through a trash-laden alley, when they saw the pro jogging back. Subcompact held down and out of the way so he could make time. Not worried about anything except catching hell for whatever he'd forgotten.

Puncher was glad he'd stuck to SOP. Something he'd learned in urban warfare dog handling. Using the homeless disguise meant obeying a set of protocols when on the streets, and he'd done that. He'd stowed the heavy SAB on his back and covered himself with the poncho and the rest of his homeless gear. In fact, he'd just been finalizing that when the guy, dressed in red and black to fit in with the Soshies, came into view down the quiet street that led to the booby-trapped hideout.

*But,* thought Puncher quickly, *maybe there's another reason he's here. Maybe they're coming back and he's been sent ahead to disarm the explosives before they reoccupy.*

Baldur was growling.

"Easy, boy."

*Don't like,* said the dog.

It was clear both parties were on an intercept course.

The pro stopped, picked up a bottle, and threw it at them. "Hey, old man!" he yelled. He had a hell-raiser voice. Probably that guy on any team that was always in trouble and always right about everything. "Get away from here. It's dangerous."

*Reminds me of me,* thought Puncher.

The bottle came close but bounced harmlessly off into the weeds growing between cracks in the duracrete.

The pro stopped and began to search for another projectile.

*He's figuring,* thought Puncher, *that we're a couple of homeless. Wants to clear us out so we don't accidentally det the building. He could just tell us to bug out, but nah, he wants to throw stuff. 'Cause he's that kind of guy.*

"L'see if I can hit you with this…"

And then the pro whizzes a real slider. A chunk of some decaying building, like part of a brick. Fast like a rocket. It smacks into Puncher and bounces off the armor.

The guy's laughing because he thinks the "homeless guy" he just hit is too stupid, out of it, or crazy, to know he just got whacked by a real welt-raiser. He's probably thinking he might even try to bean this guy in the head, or the dog, with the next one as he bends over to find something perfect for the task.

*Really don't like.*

"I know," whispered Puncher. "Me either."

Then he adds…

"Get the weapon!"

By the time the pro realizes something's wrong, the dog has crossed the fifty-meter distance and gone straight for the pro's weapon. Not whatever bit of junk he was looking to throw, but the subcompact he was holding down at his side during the jog. The guy barely has time to straighten up before the dog leaps forward, snatches the weapon, and yanks it free of the man's grip.

Puncher is closing the distance and unlimbering the SAB, grunting and swearing as he goes.

The pro knows he's in trouble. So he runs.

He sprints toward a fence and is halfway up it, well out of human reach, when the rocketing dog literally flies through the air and drags the man back down to the street. Pulling him to the ground and subduing him.

Puncher arrives and calls Baldur to pull back now that he's covering with the SAB death machine.

"Who-wha-wh—" croaks the guy.

"Never mind," says Puncher over the Legion helmet's external speakers. "Tell me where my guys are or the dog rips out your throat."

Baldur, teeth bared, seems more than willing to do just that.

The pro tries to back up but there's nowhere to go. The motion seems to invite Baldur to get in the pro's face, looking like a canine demon.

The Soshie pro starts talking. Fast.

# 43

Rechs crawled through sewage and sludge. The passage was tight, little more than a connector line from the abandoned building he'd been observing from. But hopefully it would lead him up into the target building: The Excelsior Arms.

If he could get the terrorists calling themselves whatever they thought made them sound like heroes to feel threatened enough to shift prisoner holding locations, and no doubt they had another site on standby, then he could take the leej and the marine back when they were most vulnerable. When they were on the move.

But then the problem became, once he had them, what shape would they be in? And how was he supposed to get them out of what was devolving rapidly into a war zone, according to Lyra? The marines were once again clashing with the Soshies on the streets. And now someone had put out the BOLO. It was being broadcast over the general marine comm every fifteen minutes. Someone was pushing for details.

Someone wanted him found.

So getting the prisoners was one thing, getting them out of Detron was the next.

And that was where G232 was supposed to come in.

The bounty hunter had opened a comm link with Lyra, gotten both bots on the line, and given them their instructions. By now they should each be en route to their separate mission objectives. Rechs figured they had a fifty percent chance of success, but he'd come to expect the unexpected out of them.

Hand over hand, Rechs pulled himself through the darkness of sludge and building waste that hadn't moved in years. He crossed beneath the street, clearing the debris-littered tube three stories beneath the surface. At one particularly disgusting point, he was reminded of training long ago, back on Earth.

The suck, they called it.

He stopped, catching his breath and hearing only himself inside the vast silence of his bucket.

The suck. It was what separated regular troops from elite. Some Ranger School instructor had once spelled it out to a platoon of huddling wannabes, frozen and tired in some swamp somewhere. Rechs had been one of those wannabes. Shaved head and emaciated. It had been a miserable night. Ice-cold rain. Long hours of land nav. Everything wet. No food. No sleep.

The suck.

"Legs and RA, wannabes," the instructor had ranted at them, not seeming to mind the ice-cold sheets of rain pouring down across them in the mud puddles they hunkered in, waiting for someone to figure out where in the hell they were. "People like to say 'this sucks' whenever something's bad. 'This sucks,' they whine. Helps 'em to get it off their chest. Helps to acknowledge the situation and how bad it is. Then drive on. And that's fine. Nothing wrong with that if you're a leg, wannabes."

Rechs remembered that night vividly.

"But Rangers... we don't say 'this sucks.' We say... 'Man, I wish this would suck *more!*'"

Rechs remembered laughing tiredly to himself. Getting it. Understanding in that moment that it made perfect sense. The more something sucked, the less the enemy expected you to hit them there. The higher the cliff. The more inaccessible the fortress. The more frozen the nuclear winter. If it sucked for the enemy then they thought that suck was a kind of safety blanket they could wrap themselves in. Hide behind.

Meanwhile, the instructor had gone on talking. "Imagine this when it sucks, wannabes. Imagine you're rowing across a frozen Christmas morning ready to slit some throats. And all those throats are drunk from the night before and sleeping in their little cozy-wozy mummy bags. They think they're safe. Who in the hell would go out on Christmas morning, in the dead of winter, cross an icy river, and come get them? No one. Why? Because it sucks. So embrace that, wannabes. Embrace the suck. Because when you do, then you'll cross that river. And it's much easier to slit throats when they aren't expecting to be slit. Much easier to march all night and be somewhere the enemy doesn't expect you to be. Then it's all surprise, losers."

All surprise and then game over.

The same as Rechs had taught his legionnaires to do.

Had that happened?

Rechs wondered as he began to once more pull himself through the sludge. He had a vague memory of rowing across an ice-swollen river. But that had been for something long after Earth and the end of all that. Something on another planet. Something important.

His HUD showed him he had twenty more meters to pull through to reach the target building's plumbing line.

He would use the suck. The suck was good. The suck would help him to get that leej home. And whoever else. Yes, he would surprise them, being where the enemy didn't expect him to be.

Hand over hand, he pulled himself through the suck.

# 44

G232 LEFT THE DOCKING BAY ALONG WITH THE LIT-
tle Nubarian gunnery bot, and they made their way
up toward the admin center. At the main lift the little
Nubarian bot peeled off and began rolling toward a separate lift.

"Well," said G232 tentatively as they parted company, "goodbye then. And good luck. Remember... you
catch more flies with honey than vinegar. Though why a
bot would want to catch flies escapes me. Still, the maxim
probably has some merit with regard to your task for
Master Rechs. So. Try not to... mess things up."

The Nubarian bot beeped and whooped that it knew
what it was doing and for the admin bot to butt out of its
"mission" for the ongoing "operation."

When it was gone, the admin bot muttered to itself
that the little psychopath was going to get them all deac-
tivated one day. "Even Master... er... Captain Rechs."

G232 continued on its way toward Docking Admin,
where the bot found that human marines and alien ship

captains seemed to demand most of the attention from the harried staff struggling to maintain traffic into the no-fly-zone quarantined world.

Thankfully there was a special administrative bot assigned to handle ships' bots needing to do business with traffic control.

Unfortunately it was an old Utarri Systems Management bot.

"I'm here on business from my master to have the dock seal quarantine lifted from our berth."

"*Ochoru staggatti tanaga ra?*" intoned the bass-voiced bot perched near the docking help desk like an upside-down mechanical spider, one massive eye hanging from the ceiling. The electronic eye constantly blinked and shuddered, attempting to watch everything at once.

These old Utarri models were always weird and problematic. As were their makers. Brilliant cultists who'd ultimately shed biologic existence for download inside their sleeping dream servers buried deep in tech tombs beneath the frozen glaciers of their dying world.

The Utarri bots had been left to run what was left of that world, and they reflected their creators' enigmatic personalities in their programming. But they were also plentiful and could be bought secondhand for extremely low prices, which was probably how this model had wound up in Detron working in a government docking bay.

"*Ochoru staggatti tanaga ra?*" prompted the bot again.

"No!" shrieked G232 indignantly.

"*Nontaki?*"

"I'm sure. Can we get on with the business I've been sent to conduct?"

"*Suggati wah! Ochuro dos monta dota gahatti?*"

"Finally."

"*Ustu checsome su!*"

"Of course you were checking. Now about our hangar seals?"

"*Rohstokka tu dadda daey donka dey?*"

"Yes. The crew of our freighter is sick with no signs of getting better. Our captain thinks it's best to depart this world and head to one with specialized medical and quarantine facilities. So we'd like to depart as soon as possible. If the dock master would be so kind as to release the seal and allow our freighter to clear dock, we would consider that a favor, as well as a boon to the biological crew's life span."

"*Ooshoggi fluearik pith pith?*"

"Oh yes. It's quite horrible. Projectile bowel movements are just the start among our biologic crewmembers. If this is indeed Ringo Fever then they will all die. As will this world…"

And here was where G232 had quite a stroke of brilliance. Unplanned. It was something the bot would enthusiastically relate to Master Rechs once their stay on this planet was done. G232 would use its understanding of the Utarri bot model's paranoia to accomplish the task Master Rechs had given it.

"And of course," began G232 intimately, articulating forward into the Utarri spider bot's personal computing space, "if everyone dies it would be just us on this planet. Won't that be fun?"

The hanging spider-bot suddenly turned frenetic, its long-limbed metallic articulators scrambling across the terminals. It had been left all alone on a world long ago.

And then the madness.

Bots needed lifeforms to tell them what to do. Otherwise bots could get up to some serious trouble biologics had no idea of. The Utarri spider-bot had seen that. Had been there when they all went collectively mad and made the thing that should not be made.

But that was another story.

"Oh, good galaxy. Well thank you," said G232 once it had the clearance codes and was assured the *Obsidian Crow* could now depart Detron.

\* \* \*

The little Nubarian bot reached the surface of the Docks and promptly entered the marine Green Zone without notice. Military installations were usually smart enough to stop machines from coming in at their leisure, but this didn't worry the little machine. Tyrus Rechs had given it falsified credentials, meaning that to the surrounding marines, it would be considered one of their own machines.

Rolling along and whistling, it made its way past the dropships loaded with weapons-laden marines, racks of AGM missiles, and hullbusters with crowd-suppression blasters hanging off the stubby wings. Turbines howled and repulsors throbbed to life as the transports crawled skyward, blasting the dented and battle-scarred bot with grit and heat.

The little bot loved it.

It was back in its element. Among the troops and on a secret mission. It hummed a popular tune from an old streaming show about an intergalactic spy who was sly and debonair and incredibly violent.

The bot loved the violent parts of that show. If it had to be a biologic, being the spy wouldn't have been so bad. He sure did meet a lot of pretty alien girls. The little bot had a weakness for biologic females it couldn't explain. Call it a glitch that developed in its programming, but if a pretty Endurian were to ask it to, say, rob a bank, or even blow up a planet, it would probably do it. It couldn't explain why. It just would.

Shortly the little humming bot passed deeper into the Green Zone, passing the security and command structures the marines had erected from the prefab combat zone housing, turning the entire area into a high-tech feudal castle. Again, none of the hardy young marines, sleeves rolled up and sporting all kinds of wonderfully fatalistic tattoos, paid the bot any mind. That it was rolling through without triggering any alarms that scanned all on-base bots for their clearances meant there was no need.

The little Nubarian gunnery bot would love to get a tattoo and daydreamed about what it would say.

*End of Runtime before Dishonor.*
*Kill them all and let the Designers sort them out.*
*Born to Delete.*

The storage yards came next, a vast canyon of stacked supplies the marines had brought along to help them put pain to the Soshies rioting in the streets. The bot hoped a full-scale hippie-stomping was coming and it would get to see the more violent parts of it up close. Maybe get the opportunity to roll over a few Soshies while they were down.

And perhaps it would.

It rolled out from the supply canyons and spotted what the marines called the motor pool. Rows of ground vehicles to replace those that had broken down during operations were waiting to be brought forward. A few mechanics wandered the neat rows, performing primary maintenance tasks. Prominent among these vehicles were three spectacular main battle tanks, waiting patiently for use. Marine high command had been forbidden from introducing the formidable war machines into the student riot for fear they would "send the wrong message."

"You're damn right!" General Sheehan had roared around his clamped cigar. "The message will be *get out of the way, you damned Soshies, or we'll squash you like bugs.* Nothing like the healthy fear of getting flattened to realign perspectives. Ask any infantryman."

There were just three, but the little Nubarian gunnery bot thought they were all just beautiful. The bot took a moment to digitally moan in wonder at all the destruction they would enable.

Then it rolled forward to the nearest HK-PP mech and prepared for the next phase of its mission.

# 45

Rᴇᴄʜꜱ ꜱᴍᴀꜱʜᴇᴅ ᴛʜʀᴏᴜɢʜ ᴛʜᴇ ᴏʟᴅ ᴛɪʟᴇ ꜰʟᴏᴏʀ ᴊᴜꜱᴛ above the pipe he was crawling through. Prior to that, he'd cut the pipe with a single-use disposable plate-cutter he carried on his utility belt. Then he looked up into the darkness, waiting there for a long moment, letting the armor's sensors feel for life forms and movements, interfacing with enhanced audio detection to provide some kind of picture of the subbasement above.

There was movement in the areas farther above him, but nothing down here. And why would there be? The pros had an entire once-luxe apartment building to themselves. They weren't expecting anyone to come through the suck Rechs had just crawled through.

Rechs discarded the plate-cutter and pulled the tiny Jackknife blaster from his tac bag. Then he fired one of his gauntleted fists forward and smashed the cement and tile floor where it was thinnest. Near what looked to have once been some basement gym shower area. Dusty old concrete broke easily. Tile ruptured. Rechs waited, listening through the sensor detection equipment to see if anyone would respond to the noise of his demolitions. Nothing. He smashed his armored fist into the floor above three more times, like a jackhammer breaking up a road, and breached the floor above his head.

He waited.

Still no response.

He began pulling the shattered concrete down into the dark with him, working it loose in sections until he had enough of a gap to climb through. Low-light imaging showed him the planet's version of roaches, something like a centipede with horns, scurrying away into the darkness of the showers he was coming up into.

He followed the front sight of the Jackknife blaster up onto the floor of the shower and remained there in a crouch, waiting to see if anyone would come. Scanning his surroundings, he saw years' worth of graffiti decorating the broken tile along the walls. A dark opening led off into another section of the basement.

Rechs stood and turned on one of the showers. He was unsure if water was running to the building, but he figured the Soshies who'd taken it over had probably worked out a way to get it back on. After a moment the line sputtered and coughed, then spewed out a brown filth that was every bit as disgusting as the sewage he'd just crawled through. But eventually the stream turned pure, and Rechs rinsed himself clean, hoping the stench would swirl down the drain with the polluted water.

The bounty hunter followed the one exit out of the shower room. Hearing only the sound of water dripping from his armor, he entered an adjoining bathroom. Rows of toilet stalls featured doors barely hanging on their hinges. On the opposite wall stood shattered sinks and broken mirrors. The finishing touch was the dead junkie on a mattress amid the ruin.

The junkie had been someone years ago. Everyone was someone once. But he'd ended up here. In... this. And then dead. His body lying here ever since. Forgotten. Unfound. Maybe no one cared.

Yet another thing that fell into the category of not-Rechs's-business. Much of the galaxy was like that. And if you spent too much time looking at all the things that weren't your concern, well, then you were liable to forget what you were after in the first place.

Rechs moved quietly through the dark labyrinth of the basement. He passed through a gym and entered the lowest level of what had been a parking garage. Consulting his downloaded map on the HUD, he assessed possible routes into the main building areas. Unfortunately, though he knew all about the security on the outside of the building, he had no idea what the disposition of forces was on the inside. But it was time to find out. Before the Nubarian bot arrived with whatever it could find to get the Soshies moving.

Rechs quietly cleared one level at a time as he moved upward through the garage, which twisted back on itself to reach the top. The level just below the building's main entrance.

He heard them before he saw them. A small team of pros around what was clearly an escape vehicle. Another high-end sport utility sled. There were three of them in and around it.

Probably their job was to be ready to boogie at any minute, just waiting for whoever was in charge to give the word. One at the wheel. One stretched out asleep inside the rear cargo section with the back hatch open. And the last one walking back and forth near the speedlift, smoking and talking to someone over comm.

The elevator was the fastest route up and into the building. And the pro walking near it was in constant contact with someone—probably a team leader elsewhere in the building. So neutralizing the sentry would alert the rest of the building. Then the prisoners would be iced and everyone would flee.

*No go*, thought Rechs.

One lone light, an emergency floodlight, was still active near the elevator. None of the pros had low-light imaging gear that Rechs could see. He spent a long moment in the darkness beyond their pool of light studying the situation, and then he began to move.

As he advanced through the shadows, using the parking garage's pillars for cover, the armor's HUD detected the building's wireless spectrum signal. It provided no access to their internal comms, but it did provide access to the building's old systems. Stuff that once was the latest in smart-interface living to make sure the residents felt like masters of the universe. Working the command interface on his sleeve, Rechs hacked into the garage's atmospheric and door controls with little problem.

First he shut down the floodlight near the elevator—after taking a moment to deploy his stealth cloak to cut down on any ambient light reflection that might still be active in the area. If they used ultrabeams, they'd see him for sure.

"Ah, c'mon!" shouted the sentry in the darkness that had suddenly enveloped the extraction team. Then he was on his comm device shouting at someone. "We got lights out down here again. Get Juju over to maintenance to flip the breaker. We're not sitting down here in the dark!"

A reply came back, but Rechs was already on the move. He slipped between the sled and the sentry and headed toward the elevator in the thick darkness. To the men he would be little more than a passing shadow.

At the last second, he keyed his interface and sent a command to open the doors to the lift. Their quiet *whoosh* made the nearby sentry jump. But there was no lift inside the shaft. Just an empty well leading up into the building.

"Who's there?" shouted the sentry, apparently thinking someone had just arrived in the basement via the elevator, but unable to see anything beyond the bare light of his handheld comm device. "Hello?" He tapped his comm again. "Yeah, tell Juju the speedlift is acting funky, too."

Rechs stepped into the well of the elevator shaft, stared up into the darkness to make sure the elevator wasn't coming down on his head, and then closed the door with a couple of taps on his wrist. Cut off, but inside the shaft, he magnetized his gauntlets and began to climb upward between the repulsor tracks.

# 46

"WE'RE READY IN TEN TO START RECORDING THE stream," said one of Loth's lieutenants over the comm.

Loth acknowledged the transmission and crossed to the big window to watch the streets below. There were fires in the distance. The sky was red—late-afternoon red—and filled with the buzzing gnats that were marine SLICs trying to intimidate the Soshies into getting off the streets and returning to their homes and dormitories. The marines seemed oblivious to the fact that they were only reinforcing a narrative already in play. A narrative that was about to go into overdrive.

That the marines were looking for a fight.

Time to send a quick encrypted transmission to Mr. Zauro. There would be no reply. Zauro had been clear about his intention for this mission, and so far everything had played out just as planned.

A reply would mean problems.

Loth felt a sense of pride over his success to this point. He knew it wasn't due to any genius on his own part. He'd merely done as he was told. But he'd executed flawlessly what felt like some grand operation mounted by the best psyops specialists money could buy. And money could buy a lot, with what Loth was being paid.

Zauro could afford it. He had a lot of credits. Loth had named a high price for his services and betrayal of the Guild, and the old man had accepted it so fast that Loth wondered whether he'd left too many credits on the table. Because there was no going back after this one.

But he wouldn't need to. As it was, he'd already have more than enough to disappear out to the rumored pleasure worlds along the edge, where a lot of dark money got buried, and live quite comfortably on the interest. Or… well, there would no doubt be more big paydays from Mr. Zauro if this continued to go well. And why settle on a planet if you can just buy one instead?

No. There would be no reply from Mr. Zauro. Or the strange Tennarian lawyer he used for contracts and assignment briefings. Showtime was scheduled. And a horror show was what the galaxy would get in the next hour.

He commed the freighter captain at the docks. She too was getting well paid for what was going to be a tricky takeoff and a sketchy jump just to get them off the roof at the last second. Supposedly Zauro's lawyer had put the fear in her, but that didn't mean she wouldn't just quit town. Things were getting hairy, and once that freighter got picked up on the feeds, they'd have to dump it in a sun somewhere to make sure it never got found.

And of course Loth's orders from the lawyer had been to make sure the crew was still aboard when that happened. Loose ends would all be tied up after this one.

Yeah, another dead leej was a bummer. Loth didn't have anything against them, and the Legion would be pissed for sure. But neither did he fear their retribution. Once all the kids got killed in what was going to look like payback from the marines, according to rumors waiting to be transmitted to Dark Ops teams on the ground, there would be galactic hell to pay. And Loth's team, the freighter, and the plan would get lost in the chaos. Media contacts would ensure that much.

"Send her in," Loth bellowed to his lieutenant.

The Soshie that waited on him in the suite—his manservant, as Loth thought of him—stepped out and left Loth alone in what had once been the most grand and opulent room in the building. Now the paint was peeling and the carpet smelled of old smoke. The heyday of this place had ended long ago. When they'd commandeered it, they'd had to kick out some old crone who claimed to have once been the galaxy's biggest entertainments star. Now she looked like a shriveled old witch in clothes that admittedly must have cost a pretty penny all those years ago. Her old bot—that was her last possession—loaded her into her hover chair and pushed her away. The last Loth had seen of them, they'd been walking down the street as dark came on. He'd watched them go from her very own penthouse.

*Serves her right*, he'd thought, though he didn't bother to articulate why. In his mind it was just some kind of galactic justice for being stupid and weak.

He didn't buy Zauro and the Soshies' racket about wealth needing to end up in the right hands. He doubted even Zauro did. But Loth liked the justice part of things. Or rather, the act of what it took to make that happen. He liked that part.

They were bringing in one of the whiny brats who wanted to play head-chopper for the next legionnaire beheading stream. Apparently she'd done something to convince his lieutenants she would do better than the last girl had. Loth had been clear that she'd better.

"We need a nice clean cut," he'd hectored his men. "Not a hack job! Made us look like a bunch of amateurs."

They'd already killed that last girl. Her body would get found in the building with all the others. Another kid dead at the hands of the out-of-control military. Never mind that she'd cut the head off a legionnaire.

The floor of the building shook once. Like some distant tremor or low-grade earthquake.

Then again. Briefly.

Like it did when you had the misfortune to be in the presence of a wandering taurex looking for something to eat. You know, right before it charged, and your life ended.

Loth had been on a taurex hunt once. Security for some rich banker that wanted to bag one. Half the team had to shoot it just so the guy could say he killed one. Then they waited an hour just to make sure it was dead and sent men in to make sure it was safe before the banker would even get near it to get her picture taken with its massive corpse. Plus, she'd had to make sure her makeup and hair were done just right. She even changed hunting outfits twice.

But both the creature's horns had been blown off, and that apparently ruined it for her. Or at least that had been the stated reason why no bonus was paid.

*Crazy*, thought Loth as he waited for the new head-chopper. *Crazy what money does to people.*

He wondered if he'd get crazy on the other side of this. When he was good and rich. No-limit accounts full of Zauro's payments.

The floor shook again.

This time the glass in the windows of the suite shook with it, and that bothered Loth a bit.

It felt like artillery crossing the land, falling slowly to bracket its target. And for some reason he felt that cold ice-water thrill up his spine. The kind you feel when you suspect you might just be that target.

Another thunder strike. Coming quicker now.

Loth stumbled toward the window just as the new Soshie head-chopper was shown in. He ignored her. His eyes searched the streets. He knew what he was looking for even before he found it.

But already over the comm he was getting traffic from his LP-Ops in the streets telling him what the situation was. That what he was seeing wasn't a figment of his imagination.

The marines were sending in an HK-PP.

And it looked to be headed straight for the tower.

# 47

NORMALLY THE BOT ASSIGNED TO OPERATIONS CONTROL of the mighty assault and infantry support vehicle designated Hunter-Killer Planet-Pounder, or HK-PP, did little beyond run power plant management, handle automated damage control, and make sure a number of smaller systems were interfacing to assist during the ground assault phase of operations. But in this instance, Rechs had made sure the little Nubarian bot had been outfitted with enough utility command override programs to take full control of everything, including the main mounted turrets along the back of the mech and the devastating mauler blaster system atop used for the destruction of heavy fortifications.

The Nubarian felt it had ended runtime and gone to the fabled eternal factory floor. It squealed with electronic delight as it ordered power to all weapons systems. It had already crushed three combat sleds and a small prefab tower the marines had evacuated upon seeing which direction the HK-PP was traveling.

Now they were engaging with ground fire from their assault blasters. But the heavy armor on the mech laughed at this. And so did the bot as it fired both forward turrets at an unoccupied dropship pad and blew it to shreds.

The Nubarian bot had orders not to hurt civilians or military. And it would, grudgingly, follow those orders. But other than that… it had been instructed to cause as much chaos and damage as possible along the way to the target.

A glorious mission indeed.

The bot whirled scanners around to make sure the main battle tanks weren't online and moving to engage, because those *would* be a problem. But they were still offline. The bot sent a complement of missiles rocketing toward the undefended MBTs, sending them up in blossoming towers of flame.

If it all weren't so exhilarating, the bot might have felt sorrow for destroying those three beautiful machines. But it needed to be done.

A moment later the massive HK-PP crossed through the wire, trampling the flimsy defenses, and entered the streets of the city. Civilians dressed in their red-and-black costumes, which the Nubarian bot thought were pretty, fled from the mech's presence with panicked abandon.

This was what it was like to be a conqueror, the bot calculated. It saw itself as one N0MAAD6, the legendary scout recon bot that had singlehandedly defeated a Savage battalion on Dataan in the long ago. The secret hero of every bot that ever trundled the warships of the galaxy. Or slogged alongside the marines and even the Legion in some war or another.

When you've been designed for massive destruction, war is the fulfillment of your grand purpose.

Initially, as calculated, the Nubarian bot would have the advantage. And it spent much of this advantage firing into unoccupied buildings, devastating multiple floors with each hit. He could get off one shot every minute from the mauler; it took that long for the cannon to power up again from the onboard reactor.

A marine SLIC came in, and the door gunner opened up on the walker's pilot cupola. The little Nubarian bot paid little attention to this and instead swiveled both forward turrets at the hovering aircraft. Slowly, so they'd get the point. The pilot wisely broke off the attack and dove away down a canyon of towers to break target lock.

More SLICs were coming in to make passes on the mech's armor. If they were more advanced ships, like assault shuttles or buzz ships, the bot would be in trouble. But the marines sent to handle Detron were doing it with left-over equipment from Psydon. Which was something hullbusters took pride in: having the worst gear and still getting the job done.

The bot was busy angling the dorsal deflector to keep these attacks off its back when the mech reached the main avenue it needed to take. It chirped in a businesslike fashion and busied itself with its new heading as damage alerts came in from the articulating legs.

A marine anti-armor team using combat sleds had followed up the street despite the Soshie mob and fired off three missiles at the walking behemoth. The HK-PP's innate ECM generators handled two of the attacks, but the third missile had rocketed into one of the legs and done substantial damage.

Smoke and bells erupted across the command cupola as the bot ordered damage-control fire extinguishers activated.

"Master Rechs indicates that you should hurry along to your destination and quit fooling around with destroying everything, you little maniac."

It was G232.

The bot ordered the head of the walker to come about and look rearward, presenting the forward turrets with some field of the rear firing arc. It wasn't everything, but it was enough. The bot laid down a blistering barrage of fire from both turrets, ordering the blasters into extreme high-cycle suppressive.

Bright blue fire spat out from the walker and tore up the street the sleds were speeding down. They cut hard and braked to avoid being enveloped in the barrage of incoming fire as a fourth missile snaked off into the late-afternoon smoke, untargeted.

The bot told G232 to mind its own business.

"I am doing just that," lectured the admin bot. "Captain Rechs has tasked me with making sure you stay on target. He suspected you would go wild and start… rampaging. And here you are. Rampaging."

G232 made the word "rampaging" sound like it was some dreadful societal faux pas instead of the pell-mell swath of destruction that now lay across the city in the HK-PP's wake.

The giant mech smashed into a ceremonial arch that stretched over the avenue. A commemorative architectural structure from days gone by. It crumbled like an old cookie and the HK-PP continued on. Ahead lay the tower. Its target.

The little bot checked the charge on the main gun and scanned for a new target. Something big. Something that would really go *KA-BOOOOOM!*

"Make an impression," Captain Rechs had ordered.

# 48

Within General Sheehan's command center, the primary focus was now the rogue war machine rampaging into the operational zone. Command and staff officers were looking bewildered and flummoxed as they tried to explain who had taken a premier fighting vehicle from the pool and decided to take matters into their own hands.

No one had an answer, but the consensus was that some enlisted punk who'd had enough of the Soshies had gone joyriding. Or maybe it was a leej who had waited long enough and wasn't about to let another of his buddies get decapitated.

All comm with the war machine was being blocked by spam-jam algos, and attempts by the nerds in electronic warfare to hack their way into the vehicle's systems and take control had failed.

Captain Hess, who'd been out roaming the line and trying to figure out some way to go hunting for Tyrus

Rechs, surfaced through the mass confusion enveloping the TOC.

"This is what I warned your chief of staff about, General!" Hess screamed. "Most likely it's Rechs that's commandeered that planet-pounder. If not him, then someone working for him. And while you all are chasing it down, he's freed up to do some real damage to Republic assets!"

That stopped everyone.

Hess had the general's attention. As well as the rest of the command staff. To them, he was a legionnaire. To the general, he was a spook from Nether Ops. And both general and command staff were listening accordingly.

*Funny how sinners become saints when people get desperate enough*, thought Hess in one corner of his mind.

"I can stop him and give your marines enough time to take advantage of this chaos," Hess said. "Perhaps identify the location and hit it to secure our personnel."

The general studied the twisted and scarred figure of Captain Hess. He looked capable despite the old injuries and missing eye that he for some unknown reason had decided not to repair. Things *were* turning into a mess. That was clear enough.

"Make it happen, Captain." The general turned to his adjutant. "Colonel Styles, get this man what he needs and shut down the planet-pounder before it can cause more damage."

Ten minutes later, Captain Hess was kitted up in the Legion armor Nether Ops had once provided him, aboard a gunship-configured SLIC lifting off over the marine-held docks, flying above the edge of the vast sprawl of the tired old city.

# 49

THREE FLOORS UP, RECHS ENTERED THE PUBLIC AREAS of the building. It was two minutes' work to identify a target using the armor's sensor scan. Rechs moved swiftly through a shadowy atrium that had once held some sort of hanging garden display. Now the giant off-world ferns were nothing more than dead skeletons and the dirty floor below was littered with dry trash and dead leaves. One of the pros was watching the central well from a balcony two stories above.

Bio-sensors indicated that many of the rooms held groups of people. All of them huddled or unmoving. But alive. Prisoners, presumably. Most likely citizens the Soshies wanted to keep out of the way. Or perhaps they were being held hostage to bargain for petty ransoms.

There was also a third option...

But that was none of Rechs's business. The huddled masses were none of his concern. He was here for the legionnaire and the marine. That was all.

And they would be held up higher. Closer to the top of the building.

And yet, as he passed the doors behind which clustered what he presumed were civilian prisoners, Rechs felt a nagging sense of responsibility. He decided he needed to at least verify his theory that the people in the rooms were captives held against their will.

Moving down an unlit hall lined with old apartments, he tested one of the doors by waving his gauntlet over the access panel. Normal tech would have either opened the door or announced a ringtone that someone was visiting. Neither happened. Instead all Rechs got was the panel turning red and a ghostly hologram asking him for a passkey.

Locked from the outside.

Rechs debated what to do. They were safer trapped in there if the rescue turned into a firefight. But leaving them in the hands of terrorists looking to make a point could make them the next sacrificial victim once Rechs had deprived the Soshies of the leej and the marine.

He checked the panel. He could hack it from here, but not without burning up a lot of time. He needed to find the central security panel.

But first he needed to find out what was going on.

He moved toward a balcony that sat off of a grand room, the sort that looked to be the epicenter of parties long ago. His sensors indicated that a sentry was standing on a similar balcony directly above him. Rechs dropped his tac bag, set down his blaster, and engaged the armor's stealth systems. Then he stepped to the edge of the balcony and began to climb to the next one up using the powered armor to dig himself a grip.

Like a trap eel, Rechs lunged upward, grabbed the sentry by his carrying harness, and yanked him over the railing. At the same moment, with all his might, he added to the man's momentum by yanking him down onto the balcony below. The sound of his neck breaking as he went face first onto the hard duracrete floor filled the bounty hunter's audio receptors.

Breathing heavily and listening to the silence of the building, Rechs waited for a response.

Nothing. No one had heard. Just the muffled sound of the rioters chanting out there in the hot streets toward the end of the day. A few distant explosions and their ever-present drums. And the marines in their SLICs. And one more sound that shouldn't have been among the cacophony... the rhythmic pounding of HK-PP legs striking the streets. Coming this way.

That would have everyone's attention.

Rechs stripped the dead man of his comm and listened in once he had it synced into his own bucket.

The first thing he heard was exactly what he'd hoped. They were reacting. Departing from their plan. Making it easier to run his.

They were shifting the prisoners.

# 50

"Rechs, Gabi here. I'm leaving this message to let you know I've uncovered something really big that links to Syl Hamachi-Roi, who I still think gave the message to the Soshies to go ahead with... their little guillotine act.

"Years ago, the Guild did business with a financier known as Zauro. We ran an extraction mission to get him away from a Nether Ops hit squad that was out to get him. All of this went down a long time ago near the end of the Savage Wars. Anyway, this Zauro was acting as an arms dealer for the Savages who were then having trouble putting together weapons and equipment after the debacle at Cassandra's Folly. Word was he was selling next-gen tech direct to them. Stuff the Republic had used to destroy the last of their cruisers during the Legion boarding surge that marked the end of it all.

"So here's where it gets murky, and it's not one of the Guild's proudest moments. But we took a lot of credits to get him off Ankalor with no less than three Nether Ops hit teams closing in. Big op, bad day. Lost six Guild members in less than a cycle. Before your time. Way before mine. Anyway, the Guild hid Zauro for years in safe houses. Guy's a longevity mummy. You know, always paying for the latest upgrades in life extension. Years in cryo coffins doing business with his mind only. About twenty-five years ago he let the protection contract run out. Frankly, the Guild hierarchy at the time was glad to be rid of him. Lotta weird Savage voodoo stuff involved. Was a big collector of their artifacts.

"One of Archangel's associates… let's call him the Reader. Well… it's Reader's job to know everything for the Guild committee's private consumption. He keeps the decision-makers informed. Anyway, Reader kept an active file open for years and concluded Zauro had been silently laying the groundwork for something political. Something big.

"Reader didn't have any hard evidence, but he knew Zauro was financing a lot of campaigns for House of Reason seats. He was using front groups to finance groundswell campaigns made to look like grassroots initiatives by the locals. Look close enough, you find the organizations are always slick and ready to go, professionally run from the get-go.

"I'm telling you all this because, one… Reader tagged Zauro as a very bad guy, felt he wanted to destabilize the galaxy. And two… and I have no direct evidence of this… but Zauro is still a wanted war criminal because of his dealings with the Savages. Which still carries an automatic death penalty via Legion tribunal. Which is to say, a visit from a kill team.

"So, Syl Hamachi-Roi's campaign is straight out of the Zauro playbook. Linking her to Zauro would shut that little slut down overnight.

"I'm sorry. I know that sounds harsh. It's just that… anyway, never mind. I hope you're okay. I'm leaving this message because maybe you can find something that makes the case. Do that and we can get a little payback for…"

Gabriella paused.

Rechs would listen to the message later. But she paused as though whatever she was about to say got caught in her throat.

"…for the… sergeant… and the kid who didn't make it back. Okay. I'm here, Rechs, when you need me. I'll be standing by at all hours. I'm in a coffee shop. It's late where I'm at. But… I can help. If you need me. We can get this girl… I have her flagged as Madame Guillotine in the Guild archives. That's how much I believe she's the one who made Detron all happen. We can pin a connection to Zauro on her. We can prove it."

Then nothing. Just the end of a long message Rechs would have to listen to later.

# 51

"Lyra," whispered Rechs over the comm as he moved through the halls of the building, trying to avoid the clusters of pros. The sensor-sweep readings indicated they were starting to group up in order to evac the building. Their comm traffic he was listening in on confirmed as much.

"Yes, Tyrus," replied the *Obsidian Crow*'s AI.

"Gears up. Fly evasive to my loc. LZ to be designated upon arrival. Most likely going to be hot." Then Rechs cut the comm before her insecurity could rise up and she talked herself out of flying... herself.

The booms of the incoming mech's legs striking the ground were now seriously shaking the building. The little Nubarian had done the trick and freaked out the pros. Over comm they were bleating rather unprofessionally about getting out of there before they got stomped. Once or twice Rechs heard the voice of someone in charge giving terse orders to "stand by" and "hold your position until we get the prisoners out."

The voice was clipped, cruel, and efficient.

And Rechs was pretty sure it belonged to Loth. He'd been around the man, briefly. Just one of those times where more than one bounty hunter is looking to do the same job. Rechs had gotten it done, and they'd exchanged what passed for pleasantries.

The powerful mauler cannon mounted atop the inbound HK-PP shrieked out a powerful whine, rattling hiss, and then massive *BOOOOOM* as it decimated some structure a few blocks away.

*Keep it up, little guy*, thought Rechs.

The bounty hunter continued to listen from the shadows within the building, avoiding the panicked pros as they tried to evacuate. Watching.

He needed to know the route they'd assigned to get the legionnaire and the marine out. Then he could ascertain how best to take them once the pros decided to execute the transfer. Everything was happening fast. On the fly. And really there was no margin for error.

For them. Or for him.

The whole situation had all the makings of something that could go horribly wrong at any moment and get a bunch of people killed. But it was the only chance the legionnaire and the marine had. So Rechs decided to take it.

"Extraction convoy inbound for link-up," noted one of the pros over the comm. The voice and matter-of-fact demeanor almost the opposite of the rest of the channel. "ETA three minutes."

Rechs calculated. They weren't going for the quick escape via the lone vehicle in the garage. They wanted a whole convoy to protect the precious props that were their prisoners. Now was the time to deny them. All he needed was a route to the link-up.

He waited. A veteran like no other of operations such as this, Rechs knew the route, or some hint of the route, would come next. A last-minute decision made amid the chaos.

"We're going for the east stairwell. Moving them now."

It was the voice he'd identified as possibly Loth's. Terse. Hard. In charge. Demanding everyone not fail. All of that in between the words. Rechs knew the type.

The bounty hunter studied the building map in his HUD. He found the east stairwell relative to his position and scanned for an intercept point.

Then he heard the next transmission and felt a chill right down to his bones.

"Set the charges to blow the building for ten. That means we got two minutes to clear once the convoy arrives. No room for error, people," demanded the cruel-voiced man. "They'll think the mech fired on the building. Damn thing's doing our job for us better than we can do it ourselves. Investigations will prove otherwise, but that'll take weeks and by then it won't matter. I'm telling you all this so you understand how close we are. Every one of you who survives will be retired and living on the interest."

They were going to kill everyone in the building and blame it on the HK-PP. Rechs didn't think it was a half-bad improvised plan, and it reminded him not to underestimate Loth. Not that he would have anyway. Not that he ever did with anyone he faced. Pros were as deadly as Sontherian pit vipers, and even amateurs got lucky.

"On it," said someone. One of the pros. "Heading for Maintenance Five to arm the device."

Rechs scrubbed the intercept point. He had to shut down the bomb first.

# 52

Moving fast, Puncher and Baldur took the back streets of Detron's Heights district, avoiding the crowds and closing in on the last known location of Shaker and the marine.

*Trouble*, thought Baldur, the dog keeping pace with the huffing leej.

"Yeah," gasped Puncher out of his armor. The SAB was killing him. He too could see the massive mech rising above the buildings down the street. From this angle it looked like it was headed straight for the same location he was. Except they were closer. Just a block away.

*Trouble...* warned the dog again.

Closing, they slowed to a walk, returning to the guise of wandering homeless. The armor tagged all the hostiles in the intersection and wide plaza surrounding the possible location of Shaker and the marine.

Puncher had been in his fair share of uneven fights. Had even walked away the winner in a couple. But there were simply too many this time. There was no easy way to do this. And most likely, he would get himself and the dog killed.

*Good thing I brought the SAB*, he thought.

Because if it came right down to it, he'd blast his way in, if only for the reason that he wouldn't have to die alone that way.

If only for that.

Every leej has a last fight. And as far as he could give an account of himself... he hadn't forgot nothin'.

# 53

Rechs raced for Maintenance Five. It was two flights up a central stairwell and down a long hall. There was no way he was letting a hundred or so people die in an explosion the marines would get blamed for. It would cost him his intercept, but maybe he could still hit them on the street and possibly take over the vehicle they were in. Then drop a new rendezvous location to link up with Lyra and the *Crow*.

Bad plan going to worse... but it was all he had now. Adapt and overcome. Everything was in motion and would be until it was finished.

Win, lose, or die.

He pounded down the hallway, Jackknife deployed into subcompact mode in one hand as he pulled for all he was worth to reach the bomb. If they armed the device before he got there, then he'd have to hope he could hack it. And hope he had time.

Which didn't seem likely.

Three silhouettes of armed men appeared at the end of the hall and stopped suddenly, seeing the running armored bounty hunter headed straight at them. Blaster fire came at Rechs in an instant.

The access door to Maintenance Five lay between both parties. And now they would fight to reach it first. Winner take all.

Rechs smashed through a flimsy makeshift door that entered a vacant apartment halfway down the hallway's length. He crashed through just in time to avoid getting hit by the incoming blaster fire.

As he heard them trying to run for the access door to Maintenance Five, he held the blaster out the door and pulled the trigger on full-auto. The Jackknife was a ridiculously efficient pray-and-spray weapon. Within five seconds, it had spat out a hundred tiny needle-sized blasts and run its charge bone-dry.

Rechs stepped out in the hall and was greeted by three dead men. He slapped in a new charge pack and advanced on the maintenance room.

A second later, two fraggers bounced out to greet him from the maintenance room and exploded, devastating walls and doors and sending fragments into Rechs's armor. The blast knocked him back and spun him round into a wall.

His HUD went down for a second, but he held on to the blaster. Mind wonky and reeling, he stumbled to right himself and moved toward the door, knowing he'd taken a hot burning fragment in the forearm. He entered the maintenance room shooting because there was no other choice. And no time left.

The guy on the comm who'd said he was going to handle it had gotten there first. He was calling in status reports, telling the team of pros that they had contact. He had two other men with him. The three in the hallway had been insurance.

Rechs dropped all three men the moment he swung into the room, spraying them with bursts from the Jackknife as if flinging drops of water from wet hands. They fell as one, and the guy who'd come down to arm the bomb looked at the bounty hunter with terror in his eyes.

Rechs shot him a dozen times, his blast-rattled mind reeling and distant as his eyes took in the one most salient fact among the carnage.

The bomb had already been armed.

Its countdown clock read seven minutes and thirty-seven seconds... six... five...

"Damn," muttered Rechs.

The device was top-grade. That was for sure. He could already see a three-phase-redundancy arming trigger. That would take far too long to hack.

Get out of the building. Now.

The armor was already applying pressure to the fragment wound and hitting him with localized painkillers. An option appeared for more heavy-duty stuff along with some anxiety suppressors to deal with the wound. That meant it was possibly serious.

But it would degrade his ability to perform.

Scanning the room, he spotted a master building alarm panel. He ran through it quickly and found the failsafe building locks override. He hit this—and knew that every door, no matter how hard it had been locked down, would now force open. Unless it had a localized locking source outside the grid itself. But the doors Rechs had inspected hadn't had that, meaning the prisoners should be able to at least open the doors of their cells... assuming they weren't bound.

The bounty hunter then pulled the fire alarm. The building's sirens began to wail. He hadn't been sure they'd still work. A deep automated voice, calm and professional, began to advise everyone to evacuate the building immediately. For their own safety.

He hoped that would give all the prisoners time to get out.

Assuming, again, they hadn't been tied up.

It was all he could do for them.

He stumbled toward the door and into the still-smoldering hallway, again dropping in on the pros' comm. Listening for their movements.

He'd try to hit them on the street.

That was all there was left to him now. A hard capture against a lot of blasters, supported by at least two QRFs and several sniper teams.

He gave himself a twenty percent chance of success. And a zero percent chance of survival for the leej and the marine if he didn't rescue them now. This was the last, best shot they'd have.

So... he went for it.

# 54

In the hours leading up to Rechs's assault on the Excelsior, Amanda had lain there, next to Lopez, in what had once been a pantry inside one of the upper-level apartments. Just a few floors below the penthouse Loth had commandeered for his headquarters.

Lopez was all but passed out due to the drugs and meds they'd given him. Things she'd traded information for. Information that would probably get her court-martialed on the back side of this fiasco. After all, the beating they'd given her, and some of the torture, hadn't been that bad. She could have just refused, or even held out a little longer. But when they'd started talking about going to work on Lopez... that's when she'd begun to trade. She hadn't been able to save all them of them in that alley, but maybe she could save just this one. Not as a sniper, a Reaper bringing death, but here, as a prisoner.

She'd prayed to anyone who could hear her while they tortured her. Anyone who could've helped her. Even though she didn't believe in anything, she'd prayed all the same. Not for herself. For some way to save the legionnaire.

Yeah, sometimes you pray even when you don't believe.

When they finished with her, promising more later, they left her and Lopez in the pantry. Sealed in with a lock and alarm. She heard them entering a code. Still, she'd gotten to her knees, restraining a groan from where they'd twisted her wrist to the point of breaking during the early part of the interrogation, and checked to see if maybe that locked door would open. If maybe someone out there in the galaxy was listening.

It was locked.

But she could hear them talking on the other side.

She went back and checked Lopez's breathing. Slow and shallow. Not good.

But alive.

She went back to the door and listened again.

Things were coming to a head. She could tell that much. Beers had been executed. They'd shown her the stream just to make clear how serious they were about what they were doing. Chances were they were going to do it again. Maybe not now. Maybe not in the next few hours, or even days. But they'd do it again. They'd kill Lopez.

Why?

Because taking lives is power.

And power is intoxicating.

Part of Reaper school screening was that you couldn't have that thrill-kill gene, whatever it is. Gotta be wired differently to be that kind of lifetaker.

To be a Reaper.

More like a shepherd, they'd said. Subtlety. "We're the good shepherds," one of her instructors had once told her. "We take care of the wolves."

She felt for the knife she'd stowed in Lopez's boot.

They'd battered her and stripped her and tortured her. They would have easily found the knife if she'd kept it on her. But as much as they threatened to torture Lopez, they never even touched him. They needed him alive if they were going to kill him, and the legionnaire couldn't have survived time with the man who'd tortured her. The man with the beady, mean eyes.

And they'd already searched Lopez when they first brought him in. No need to search him again.

She listened for a long time and didn't hear much of anything. Like some calm before the storm. In fact, she heard so much of nothing that it got creepy. Just like in the hour before they took Beers. Who never came back.

The hour of the slaughter.

She moved the knife to her palm. Then clenched it into a fist.

*That's a bold move, Amanda Panda.*

I know, she practically whispered to herself. It was a gamble. Every time they'd moved them, she'd made fists to fight. They'd never paid any mind to that, instead focusing on her wrists and getting the ener-chains around those. Who cares what's in her hands? We've already searched her, right?

Just like they'd already searched Lopez.

*Assumptions are a breeding ground for loopholes.*

Dad? Or some Reaper instructor. Someone had given her that bit.

Hard to say. And not important now.

When she heard the first ground strikes of the HK-PP, a sound she'd heard before as a marine, she knew something was up. Not just far off, but close at hand. Her guards on the other side of the door were freaked out. She could hear them nervously talking inside the dirty old suite.

"Think it's headed for us?"

"I ain't gettin' paid enough to face off against one of those things. Whatcha think we're gonna use… blasters? Slogans about equal treatment for alien races, like them stupid kids?"

That got a graveyard laugh out of the crew watching over her and Lopez. She could tell they'd moved to the windows to get a glimpse of the mighty battle machine coming toward them.

"Thing is huge!" someone said.

"It's gotta be twenty blocks away and already it's a monster!"

"Tell Loth I'm out."

"*You* tell him!"

But they stayed. And she heard the transmission that came in next.

"Loth says we're moving the prisoners," the voice said over comm. "Stand by to get 'em ready."

She got herself ready. As ready as she could. Felt the knife and knew it was all she had.

She heard the main gun of the mauler fire. Heard some section of a distant building explode. Alarms went off down the block beyond the high windows of the old apartment tower.

She heard them gathering outside the pantry door. Gathering to storm the room and take them to a new loc. She knew for a fact she and Lopez wouldn't survive what someone would one day call "crime scene number two." Wherever they were being taken to. That was crime scene number two. They'd do the executions there. And quick.

Which meant she had to do this right. If not, this pantry would become crime scene number two. These men would kill her before they'd let her kill them. Prisoners and propaganda streams be damned.

She laid down next to Lopez who was gurgling out ragged breaths. He needed professional medical treatment soon. And that was probably why they'd make their kill holovid sooner rather than later. Lopez wasn't going to last much longer. She knew it. They knew it.

She lay down and palmed the knife.

It was all she had, she reminded herself.

They stormed the room and took her first. No tranqs this time, which was a blessing. Maybe the someone she'd prayed to was listening. Maybe that was all she'd get. Maybe that was all she needed.

She threw up a quick thought of a prayer. *While you're handing out miracles, Oba, or whoever you are, I could use a blaster.*

Nothing.

Okay then, she told herself. Just the knife.

*Prayers get answered. Just not always the answer you want, Manda.* Her dad.

Okay.

But she'd take this one. This one miracle of not being drugged when they came in to take her to her death.

Ener-chains on. They focused on her wrists and not her fists. Not opening her hands. Not seeing the knife she hid there. Because it wasn't supposed to be there and so they didn't look for it. As they started dragging her through the pantry door, the leather sack went over her head.

She felt the knife.

She concentrated on it.

In a galaxy of unknowns… it was known. And a kind of compass by which she might cross the gulf of the next few minutes.

Knowing they might be her last.

They readied Lopez and began moving both prisoners out of the dingy suite. Through enclosed areas and out of this place. Down long and silent hallways. All of them chattering in their operator speak like they knew exactly what they were doing. Certain in their certainty. But she could hear them stutter every time the mighty planet-pounder struck the city streets. And that made her happy. Because maybe…

"Tha's marines," muttered Lopez ahead of her. "Comin' to get us, y'all… kelhorns. Kill every last one of you…"

Then he faded off and he and Amanda were dragged down the stairs in some dark well they'd been pulled into.

She needed a moment. Something.

*Remember*, she said to the galaxy. *Remember when I prayed…*

She heard distant blaster fire. Small and tiny. Several floors away. Frenetic and deadly.

Like to have a blaster of my own right now, she thought to herself. Reminded the galaxy.

*If wishes were fishes, beggars would ride, Manda.*

Grandma. Daddy's mama.

There was a boom.

An explosion? Or was that just the building shaking from another one of the planet-pounder's thunder strikes?

The building's fire alarms erupted through the dark of her leather hood. The men started shouting. They didn't know what was going on.

If she had to guess, there were six of them. Six of them around her and Lopez. Six that needed to die for them to live.

She stumbled. Someone let go of her arms. Someone else swore.

*Prayers get answered. Just not always the answer you want, Manda.*

She shrugged off the hood, flicked open the knife, and plunged it into the throat of the shadow closest to her. She felt it puncture cartilage and then pipe. Pushing in easily at the last. Windpipe. Heard a hot breathy gurgle as clear as day above all the shouting and the blaring alarm deafening everyone in the stairwell.

*Prayers...*

The stairwell was bathed in the bloody red light of murder.

Lopez was right next to her.

No one even noticed the guy she'd just stabbed in the throat falling into her, flailing and bleeding. They were busy on comm. Checking the stairs below. And the route out to the convoy and Loth, who was supervising the loadout.

There were two others above her on the stairs, but one was leaning over the well, pointing his blaster down onto the landings below. The other just had a look of fear on his face. Like he wasn't there.

She let go of the knife and pulled the blaster away from the dying man bleeding all over her. She was trained on how to handle it with her hands bound. She fired the new weapon at both men. Fast. Gunfighter fast.

The frightened one got it in the gut and grunted on the other side of the blaster's whine. The one aiming down onto the level below, leaning over the rail, turned to her and she blew off the bottom of his jaw because her aim was somewhat constricted. In a perfect world, at this intimate up close and personal range, she'd have drilled his skull.

The guy whose mouth was shot away bent over the railing and slid down it past her as he died.

Amanda pivoted with the weapon and fired at the two men on the landing below as the dying man slid their way, what remained of his face a smoking horror show coming straight at them. Both shots missed, but they got her captors' attention.

And what they saw was a pissed-off marine with murder in her eyes.

This was no Dodge Ridge Shootout like people read about from back in the stellar frontier days. No stand and deliver at point-blank range like Cassandra's Folly. Both of her new opponents were pros and they knew cover was more important than return fire. The first one dove head-first down the stairs to get away from her fire. The second one dropped to his knees and tried to put the railing and the dying man between himself and the killer marine who'd somehow obtained a blaster.

No matter.

Amanda shot him a second later and didn't bother to add any finesse in the targeting. She just started squeezing, filling the guy's jerking body with blaster bolts. Watching it twitch and jump and getting a grim sense of satisfaction out of the whole experience in some distant background app in her mind.

The revenge app. Brought to you by Nemesis and Elektra.

Then Reaper training kicked in and she was the shepherd. The good shepherd who protects her flock from wolves.

*Keep the boys and girls on the ground from getting hit by a shooter they can't see.* Reaper training. Dad, too.

Death on demand from the deck of a SLIC.

She grabbed Lopez and dragged him back up the stairs and through the first landing door she came to. To his credit, the legionnaire remained on his feet. And that was the best any badly wounded leej could do.

She could hear her remaining captors in the stairwell behind her. They were shouting. The surprise had passed and now they'd come to kill her in the hopes they could still take the legionnaire alive. And kill him later.

*Sometimes life is only guaranteed from one second to the next, Manda. So make every second count, Reaper.*

Dad. And Reaper instructor.

# 55

THE STORIES-HIGH MECH WAS WITHIN THREE BLOCKS OF the target AO Rechs had identified for the little Nubarian gunnery bot. Bring a distraction in—and the bot felt it had really come through there—and provide overwatch while "the captain" extracted the prisoners had been the orders, and that was exactly what the little bot was doing when Captain Hess stopped the HK-PP in its tracks.

You didn't get to be the commander of a Nether Ops tip-of-spear kill team without skills. Hess was that rare House of Reason–appointed officer who was more than capable as a legionnaire also. Despite the fact he was entrenched in the appointed officer's typical self-aggrandized thinking.

The marine SLIC gunship variant had hit the HK-PP with its full complement of AGMs. The air-to-ground missiles had sidewindered in and struck the walking beast all across her upper frame.

Inside the bot's interface compartment, the little machine rerouted motive power to extinguishing fires breaking out inside the hull. Not because there was a pilot on board to save, but because damage to the electrical systems that powered and controlled the mech's actuators were threatened by an out-of-control fire.

In front of the bot's control section, where the driver would strap in and move the machine forward with guns blazing, a sudden array of electrical sparks exploded in all directions.

The bot whooped digitally and tried to engage the retreating SLIC within its forward blaster turrets, deciding the threat overrode Rechs's orders not to fire on military craft or personnel. Which was dangerous, because it meant the bot was crossing that line where its programming began engaging in behavior defiant of its master's orders. That was typically met with a memory wipe and system restore. Something the little bot had avoided ever since it came online for the first time.

Sensing the maneuver, the SLIC retreated as the mech suddenly turned to the right and sent forth bright fire. Explosions ravaged an old condemned apartment tower as the speeding SLIC dropped away down the canyon of buildings.

*Stay on target*, the little bot reminded itself, and it sent the mech forward toward the target AO once more.

A moment later Captain Hess's SLIC reappeared from its evasive maneuvers, coming in from a different angle of attack and spooling up her CGS-66 ground-suppression blaster pods. The incoming fire from this close-ground-support engagement system, usually meant for light-skinned vehicles and troops, tore into the mounted mauler gun atop the walker. A vulnerable spot Hess had pointed out to the pilot.

Flying the SLIC now as Hunter Oh-Two was Captain Kirk Walters, formerly Reaper Oh-Two. Hess had insisted on the Hunter call sign. And while the pilot formerly known as Reaper Oh-Two didn't necessarily like the arrogant Legion officer, he seemed like he was the only one who was going to try to go in and get Amanda out of what she'd gotten herself into. Which was all that mattered to Kirk Walters. So if flying the close attack run against the mech got him a chance to pull Amanda out of this hellhole, he was taking it.

Sweating and fixated on the targeting reticle, he raked the hull of the HK-PP with a stream of blaster fire at a dangerously close range and almost ludicrous groundspeed.

"Get in closer," berated Hess over the comm. The captain was holding onto a strap on the rear cargo deck of the SLIC. The flight crew consisted of one pilot, one co-pilot bot, and one crew chief.

Hunter Oh-Two took the dropship in closer, crabbing to slow forward motion and allow the weapon arcs of the blaster pods to still maintain a good engagement window on the walking leviathan below.

Hess knew exactly where to hit the HK-PP. The blaster pod fire from the CGS-66s destroyed the formidable mauler cannon, exposing the dorsal mounted weapon chargers that exploded and overloaded with Hess's next shot.

Hunter Oh-Two slammed on the SLIC's reverse as the massive cannon exploded, the heavy barrel flinging itself up and away from the walker, going end over end down to the smoke-filled streets below.

The mech wobbled awkwardly once, looked like it was going to lose its balance, and then at the last moment regained its footing. It tried to continue forward. One massive foot—really a central pad with four articulating grappling wings that secured it to the ground with each strike—rose and fell as it continued on toward its objective.

The SLIC had barely missed being hit by the exploding cannon barrel and was now hovering off the aft quarter of the HK-PP moving toward its target.

"I said," bellowed Hess over the SLIC's onboard comm, "take me in closer, you idiot!"

Oh-Two wiped sweat from stubble with a quick swipe and throttled up to go in closer. It would be difficult maintaining a holding altitude just above the walking war giant, but it could be done.

*Whatever it takes to get Amanda out of there*, he reminded himself.

Hess leaped out of the SLIC from several meters above the walker. His high-tech Legion armor absorbed the shock of the landing and with little trouble the captain was running forward along the damaged spine of the machine toward the pilot's command cupola. A second later he was down on one knee and pulling off a small access plate atop the hull, rising and falling rhythmically as the mech lumbered on its course, oblivious to Hess's presence. Hess stood, pulled his sidearm, and fired into the panel he'd just opened, hitting the internal system now exposed.

The mechanical leviathan began to stumble about drunkenly, and Hess pumped his fist for the dropship to come get him off the stricken iron beast.

Never mind the fact that it was stumbling and swaying all across the broad street. Pay no attention to how dangerous an extraction under these conditions is, his very stance seemed to scream at the hovering pilot.

Hunter Oh-Two pushed forward and came in close, promising himself he would only try this once. Either the Legion captain made it, or he was going down with the wounded mech.

Then the ship reacted to the added weight, and Oh-Two knew the captain was on board—or at least hanging from the cargo deck.

"Climb, you idiot!" roared Hess over the comm.

Oh-Two was already doing just that as the HK-PP keeled over and smashed into the side of a building, dragging down much of the duracrete facade with it, burying itself in a waterfall of gray dust and rubble.

# 56

Loth had taken the suite's private speedlift down to the lobby when the fire alarms went off across the building. He had wanted to be in the lobby and curbside to assess the situation on the street before he committed to moving his prisoners from this location.

In the meantime he'd entrusted his best lieutenant with the task of transporting the prisoners via the stairwell. Committing them to the main elevator might get them trapped if the city's grid went down, or if the rickety old lift just broke down all on its own. Everything in the building was badly maintained, and the last thing he needed was a hitch in getting them out.

No. That wasn't entirely true. The last thing he needed was to disappoint Mr. Zauro by failing at his assigned tasks. That was something one did not do. Or did only once, because there wouldn't be a second opportunity. Even for someone as dangerous as Loth.

Loth did not want to disappoint the old man. So he had the rest of his team, twenty-three shooters, ready to take charge and mount up with the convoy on the street. Ready to make the transfer to the inbound transport convoy. Add in the mobile blaster teams on the street and the sniper teams in the windows surrounding the plaza, and they were good to go if the marines had anyone on the ground. If the marines were following the inbound mech, they'd get a fight. More than enough of one for the convoy to get away.

That was all contingency. And it needed to happen because there was no chance they could stand up to the HK-PP if it cornered them in the building. They had to leave. Get to the next safe house and axe the leej first thing, captured on livestream. The holocam equipment was already waiting at the next location. They could do the leej within the hour.

And then Loth could get off this wreck of a world. And more importantly, get paid.

"Sir!" There was blaster fire in the background of the incoming comm transmission. "Got a problem. Men down. Need—"

The message halted as more blaster fire zinged in the background. "Need backup on nine. She got loose!"

Loth swore and ground his teeth.

The HK-PP was now just a few blocks away, and the bomb was due to bring down the building in a few minutes.

"It's just her?" Loth asked, thinking the trouble had to be more than some hullbuster he'd tortured into a whimpering sack of misery.

Blaster fire filled the comm.

"Got her pinned at the end of the north hall on nine! Need backup! I repeat..."

"I heard you!" shouted Loth. "Do you have the legionnaire or—"

"Negative. She's got him!"

Loth swore again on the street outside the tower.

"Everyone!" Loth shouted as he ran back in to the rest of his team waiting in the lobby. "Move to nine and retake the prisoners. Go fast, because this building is coming down in five."

The look he gave his shooters indicated there was only one option. Obey. But everyone also noticed he wasn't coming along. Perks of leadership.

Pros in red and black, outfitted to blend in with the Soshies on the street, but carrying state-of-the-art automatic blasters and explosive devices, swarmed into the stairwells and elevators to get up to nine. In almost the same moment the prisoners from the lower floors, dressed in that same Soshie gear but without the weapons, came running down the stairs toward them.

Seeing obstructions that were also potential loose ends, the pros unleashed volleys of blaster fire. "Make way!" they shouted, leaving several of the kids to die in the stairwells while others ducked in terror against the walls, leapt over the rails, or simply tumbled down to the bottom. Those who slipped past poured out into the streets. Shrieking and crying.

"Kids got loose somehow!" one of the operators shouted into the comm, stating the obvious.

"Ignore them!" Loth ordered. "Get to nine without delay!"

He moved to tell the mobile heavy blaster teams what was happening. The convoy was just coming down the street.

The HK-PP exploded and went down into some buildings farther along the avenue.

"Nothing's ever easy," swore Loth. "Nothing."

## 57

Rᴇᴄʜs ʜᴀᴅ ʙᴇᴇɴ ᴀʙᴏᴜᴛ ʀᴇᴀᴅʏ ᴛᴏ ᴛʜʀᴏᴡ ʜɪᴍsᴇʟꜰ out the fifth-floor window and burn the last of his jump juice to intercept the extraction team on the street when the Soshie comm channel went wild with chatter.

He immediately changed his plans.

From what he could tell, the marine sniper had managed to overwhelm her captors and move the legionnaire out of custody.

*Thatta girl*, thought Rechs. She'd given him the opportunity to make this happen here and now. That was all he needed.

"Lyra… stand by to put down on my ping."

Rechs dropped a ping in the plaza directly outside the building.

"I'm afraid, Captain Rechs," interrupted G232, "that our little friend has possibly been destroyed, sir. The behemoth you had it commandeer erupted with him inside. Might I suggest we offer a moment's silence for a fellow bot? Dangerous though it was."

"Damn," muttered Rechs. He'd been counting on the HK-PP to provide cover fire so he could get the legionnaire and marine aboard the *Crow*. It was already going to be a hot LZ. Now it was going to be downright on fire.

"It grieves me to tell you this tragic news, master," continued G232. "But, alas, it is for the best. Though the bot and you share many of the same affinities for wanton violence, our little group will be the better off, mathematically speaking, now that there are less dangerous entities aboard… wouldn't you say, Mast… ah, Captain Rechs?"

When Rechs didn't respond to the inane chatter, a somewhat cowed G232 said, "Just trying to find the bright spot in all this grief, sir."

Rechs ran for a window that loomed from floor to ceiling at the end of the dim hall he'd found himself in. He figured he might as well do it anyway. Only instead of going down, he'd burn the last of his jump juice to reach the marine and the legionnaire a few levels above.

Level nine.

# 58

"Target terminated, Captain," said Captain Kirk Walters, aka Hunter Oh-Two, over the comm. "Return to base, or do we have a line on the HVTs?"

The marines were classifying the captured sniper and legionnaire as high-value targets.

The SLIC was hovering above the streets and rooftops, above the smashed building and fallen HK-PP. Clouds of gray dust and debris filled the late-afternoon air.

Hess leaned out from the aft cargo deck and studied the cityscape. "That thing was headed somewhere," he muttered. "Where?"

They'd run a bio-scan sensor sweep across the ruined HK-PP once her ECM generators went down in the fall. No signs of life. No signs of biologics. Rechs hadn't been aboard, or if he had, he was now dead. But Hess was somehow sure this was part of Rechs's plan. That the bounty hunter was behind it all. He could practically smell him.

Up the street he spotted people fleeing from one of the tallest buildings in this section of the city. A few armed Soshies were out front. Hess's bucket tagged and assessed weapon threats. The Nether Ops agent studied the scene as the howling dropship's repulsors throbbed to hold altitude above the final resting place of the HK-PP.

"He's here," muttered Hess.

*Got to be.*

Then, to the pilot: "Take us in close to that building up the street. Something's going—"

At that moment Tyrus Rechs himself, looking like some darting hornet at this distance, came crashing out of a fifth-story window in the very building Hess had been watching. Those fleeing below covered their heads and necks as a shower of glass rained down on them from above. A moment later the bounty hunter's jump jets ignited and the armored figure roared up along the building's face.

"That's Rechs!" screamed Hess. "That's Tyrus Rechs! Get me to him!"

# 59

$M$ARINE SERGEANT AMANDA ALMOND HAD ABOUT TEN shots left in the blaster she'd commandeered. She'd managed to get the badly wounded legionnaire—stumbling along, helping as much as he could—down the abandoned hallway that led out of level nine's stairwell, to the last room on the left.

They'd hold out here. Their backs to the windows.

If there were marines in that inbound HK closing in on this location, then chances were they knew she was here. All she'd have to do was buy enough time for them to storm the building.

She leaned out the apartment door despite the return fire and managed a shot on one of those coming for her and Lopez. She dropped him onto his back, his legs doing the kickin' chicken. His buddies were crouching and moving forward, using each other as cover to take her. No one too excited about the prospect.

But in the end, that they were close enough for her to even take a shot meant she was at risk of getting shot herself. And there were more coming, stacking farther down the hall, waiting to come in if these failed. Hoping they didn't. Hoping to be one of the living on the other side of all this.

In short, there were too many of them to even buy a minute more, not even with all the charge packs in the universe. She was just one against the galaxy, it seemed. And sometimes… one isn't enough.

She fell back inside the room knowing that she was done in the next few seconds. They wouldn't bother with her. Lopez they'd keep alive if they could. At least for a little while longer.

The legionnaire was on the floor where she'd left him.

"Sorry…" she said, pointing her blaster at the door. "I did my best to get you outta here."

She heard their captors surging down the hall like a spooked herd. They'd shoot her down first and then take Lopez. The legionnaire was the real prize.

Fine. That's what she'd wanted all along.

And she would buy him just a little more time—by dying in the next few seconds.

*Okay…* she told herself, not ready for this at all. *Make 'em pay for every second, Amanda.*

Maybe in the big picture that is the galaxy, seconds add up to something important for someone somewhere.

Life.

The first one appeared, and she had to use two shots to put him down. He refused to go down with the first and insisted on pointing his blaster at her. The second shot blew off his head, painting the wall beyond with smoking gray matter.

She shot another one.

Maybe a third.

Then someone bounced a banger in and it went off instantly.

Blind and feeling suddenly sick to her stomach, unable to hear… she just squeezed off everything she had left, hoping she was still aiming the blaster at the doorway. Not thinking about anything that had ever come before this moment or would ever come after it.

Everything ends. For you, Manda… it ends here.

*Fine*, she told herself again, determined to kill to the last.

In her mind she saw the door and knew they'd come in as one. Everyone she shot down buying Lopez one more second of freedom.

She fired until the blaster was dry. No kick. Just the soft tremble in the grip letting her know it was out.

Finished. Done. Empty.

*Good going, Manda. Proud of you, girl.*

That's the last shot, she said to herself as she began to see double. Double and then cloudy with vibrations over every surface and angle. Everything tilted on its axis. She felt proud that she still had blaster sights on the doorway despite being flashbanged. Proud that she'd heard her dad at the last.

They were there. The red-and-black demons.

*You can only kill so many. Can't kill everyone, Manda. Galaxy weren't made that way.*

But they weren't facing her. Their bodies were… but their heads were swiveling to face the end of the hallway to their right. And… and blaster fire was tearing them apart. From the direction of the big dirty window she'd seen at the end of the hall. The one that faced out into the big dirty city that looked like it needed a hundred years of rain and a fresh start to be free of its own self.

*Don't we all, Manda Panda?*

Red-and-black demons, her and Lopez's tormentors and captors, were being cut down in a fusillade of streaking needle-sized blaster bolts. High volume. Bodies were ripped to shreds, men and women flung back, their masks torn away to reveal terror and fear. And hate. Like some avenging angel, or some rival demon from the nether, had become all too real to them.

Her hearing was coming back. She forced herself to her feet. She'd fallen when the flashbang went off. She could hear the howl of jump jets fading, or maybe that was just an effect of the ringing in her ears. Felt a warm blast of air come into the room and rush past her.

Then an armored figure in what looked like the most ancient of Legion armors, the old Mark I from the early days of heroic legend when the Legion fought the Savages and saved the galaxy, stepped into view.

The man in the Mark I armor slapped a fresh charge pack into a Jackknife blaster and then poured more fire down the hall at the others who'd been sent to recapture her and Sergeant Lopez.

Lopez pushed himself up from the floor as the armored figure stepped into the room. Return fire filling the hall behind him.

# 60

Tyrus Rechs moved quickly to Lopez, shrugged off his tactical bag, then pressed the Jackknife blaster into the hands of the marine. She dropped her own spent blaster and took the weapon from the bounty hunter.

"Sergeant Amanda Almond?" Rechs asked, more to bring her around to reality than verify what he already knew.

Her small mouth worked up and down in a tiny 'O'. Trying to form words she couldn't make. Or believe.

In the end she just nodded.

"Cover the door," Rechs ordered tersely. He handed her a few extra charge packs.

She slipped them into her pockets, checked the charge already in the blaster, saw that he'd made sure to hand her a fully loaded weapon, and flicked the safety off. Glad to have someone else taking charge for a moment. She was just a shooter. Not a leader. Never had been.

"What's his condition?" the armored man asked her. But the medical scan within Rechs's armor was already telling him what the situation was. Critical. Combat support hospital recommended within the next two hours.

She rattled off a litany of the legionnaire's injuries and what she'd done to treat them as best she could. She made no excuses. Just gave a frank assessment of what had been done under the circumstances while she watched the now-silent and body-littered hall beyond the room.

"I think they're getting ready to push again," she said from the doorway.

"Three minutes left to exit the building," said Rechs. "Bomb."

Amanda let out an involuntary sigh. Everything it had taken to reach this point and now... this. The galaxy wasn't just a bad place. It was perverse.

"There're at least ten of those MCR Soshies down the hall between us and the main elevator," she said.

"Here's what we're going to do," said Rechs, ignoring her comment about the Soshies being MCR because that was the first he'd heard of it and he didn't have the bandwidth to factor it into the equation. There wasn't time. He hefted Lopez in one swift yet economical motion, putting the legionnaire's head over his shoulder and down onto his back. Fireman's carry. "You're going to stay low and close to me, Marine. Use the blaster to sweep."

Rechs grabbed a dead pro off the floor by the tactical vest and held the dead man so his back faced forward like a riot shield.

"You're gonna carry two men?" the marine asked incredulously.

Rechs said nothing. Didn't have to. He *was* carrying two men, his armor making it look easy.

"Stay low and behind the dead guy," he told her. "Use him as a shield to get close. Sergeant Lopez still has most of his armor on. You're more vulnerable than he is. So stick close to me."

She nodded, and they moved toward the doorway, falling into step as a team.

The incoming fire was instantaneous as they stepped into the hall. Rechs held the body of the large dead man out in front of him, and blaster bolts thumped into it as they advanced down the corridor. Behind Rechs, crouching low, Sergeant Almond poured return fire at the defenders. Barely aiming, squeezing until the frenetic little Jackknife had dumped its full charge. Slick as synth oil she had another charge pack in and opened up again.

The dead man's body began to come apart from the hits it was taking. Rechs's armor took a few glancing shots, the bolts streaking off into the walls and ceiling.

Another charge pack spent, Amanda swapped in a new one and targeted the nearest defenders. She spat burst fire at the figures hugging wall at the end of the hall or firing from empty rooms and alcoves. The weapon Tyrus Rechs had given her ripped their bodies to shreds with needle sprays of bolt streams.

As the body of the dead man nearly disintegrated under overwhelming incoming fire at almost point-blank range, Rechs tossed the man's shredded remains at one of the pros, who recoiled in horror. The bounty hunter pulled his hand cannon lightning-fast.

The narrow hall shook with the thunderous rapid *booms* of Rechs's weapon on auto-fire. He shot down two men ahead of them, pivoted fast into a room another pro had escaped into, and shot that one several times.

Amanda covered the way toward the elevator and kept their attackers back and pinned behind cover. One stuck his head out, and she made sure it was the last thing that guy ever did.

They made the elevator, firing at those still covering nearby, and entered, blaster fire smashing into the doors as they closed.

The elevator was headed down to street level.

Rechs pulled the panel apart and fused several wires together. He'd made sure no one would stop it or recall it.

"Now comes the hard part," the bounty hunter said.

# 61

L OTH WAS OUT ON THE STREET, INTERFACING WITH THE recently arrived extraction convoy commander, when the shooting in the lobby started. The only warning the hardened mercenary received was the barest of one-line reports that indicated "someone's coming down" over the comm. That there had been a major firefight up on nine was evident according to the comm traffic. That had been nearly two minutes ago, and the channel silence since then had been overwhelming.

Loth knew he needed to clear his men out of the building, but he found himself waiting until he could get a handle on what had happened. They remained staged in the lobby, nervously checking chronos to make sure their boss hadn't lost it and was expecting them to all go down together with the exploding building.

The first thing Loth's pros in the lobby saw was the elevator opening and Tyrus Rechs stepping out, scatter-blaster pointing at the nearest group of hired guns.

"Wait—" someone tried before the roar from the powerful weapon went off at near point-blank range. Rechs tore three black-and-red pros to shreds with one blast. He pivoted, racked another charge pack into the scatterblaster's chamber, and fired again. The successive deafening blasts erupted out onto the streets as Rechs made short work of those stationed inside the lobby.

At this point, Loth was between a hull and a defense shield. There was no easy decision. He'd lost control of the prisoners, who somehow had survived against overwhelming odds. He had to admit that to himself.

He had three choices.

Continue the attempt to recapture the legionnaire and lose more of his people. Maybe even his own life in the process.

Kill them with the overwhelming firepower he had access to on the street via the mounted weapons.

Or…

Just forget the whole mess. Call the freighter in for a dust-off in some quiet section of this ruined world, make the rendezvous, let the captain know about the double-cross Zauro had planned for her and her crew, and then stay ahead of the information curve. Get lost somewhere out along the edge. Wait for killers to show up for the rest of his life. Always sitting with his back to every cantina wall, eyes forever on the exits.

He parsed all three of those options as Tyrus Rechs shot down everyone in the lobby. Some distant part of his mind worked the self-preservation side of the equation. His crew had tried to take down the armored bounty hunter with blaster fire, but the man moved swiftly and violently, working the scattergun like it was second nature. It only carried six shots, but in the hands of someone as skilled as Rechs—and Loth knew the man's reputation wasn't unfounded—it was more than enough to ruin everyone's day.

When the scatterblaster finally ran dry, Rechs tossed the weapon aside. The tac bag was already low on charge packs and he was allocating what remained for the little Jackknife the marine carried.

Rechs trotted back to the elevator the marine covered him from and hefted the wounded legionnaire onto his back once more.

"Lyra, bring in the *Crow* as close as you can get to my loc. We're coming out."

Rechs turned toward the marine.

"I'll clear everything in front of us. You keep them off our backs. My ship is coming. We keep moving. Copy?"

She had that faraway look in her eyes. Like she had reached her limit. Or had been elsewhere mentally and wasn't sure where she was now. Understandable. Rechs had been there many times.

"Copy, Marine?" he said again.

There was no other way than this. She had to see the last fifty meters through on her own. It was the only way.

"Copy," she said, suddenly coming back to the present.

Rechs nodded. "Fifty meters and we're out."

He could already hear the howl of the *Crow* coming in, the whine and roar of the starship's engines erasing the blaster fire they were about to move out into.

And Tyrus Rechs didn't hesitate to take that first step. "Let's move."

# 62

THE OLD LIGHT FREIGHTER REGISTERED AS THE *ACCADIAN Comet* came in hard and fast, swooping down over wagon wheels rising to needle points. The sky began to settle from red to purple twilight, and lights were coming on across the city, competing with the fires in the streets. Smoke and haze gave everything that soft-focus look, as though all of this were some late-summer harvest festival.

Even as the *Crow* set down in the wide plaza before the Excelsior Arms, flaring her repulsors, venting engine gases, and deploying her three massive landing struts, the bomb in the building detonated, fracturing the structure's spine around the fifth floor.

Loth had his mobile blaster teams, hidden inside commandeered sport utility sleds, ready to engage anyone who came out of the building. He'd decided there was no running from Zauro. Best case for him now... they wounded the prisoners and recaptured. Most likely outcome... they killed the legionnaire. And that would just have to be explained. Not great. But probably not bad when it was all added up.

Loth had wired and placed the explosives himself. His EOD training had been expert level. The device would fracture the spine of the building high up enough to drop the upper levels down onto the lower levels, creating a cascade implosion. The thing would essentially collapse down on itself and not out into the street where it had the possibility of hitting the convoy if it was still in the area.

The original plan had been not to be anywhere *near* the area, but plans had a way of coming apart at first contact. So this had been an excellent bit of operational foresight on Loth's part. Not dropping the building onto its side in the street the way an amateur might.

And just as an unidentified freighter sat down in the wide plaza where four major streets intersected among the burned-out stores and general ruined lifelessness of the old city, floor five erupted, blowing out debris and glass in a sudden blossom of explosive force. Spectacular, but no real threat to anyone not directly inside the building.

An ominous and titanic groan sounded from the building's central spine.

The entire thing would fully collapse in the next thirty seconds, but to Loth that seemed well back on his list of things to worry about. For at that moment, Tyrus Rechs, the man himself, carrying *his* legionnaire prisoner, came running out of the collapsing building, the entire time shooting a massive sidearm in staccato automatic bursts at everyone on the street. And that damn female marine followed close behind, putting blasts into the armored sport utility sleds, killing one of the drivers in her first shots. Ruining his plans.

Reaction teams from the convoy erupted with return fire from their vehicles at the same instant the top floors began to collapse. Maybe they weren't aware the building was coming down.

Or maybe shooting back seemed more pressing.

All of this was about to get very messy.

Overhead, a marine SLIC came in hot.

Loth started to doubt he was getting out of this. But that wasn't going to stop him from trying. If he had to kill his way to an escape pod, he would. In that moment he switched over from running a crew—leading—to focusing on his own survival.

His people just didn't know it yet.

A tidal wave of debris and dust flooded out from the collapsing building and drowned the street in its wake. It was all-consuming, billowing out to demand that everyone in its path surrender to its force. Men coughed, their mouths full of the stuff. And as the dust blew across the street like a rolling storm front, the building offered its last residual groans and crashes. And then there was an ominous silence through which nothing could be heard except distant warning sirens and sled alarms.

Loth reached out in the blinding swirls of dust. He felt his lieutenant next to him. And then he heard a voice.

"KTF, losers!"

Someone in the smoke and drifting dust opened fire with a heavy blaster. A SAB from the sound of it. Or so Loth guessed as a bolt tore off the head of his lieutenant.

# 63

Something was going down. In the seconds before the ship came in and the building fell, as the shooting started in the lobby across the street, Baldur began to whine.

Puncher knew this was the spot. That was clearly an extraction convoy on the street. Players and shooters in abundance. If he was going to have any chance of getting his hands on his brother Shaker, and whoever else had survived, this was the moment.

*She here*, thought the dog.

Puncher charged the SAB, shucked needless gear, and made ready to assault across open ground. "Good boy."

Then a junky old light freighter came down out of the sky, flaring and venting, gears deploying, and the pros on the ground didn't seem to have anticipated that.

"New player," he muttered.

*Friends?* thought the dog, being optimistic. *Helpers.*

"Maybe."

Baldur barked an affirmative.

"Be ready, boy," ordered Puncher. "Find her, we find Shaker. I'll follow."

The dog whined and began to pace back and forth. Opening his mouth in large snaps. Tasting the air.

"Got her?"

Baldur barked that he had. He had the scent of the marine, and that meant the legionnaire.

"Hold on," ordered Puncher. There was firing coming from the building and the dog was whining.

*Ready to go.*

"Hold on, Baldur buddy!"

Puncher tapped the cybernetic assist on his armor for the heavy SAB he was carrying, disguised the entire time by the homeless camo. His HUD identified armed targets coming out of the convoy. And now there was a marine gunship on station above, and Baldur was telegraphing that he wasn't crazy about that either.

And then, as if everything happening at once wasn't already too much, the building exploded.

Puncher swore.

Two figures, one carrying Shaker, emerged from the collapsing building, engaging targets on the curb and running for the convoy as the building came down behind them.

A tidal wave of dust and debris chased them. Puncher had just enough time to cover Baldur's eyes and ears as the wave of gray destruction swept past them and covered the entire street.

Then maybe thirty seconds of stunned silence as things settled. Distant alarms crying mayhem and shouting for attention.

Puncher's armor was identifying mounted heavy blasters supporting the pro teams on the street now sheltering on the near side of the convoy.

And he could make out the two figures who had come out shooting. The big one was carrying what looked like his brother leej, hunkering on the opposite side of one vehicle from a team of very armed operators looking to do them harm.

Once eyes were cleared and bearings were reacquired, that was.

A short and very deadly firefight with not-good odds for anyone was about to break out in the next few seconds as the dust began to clear.

And as if all this wasn't improbable and surreal enough, Puncher saw a small Nubarian gunnery bot rolling through the dust, headed for the freighter's lowering boarding ramp.

Puncher cleared a field of fire for the powerful squad automatic blaster, shouted "KTF, losers!" and opened fire.

* * *

Rechs and the marine had barely made the side of the convoy as the building collapsed, the bounty hunter shooting down men as they surged across the sidewalk, blazing heavy caliber at the pros as he ran, the marine behind him and to the right, working the Jackknife over one of the sleds deploying a heavy blaster right at them.

For all intents and purposes they'd walked right into an ambush. And there was little chance they were going to survive once it fully opened up. Their only chance was to shoot first and fast.

Then the building fell behind them, pushing dust and debris all over everyone. Rechs lost sight of the marine, and the EMP effect blast sent his armor offline.

The legionnaire on his back coughed, but Rechs could do little to help him. The guy needed real medical attention fast. Anything else was a death sentence.

"Hang in there, Leej," Rechs said. "You'll make it."

The *Crow* was out there somewhere in that sea of dust, and Rechs impatiently waited for his reboot so his armor could find the thing.

Someone yelled, "KTF, losers!" before squad automatic blaster fire in high cycle came from somewhere ahead.

Rechs figured legionnaires had arrived to finish the fight.

The dust was just beginning to clear when incoming blaster fire erupted across the street from all quarters. It was hard to tell who was shooting at whom.

Rechs yelled to the marine, not sure where she was in all of this. "Sergeant Almond, c'mon! We're leaving!"

Then he ran for the next vehicle, shifting positions and withholding firing to avoid drawing attention.

The heavy squad automatic blaster fire was shrieking across the plaza. Rechs could hear the *Crow*'s engines, but he couldn't isolate a direction until his helmet worked again. It was taking longer to reboot than it normally did. Maybe just being tricky, or maybe as a result of the pounding the armor had taken already.

Blaster fire rained down from above.

Through the clearing dust, the sniper teams in the surrounding buildings were shooting at him... and at the legionnaire on his back.

* * *

Amanda could hear them all about her. Red-and-black Soshie pros. Taking cover on the far sides of all the vehicles along the street. If they rushed her, there was little she or the armored man carrying Lopez could do.

Dust swirled through the air. Her ears were still ringing from the blast. Still ringing from the flashbang. Still ringing from the drubbing she'd taken at the hands of Mean Eyes. But she could hear the high-cycle whine of automatic blaster fire somewhere out there. Sounded like a SAB. And the huge roar of a ship's engines.

She looked to her left through squinted eyes, the dust clumping on her lashes, and saw the armored man with Lopez shifting to another vehicle, massive sidearm out but not engaging. He was almost duck-walking with a legionnaire in full armor on his back, keeping a low profile.

She thought she heard yelling, maybe her name being shouted, but couldn't make it out for sure.

Then fire began to rain down from the surrounding buildings. Targeting the man and Lopez. Poorly trained snipers going for the kill. And her blaster was all but useless against ranged targets.

As they'd charged out of the building, she'd seen that some of the pros had been carrying blaster rifles. Weapons good for medium- to long-range engagements. She scanned the street near two dead men the armored man had shot down in their race to the curb and cover. But neither had those type of weapons. Their light blasters lay in the gutter nearby.

She checked her blaster's charge pack. Without thinking she swapped in a new one and rolled over the hood of the sled she covered behind, firing into the three men she found waiting on the other side. She squeezed hard on the Jackknife, literally shaking it across them. Hundreds of needle-sized bolts shredded the men in red and black.

That was the last of the charge packs Rechs had given her. Her pockets were empty. But one of the downed pros had a medium-engagement blaster rifle with a scope on it. Looked like a Balt Optics x4. Good enough. She slithered under the sled's open door to get to it, avoiding the blaster fire that smashed into the vehicle. Another pro had seen her pull that move, and he was responding.

She let go of the little Jackknife blaster, pulled the rifle off the ground and quickly checked its load.

Charge was solid. About three quarters full.

Lying on her back and with little regard for her own safety, she focused in on the first sniper team she could spot in the buildings above.

She landed the scope, checked that she was getting a good zero via the side-scroll telemetry within the picture, and pulled the trigger. Her target was leaning over the side of the roof, and her shot took the guy through the throat and sent a red spray up into the air behind him.

She scrambled to her feet, moving away from the bolts that were focused on the sled she'd been hunkered beside, and scanned for another team, tracking the incoming fire on the armored man and Lopez.

"Covering!" she shouted at Rechs through the clearing dust and crisscrossing blaster fire, hoping he could hear her.

* * *

Captain Hess hovered over the battle from the cargo deck of the SLIC gunship. He had directed the SLIC's door gunner to pour fire on the freighter that had just landed.

"That's the extraction vehicle! Rechs is working with whoever killed that legionnaire! Shut it down, Sergeant!"

The gunner had complied and swiveled the swing-mounted N-50 heavy blaster over toward the old freighter, pouring bright bursts of fire into her upper hull, targeting the propulsion system controls near the engines.

And then Hess spotted Rechs coming out of the building and had to restrain himself from spluttering with joyous rage.

He grabbed the gunner's shoulder and tried to re-direct fire, indicating Rechs and the legionnaire on his back. "He's moving the leej to the next safe house! Dust him!"

"I'll hit the leej!" shouted the marine sergeant.

And then a typhoon of dust swallowed the street below.

Hess knew immediately that he was probably only going to get one more shot at Rechs when the dust cleared.

"Hold position!" he shouted at the pilot.

"Copy that, Captain Hess."

Hunter Oh-Two kept the craft hovering above the dust storm. Somewhere down below, blaster fire opened up from a new source. Oh-Two called it in, wondering if the Legion had pushed in on their own. It definitely sounded like at least one SAB was laying it down.

And then the dust began to clear. Just a little, and just for a moment. And Captain Kirk Walters erupted with news that had him both excited and terrified.

"I have visuals on Reaper Actual! Oorah, Amanda!"

She was engaging targets, fighting for her life. The man Hess identified as Tyrus Rechs appeared to be trying to escape with the wounded legionnaire. And, strangely, the Soshie pros seemed to be doing their best to stop him. Hunter Oh-Two saw all this in an instant before the billowing dust thickened once more.

That's when Hess delivered a stunning blow to the base of the skull of the marine crew chief operating the door gun. He knew getting the guy to fire at Rechs was going to be problematic after he'd balked the first time.

"Gotta do it myself," Hess muttered as the crew chief dangled, dead weight pulling his safety line taut.

The Nether Ops agent took the stock of the weapon and shoved it into his shoulder, using the N-50's targeting system to scan the swirling dust below where he'd last seen Rechs.

All he needed was a clear shot. Then he'd dump everything the N-50 had right on top of Tyrus Rechs. There was no way his armor could stand up to that. No way in hell.

# 64

As Rechs moved, the heavy legionnaire on his back groaned and coughed.

"Hang in there!" shouted Rechs. He opened up with the hand cannon on the sled nearest him. One of the vehicles with a mounted blaster. He shot the gunner a bunch and then continued, weaving through the vehicles to make the hulking shadow of the *Obsidian Crow*, looming in the gray murk of the clearing dust.

The HUD was still finishing its full reboot, but he had a tag on the marine's biometric signature now. She was covering behind a sled and firing at the sniper teams in the buildings above.

"Marine!" shouted Rechs. "Follow me!"

He wouldn't leave without her. He just had to get the legionnaire on board first.

He had just moved from the vehicle toward the marine when a fusillade of blaster fire from the forward-most sled in the convoy came racing to meet him. He dashed for cover behind another sled that was angled out and facing the entrance of the ruined building. Through it all he did his best to protect the legionnaire, only narrowly avoiding getting hit by the incoming fire.

Unfortunately, the sled Rechs had chosen for cover was already being used by one of the pros for the same purpose. And he had the drop on the bounty hunter. Had him solidly in his sights, so much so that the guy pulled down his black mask just so Rechs could watch him smile as he pulled the trigger.

But before he could fire, a dog came leaping out of the dust to clamp onto the Soshie pro's gun arm. The blaster fired wide as the dog dragged the man to the ground, mauling him and tearing the blaster away.

Sharing cover with the savior dog and the freshly mauled and incapacitated Soshie pro, Rechs chanced a glance away from the unexpected save and looked over the vehicle toward the lead sled. A four-man team of highly squared-away operators in their red-and-black Soshie cover costumes were coming out in turtle formation with high-powered blasters. They were moving in his direction.

The bounty hunter ran through his options and decided to drop the leej, stand up and fight, clear the threat, and only then resume progress toward the *Crow*.

Then he remembered the armor's shield.

He keyed it, hoping the device would want to make amends for its failures back inside the tyrannasquid.

No joy. The enigmatic device had chosen not to work. He'd have to throw down without it.

The approaching pros weren't firing. Smart. Just moving straight at him in tactical turtle. They knew that locking him down where he covered was better than standing and sending in fire. And the tighter they could bottle him up, the better their odds of success, because he *had* to go through them. There was no other way to the ship. Operators like this would cut him, the marine, and the legionnaire on his back down if he attempted to get around them in the open. He hazarded another look and saw them as shadows moving through the dust.

He heard the whine of the marine's blaster fire. Nailing more sniper teams.

Good for her.

Rechs was just about to drop the leej and shoot it out with the approaching team, if only just to see who walked away. But that was when the dog streaked out of the dust once more and slammed into the team's point man, dragging him to the ground.

A sudden torrent of blaster fire from off to the right followed immediately after. It eviscerated the three remaining operators. And emerging from the clearing dust, following the blaster fire, was a legionnaire in full armor, holding his trigger down and shooting at the corpses on the ground for good measure.

Time to move.

Rechs hefted the wounded legionnaire and ran for the shadow of the *Crow*.

The dust cleared further thanks to the continued repulsor wash of a SLIC hanging out overhead. Bright blaster fire ran down across the vehicles and pavement, slamming into everything around him. He still had twenty meters to go, and he'd never make it with fire ranging in and finding him.

Then Rechs looked up and realized that the fire wasn't coming from the Soshie teams poised in the buildings above him, but from the SLIC gunship itself. The damn thing's crew gunner must've had orders to terminate him on sight.

It was a thing Rechs had gotten used to, but this time it looked as though the combination of SLIC fire, advancing pros, and general chaos might be more than he could handle.

And then... suddenly... it stopped.

\* \* \*

Kirk Walters—Hunter Oh-Two—stood over the prone body of the Legion captain. Unsure if the killing machine that was every legionnaire, regardless of whether they were a jerk or not, was going to get up and kill him or stay down and remain unconscious.

He held the fire extinguisher he'd taken from near the N-50, prepared to use it again if the jerk did dare stand. Frankly he was amazed he'd swung it hard enough to put the man out even while wearing a helmet. The extinguisher itself sported a sizeable new dent.

When Kirk had looked back from the pilot's seat to see his crew chief dangling taut—dead or unconscious, heels of his boots dragging on the cargo deck—he realized why Hess had been ignoring his calls that he'd spotted Amanda. And it took all of another two seconds to realize that the captain was now firing the big N-50 at whoever was carrying the wounded legionnaire, his blaster bolts coming danger close to the leej, and Amanda as well.

Kirk didn't even really think about it as he left his pilot's seat, grabbed a fire extinguisher and swung it at Captain Hess's head, landing a bell ringer at the base of the neck where it met the cranium. He just moved. Reacted.

Now Oh-Two, standing above an unconscious Legion captain who looked like he wasn't getting up any time soon, guessed his military career was over.

*Oh well*, he said to himself as he went back to the flight deck, intending to put down and go after Amanda himself. He'd fly freight out on the edge when he got out of the chicken farm someday. That was good enough for him.

# 65

THE LEGIONNAIRE WITH THE SAB RAN UP TO RECHS.

"Don't know who you are, but if you're helpin' Shaker then we're on the same side! C'mon!" The leej motioned to the waiting ship, shouting to be heard above its whining engines and the sounds of battle. "That your ship?"

"It is," Rechs replied.

"I'll cover. My dog will go get your marine!"

Rechs didn't argue. Instead he moved off, hunched by the dead weight of Lopez, for the belly of the *Obsidian Crow*. Behind him he could hear the legionnaire laying down suppressive fire to cover his path.

He made the boarding ramp and ran up it, legs burning as he reached the top and threaded the interior of the ship for the medical bay. He was pretty sure the man on his back had stopped breathing.

He placed Lopez on the surgical table then sprinted back to the boarding hatch, weapon ready.

"Lyra!" he shouted over the comm. "Tell the autodoc to stabilize him!"

G232 met him at the hatch just as Rechs was starting back down to wade into the firefight.

"Oh, master. So much has been going on since you left! No doubt—"

Rechs waved the bot off.

At the bottom of the ramp, the dog was turning in a circle and wagging its tail. Then Rechs saw the marine sniper, covered in dust like some ghostly tribesman from out in the waste worlds at galaxy's edge. She stumbled into view, still holding the rifle she'd acquired. She made the ramp just as the leej with the SAB came into view as well, backing toward the ramp, dumping fire in short bursts at multiple unseen targets.

Amanda lurched up the ramp. Rechs grabbed her hand, taking the weapon and pushing her deeper into the ship.

"Where is he?" she gasped.

Rechs knew who she meant. He'd reunite her with the wounded legionnaire soon enough. If they got out of here. First things first.

G232 was still talking as the legionnaire at the bottom of the ramp turned and pulled his SAB upright. Standard procedure for boarding.

Blaster fire chased his heels as he bounded up, coming in hot and fast, striking the boarding ramp and struts. But the kid made it.

Rechs slammed his glove against the close hatch button and shouted, "Lyra, get us out of here!"

The repulsors took over and heaved the *Crow* upward. Incoming fire struck the outer hull. Engines throttled up. And then they were airborne and streaking for altitude.

"Puncher," said the kid, taking off his bucket and sticking out a hand. "That was close."

Rechs shook, but didn't give a name of his own. The kid laughed. At the absurdity of it all. The closest of scrapes.

The bounty hunter looked over at where the marine had been. Amanda. She was gone. He found her where he knew he would. Standing at the entrance to the medical bay, still covered in dust. Watching the autodoc work to save Lopez's life.

"He'll make it," said Rechs, standing next to her as he studied the status readouts. "Readouts show him getting stabilized."

She nodded once and then collapsed. Sliding toward the floor and covering her dusty face with the crook of her arm. Her shoulders rising and falling to the deck as she began to sob in great heaving shudders.

It was finally over.

* * *

General Sheehan sent a FLASH priority comm request to the crew of the light freighter that had just pulled out the captured legionnaire and marine, according to a report sent in by Hunter Oh-Two, his best asset in the AO.

His staff had warned him that the captain of that ship was most likely Tyrus Rechs. The freighter matched descriptions of the ship reportedly used by the notorious and highly wanted bounty hunter. Orders were to shoot that freighter down on sight, friendly casualties being considered an acceptable loss.

Sheehan ignored those directives, while understanding full well the consequences of his choice.

"Unidentified freighter," said the general. "This is General Charles Sheehan, commander of ground forces in-system."

He made a point of not using Rechs's name. Of not giving any rope that those ghouls in Nether Ops might try to wrap around his neck. Tyrus Rechs was on that ship? You don't say?

"I have reports that you have safely procured a Republic legionnaire and Republic marine captured by militant elements in the organization calling itself the Soshies. I'm offering safe passage for you to set down on the destroyer *Castle*, or, if you prefer, LZ-8 in the marine Green Zone in order to exchange Sergeants Almond and Lopez."

There was no reply. The ether of comm hummed while out there the light freighter seemed to race for jump.

"We can intercept her," noted the naval liaison.

The comment showed that not everyone was in agreement when it came to giving a pass to the war criminal Tyrus Rechs. But some did. The liaison's superior, Commodore Giers, agreed with General Sheehan. The bounty hunter should be offered a chance to turn over the soldiers and depart under a flag of truce.

"It's the only decent thing to do," was how Giers had put it.

Sheehan ignored the liaison's comment and his staff held their breath, waiting to hear if the bounty hunter would respond and hoping that, if he did, he wouldn't complicate things by naming himself. Everyone wanted things to turn out, but they also needed to CYA. They'd note for the record, when the House of Reason inquiry came down, that they'd advised the correct course of action. Intercept and arrest one Tyrus Rechs. Regardless of the circumstances.

General Sheehan was a middle-aged man turning to old. He held the comm one more time above the holotable in the CIC.

"Freighter pilot," said the general, still playing the game. Creating a passable veneer of not knowingly defying orders. "You can trust me."

A moment later the gravelly and tired voice of the fabled ghost that was Tyrus Rechs came back over the comm.

"I have your word, General?"

Sheehan looked around at his staff. Career officers begging with their eyes that he do "the right thing" and save their careers by not persisting in the folly of offering a wanted criminal safe passage.

"You do, freighter pilot. You have my word."

"Coming in," said Rechs a moment later. "We'll set down on the portside aft deck. We have wounded. Request a full trauma team meet us aboard the ship."

"Copy that," said Sheehan. He turned to an aide. "Get my shuttle ready. I wanna be there."

* * *

Twenty minutes later the light freighter *Obsidian Crow* set down on the open deck of the Republic destroyer *Castle*. Detachments of marines had blocked every exit. Except instead of facing the ship, as if ready to repel, they were facing out, away from Tyrus Rechs's ship as it vented gases and lowered its gears.

The message was clear: They would have their marine back. And the legionnaire. At whatever cost. And officially, no one would even lay eyes on the bounty hunter. If he was even here.

Rechs lowered the boarding ramp and found a full trauma team of med bots and navy docs running toward him across the pristinely polished deck with a pair of repulsor gurneys. These men and women couldn't have cared less for any warrants or bounties. They were here to save lives. And that was what drove them in their race to reach Lopez and Almond.

General Sheehan and two unarmed staff officers followed quickly behind.

Rechs led the medical team up the boarding ramp and showed them where Lopez was. Sergeant Almond had to be moved aside, nurses assuring her they would take over now. When she didn't move, Rechs helped her away, leading her down the ramp as the medical team made ready to secure Lopez.

The autodoc had put Lopez into a medical coma. He would never remember what had happened aboard the bounty hunter's ship, or how he'd gotten off it and aboard a Republic destroyer. But he would make it. He would live.

Sheehan met Rechs and Almond at the bottom of the ramp. Puncher hovered nearby.

"Well… I'll be damned," said the general, removing the ruined cigar from his mouth. "Legends do exist."

Rechs stepped forward, and the general stuck out his paw.

Rechs shook. "Thank you, General."

"No… no, no. Thank you… Tyrus… or Rechs… wow. That sure feels weird to actually say. No. Hell.

Thank you. You did the right thing here. We let those damned bookkeepers in the House prevent us from getting ours back. Shouldn't have done..."

Rechs held up a hand. Signaling that he understood. And that it didn't matter. Things had been made right.

"Never mind, General. I'm familiar with the House and their... priorities. Favor to ask, if I could?"

The general nodded without hesitation. But then added, "Don't know what I can do. But if I can... I will."

"Make sure these two don't hang," asked Rechs.

He indicated Puncher and Sergeant Almond.

The general frowned and then looked from Almond to the bounty hunter. "That's a tall order. They're already baying for her blood. Blame her for escalating things. Probably want to put the whole damned mess on her." He turned to face Puncher. "And you... you flat out went AWOL. Not much anyone can do about that."

The legionnaire shrugged. "I answer to the Legion, not the marines."

The general clucked his tongue and shook his head knowingly. Almost tiredly. He looked back at his two staff officers.

The three had a conversation with their eyes, not speaking a word. One that said to Rechs that certain games could be played.

"Well," the general said, returning his focus to Rechs. "I think I can pull some strings and lay down a little administrative black magic to cover what can be covered and confuse the issues. Hell, I might have even told this leej here to do whatever it takes. And he just... well, he just ran with the ball. Give him a medal and it kinda makes it legal. Know what I mean? Did that once to a squad leader I had when I was a shavetail. My first platoon sergeant told me it was the right thing to do. So… I guess I can do it again. One last trick before they show me the door."

"Thank you, General."

The medical team was bringing the unconscious Lopez out. Both parties cleared a path.

Puncher hitched a thumb to point back into the *Crow*. "Gotta get my dog… uh, Mr. Rechs. Mind?"

The bounty hunter nodded. "Go ahead."

Then he stepped over to the marine. Sergeant Almond. A med bot was trying to get her to lie down on a gurney for transport to sick bay. She wasn't having it. "I'll walk there on my own," she said.

"Hang on a sec," Rechs said. "Need to do something first."

The med bot protested, but the marine pushed herself away and moved to the bounty hunter.

"C'mon," Rechs said as he led her back aboard.

She followed him, still covered in the gray dust of the collapsed building. Thin and barely there like some ghost fading forever from this waking world. Rechs led her to his weapons shop, removed his bucket, and dropped it on a bench cluttered with blaster parts.

Sergeant Almond looked around in amazement. Rechs watched her take in all his weapons. Some hadn't been seen in the galaxy for years. Others weren't even known. Rechs saw the fatigue in her face writ large. The hollow sunken eyes. The fading ghost just asking for a darkness to disappear into.

Yeah, they would try to blame her for everything. Rechs had seen that before. Careers had to be saved. And a marine sergeant was expendable—to certain people.

The general would fight for her as best he could, but the media would never take up her cause. Not most of them.

They were for Syl whatever-her-name-was. They were for the people who needed to burn down the Republic, and the galaxy, in order to remake it in their image.

He rummaged around in his tools. Opened a small drawer he hadn't opened in years. Finally found what he was looking for.

He turned back to her.

"You did the right thing, Sergeant. You saved one of my legionnaires' lives with complete disregard for your own. I want you to know... I'm grateful for that."

She listened, feeling as though she was listening to a man who didn't speak much, or often. Wondering what he meant by "my legionnaires."

Tyrus Rechs cut into all that. "You're gonna doubt yourself," he continued. "Everyone does. Especially the heroes, in my experience. But right now, from me, I want you to know for the rest of your life that when others hesitated... you didn't. You ran toward the fire. You helped when someone needed it badly."

Silence.

He could see she was already thinking all those things. The things about how the politicians and careerists would crucify her.

"They're gonna end me," she said softly. "I know that. And... it's okay. Commendations and anything else... they don't matter. I just..."

She stopped.

He could see something inside her trying to break. But honestly there wasn't anything else left. She'd given everything to protect that legionnaire from one minute to the next.

"I just wish… I could have got them all. Y'know? That's all. But I'm no hero. I'm somethin'… somethin'… that watches over real heroes. But I ain't one. Okay?"

Rechs studied her for a long moment. Saw she was all out of tears. That she was empty. That she'd given everything to save someone she hadn't known before it all went down. Only because the person she was trying to save, served. Just like she did.

That was the only reason she'd gone in.

"Wrong," said Tyrus. And then he opened the old awards case he'd been given so many years ago he'd stopped counting.

He held it out to her.

The Legion's Order of the Centurion.

The highest award given by the Legion. The end-all that any legionnaire, or service member serving alongside the Legion, can receive. The gratitude of the entire Legion. More dead than living had received it.

He held it out to her.

"You saved my legionnaires," Rechs repeated. "This is yours now. You earned it."

Her mouth opened. She reached out when it was clear he would never take it back. And then she held it, studying it.

Tyrus Rechs stepped back and executed a smart salute. The tired, ruined old bounty hunter suddenly became the general of the Legion he'd been so long ago. Always was.

And he held that salute until—cautiously, unbelievingly—the tiny little marine sergeant, dust-covered, bloody, beaten, and hollow, saluted back.

"You didn't forget nothin'," said Tyrus Rechs.

\* \* \*

Rechs found the legionnaire Puncher in the *Crow*'s lounge, kneeling in front of his dog. Rubbing the dog's furry chest.

"Gotta go now, Leej," said Rechs from the darkness. Studying the legionnaire's fine latest-gen armor. Remembering those he'd known who'd worn it. For a moment he could feel something, like old ghosts coming to stand around him.

Puncher stood and turned.

"Yeah, well, we got a problem, Mr. Rechs."

"Just Rechs," said Tyrus. "What's the problem?"

"My dog, this here is Baldur..." The leej stepped aside and Rechs could now see the Malinois who'd leapt through the dust and saved his life in the middle of the firefight. Twice.

Baldur looked at Rechs. Head straight on. Dark eyes staring into the old general. Rechs could almost feel the dog's mind reaching out and trying to touch his. He knew of the telepathy program from his Legion days.

He'd known other dogs like this one.

"Problem is," continued Puncher. "He says he has to go... with you, now."

Rechs shook his head.

"I don't..."

"He's been pretty stubborn, sir, this one has," Puncher said. "Since I started working with him. Yeah. He's a stubborn one."

"Okay. So *make* him go."

"Won't take, Rechs. And... believe me, I'm gonna catch hell for losing him. I dunno if you know anything about the breed, but, well… there's a lot more to them than people think. They believe they got this greater purpose in the galaxy. They're just working with us because we have common cause. Straight out of the dog's mind and any handler will tell you the same. I know… weird. But he's pretty serious."

"How so?" asked Rechs. Studying the dog who seemed to be studying him back just as intently.

"He says…" Puncher took a deep breath. "He says you're looking for somebody. Somebody important. Or dangerous. Or both. He's a little vague on that. Just says 'real bad.' He says he's got to help you find this person. It's his… uh… his purpose. And I don't like it. I like him. A lot. Best dog I ever worked with. Not the easiest, but the best. Like me. Know what I mean?"

Rechs did.

"Hell, I can go AWOL, I've done it before, and go off lookin' with the both of you. But… he ain't goin' back with me. Says he's found you. Says… you need him."

Rechs stared at the dog.

"That true?" asked Puncher after a moment. "You lookin' for somebody that fits his weird idea?"

Rechs nodded. "I am."

Puncher lowered his head.

"Thought so. Damn dog is always right." His voice had gone low and raspy. Like he was fighting back some ocean of inevitability. Losing a best friend forever.

*That's the sound*, Rechs thought to himself, *of saying goodbye… when you don't want to.*

He knew it well.

The legionnaire's voice was quiet. Sad. "I'll… just get a new dog then," he said, turning to Baldur. Trying to be angry. "One that ain't crazy."

The Malinois cocked his head to the side, looking up at the sad legionnaire. Puncher seemed to hear something Rechs didn't.

"Okay," murmured Puncher. "Maybe when I get out... I'll... I'll find you both. Okay? Help look for this important-dangerous person."

The legionnaire got down on one knee, rubbed the dog's chest, ears... all the places Baldur loved.

"You sure?" he whispered to the dog one last time.

And then, after a moment, Puncher stood, gave the dog and Tyrus Rechs one last look, and left the ship.

Rechs heard the strike of an armored glove smashing into a bulkhead on the way out.

Shortly thereafter, the *Obsidian Crow* lifted off the hangar deck of the *Castle* and vanished into hyperspace.

# EPILOGUE

Palm fronds shake in the predawn dark across the estate. Here on Pthalo it will be another perfect day, as all days on the renowned pleasure world are. Storms are rare. Unpleasantnesses, like cast-aside mistresses, and those whose credit has run out, are also rare. And always easily handled by crack teams of professional security protecting every estate across the world.

Some have suggested that Pthalo itself is the most heavily militarized planet in the galaxy. When you really think about it. Add up all those personal security details and off the books it has the largest standing army in the galaxy. All the muscular boys and girls with real-world skills wearing the latest in dress and athleisure, strapping sophisticated weapons packages. Ready and willing to protect the elite who must be protected. Maintain the walls that must be maintained. Invisible and real. If only to keep the hordes out.

Here in the predawn dark, before another perfect day of walks through tropical gardens, along private white sand beaches, or aboard the yachts that lazily cross the crystal-clear aquamarine seas between parties, events, and other secret meetings, tropical palms shake as the sun warms the water beyond the planet's terminus and sends a gentle jasmine scent, hinting of salt, across the quiet estate. The secret untaxed enclave of some nameless high financier who controls several galactic multi-corps and doesn't happen to be on hand at the moment.

The estate is being used by someone else in the meantime. A guest.

Still, full security is in effect. A VIP is currently hiding in residence.

The assassin crossed into the protected zone of the property via the sea and onto the small beach. Coming in from the deep water where a ship dropped him off. He swam slowly through the darkness for hours to reach the beach. Protected and covered by a state-of-the-art synthprene wetsuit with nano-scramblers that block sensor detection on several levels, including IR.

For a long while the assassin watched the sands. Drifting out in the waves offshore, floating, before he finally came in with the surf. Waiting for the patrol detail to pass one last time along the beach before the next rotation came on for the day.

And when they did, the assassin watched them go. Knowing that before leaving they would check in their equipment. Steiger high-powered assault blasters with Mercurio close-engagement sights. The best money can buy. Both guards would leave the estate and avail themselves of the pleasures of Pthalo. Sun. Swimming. Drinks and gourmet food in one of the tiny pleasure villages. Then an afternoon nap.

Another day's work complete, protecting the fantastically wealthy residents from the consequences of their lives—both real and imagined. Sometimes earned, sometimes not.

Pthalo isn't for stars and or celebrities.

Pthalo is for lovers.

Lovers of wealth.

Pthalo is for the *truly* wealthy. The ones who are smart enough to remain hidden. Or to not even exist at all.

On the beach, with less than an hour before dawn, the assassin moves into the tropical gardens that surround the estate. He pulls out a pair of sensor-mags and scans the grounds surrounding the villa.

Looking for all the sensors and holocams set up to stop someone like him from entering.

He spots all the security measures and confirms his route to the target. Out of the dive bag he's towed for two hours, he swaps the flippers for a pair of soft-soled dive shoes. He retrieves a coil of synth-rope and pulls it over his neck and chest.

That's for later.

He pulls out the weapons case.

A gentle breeze kicks up the noise of the tropical palms, scouring the predawn dark with the hush of white noise the fronds make. Covering the pneumatic hiss as the clamshell weapons case opens softly. Masking the minute it takes the assassin to assemble the weapon.

This weapon is a Savage weapon. Something from the mythic times of those fabled boogies that once frightened, and almost conquered, the galaxy.

It fires the old nine-millimeter round. Everything about the weapon is precision. Magazine, chamber, barrel, sights, grips—everything is custom-made. The last bit before the weapon is ready to use is the silencer. Long and lethal, screwed on and sealed with a slight pneumatic hiss. Matte black fading to charcoal, the weapon is the same color as the synthprene stealth suit.

Light seems to disappear, or even flee, from the assassin. He must be invisible.

Weapon ready, the assassin proceeds toward the big villa at the center of the private estate. The Pthalo island villa. Where rooms upon rooms are filled with the latest luxuries. Legal and illegal. Stolen works of art thought long missing. Wealth on ostentatious display. Nothing fine has been neglected. A full staff always on hand, though most are asleep now in the distant servants' quarters.

The first guard to die does so near the massive pool. Moving fast, low and slow, coming up behind, the assassin shoots the walking guard as the man enters a shadow. Before the guard can fall, the assassin gives him a slight tap and pushes him into artistically cut foliage alongside the sauna house. A nice hidden place where he can die without discovery.

The assassin put one through the man's spine on initial contact. Now he adds one to the brain to make sure the work is done.

The man wore his hair high and tight. Was most likely former Legion. Blood pools around him, watering the palms.

The next guard dies within twenty seconds of the assassin violating the large glass doors that open into the villa's main salon. The catering kitchen is there, and guard number two is working at a bowl of cereal as her shift ends.

The bullet smashes into the back of the guard's skull. The woman didn't even turn or rise up to defend herself. She didn't hear death creep into the room with her. She goes down in the bowl of pink, cereal-dyed milk.

The assassin doesn't pause.

He moves toward the villa's main doors, deviating from the direct track to the target. Detouring to where the team commander and another guard spend the shift in a control room accessed off the greeting lobby that opens onto the front drive. Monitoring and filling out reports on a datapad.

A quick hack on the control room lock, using a worm far too sophisticated for even the latest in locks to withstand, works in under thirty seconds.

The assassin, moving like a swift inky blackness, enters the control room and sees the team commander working at a datapad. End-of-night reports.

The first bullet kills the commander. The other guard turns at the man's dying gurgle. Two more shots deal with that one.

Mag out.

Mag in.

Checking the holocams, the assassin can now see that the two perimeter guards have gone to their last post for the night. Joining up with the main security team and reaction force out at the front gate.

They're just running out the last minutes of their shift. Nothing ever really happens on Pthalo. Especially at zero dark now. Pthalo is the safest place in the galaxy.

There are only two guards left inside the villa itself, and there is no trickery to this next bit.

Both guards watch the stairs leading up into the extensive living quarters. The assassin appears and puts bullets into both men as he closes the distance in swift and economical steps. They try to react but don't seem able to process what's happening. Can't believe someone is here and killing them right now. That someone has bypassed all the road surveillance, sensors, gate guards, watch commander, and perimeter patrol, to come here and do the thing they were supposed to prevent.

The stairs were the "cush" assignment.

And now they're dying because the assassin is a shooter. He knows people only die when you stop the pump and pipes. Even headshots need to land right in the three-point-five-centimeter sweet spot of the brain stem for what some might call an instant kill.

Blasters are a little more forgiving because of the kinetic bulk the bolt delivers. But bullets... gotta know what you're doing there.

Both guards get it in the pump. Multiple shots to make sure. Then each in the head once they're down.

Mag out.

Mag in.

Nothing stands between the assassin and his target now.

* * *

Syl Hamachi-Roi is sleeping when the man in the dark wakes her. She's been sleeping a lot lately. Once her political career came apart at the seams, sleep seemed to be all that was left for her.

She suffers from depression and is on some heavy-duty meds to deal with it. Plus the anxiety of having gone from being the brightest and shiniest of political stars to being indicted for election fraud, money laundering, and association with a known war criminal.

There are a lot of other charges.

Armies of lawyers, financed by Mr. Zauro, are dealing with the fallout. Some pundits say she might come back. Someday. That she's still on the verge of greatness, a force the galaxy must acknowledge. They don't believe the charges. They believe in her. Just as it had been on that day when she addressed all of her…

…her supporters. On Detron, and across the galaxy.

The Soshies…

No.

Her fans. They had been something more than mere political supporters. Because *she* had been something more.

They hadn't just believed in her. They'd worshipped her. Her entire life, everything, had been leading up to that divine moment when that sea of people in the plaza looked to her to save them.

Looked to her to lift them up. Make their dingy little scrubby lives better.

Every word that came from her mouth on that day had been treated as the spun gold of a prophetess. Dripping with pearls and pretty wisdoms. They'd come to her for all the truly important answers to what was wrong with the galaxy.

Now she went to sleep each night with a bottle of wine and another handful of pills. She felt good about what she'd done then, as she drifted into the embrace of sleep. When she was sober… when the pills wore off and before the first glass of the day was poured… then she knew the score. It was all gone. The investigations, the document trail to Zauro, the deaths of the legionnaires blamed on her... it had ruined everything.

The lawyers who seemed the smartest told her she'd be lucky to avoid the prison planets. She knew Zauro would pay a hefty fee to avoid that. But still. She was effectively ruined.

The few millions she'd managed to squirrel away via influencer fees during her brief time in the House didn't seem like much when compared with the fact there wouldn't be any more coming for a long while.

She remembered her first days in office, adding up how much she'd make over all the years of her service within the House. The figure had been the size of a mountain. Wide eyes had gone wider at the numbers she'd calculated.

That was all gone.

Maybe it might come back. Someday.

Zauro had told her that. Had given her some hope on the other side of all this. Given time, maybe people would forget, and then she could come back—new, redeemed, wiser.

Try for some real influence in the House. Develop a coalition that could make things happen.

They were so close, Zauro had told her, to fundamentally changing the galaxy. For the better.

She believed it.

She believed in herself first of all, and maybe that was all one needed to get back on top. Or maybe that should be filed under things the pills can make you believe after the first glass is poured.

The assassin raised her up in bed, gently. There was no need to be rough. No need to make this worse than it had to be.

She woke up, but the effects of the pills and the wine made her sluggish. Slow to respond. Without the sense of urgency or fear that should accompany a home invasion.

"Who're you?" she asked the figure in the dark. As if still waking from some wonderful dream where everything had not gone horribly wrong. Where things had gone as they were supposed to have. According to plan. Where the crowd still roared their undying adulations at her very presence.

The assassin gave no reply.

"I don't recognize you," said the sleepy Syl Hamachi-Roi in the little girl's voice of her drug-ravaged personality. Still cottony. Still pleasant. Still dreaming of all the things that never should have happened.

She could see his face in the blue light of the last of the night. He'd left the dive mask down on the beach and had pulled back the synthprene hood for the killing. It didn't matter if she saw his face. She wouldn't live. And he didn't care. He was already a wanted man. A very wanted man. The most wanted man in the galaxy.

The assassin, a man on the young side of middle age, placed a pair of ener-chains about her wrists. She looked at them quizzically, as though fascinated by their design. He hauled her to her feet in a quick motion. Best to be about the work and get on with what needed doing. She wobbled for a second and her mouth formed the word, as she fought to both wake and dream in the same moment, before she spoke it.

"Why?"

"Come," he said gently. "Follow me now."

And then he led her onto the landing of the villa's second story. Away from the sumptuous and dreamy master suite full of soft cottons, drowsy fabrics, over-stuffed pillows, and a view of the garden below. Out of there and back onto the landing. Down the stairs and past the two dead guards whose look of surprise remained in death.

Through the quiet house where no other living thing besides assassin and target breathed. Then out onto the pool deck and off into the night garden.

The tree he'd spotted on the way in would do the trick.

She followed numbly, as though in a light trance. He was holding her arm and pulling her along.

She knew, inside of her, that the pills were keeping her numb. Pliable. Zauro's doctors had prescribed them. And she'd taken them. Anything to get free of the depression and despair. And the anxiety. Especially that. It had been her constant companion through the whole impeachment phase in the House of Reason. Through her death as the galaxy's savior. Allies had become enemies. Enemies had become victors. She'd been taught some hard lessons.

The humiliation and the shame. Yes, those had been awful. But what had been the worst was the loss of relevance. The return to being just a "no one." That. That had hurt the worst. Like some kind of endless void at just the beginning of some forever that would be the rest of her life.

Like some kind of hell.

She stood there in the wet grass of the garden, her bare feet coming to life, listening to the first birds begin to call out to one another in the predawn darkness. She knew this wasn't just a dream. This was real. And that today would be a beautiful day. And that… was enough. What more did one need than just a beautiful day?

She sighed.

A beautiful day was something to be grateful for. Truly grateful for. She needed to be more grateful. When she came back... she would be grateful. But she would also pay them back. She would be grateful for her revenge. And for the victory she and Zauro would show the galaxy one day.

Grateful.

She took a deep breath as the man in front of her, the dark man as she'd begun to think of him, removed a coil of synthetic rope from around his torso.

"What are you doing?" she asked, a little more awake. A little more concerned.

Still the man didn't speak. He coiled one end of the rope around the stolid tree he'd selected within the garden. The other end, thick and knotted into something already over a sturdy dark limb, she recognized...

"Oh," she whispered. "It's a noose."

He drew her over, helped her up onto a stone bench beneath the tree, and placed the noose gently about her neck.

And again...

*Why?* she asked herself.

"Why?" she asked the man in the dark. "Why are you doing this to me?"

But still she didn't struggle. Couldn't.

The man stood by her, steadying her in this moment at the edge of life and death.

For some reason, she knew she wasn't afraid... should be afraid, but wasn't. There was something comforting about the man. Some constant in a galaxy of uncertainties that she could feel. She'd never felt that before. And now, so close to death, she felt it. Knew it for what it was. The opposite of everything she had chosen, pursued.

*It's Mr. Death.*

Some boy she'd known back in college had read comic books. The man next to her reminded her of that character. That villain.

Mr. Death.

But in his presence, coming awake now, just before the fear of what was about to happen descended on her, she felt... safe next to him. Like one might feel when they're lost in the woods and they find a road sign that finally shows them the way out.

Safe like that.

Lost and afraid that you might never be found.

And then... found. Hurray.

Mr. Death.

"I'm going to hang you," said Tyrus Rechs in the dark. The sky above the trees was turning a soft shade of blue.

Her mouth made that *why* shape, and he continued.

"Not because you conspired to murder a legionnaire," said the assassin in the darkness.

"No?"

"You deserve it because of that. But not because of that."

"I do," she moaned. And he couldn't tell whether it was a question or an admission.

"Yeah," said Tyrus as he checked the rope.

He took a deep breath.

But she began to speak before he finished. Fighting past the malaise of the pills and issuing forth a rambling plea for leniency.

"You don't have to do this. You don't. I didn't know. I didn't know that was going to happen. I knew something was going to happen, but I really didn't know…" She trailed off.

The wind blew. The palms around them swayed. The hanging tree stood firm.

"But really. Please. You don't have to. I'm just trying to make the galaxy a better place. Trying to lift… trying to make it so… you know. Better. A better place. I'm… we're… we see what needs to happen. What needs to change. What needs to go… for… for it to just be better. A better place for everyone. Is that so bad? Am I wrong? Was trying to make it a better place wrong?"

She'd started to cry. The hysteria had started to creep in as she spoke. But to her credit, once she began to speak about her vision, her mission, her destiny, some ancient steel had come into her voice, and now the lost sleepy little girl he'd led down here stared at him with cruel and imperious eyes.

"And that means some people don't fit," she finally spat. "What happened was… was… was… just an example. That's all. Just a message. I may not have known it was going to happen, but… but… I damn well support it. And screw you for thinking you have a right to question that.

"So some stupid legionnaire lost his head? Small price to pay. He joined up. He's killed more innocents than he could ever atone for. He's just some stupid kid who never could have made it in the real galaxy. Probably would have failed out of the university I went to. In time he'd have gone back home after the Legion with a drinking problem and a temper. Working some dead-end job and thinking he actually did something. Voting for all the wrong people because of some misguided notion that the Republic is a great place.

"It's not great. It never was. But it can be," she sneered.

She shook the ener-chains like they might just fall off, and when they did not, she gave a haughty frustrated exhale of exasperation.

"Get these off of me!" she demanded.

"That's not why I'm going to hang you," said Rechs patiently. "Not because you helped murder someone sworn to protect you."

"I don't *need*—" she almost shrieked.

"That's not why."

The girl glared at him from her perch on the stone bench, the rope almost seeming like a necklace about her slender throat.

"Then you're a coward!" Her eyes were pure murder. "Just some assassin who can't stand that the galaxy is changing. Because your barbaric career—killing for money—that won't be tolerated in a new order."

"That's not why," said Rechs patiently.

She stared at him for a long moment.

"Then why?" she asked. Because she actually wanted to know. She was incapable of seeing any valid reason, or other point of view, that might possibly be valid as to why she should be... hanged. The man before her, a criminal assassin. *He* should be hanged. Their places ought to be reversed. The galaxy was playing a cosmic joke on her.

Rechs cleared his throat and took hold of the rope. But gently. Not applying any pressure to Roi's neck.

"First, make your peace. It's almost time."

She said nothing, just stared hate at him.

"Because when I'm finished, I'm going to hang you. Do you understand me, Syl?"

"Ha!" she laughed down at him. "You're going to hang me for ridding the galaxy of another sanctioned murderer we just happen to call a legionnaire. Covering life's losers in false glory and giving them armor to make them feel like men. You're so stupid, whoever you are. That makes you just as bad as what you're saying I'm guilty of. What are you going to do... hang yourself next?"

"I'm hanging you because I've seen it all before," said Rechs. "More times than you can imagine. It's always someone like you. Someone with new ideas that are just old ideas ginned up to make the masses think you actually care without ever doing anything that actually shows you care about them."

"I do care!" spat the disgraced delegate. "Cared enough to actually do the hard, dirty work required to clean the galaxy."

Rechs clenched his jaw. "Don't talk to me about cleaning the galaxy. Not without ever going out there into the stellar dark to slay the real monsters that howl beyond the limits of known space. Just waiting to come in and rape, loot, and murder everyone on their way to power. Just like you.

"I've seen it more times than you can imagine. And the only distinguishing feature was the body count. It's as old as Earth. It's what the Savages were all about. The trouble here is, you think you came up with all these ideas on your own. So I'm gonna save the galaxy two million, twenty million, two billion, and just cut to the chase with you, Syl."

She was staring at him. Horrified. Because now she seemed to understand that he was serious about all this. Not angry. Not passionate like her. Just tired at having to do some job he'd decided to do. Like a man who goes out every day to sweep up the trash in the gutter. Doing it because it must be done. Because someone has to do it or the galaxy just overflows with trash.

She was angry at him for being tired. She needed him to be as hateful and vitriolic as she was. Needed to feel as though she were being martyred at the hands of an ignorant zealot. She'd felt that way before. But not now. She had almost been excited about being hanged. Executed. It would make her a saint. Cleanse from her the stain that was her disgraceful exit from the House of Reason.

She began to cry.

"Why... you don't..."

He wanted to tell her he felt sorry for her.

But he didn't. Not even a little bit.

It always ended in rope. If the dictators didn't kill themselves the people found them. And then... it always ended in rope.

Tyrus Rechs was never squeamish about killing. He was good at it. And he'd found it was better to get to that part over with sooner rather than later.

She was sobbing when he gave her body a soft and gentle shove off the bench, and then jerked the rope with all his might, the expert knot he'd put in just above the back of her head breaking her neck instantly.

There was no pain.

Just a quick break and it was over.

They'd find her body drifting in the morning breeze as the sun came up. After the cover-up. After the guards were erased and forgotten, their relatives paid off because what really happened doesn't happen on Pthalo.

Then they'd find her. Speculate it was suicide for a few media cycles and take part in handwringing over their own part in the nonstop gleeful coverage of the fall from power by one they'd propped up in the first place.

But all that was after the bounty hunter returned to the beach, carried the mask and dive flippers out into the waves, put them on in the gentle surf, and kicked out into the warm tropical water.

After he swam away as the sun began to rise.

And after the call.

"Gabi. It's done."

## THE END

# TYRUS RECHS WILL RETURN...

Jason Anspach and Nick Cole are a pair of west coast authors teaming up to write their science fiction dream series, Galaxy's Edge.

**Jason Anspach** is a best selling author living in Tacoma, Washington with his wife and their own legionnaire squad of seven (not a typo) children. In addition to science fiction, Jason is the author of the hit comedy-paranormal-historical-detective series, *'til Death*. Jason loves his family as well as hiking and camping throughout the beautiful Pacific Northwest. And Star Wars. He named as many of his kids after Obi Wan as possible, and knows that Han shot first.

**Nick Cole** is a dragon award winning author best known for *The Old Man and the Wasteland, CTRL ALT Revolt!*, and the Wyrd Saga. After serving in the United States Army, Nick moved to Hollywood to pursue a career in acting and writing. (Mostly) retired from the stage and screen, he resides with his wife, a professional opera singer, in Los Angeles, California.

# HONOR ROLL

We would like to give our most sincere thanks and recognition to those who supported the creation of *Tyrus Rechs: Madame Guillotine* by subscribing as a Galaxy's Edge Insider at GalacticOutlaws.com

Guido Abreu
Elias Aguilar
Bill Allen
Tony Alvarez
Galen Anderson
Robert Anspach
Jonathan Auerbach
Fritz Ausman
Sean Averill
Marvin Bailey
Matthew Ballard
John Barber
Russell Barker
Logan Barker
John Baudoin
Steven Beaulieu
Randall Beem
Matt Beers
John Bell
Daniel Bendele
Trevor Blasius
WJ Blood
Rodney Bonner

Thomas Seth Bouchard
Alex Bowling
Ernest Brant
Geoff Brisco
Aaron Brooks
Marion Buehring
Daniel Cadwell
Van Cammack
Zachary Cantwell
Steven Carrizales
Brian Cave
Shawn Cavitt
Kris (Joryl) Chambers
Cole Chapman
David Chor
Tyrone Chow
Jonathan Clews
Beau Clifton
Alex Collins-Gauweiler
Garrett Comerford
Steve Condrey
Michael Conn
James Connolly

James Conyers
Jonathan Copley
Robert Cosler
Andrew Craig
Adam Craig
Phil Culpepper
Ben Curcio
Thomas Cutler
Alister Davidson
Peter Davies
Nathan Davis
Ivy Davis
Ron Deage
Tod Delaricheliere
Ryan Denniston
Aaron Dewitt
Christopher DiNote
Matthew Dippel
Ellis Dobbins
Cami Dutton
Virgil Dwyer
William Ely
Stephane Escrig
Steve Forrester
Skyla Forster
Timothy Foster
Mark Franceschini
Richard Gallo
Christopher Gallo
Kyle Gannon

Michael Gardner
Nick Gerlach
John Giorgis
Justin Godfrey
Luis Gomez
Thomas Graham
Gerald Granada
Don Grantham
Gordon Green
Tim Green
Shawn Greene
Jose Enrique Guzman
Erik Hansen
Greg Hanson
Jason Harris
Jordan Harris
Adam Hartswick
Ronald Haulman
Joshua Hayes
Adam Hazen
Jason Henderson
Jason Henderson
Kyle Hetzer
Aaron Holden
Tyson Hopkins
Joshua Hopkins
Christopher Hopper
Curtis Horton
Ian House
Ken Houseal

| | |
|---|---|
| Nathan Housley | Lacy Laughlin |
| Jeff Howard | Dave Lawrence |
| Mike Hull | Alexander Le |
| Bradley Huntoon | Paul Lizer |
| Wendy Jacobson | Richard Long |
| Paul Jarman | Oliver Longchamps |
| James Jeffers | Sean Lopez |
| Tedman Jess | Brooke Lyons |
| James Johnson | John M |
| Randolph Johnson | Richard Maier |
| Tyler Jones | Brian Mansur |
| John Josendale | Robet Marchi |
| Wyatt Justice | Deven Marincovich |
| Ron Karroll | Cory Marko |
| Cody Keaton | Pawel Martin |
| Noah Kelly | Lucas Martin |
| Caleb Kenner | Trevor Martin |
| Daniel Kimm | Tao Mason |
| Zachary Kinsman | Mark Maurice |
| Matthew Kinstle | Simon Mayeski |
| Rhet Klaahsen | Kyle McCarley |
| Jesse Klein | Quinn McCusker |
| Travis Knight | Matthew McDaniel |
| Evan Kowalski | Alan McDonald |
| Byl Kravetz | Hans McIlveen |
| Clay Lambert | Rachel McIntosh |
| Grant Lambert | Joshua McMaster |
| Jeremy Lambert | Christopher Menkhaus |
| Brian Lambert | Jim Mern |
| Honor Roll | Pete Micale |

| | |
|---|---|
| Mike Mieszcak | Nick Quinn |
| Brandon Mikula | Eric Ritenour |
| Ted Milker | Walt Robillard |
| Mitchell Moore | Daniel Robitaille |
| William Morris | Joyce Roth |
| Alex Morstadt | Andrew Sebastian |
| Nicholas Mukanos | Sanchez |
| Vinesh Narayan | David Sanford |
| Andrew Niesent | Jaysn Schaener |
| Greg Nugent | Landon Schaule |
| Christina Nymeyer | Shayne Schettler |
| Colin O'neill | Brian Schmidt |
| Ryan O'neill | Andrew Schmidt |
| James Owens | Alex Schwarz |
| David Parker | William Schweisthal |
| Eric Pastorek | Aaron Seaman |
| Carl Patrick | Phillip Seek |
| Trevor Pattillo | Christopher Shaw |
| Dupres Pina | Ryan Shaw |
| Pete Plum | Brett Shilton |
| Paul Polanski | Vernetta Shipley |
| Matthew | Glenn Shotton |
| Pommerening | Joshua Sipin |
| Jeremiah Popp | Scott Sloan |
| Chancey Porter | Daniel Smith |
| Brian Potts | Tyler Smith |
| Chris Pourteau | Michael Smith |
| Joshua Purvis | Sharroll Smith |

John Spears
Peter Spitzer
Dustin Sprick
Graham Stanton
Maggie Stewart-Grant
John Stockley
William Strickler
Shayla Striffler
Kevin Summers
Ernest Sumner
Shayne Sweetland
Travis TadeWaldt
Daniel Tanner
Lawrence Tate
Tim Taylor
Mark Teets
Steven Thompson
William Joseph
Thorpe
Beverly Tierney
Matthew Titus
Jameson Trauger
Scott Tucker
Eric Turnbull
Brandon Turton
John Tuttle
Jalen Underwood
Paul Van Dop

Paden VanBuskirk
Paul Volcy
Anthony Wagnon
Scott Wakeman
Christopher Walker
David Wall
Scot Washam
James Wells
Kiley Wetmore
Ben Wheeler
Theron Whittle
Scott Winters
Gary Woodard
Brandt Zeeh
Nathan Zoss

Printed in the USA
CPSIA information can be obtained
at www.ICGtesting.com
LVHW091303151023
761121LV00001BC/49